COWBOYS & ANGELS
Book 7

Reckless Love

NEW YORK TIMES & USA TODAY BESTSELLING AUTHOR
KELLY ELLIOTT

piatkus

PIATKUS

First published in Great Britain in 2019 by Piatkus

1 3 5 7 9 10 8 6 4 2

A CIP catalogue record for this book
is available from the British Library.

ISBN 978-0-349-41852-0

Printed and bound in Great Britain by
Clays Ltd, Elcograf S.p.A.

Editing by Cori McCarthy, Yellowbird Editing
Proofing by Amy Rose Capetta, Yellowbird Editing
Developmental editing by Elaine York, Allusion Graphics
Cover photo and design by Sara Eirew Photography
Interior Design by JT Formatting

Papers used by Piatkus are from well-managed forests
and other responsible sources.

Piatkus
An imprint of
Little, Brown Book Group
Carmelite House
50 Victoria Embankment
London EC4Y 0DZ

An Hachette UK Company
www.hachette.co.uk

www.littlebrown.co.uk

Kelly Elliott is a *New York Times* and *USA Today* bestselling contemporary romance author. Since finishing her bestselling Wanted series, Kelly continues to spread her wings while remaining true to her roots and giving readers stories rich with hot protective men, strong women and beautiful surroundings.

Kelly has been passionate about writing since she was fifteen. After years of filling journals with stories, she finally followed her dream and published her first novel, *Wanted*, in November of 2012.

Kelly lives in central Texas with her husband, daughter, and two pups. When she's not writing, Kelly enjoys reading and spending time with her family. She is down to earth and very in touch with her readers, both on social media and at signings.

Visit Kelly Elliott online:

www.kellyelliottauthor.com
@author_kelly
www.facebook.com/KellyElliottAuthor/

Also by Kelly Elliott (published by Piatkus)

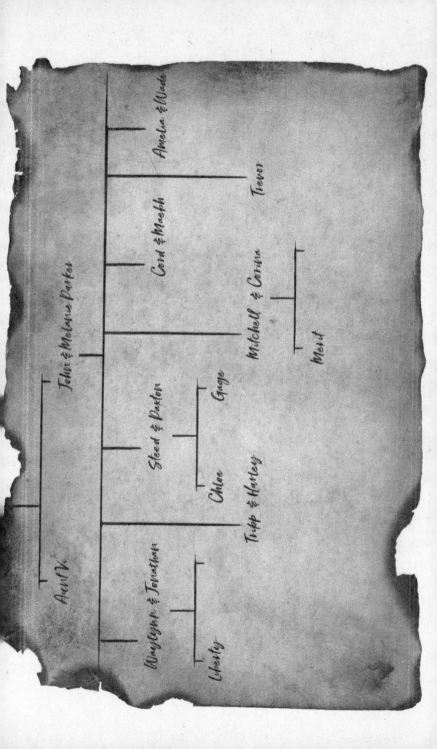

Aunt Vi

John & Melanie Parker

Waylapper & Jonathan

Liberty

Steed & Paxton

Chloe

Gage

Tulip & Harley

Mitchell & Carina

Merit

Cord & Maeph

Trevor

Amelia & Wade

Reckless Love

CHAPTER 1

Dear readers,

Reckless Love is the last book in the Cowboys and Angels series. I've loved writing these books and have come to love the Parker family so much. I hope you have as well!

Please remember these are not standalone books. You must read books 1 – 6 first and they are all listed in order in the front of this book.

Happy reading!

Trevor

Senior Year of High School

"That is someone I'd like to tap."

I gazed past my best friend, James Larson, to Scarlett Littlefield.

"Scarlett?" Jim Montigo asked. "I didn't know she was back from Boston. Wasn't she quite the prankster in middle school? Set a garbage can on fire outside the courthouse or something?"

My eyes roamed over Scarlett's body and I smiled. She'd always been beautiful, but now she was all grown up with a body to die for. Even under the dim lights of the backyard party we were all attending, my breath paused at the sight of her.

"She was known to pull a prank or two." Turning to James, I added with a smirk, "I don't think she's your type though, dude."

He huffed as I glanced back her way and tried to pull my eyes off of her.

Jim chuckled. "Because she's your type, Parker?"

With a shrug, I replied, "She doesn't seem the like the type of girl who would be any of our types."

Jim nodded.

"She's going to school in Boston you said?" James asked.

She turned, and my eyes met Scarlett's. What in the fuck was that feeling in my chest?

We locked gazes and when she smiled, my damn knees wobbled, and warmth filled my entire body. I returned the smile, and I swore she swayed.

"What the fuck, Parker? All you have to do is smile at a bitch and she melts on the spot?" James joked.

"Don't call her that," I said, not pulling my eyes off of her.

A hand waved in front of me, "Jesus, dude, are you drooling?" Jim asked.

I slapped his hand away. "Knock it off, asshole."

Time moved slowly as I watched Scarlett make her way around to her friends, hugging them and saying goodbye. She was leaving, but not before I got the chance to talk to her. I remembered her from elementary school and middle school. She'd been the first girl I ever danced with at a school dance, and definitely the last. Not that anyone else knew that.

Following her out of Mitch O'Conner's backyard and onto the street, I called out her name before she got into her little sporty BMW. She was an only child and spoiled rotten, or that was the rumor.

"Scarlett!" I called out. "Hold up!"

She paused, then turned to face me. A smile lit up her entire face.

Stopping in front of her, I pushed my hand through my hair and said, "Hey, I'm Trevor Parker."

Her cheeks turned a slight pink, and my cock jumped in my pants.

"Our mothers are best friends. I know who you are, Trevor."

My brow lifted. "Is that a good thing or a bad thing?"

Leaning against her car, she folded her arms over her chest, lifting her already perky tits. My damn pants grew a little bit tighter. My mother would kill me if she knew the thoughts that were running through my mind right now.

"I'm not sure I know you enough to answer that. If rumors are true, I'd say it was a bad thing."

With a hurt expression, I slammed my hand over my heart. "Ouch. You wound me so, Ms. Littlefield."

She chuckled and rolled her eyes. "You probably don't remember this, but you were the first boy to ever ask me to dance. At our sixth-grade winter formal in middle school."

With a crooked smile, I placed my hand on her car, bringing our bodies closer. It wasn't lost on me how she shook a little and sucked in a breath as I drew closer to her.

"I remember. You were the first girl I ever asked to dance with me."

And the last.

Glancing to the ground, she dropped her arms to her sides nervously before looking back up at me.

"So, how have you been?" she asked. Her voice was so fucking sexy. "My momma said you're going to be taking over your family ranch after college."

"That's the plan. Ranching is in my blood and it's something I love. Can't really see myself doing anything else."

"You look good in Wranglers, so that's a plus." Her cheeks turned a soft pink at the innocent flirting.

"That is a plus," I replied with a wink. "How do you like going to school in Boston?"

Scarlett exhaled loudly. "It's cold. We had a mid-term break so that's why I'm home for a visit."

"You going to college up there also?"

Her eyes looked so sad. "Yeah. Probably."

"How long are you in town for?"

Her teeth dug into her lower lip, and I was pretty sure I let out a groan as her pink lip turned white.

"I leave tomorrow."

My heart dropped. "Tomorrow?"

She nodded. "Yep."

It was out of my mouth before I could stop myself. "You want to go grab a cup of coffee at Lilly's?"

Her face lit up again, and I decided right then and there I loved making her smile.

"I'd love to," she replied.

"I'll meet you there."

Scarlett flashed me another breathtaking smile and slipped into her car while I jogged over to my truck. I hadn't told James and Jim that I was leaving. The last thing I wanted was to catch hell from them. The less they knew the better.

The entire drive to Lilly's my hands shook. *What in the hell did this girl do to me?* For the first time in my life, I wanted to be with a girl not only for sex, but to find out more about her. I was curious about Scarlett. Curious about why my heart seemed to beat faster when she looked at me. The little girl with the braces and braided pigtails was fun to play tag with when our mothers would visit, but now she was fucking stunning. I wanted to get to know everything about her, and I wouldn't turn down a game a tag, if she insisted.

Walking into the café, I spotted Scarlett in a booth. She glanced up and waved to me as I made my way over to her.

"Hey," I said, slipping into the booth.

"You made it."

I frowned. "You didn't think I'd come?"

She shrugged. "I wasn't sure. I guess I shouldn't put too much stock into those rumors after all."

I tried to smile, but it fell short. What if she knew all those rumors were most likely true? Most of the girls I asked out were sure bets who I'd be making out with within an hour of said date, and if I was lucky, sleeping with that night. Hell, most of the girls were only interested in hooking up as well, just so they could say they had fucked me.

After ordering two coffees, Scarlett and I were lost in conversation. I'd never been able to hold conversations with any of the girls I took out. Scarlett was different. So fucking different. She laughed at my stupid jokes and listened when I talked. She asked what having six siblings was like, told me she hated Boston but didn't want to disappoint her parents, and said she planned on moving back to Oak Springs after college. I told her my plan was to go to college and work on the ranch with the goal of someday running it. Hopefully with a couple of my brothers.

With a sigh, she dropped back against the booth seat. "It must be nice to have a dream."

"You don't have a dream?" I asked, watching those beautiful light brown eyes study me before she answered.

"Not really. I mean, I want to go to school, but there's nothing I feel passionate about. I love animals and wanted to go to vet school, but my parents didn't think that was something I'd stick with."

I frowned. "Why would they say that?"

She shrugged, her eyes turning sad as she glanced down at her coffee cup. Running her finger over the rim, she stared at it, lost in thought.

I studied her hands. Moving up, I watched her chew on her lip, and I ached with a need to kiss her.

"I want to kiss you, Scarlett."

Her eyes jerked back up to meet mine. The corner of her mouth rose slightly as she asked, "Why?"

With a laugh, I shook my head. "I don't know."

Her brow rose.

"I mean, I know *why*, but I don't know…why."

She giggled. "That makes zero sense, Trevor."

I cleared my throat. "Okay, I want to kiss you because you're beautiful. Funny. I like you, and you're different from any other girl I've ever talked to."

My tongue darted over my lips, her gaze taking in the motion. When her eyes lifted back to meet mine, she said, "Then maybe you should kiss me."

I smiled.

She smiled.

And my heart felt like it was going to explode on the spot.

"You kids want anything else?" Lilly asked, glancing between me and Scarlett and breaking our intense connection.

"No thanks, Lilly," I said with a polite smile. Scarlett pulled out the money for her coffee, but I tapped her hand. I barely noticed the slight gasp she made from my touch because it felt like a zap of electricity.

"I got it."

"Thank you," she said, blushing. She started to slide out of the booth.

"Where are you going?" I asked.

"I have to leave for the airport early in the morning. I better head home."

"Your folks taking you?" I asked.

She nodded as I tossed a ten onto the table and followed her out of the café.

We walked toward her car and with each step closer, my heart raced in my chest.

Scarlett stopped at her door, then faced me. When she looked up and smiled, I knew that Scarlett Littlefield made me feel something I'd never felt before and that scared the shit out of me. Maybe it was a good thing she was leaving town. I had a feeling she would keep my stomach in knots if she stayed in Oak Springs.

"Thank you for the coffee and conversation, Trevor. I really enjoyed it."

The way she said my name made my chest squeeze even more.

I stepped in, making her lean back against her car. When I lowered my mouth, I paused inches from her lips. Closing my eyes, I breathed in her scent.

Fucking heaven. I'd never forget that smell of vanilla and coffee mixed together.

"Trevor," she whispered, right before I pressed my lips to hers. Her hand landed on my chest, and I thought for a moment she was going to push me away, but she gripped onto my T-shirt and pulled me closer to her while she raised up onto her toes. Our kiss deepened as I pushed my fingers through her hair and held her tightly. I'd never in my life experienced a kiss like that.

When we broke apart, our breath was deep, labored. Leaning my forehead against hers, I was about to ask her for her phone number when she spoke first.

"I'm not like the girls you're normally with, Trevor."

My eyes closed. What did she mean by that? That we could never be together? I wanted to tell her I didn't want her for that reason. That I knew she wasn't the type of girl to love 'em and leave 'em. Hell, I wanted to get to know her. Talk to her. Find out what she loved, hated, dreamed about. But none of that would come out. I could only manage to get two words out.

"I know."

Taking a step away, I stared into her eyes and willed myself to say the things I had just thought.

Nothing came out.

My hands were shaking so I slipped them into my pockets. It was like she was waiting for me to say something, and I had no fucking clue what to say.

Pulling in a deep breath, she let out a gruff laugh and shook her head.

"Right. Okay, well, thank you for the coffee."

Scarlett spun around and opened her door. She went to close it, but I grabbed it before it could shut.

"I...I really enjoyed talking to you, Scarlett."

With the most beautiful smile I'd ever seen, she replied, "Me too, Trevor. See you around."

Nodding, I let the door go and took a few steps back. The car started and I stood on the sidewalk and watched until I couldn't see her anymore.

My head dropped back as I closed my eyes. It was the first time in my life I felt like I had just lost something. Something special.

CHAPTER 2

Trevor

Present day

I downed another shot and stared straight ahead, watching the scene play out at my old high school buddy's bachelor party in the private room at one of the local dive bars in Oak Springs. I was buzzed and that helped me to forget that Scarlett was still ignoring me.

"Why don't you let me give you a ride home? You're pretty trashed," Wade yelled at me.

"Fuck no! It's Brad's bachelor party. I'm not leaving until I make sure he gets fucked by the stripper…and I'm not trashed."

Wade rolled his eyes. "Dude, he's not fucking a stripper a few days before his wedding."

"Why not?" I asked as I eyed the blonde. Those seemed to be the type I was going for lately. They had to be blonde, or I couldn't fuck them. As a matter of fact, I was finding myself having a hard time fucking any woman lately. I hadn't been with anyone in weeks. Hell…it had been months—if I didn't count Scarlett. I messed around with a few girls, but I couldn't get past that. I didn't want them.

I wanted Scarlett.

"I'd fuck her," I deadpanned.

The stripper looked my way and grinned before she walked toward me. She had wrapped up her little dance and had been talking to Brad before she heard my comment. She sat right on my lap, her glorious tits all in my face.

"Want to go home with me, baby?" I asked, my mouth against her ear, my hand on her thong-covered ass. She winked as she pushed into me. Too bad my dick wasn't really in the mood. Pushing her off, I stood.

"Hell yeah. I'm getting lucky tonight," I said, reaching for her hand.

Wade pulled me to a stop and shook his head. "Damn, Trevor. Are you sure you want to do this?"

"Why wouldn't I?"

He shrugged and then leaned in closer. "Scarlett?"

I tossed my head back and laughed—even her name felt like a knife in my chest. I acted like I wasn't slowly dying inside. I'd tried calling her earlier when I was still sober. I wanted to stop by and talk, but she sent me to voicemail. Like she did every time I called her. She'd been avoiding me ever since that day she saw me talking to Traci Stephens, Sierra's best friend, and the maid of honor in Brad's wedding.

We'd all met that day to talk about the destination wedding Brad and Sierra were having. I hadn't met Traci before and she was flirting with me something fierce. I gave her some harmless flirting back, with no intentions of doing anything. Scarlett had seen it all go down. I knew what it looked like. I also knew I was a motherfucker for the way I had treated Scarlett a month before that. It was the last time we'd slept together, and the only time I'd ever been reckless while having sex. The memory of that night came crashing back to me.

I vowed to myself I wasn't going to sleep with her again, but I saw her out running near her house. And there was no way I could stop the attraction I had toward Scarlett. I'd tried to push her away, but she always pulled me back. I felt things for her I'd never felt with another woman, and I had told her that, more than once.

Parking in front of her house, I got out and made my way up the porch. All I wanted to do was talk to her. She'd been so upset with me the night after she admitted her feelings, and I basically told her there could never be anything between us. I couldn't tell her that I was scared to death. If I gave her my heart, I'd be giving her the power to destroy me.

I hadn't been able to sleep the whole night. All I saw was the hurt in her eyes when I told her I could never settle down. That I wasn't a one-woman kind of guy. She nodded and walked to her front door. When she turned back to me, I saw it in her eyes. She was giving up on us.

"It's over, Trevor. I'm not doing this anymore. I need you to leave and not come back."

Scarlett's words were haunting, keeping me from sleeping.

That day I saw her out running, I waited until she went inside her house, then knocked. When Scarlett answered, I pulled her into my arms and kissed the living fuck out of her. Soon we were in her house, clothes being ripped off on the way to her bedroom. We didn't fuck that day. We made love. I went slow, and it had never felt so good in my entire life to be with a woman. It was too late before I realized why it felt so damn amazing. We'd gotten so caught up in each other we had made love without a condom.

When I realized what I'd done, I jumped out of the bed. I never even looked back at her after I got dressed and rushed out of her house. The only thing I heard was a sob coming from her as she called out my name.

Asshole.

I was a fucking asshole.

I shook the memory away and slapped Wade on the back. "Dude, Scarlett is done with me, and I'm done with her."

"You're done with her?" he asked, anger filling his eyes. "Was she a used piece of furniture or something?"

Anger hit my chest and nearly knocked me on my ass. "You know what? Fuck you, dude. You don't know anything."

Wade's hands slipped into his pockets as he looked at the girl to my side. "I know if you leave here with her, you're going to regret it."

Forcing myself to smile, I lied. "Yeah, I don't think so."

As the blonde and I walked toward my truck, Wade's words hit me again.

"You're going to regret it."

The stripper was all over me. Her hand landed on my deflated cock that wasn't the least bit interested as she pushed me against the truck and licked my neck.

"I can't wait to have your strong arms holding me up while you pound into me," she said against my lips.

What in the hell am I doing?

I didn't want this. No, I *did* want it. I wanted to fuck her brains out; I wanted to fuck someone's memory out of my own head, but a part of me wanted to push her away. I was so fucking confused, but once I came to my senses, I knew what I needed to do.

I needed this woman to get the hell away from me right now.

Pulling my mouth from hers, I saw her out of the corner of my eye.

Scarlett.

I pushed the stripper away and shouted, "Enough." When I turned to look at Scarlett, she was leaving. A guy was walking with her, his hand on her lower back, guiding her away from me. He whispered something to her as they kept moving.

"Scarlett? Scarlett! Wait!" I shouted as I made my way toward her. "Please, wait! I wasn't going to do anything with her."

The guilt hit me right in the gut. I had let this woman touch and kiss all over me not two seconds ago.

When the guy glanced over his shoulder, I stopped in my tracks.

Eric.

The guy from Maebh's restaurant. He shot me a dirty look, ushered Scarlett into her car, and climbed into the driver's seat. My eyes darted over to her. She was crying. My legs felt like they were going to give out when I saw exactly how *hard* she was crying.

"Scarlett!" I screamed, causing her to look up and then say something to Eric. The bastard pulled out and did a U-turn on Main. I stood there and watched her car until I could no longer see the red taillights anymore.

Dragging my hands over my face, I let out a frustrated groan. "What did I do? What the fuck did I just do?"

"So, are we leaving or not?" The stripper's voice pulled me out of my daze.

Turning, I took her by the arm and led her back to the bar. "I'm leaving, but without you."

"What the fuck is this shit?" she demanded.

We ran into Wade as we walked back into the bar.

He looked surprised to see us. "What happened?"

The stripper walked away, but not before calling me a few names.

"Scarlett…she saw me with the stripper."

Wade groaned. "Damnit, Trevor. I told you not to do it."

My hand rubbed my buzz cut. "I wasn't going to. I was about to tell her I changed my mind, but Scarlett saw her kissing me."

He narrowed his eyes. "It takes two to kiss, dickhead."

I shook my head, trying to clear my thoughts. "She was with Eric."

Wade's head pulled back in surprise. "Eric, from Maebh's place?"

"Yeah, and they looked pretty cozy together. He was driving her car."

"What are you going to do?" he asked, worry in his voice.

"I'm too drunk to drive. I need you to take me to her house."

"What? Trevor, maybe you need to go home and sleep this shit off. Talk to her when you're sober."

"Please, Wade. *Please*."

He sighed. "Fine. Let's go before I change my mind."

Ten minutes later, he pulled up to Scarlett's house and parked out front. Her BMW was in her driveway and a weird feeling hit my chest. What if she was with Eric in the house? Were they dating? Was he just a friend?

"Is Scarlett dating Eric?" I asked while staring at her front door.

"Not that I know of."

Pushing the passenger door open, I stumbled out of the truck.

"Shit, Trevor, you're more drunk than I thought. This is a bad idea."

I kept walking but felt Wade behind me.

Knocking, I pulled in a deep breath. It opened, and Scarlett gasped at the sight of me. Then her eyes went past me to Wade.

"He was too drunk to drive over here and asked me to bring him. Sorry, Scarlett, I was afraid if I didn't bring him he'd try and drive."

She smiled slightly at Wade, but it faded when she looked at me.

"I wasn't going to sleep with her."

"I don't care, Trevor. You've made things clear where we stand when you walked away that night."

Shaking my head, I took a step closer, but she backed away with fear in her eyes. I stopped instantly.

Why in the hell is she afraid of me?

"I've been trying to call you. Why won't you let me talk to you?"

Tears filled her eyes, but she did a damn good job of keeping them at bay.

"Actions speak louder than words, Trevor, and I've seen plenty of action from you the last few months, with other women."

"Scarlett, I haven't been with anyone but you in months."

A shocked expression covered her beautiful face. Then she looked at Wade and then over her shoulder to someone else in her house.

"Now is not the time to talk, Trevor."

I took a few steps closer and saw him.

"What the fuck is he doing here?"

"Trev, let's go. Y'all can talk tomorrow," Wade said.

"It's none of your business why I'm here," Eric said in his stupid English accent.

My eyes swung back to Scarlett. She turned to Eric. "Please stop, Eric. You're making this worse."

"Are you fucking him?" I asked, my fists balled up.

"Trevor!" Wade said, pulling my shoulder.

"What?" Scarlett said, hurt laced in her words. "Not that it's any of your business, but no. I'm not a whore like you. He's been here for me when I needed a friend."

Eric had the decency not to smirk at that remark. He looked away from us and walked back into the room.

"I've been wanting to talk to you." My voice sounded desperate. "Why won't you talk to me?"

Her hand covered her mouth, holding back a sob as a tear slipped free.

"Scarlett," I whispered as I walked closer. She dropped her hand, and I cupped her face. "Please, please talk to me."

She pushed me away and shook her head.

"Wade, please get him out of here. He's won't even remember any of this tomorrow."

Anger filled my entire body. "The fuck I won't! I'm not that drunk. Scarlett, *please* let me talk to you. I didn't mean any of what I said that night."

She stared like she wanted to believe the words coming from my mouth—but deep inside—she didn't.

"Eric, please help Wade with Trevor."

Eric started toward me, and I pointed to him. "You come anywhere near me, and I'll punch the fuck out of you, you motherfucker."

Wade jerked me back, causing me to stumble. It was enough to get me out of the door and for Scarlett to shut it.

"Scarlett!" I yelled, but Wade stood in front of me.

"Stop it. Trevor, this is not the right time. Dude, for the love of God, let's get out of here. Talk to her when your liquid courage doesn't make you sound like a pussy."

I stared at my best friend. "I've lost her, haven't I?"

He shook his head and grabbed my arm, guiding me toward his truck.

"I don't know. I do know this isn't going to help win her back."

By the time Wade had driven me to the ranch and my place, I felt like I had sobered up. My head was pounding and I couldn't get Scarlett's face out of my mind.

"You need help getting in?" Wade asked.

I sat there for a few moments, not able to move.

I've lost her.

"Trevor?"

"Nah, I'm good, bro. Thanks for bringing me home."

I went to get out of the truck, but he reached for my arm.

"For what it's worth, I don't think she's dating him, Trevor."

Glancing over my shoulder, I forced a smile. "Thanks again, man. I appreciate it."

I slowly made my way into the house, walking straight to the bar and pouring a shot of whiskey.

After I threw it back in one gulp, I set the shot glass on the bar and whispered, "I've lost her."

CHAPTER 3

Scarlett

Sitting on the sofa, I held the cup of hot tea in my hand and stared out the back window. A bird was currently eating away at the feeder in front of my large picture window that looked out over the massive backyard.

A tear slipped down my cheek, and I didn't have the energy to wipe it away.

The knock on my front door startled me out of my daze. I froze. What if it was Trevor?

I knew I had to talk to him. I'd been avoiding him, fearing the moment he found out I was pregnant. I had no idea how he would react. Would he freak out like he did when he realized we had made love without a condom? Would he pull me into his arms and tell me everything would be okay? Or would he simply tell me I was on my own?

I knew the last one would never happen. I just didn't believe the second would happen either.

My doorbell rang again, and I heard Amelia's voice. I sprung up, nearly spilling my tea before setting it on the coffee table and rushing to the front door.

What if something had happened to Trevor?

Ugh, why do I even care?

I was reminded why I cared as a wave a nausea hit me.

I opened the door and forced a smile, pushing down the urge to throw up.

"Hey, is everything okay?" I asked.

Her bright smile seemed forced, but she didn't seem like she was coming with bad news.

"Wade told me what happened last night. I wanted to make sure you were okay."

Her gaze looked past me and into the house.

"I'm not with Eric, and he's not here."

Relief washed over her face as I gestured for her to come in.

"Scarlett, I'm not sure what is or isn't going on between you and my brother, but Wade said he's never seen Trevor act the way he was acting last night. He said he seemed destroyed at the thought of you with another man."

"Maybe you should be talking to your brother and not me."

I covered my mouth as I closed my eyes. I was never rude like this. With a quick shake of my head, I dropped my hand and looked at Amelia. Her red hair was pulled into a ponytail and there was a glow about her. One that I recognized when I looked at my own face in the mirror. For a brief moment, I wondered if she might be pregnant as well.

"I'm sorry. That was rude. I don't know what came over me and caused me to act like that. I've been working long hours at the courthouse, I think it's catching up to me."

She gave me a gentle smile. "I know what came over you. A Parker man."

Sighing, I headed toward the kitchen. "You've got that right. Hot tea?"

"Oh, that sounds amazing. You wouldn't happen to have peppermint? My stomach is…a bit upset."

"Mine too. Each morning I have to have a cup or I'm throwing…" I trailed off my words and froze in place for a few seconds.

Shit. Shit. Shit.

Turning, I smiled, but Amelia was staring at me. The look on her face seemed to be one of shock. As if we both had come to the same conclusion at the same time.

"Are you pregnant?" we both asked at once.

Amelia smiled, and I turned white as a ghost.

"Yes! I'm around thirteen weeks. We just found out and haven't told anyone!" Amelia squealed with delight.

I forced a smile and wrapped her up in to my arms. "Congratulations, Amelia. I bet Wade is over the moon."

She hugged me back tightly before pulling away. "He is. I'm due not too far behind Harley, April 30. My parents are going to be in grandchild heaven next year."

I swallowed hard, the back of my throat cramped as I held my tears back. Then Amelia's smile faded, and she grabbed my hands.

"Scarlett."

Her voice cracked, and I knew she was reading me like an open book.

"Oh, Scarlett, is it Trevor's baby?"

My chin trembled, and I opened my mouth, but nothing came out. I finally was able to nod a couple of times.

Amelia pulled me back into her arms, and I let the flood gates open. I wasn't sure how long I cried in her arms, but it felt good that someone else knew. As of right now, it was only Maebh, Cord, and Eric. I hadn't told anyone else. Not even my parents. I couldn't take my father's disappointment right now.

"Shhh, it's okay. It's going to be okay."

My body shook as another round of sobs hit me.

"Come on, let's sit down." Amelia's voice was strong and sure. That only made me feel more like an idiot. I wasn't this type of woman. I wasn't weak. I was strong, but this…all of this was throwing me, and I had no idea what to do about any of it.

"I'm…I'm sorry. I didn't mean to break down like that," I said, taking the tissue Amelia had snagged on the way to the living room.

"I take it Trevor doesn't know."

"No. The only people who know are Maebh, Cord, Eric, and now you."

Her eyes widened in shock. "Cord and Maebh know?"

"I ran into them at the doctor's office and, well, let's just say I had a breakdown. Maebh was the first person I told, and I swore her to secrecy, but she told Cord. Unfortunately, she was in Eric's office when she told him. She hadn't seen him in there."

Amelia smiled sweetly. "So that sort of makes sense why Eric was with you last night."

"I was with Maebh last night. Eric was just walking me to my car when I saw Trevor with…*um*…some girl."

She nodded. "He told Wade he wasn't planning on being with her, if that helps any."

I dragged in a deep breath. "It's hard to see the man you're in love with and whose baby your carrying hanging all over other women. Flirting with them, and not wanting to be with you."

Amelia took my hands. "I don't think Trevor feels that way."

"The night we made this baby, he realized we had forgotten a condom and he freaked. He got up and left like it never happened. He didn't say a word to me when he walked out. What's he going to do when he finds out, Amelia? I'm scared to death he'll think I'm trying to trap him."

She scoffed. "He was the one who didn't remember the condom. I know my brother, Scarlett. He wouldn't abandon you or this child."

I nodded, wiping a tear away. "I forgot too. I know he wouldn't turn his back on his child, but he doesn't want a relationship with me. He told me he didn't."

Amelia grinned. "Right now, my brother thinks he's losing you to Eric and that is destroying his entire world. He's upside down and inside out and no clue what to do about it. He *does* want you. He's just too scared to see it."

My eyes widened in shock. "What?"

"Last night when Wade was driving Trevor home, he kept repeating how he'd lost you. Sometimes men need to lose something in order to see what they had."

"I'm not with Eric, though."

"I know," she said, throwing her hand up and waving it around. "Trevor doesn't know that, and right now I'm going to guess he's going out of his damn mind thinking you moved on and you're dating Eric."

Another round of sickness hit me. I stood. "I'll be right back."

Rushing out of the living room, I made it to the half bath and dropped down. I threw up the little bit of breakfast I'd had earlier. My morning sickness wasn't just in the morning. It seemed to hit me whenever it felt like it.

"How bad is it?" Amelia asked, handing me a warm, wet, washcloth.

"It hits me at the strangest times."

Amelia leaned against the sink counter as I planted my ass on the floor and pressed my back against the wall.

"Yours?"

"Morning, first thing. Then I feel great the rest of the day."

I groaned. "I hate you."

She chuckled. "From what I've researched, it sounds like you might be pregnant with a girl. They tend to make you more sick."

My eyes widened, and I smiled. "A girl?"

With a nod, she said, "Yep. Of course, my research consists of old wives' tales, but who cares!"

We both giggled.

"Needless to say, Wade would be happy with either, but I have a pretty strong feeling I'm carrying a boy."

"A girl?" I whispered, my hands going to my stomach.

"When are you due?" Amelia asked.

"May twenty-fifth."

She smiled. "Three weeks after me. We're not that far apart."

Sitting on the floor, she bumped my knee. "Me, you, and Harley are all pregnant at the same time! How fun will this be?"

I tried to smile, but I knew it looked fake.

"When are you going to tell him? Please don't wait too long, Scarlett. It wouldn't be fair for Trevor to miss out on things."

Looking at the ground, I shook my head. "Right now, I don't really care what is fair to Trevor. He's pushed and pulled at my emotions so much, Amelia, and I'm pissed at him."

She blew out a breath. "That's fair. Listen, I know what we need to do to cheer you up."

My eyes lifted to hers. "What?"

"We need to have a girls' day."

I chewed on my lip. "I'm not…um…ready to tell anyone else about the baby."

Amelia stood, pulling me up with her. "Hell, neither am I. As of right now, you're the only other person who knows."

"What did you have in mind?" I asked, making my way to the kitchen for a glass of water to rinse my mouth out.

"I know you don't really know Waylynn and Paxton, or Corina and Harley, but they're all amazing. I know they want to get to know you, so I say we meet them for brunch, then we go to my place and have a fun-filled day. Bring your swimsuit, we'll get in the pool."

She spun around and looked at me. "You're not showing, are you? You're not that far along."

I shook my head. "Almost ten weeks."

"I don't have anything but a little pouch that honestly I've always had!"

We both laughed again.

"So, you in?"

I chewed on the inside of my cheek as Amelia tilted her head and gave me a pleading look.

"Okay, I'm in."

CHAPTER 4

Trevor

My father's truck pulled up and stopped as I drank the last of my water. It might have been mid-October, but it was still hot as hell.

"Trevor, Wade, how's the new fence going up?"

Wade walked to my father and shook his hand. "Morning, sir."

"It's going like any other fence, Dad. Mitchell send you out here to check on us?"

My father laughed. "No. He and Steed were trying to get some cattle out of the east pasture. Looks like someone cut the fence to ride their four wheelers again."

I cursed under my breath. Damn kids. When I caught those little bastards I was going to string them up by their toes.

Wade groaned next to me. "Damn kids."

Nodding, my father replied, "I'm going to string the little bastards up in the barn and lash 'em."

I couldn't help but smirk at how close my thoughts were to my father's.

"You boys want to grab some food? Melanie is meeting Joyce for lunch, and I've been abandoned by everyone. Wade, your wife is having a little party over at your house. Girls only I've been informed."

My chest dropped at the mention of Joyce, Scarlett's mother.

Wade grinned like a love-struck puppy. "Amelia texted that I wasn't allowed home until this evening. It is a girl-only zone."

The hearty laugh that rumbled from my father's chest made me smile. "It's nice to see them all spending some time together. They also invited Scarlett."

My head jerked up, and my father smiled—like he knew that bit of information would grab my attention.

"Scarlett?"

Her name was out of my mouth before I could stop myself.

"Seems Maebh and Scarlett have become friends recently."

"Really?" I said, casting a glance over to Wade. He shrugged, like he had no idea why my father was bringing this up.

With a wink he added, "Seems to me you boys should crash the party later. It could be fun."

Wade laughed, and I frowned. Was my mother getting my father involved in her plans push to get Scarlett and me together? I sure as hell hoped not. It was hard enough with her butting in; if you added my father to the mix it would be too much to take.

"I'd stay and help, but it looks like the two of you got it covered. Enjoy the hot Texas day."

"See ya around, Dad," I called after him. Wade went back to work as I watched my father turn his truck around and head down the dirt road.

"What was that all about?" I asked, facing Wade.

"What do you mean?"

"He was talking about Scarlett."

Wade shrugged. "So?"

"Did you tell anyone about last night?" I asked, picking up the wire cutters and making my way over to him.

"No. Well, Amelia. I told Amelia."

I groaned. "Why?"

He let out a gruff laugh. "Because I tell my wife everything. And, dude, do you even remember last night?"

"I remember you stopping me before I ripped Eric's goddamn throat out of his neck."

Wade laughed. "Then you weren't as drunk as I thought you were."

I huffed and got back to work. The sweat poured off of me as we got the fence up and headed over to the east pasture to fix another fence that had been cut.

"You think they're dating?" I finally asked.

"Who?" Wade wiped his forehead with his sleeve.

"You know who the fuck I'm talking about. Scarlett and Eric."

"No, I don't think they're dating."

"What makes you so sure?"

Wade stopped working and faced me. His expression was serious.

"Trevor, what's going on with you when it comes to Scarlett? It was pretty damn clear last night you're fucking around with her feelings, dude. I love you like a brother, but you need to make a decision if you want this girl or not. Right now all I see is an asshole treating a pretty damn amazing woman like shit."

"You don't know…"

Wade cut me off. "You're right, but it's obvious to everyone around you how you're treating Scarlett. I don't know why she keeps letting you in, to be honest. I'm thinking Eric is probably the better choice for her."

I stumbled back some. It felt like Wade's words had pushed a knife right through my heart. He wasn't finished either.

"For fuck's sake, even I could feel her pain from where I was standing. If you don't want her, let her go, Trevor. If you do want her and can see a future with her, then do something about it."

Wade turned away and went back to working on the fence, leaving me alone in my thoughts.

When I finally made my way over to the fence, I felt my anger building.

"I'm not the type of guy to settle down. At least, not yet anyway."

He huffed. "So you want her to wait for you? Pretty fucking selfish, man."

"No. Yes, fuck, I don't know what I want."

Wade faced me, a serious look on his face.

"How many women have you been with since the benefit dinner last spring, *not* including Scarlett."

"Why?"

"Just answer the question, Trevor."

"One."

He shook his head and took two steps toward me. "Admit it to yourself, Trevor. You love Scarlett and that scares the hell out of you. You obviously knew each other before that dinner. I saw the way the two of you looked at each other."

"We did," I admitted.

"Intimately?"

I rubbed the back of my neck. "No. We sort of grew up together off and on. Mom would bring me to her house when we were young, or her mom would bring her here. I don't really remember much when we were little. We played tag a few times. She left to go to high school in Boston. She came back into town our senior year and I ran into her at a party. We went for coffee and I…*um*…kissed her."

Wade stared at me for a few moments. "Trevor, you say you can't give up women, that you aren't ready to settle down, but let me ask you something. When you were with that one other woman, did you wish you were with Scarlett?"

My heart froze in my chest. I stood there, not saying a word.

"Yeah, I thought so. Why are you so afraid to commit to her?"

"I don't know. I honest to God don't know. I mean, all I do know is that if I give her my heart she totally has the power to destroy me and that has me fucking sideways, bro."

He scoffed. "Well, you better figure it the fuck out, dude. Sooner rather than later. I'm pretty sure you hold that same power over her. Her tears last night were proof."

A knock on my office door made me glance up from the planting schedule that Wade had given me earlier that week.

Cord stood in the doorway, a smile on his face.

"Hey, what brings you here?"

He shrugged as he walked in. "Maebh is over at Amelia's for some girl's day. Thought I would swing by and see what's going on."

I ignored the bit of information about Amelia's party. "You wouldn't happen to be free this week, would you? We've got to bale the south pasture, and we sure could use the help."

Sitting in the large leather chair in front of my desk, he nodded. "Count me in. Tripp coming?"

"Yeah, he cleared his schedule, but I think that morning Harley has a sonogram he's going to."

Cord moved around in his seat and started looking around the office, suddenly seeming uncomfortable.

"You okay?"

He laughed. "Yeah, it's weird thinking about Tripp and Harley. I'm happy for them."

A warm smile moved over my face. "Me too."

Cord looked at me with concern in his eyes. "You talk to Scarlett lately?"

I sighed and dropped back in my seat. "Sort of. I fucked up last night and took a stripper from the bachelor party out to my truck. Nothing happened, besides her sucking my face off, but before I could push her away and tell her she needed to go back in, Scarlett walked up on us."

Cord groaned. "Fucking hell, Trevor. Are you out of your damn mind?!"

The disappointment in his voice nearly killed me. I seemed to be disappointing a lot of people lately.

"She took off with that fucker from Maebh's restaurant."

Cord's look of surprise—and then dread—made me frown.

"Eric was with her?" he asked.

I leaned in closer. "Yeah, does he like her? Is there something going on with them?"

The way Cord's throat bobbed made me realize he knew something he wasn't telling me.

"No, I think they're friends. That's all."

My brow lifted. "You *think* they're just friends?"

He half shrugged. "I mean, I get the feeling he might like her, but…"

Cord's voice trailed off.

"But?" I replied, motioning with my hand for him to keep going.

His cell phone rang, and he quickly grabbed it. Smiling, he answered.

"Hey, Maebh, y'all having fun?"

He smiled, so I was guessing the girls' day party was a hit.

Glancing at his watch, he said, "I'll pick you up in about an hour. I'm on my bike."

I glanced down at the schedule again and made a few notes while Cord finished talking to Maebh. When he ended the call, I looked back at him. The smile on his face even made me smile.

"Jesus H. Christ, dude. You look like you're on cloud nine."

He seemed to glow with happiness. If I wasn't so happy for him I would think he was pussy whipped and call his ass out on it.

"I am. I honestly didn't think I would ever be this happy."

My chest ached because even if I didn't want to admit it to myself, I was jealous of Cord. His smile faded, and he leaned over, placing his arms on his legs.

"Trevor, I'm pretty damn sure Scarlett loves you."

Mixed emotions swirled around in my head. I was happy Cord had said that, and scared, and confused as to why he'd said it. How in the hell would he know how Scarlett felt about me?

"How do you know that?" I asked.

"Maebh and Scarlett have become close the last couple of weeks. They share…things."

"Like?"

His head dropped, and he groaned. He was for sure keeping something from me and I could tell it was eating him up. When he looked up at me, he blew out a breath.

"Listen, all I can say for sure is that if you don't figure this shit out, you're going to lose her and a helluva lot more than that."

"Lose her to Eric?" I asked, half joking, half serious. The look on Cord's face was one-hundred-percent serious.

"Yes. To Eric. I think he has a thing for her, and he's been hanging around her a lot the last few days. He knows she is…vulnerable. He's a good guy, and I don't think he's taking advantage of anything, but they're growing closer. You need to figure this out, Trev. Fast."

I dropped back in my chair, scrubbing my hands down my four-day stubble.

"I've messed things up so bad with Scarlett. I've said some things to her I know she can't forgive. I've been trying to call her and she keeps ignoring me."

"Because she keeps seeing a different woman hanging on you, dude. How do you expect her to ever forgive you or give you a chance if you can't keep your dick in your pants?"

"I haven't been with anyone in months besides Scarlett. The last time we were together, things got pretty intense. I'd never in my life felt the way I felt that night I was with her, and I sort of walked out on her."

His eyes filled with understanding. Did he know Scarlett and I had had unprotected sex?

"Did Scarlett tell Maebh about that night?"

Cord's eyes left mine, and he looked down at the floor. "Yes."

Damn.

"I've never done anything like that before, it's just, we got so caught up in each other and…hell…Scarlett has always made me feel different."

Cord's brows pulled in tight. "What do you mean, 'always made you feel different'?"

I laughed. "Fuck, I've had a thing for her since middle school."

Shock rushed over my brother's face. "*What*? I didn't think you even knew her that well before Mom made you take her to the benefit dinner. I mean, y'all played together when you were younger, but I thought once she left town for school, you didn't think twice about her."

With a shake of my head, I told him about how she had been the first…and last…girl I'd ever asked to dance with in middle school. How I never even asked anyone to dance at any school function after that. I told him about the night Scarlett and I went and had coffee and how I'd had kissed her.

"Wait, Trevor, you're telling me you've liked Scarlett for that long?"

I swallowed hard, ready to admit to myself and to him the truth. "Yes."

"What the fuck are you doing then?"

"I don't know! I guess I'm scared."

"Of?"

"The same fucking reasons you were with Maebh. I'm worried I'm going to hurt her, or worse yet, she'll hurt me."

Cord stood and started pacing. What in the hell was wrong with him?

"Trevor, you need to talk to Scarlett. Y'all need to work this out. This trying to push her away because you think you can forget how you feel about her, it's not working, and you...you...you really *need* to talk."

I stood, fear gripping my chest. He knew something. I could see it all over his face. "What are you not telling me, Cord?"

His eyes met mine. "Nothing."

I scoffed. "You always were a terrible liar."

Pushing his fingers through his hair, Cord let out a breath. "Let me just give you a piece of advice, little bro. If you wait too long, I'm not sure you're ever going to be able to get her back, and you're going to regret it. Trust me when I say that. You'll regret it for a lot of different reasons."

This had to do with Eric. I knew it did. That fucker was moving in on Scarlett, and I'd be damned if I would sit back and let that happen.

CHAPTER 5

Scarlett

I'd never laughed so hard in my life. Maebh, Waylynn, and I were sitting on a float in Amelia's pool listening to Waylynn tell the story of how Mrs. Hopkins walked in when she and Jonathon first did the deed.

"What did she do when she walked in on y'all?" I asked, giggling.

"And tell me you had finished, and she didn't ruin it for you!" Maebh added.

"Oh, I was yelling out Jonathon's name, and he was grunting like a stallion letting his shit go. When we finally came down from our orgasms, I looked to see Old Lady Hopkins standing there, her hand over her heart in shock. So shocked, she didn't move the entire time Jonathon zipped his junk back into his pants."

I laughed harder, holding my cramping side. "I can't...even..." I said between laughs.

Waylynn smiled and winked at me. "It was worth it, even with all the shit she caused me afterwards."

"I'd say so," Maebh replied, wiping a laughing tear away.

Waylynn turned to me. "So tell me, Scarlett. Is my brother Trevor as well-endowed as he makes everyone believe?"

I nearly choked on my drink. "Wh-what?"

"Come on. We want to hear details," Paxton said, giving me a wink.

"*Um*."

"Holy smokes, look at her cheeks turning pink!" Corina gasped.

Maebh gave me a sweet smile and then nodded.

"He's certainly not lacking anywhere," I said.

A fit of giggles hit everyone, me included.

"That doesn't say much. Is he big or not?" Paxton asked, taking a long drink of her cosmo. Waylynn and Paxton were on their way to tipsy, with Corina and Maebh not far behind. Harley, Amelia, and I were not drinking, but Amelia was making me and her virgin drinks, and no one else was any the wiser.

I felt my cheeks heat. "Trevor is very big."

"It's in the Parker blood, I'm telling you!" Paxton said.

"Gross!" Amelia shouted, splashing Paxton.

All eyes went to Corina. "Mitchell?" I asked with a raise of my eyebrows.

She smiled and took a sip of her drink. "I don't kiss and tell."

"What the heck!" I shouted. "I told y'all about Trevor! You have to tell us about Mitchell."

"Steed's name fits him, that's all I'm saying," Paxton added, then hiccupped, clearly buzzed.

Waylynn groaned and then laughed. Amelia looked horrified.

"Fine, Mitchell is big. Thick and big."

A round of hollers came across the pool as Waylynn splashed Corina. "Okay, big is one thing, but don't describe my brother as being *thick*. The visual makes me gag!"

Harley laughed and everyone looked at her. She grinned and that was all the answer we needed.

Then all eyes went to Maebh.

"I have no problem saying Cord has a big dick."

Laughter erupted again, and this time Amelia and Waylynn laughed. Something about Maebh's Irish accent made her stress the word a little bit more. I'd never felt more at ease with a group of women than I did with these ladies. They made me feel so welcomed, like I had been in their little group for years.

"It's a damn good thing Aunt Vi took Chloe to her place," Waylynn said, finishing off her drink.

Paxton tapped my foot with hers. "I heard a rumor about you, Scarlett."

My entire body froze. "A rumor?" I hated that my voice cracked.

"You were quite the dancer in high school."

Amelia laughed. "*I* told you that, Paxton!"

My eyes darted to Amelia with a puzzled look.

"Okay, so I remember a party I went to once. You and Trevor were seniors and your girlfriends did a group dance. Y'all had practiced it all summer when you were home from school in Boston, and you performed it at Brad's end-of-the-summer party."

I covered my face and laughed. "The one to 'Dirrty'?"

"Yes!" Amelia said, pointing to me.

Waylynn headed over to me, grabbing my float and pulling me toward the steps. "Wait, what is this dance? I need to see it."

"No way, Waylynn! It was just some silly thing the girls and I did. We made up two dances to Christina Aguilera songs."

"I want to see!" Maebh said, pushing me out of the water.

"Maebh!" I exclaimed.

"Hurry, me man will be here soon to pick me up and I want to see this."

Groaning, I let Waylynn drag me over to the deck that was just a bit higher than the pool.

"Amelia, can I connect my phone to your Bluetooth speaker?" Waylynn yelled.

"Yes!" Amelia called out. She was now acting a bit tipsy, only because Corina had asked her how come she wasn't feeling the drinks with how many she'd had. I played it safe and only had two drinks and mixed a lot of water in between, so no one questioned that I wasn't feeling tipsy.

Waylynn wore a huge smile as the notes to Christina Aguilera's "Dirrty" started playing.

"Get it, gurl!" Paxton yelled.

It didn't take me long to get into the vibe of the song. As soon as Christina started singing, my hips started moving, and the dance moves instantly came back to me. I couldn't believe I remembered it all from the music video.

I decided to have fun with it. It was just the girls and me, and for the first time in a long time, I was having fun.

Waylynn quickly joined me. Her body was amazing, and moved in perfect sync with mine. Of course, alcohol made her a little more brazen as she got super close, and I wasn't sure if I should go along with it, but when Maebh and Amelia yelled out, I knew it was okay to let loose.

Soon we were for sure dirty dancing with each other. Waylynn even slapped my ass, making me laugh. It was nice to let myself get lost in the music and fun. Soon the rest of the girls were dancing with us.

Maebh was the only one not dancing, only because she had decided this needed to be recorded. Then her face dropped and her eyes looked past us and then quickly back to our little group. She made a little motion with her finger across her neck, as if saying we needed to stop. I turned and froze. Six men were watching us. My gaze landed on a set of blue eyes that had haunted my dreams for six years.

"Trevor," I whispered.

"Holy fucking shit. That was the hottest damn thing I've ever seen," Wade said before Mitchell smacked him on the head.

"That's my wife you're staring at, asshole," Mitchell replied, making his way over to Corina and pulling her into his arms. "You're doing that dance for me later tonight," he whispered loudly to her.

My cheeks heated as I watched Wade walk over to Amelia and kiss her passionately.

I turned and made my way over to the chair that had my wrap on it. I could feel Trevor's eyes on me. Burning into me.

"Hey, I feel like I was cheated since my girl was recording that!" Cord shouted, walking up to Maebh and gently kissing her lips. The way he looked at her, like she was his everything, made my stomach drop. They were adorable. I wanted a man to look at me like that.

"What's Trevor doing here?" I asked, as Cord and Maebh came closer to me.

Cord cleared his throat and said, "My bike wouldn't start, so he offered to give me a ride and take us home."

I tried not to look his way, but I couldn't help the pull. Whenever Trevor was around, it felt like I was a moth to a flame. He could both destroy me and give me life.

But when he started our way, I held my breath, quickly looking around for an escape. Maebh saw what I was doing and wrapped her arm around mine, keeping me rooted in place.

Walking up to me, Trevor smiled and my knees went weak. *Damn it. Stop reacting to him, stupid, betraying body.* "I remember that dance. A few of your friends did it at Brad's party that one summer."

Trevor had been there? I hadn't even seen him at that party. He was probably off messing around with some girl.

"I didn't know you were there," I said, lifting my chin and trying to relay my thoughts to him with the power of my eyes.

"I only stopped by to get Amelia. I got there in time to see the dance, then dragged my sister away."

Trying not to smile, I simply nodded.

His eyes traveled over my body, and I realized I still had my cover open. Trevor was looking at me greedily and I hated the way it made my lower stomach pull with desire.

"Do you need a ride home, Scarlett?" Cord asked.

When I glanced over at Wade and Amelia, they were lost in each other. Even though Amelia said they'd give me a ride home, I hated asking.

"I hate to bug Amelia."

Cord hit Trevor on the shoulder, pulling his eyes off of me.

"Mind dropping off Scarlett?" Cord asked.

"Not at all," Trevor replied, a crooked smile on his face.

I wanted to argue, but how else would I get home? I could call Eric, but I was beginning to depend on him a little too much and didn't want to give him the wrong idea about our friendship. Maebh had already warned me Eric had feelings for me, even before we had become friends.

"Are you sure?" I asked, chewing on my bottom lip. Trevor reached over and pulled my lip from between my teeth, causing my entire body to zip with electricity.

Damn him. Damn him. Damn him.

I wanted to hate him. A part of me did. He had played around so much with my feelings, I wasn't sure I was ready to be alone with him. Maybe he'd drop me off first, and then Cord and Maebh.

"Good. I want to talk to you," Trevor stated, giving me a slight smile.

Looking away, I gathered my things and turned to the three of them. "Do y'all mind if I change really quick?"

"Good idea!" Maebh stated, following me into the house. When we were in the guest bedroom, I tried to pull in a few deep breaths.

"Are you okay?" Maebh asked.

"No," I replied. "I'm not sure I'm ready to be alone with Trevor. I'm not ready to tell him."

She took her hands in mine. "Scarlett, he deserves to know. The longer you put it off, the harder it will be, lass."

Nodding, I fought the tears that threatened to spill. "I know... I'm just not ready for how he'll react."

With a frown, she let out a breath. "Don't wait too long. If he finds out from someone else, it will destroy him."

"Like who?" I asked.

Maebh shrugged but didn't answer.

Sitting in the truck it hit me how exhausted from being out in the sun and all the activity at Amelia's place. Trevor and Cord were talking about the ranch in the front seat, and Maebh had fallen asleep not five minutes after we left. It didn't take me long to feel my eyelids growing heavy as I drifted off to sleep in the back of the truck.

A gentle movement lulled me back as I inhaled deeply. His smell filled my senses, causing me to relax even more.

Trevor.

He was carrying me.

His cologne engulfed me, instantly making me press into him. My body was exhausted. I didn't even have the energy to open my eyes. When I felt him climbing the stairs, I knew he had carried me into my house.

When he placed me on the bed, I grabbed my pillow and snuggled into it. Then the bed dipped, and I felt his presence. I didn't move, except to continue my slow breathing.

Barely cracking my eye open, I found Trevor sitting on my bed staring straight ahead. His shoulders sagged. He looked defeated and an ache grew deep within my chest. The urge to sit up and hold him was strong, but at the same time, I wasn't sure I wanted to keep opening myself up to him. I gave and he took. I couldn't take any more of that.

Trevor dragged his hands down his face and let out a soft exhale, then he spoke so softly, I struggled to hear his words.

"I don't know what to do. I love you, Scarlett. You deserve someone better than me. I'm so fucking scared and confused."

My breath caught in my throat, and I had to force myself to close my eyes and breathe.

Oh. My. Goodness. Trevor said he loved me. He loves me!

I wanted to scream out. Why could he only say this when he thought I was asleep? What was keeping him from telling me how he truly felt?

"Please, God. I just need one more chance here to get this right."

His voice sounded desperate. I opened my eyes and went to talk, but the bed moved and Trevor stood. For some reason, I shut my eyes again, making him think I was still asleep. I needed to process his words before I did or said anything.

I felt a blanket on top of me. He gently kissed my forehead and butterflies took flight in my stomach like they did every single time this man touched me.

"Sleep good, angel."

I immediately felt the loss of warmth when he walked out of my room. My eyes stayed shut as I listened to him go down the steps. When the front door clicked shut, I sat up in bed, hugging my stomach. I stared at the now-empty doorway, trying to wrap my head around what I'd just heard. Trevor said he loved me.

My head dropped back, and I stared at the ceiling. Tears quickly pooled in my eyes and released in a rush down my face.

The push and pull of Trevor Parker was taking its toll on me, and I wasn't sure how much more of it I could take.

I needed to tell him about the baby, and I needed to do it soon.

CHAPTER 6

Trevor

Cord's Place was packed, and I couldn't seem to keep up like normal. My mind was all over the damn place. Every time I closed my eyes I saw Scarlett. Scarlett dancing in that damn two-piece bathing suit. Scarlett walking into Lilly's for breakfast. Scarlett running down Main Street as I walked into the bar. She was fucking everywhere.

I called her earlier to see if we could talk. This time she answered her phone and said she had something to tell me, but that she already had plans for this evening. We made arrangements to meet for breakfast tomorrow, and I was counting down the hours until I could see her. I needed to tell her how I felt about her...how she scared the living shit out of me. I needed her to know about the stupid voice in my head that told me I wasn't good enough for a woman like Scarlett.

"Trevor Parker."

My head snapped up to see two girls I went to high school with standing on the other side of the bar.

"Well, if it isn't Channing Jones and Sydney Moore. What are you two doing in Oak Springs?" I asked with a polite smile.

"Causin' trouble," Channing said with a wink. "Want in on it?"

I laughed. Channing and I had hooked up once, the summer after my freshman year of college. We'd been drunk at the time and even though it was fun, it had been a mistake. Hell, all of my hookups felt like mistakes looking back.

"Nah, not interested."

Her lower lip jetted out. "Don't tell me you've changed your ways, Trevor. I was sort of hoping for a repeat of the last time we had...fun."

I wasn't surprised by my lack of interest in Channing. My cock didn't jump for anyone anymore but the dark-haired beauty who consumed my every thought.

"A party for three, maybe?" Sydney added. That should have caught my attention, but all it did was turn my stomach. The thought of being with any other woman besides Scarlett actually made me feel sick.

What in the living fuck is wrong with me?

Scarlett Littlefield was what was wrong.

She was the only woman I wanted. The only woman I'd ever loved. That realization hit me like a brick wall. Even though I said it to her last night in her room while she was sleeping, I needed to tell her to her face. I needed to make her see it in my eyes.

I loved her. I fucking loved her.

And I needed to see her, tell her how I felt. Beg her to forgive me for being a complete idiot.

There was no way I was waiting until tomorrow morning. I'd waited long enough.

"Ladies, if you'll excuse me, there's someone I need to see."

"Who could possibly be more important than a threesome, Trevor?" Channing asked, a smirk on her face.

"I didn't even realize exactly how important she was until just now, so thank you for that, Channing."

Her eyes widened in surprise while Sydney's jaw dropped.

"She?" Channing spit out.

I nodded, then turned from them, making my way over to Cord. Slapping him on the back, I leaned in close and said, "I'm leaving."

He laughed and looked at me. "You're leaving?"

"I need to talk to Scarlett. Now."

A smile moved across my brother's face. "It's about fucking time."

My hand landed on his shoulder, and I gave it a squeeze. "You okay here if I leave? It's packed."

"Yeah, Ross is coming in. He asked to work some overtime, so he can bartend. Go do what you need to do," Cord shouted over the music.

I jumped over the bar, ignoring the looks from women who clearly wanted something from me. I'd probably fucked at least half of them if they were locals. Hell, I couldn't even remember, which really made me realize what a complete dick I was.

Once I was outside, I jogged to my truck. I'd parked across the street and just down from the bar earlier today. When I got into the cab, I glanced across the street and saw right into Aisling. The small sitting area had a few people there, and when I saw Scarlett, I smiled. There was a girl sitting to her right and someone to her left.

Jumping out of my truck, I started across the street but stopped when I saw who was sitting on the other side of Scarlett.

Eric.

He leaned in so that both women could hear him as he spoke. Whatever the jerk said, they both laughed. Scarlett put her hand on his shoulder, and I saw red. And I kept walking toward the restaurant, trying to see if anyone else was with them. Another guy sat across from Scarlett, his hand laced with the other girl's hand on the table.

Eric leaned in closer to Scarlett to speak, clearly only wanting her to hear what he had to say. She shook her head, and Eric stood. When he leaned down and kissed her cheek, I froze in place. Scarlett watched him walk away and then turned her head and looked straight out the window, as if she could feel my presence.

Our eyes met and her smile fell. I took a few steps back and I thought for a moment she was going to come outside, but she didn't move. Turning, I quickly jogged over to my truck and got in. My phone buzzed in my pocket, but I ignored it as I pushed the button and started my truck.

The entire drive back to the ranch I felt numb.

Eric had been her *other plans* tonight. She really had moved on. Maybe that was what she wanted to tell me.

Pulling up to my garage, I slammed my hand on the steering wheel and yelled out as loud as I could.

"You stupid fucking idiot! You fucking idiot!"

I ran my hands over my face, and I shook my head as I let out a gruff laugh.

"You lost her, you damn fool."

When I finally got out of my truck and headed into my place, I pulled my phone out of my pocket. Scarlett had sent me a text.

Scarlett: *Why did you leave?*

Trevor: *I wanted to talk to you, but I didn't realize you were on a date.*

My phone rang less than a minute later. For a moment, I thought about sending her to voicemail, but I answered.

"Hello?"

"Hey, it's Scarlett."

Smiling, I replied, "I know."

"Why are you not working at Cord's Place? I thought you said you were going in tonight."

I rubbed the back of my neck. I wasn't about to tell her how I felt over the phone, and hell, I wasn't even sure if it mattered to her anymore.

"I needed to clear my head and I happened to see you when I was walking to my truck, but I saw you were with…people…so I left."

"I wasn't on a date. I'm visiting with a friend of mine. I haven't seen her since she graduated college, and she was in San Antonio with her fiancé and they drove over to Oak Springs to see me."

"You and Eric looked cozy."

Scarlett was silent for a moment. "Not as cozy as you and that stripper looked a few nights ago."

Okay, *ouch*, I deserved that.

She cleared her throat when I didn't answer.

"I don't think I'll be back home until later this evening and by then I'm sure it will be too late to talk. Are we still on for tomorrow morning?"

Forcing my voice not to crack, I answered, "Yeah, I mean, if you are. I'd like to talk to you about something. Nothing bad, I mean, I guess it's good. I think. Fuck, I don't know."

I could hear the smile in her voice as she replied softly, "Same here."

"Okay, then I'll see you in the morning?" I asked, sort of relieved that she didn't have anything bad to tell me.

"Yes."

"Good night, Scarlett."

She paused for a moment, almost as if she was debating on saying something else.

"Good night, Trevor."

I parked across the square and sat in my truck, waiting to see if Scarlett was going to show up for breakfast this morning. After last night, I wouldn't be surprised if she bailed.

When I saw her, my breath stilled. She was so beautiful.

Dressed in jeans and a light tan sweater, she had her dark brown hair pulled up into a ponytail. She walked into Lilly's and took a seat in the same booth we sat in so many years ago.

I dragged in a deep breath and got out of the truck. My feet wanted to run to her, but I made myself walk at a normal pace, not taking my eyes off of her. As I crossed the street, she turned and her warm brown eyes locked with my blue.

She smiled, and I had to force my legs to keep moving because all they wanted to do was go weak.

As I got closer, I felt someone reach for my shoulder, pulling me to a stop.

"Trevor?"

His voice was like nails going down a fucking chalkboard.

Stopping, I turned to face Eric.

"Eric."

"What are you doing?"

Lifting a brow, I asked, "What do you mean?"

"You're playing around with her emotions, lad."

I laughed, but not in a friendly way. "What the fuck do you know about me and Scarlett?"

He shot me a dirty look that said he knew plenty. "I know you're hurting her, and she can't move on because you won't let her go."

Pushing his hand from my arm, I took a step closer. "I don't know what the fuck your game is, but stay away from her. She's mine."

He had the nerve to smile. "She's not a piece of property you can claim, lad. And I'm going to be real honest. I like her...a lot. I'm tired of seeing you hurt her."

My fists balled up and I was ready knock the fuck out this ass-hole when I heard Scarlett.

"Trevor!"

Snapping my gaze in the direction of her voice, I stepped away from Eric. Scarlett was standing out front of Lilly's, her eyes bouncing from me to Eric.

"So will Eric be joining us this morning, Scarlett?" I asked, bitterness laced in my voice.

She looked confused as she focused on Eric, giving him a stern look before she looked me in the eyes. "No, I'm having breakfast with you. Only you."

Eric walked over to her. "Scarlett, you were very upset the last time you saw him. Are you sure you don't want me to stay?"

"What the fuck?" I mumbled, shaking my head at this asshole.

Scarlett's gaze looked past him at me, and I was positive I saw anger before she focused back on Eric. I just wasn't sure if she was pissed at me or him.

"I'm not a child who needs protecting, Eric, and Trevor won't upset me again."

Eric scoffed. "That's all he's ever done to you, love."

"Love?" I asked.

Scarlett looked at me again. This time, something else was in her eyes. Something that scared the piss out of me, but I couldn't place what it was.

"What's going on with you two?" I demanded. Eric shot me a shit-eating grin.

Scarlett, on the other hand, gave me a look of pleading. "Nothing is going on between us!"

Before I could ask anything else, my phone rang with my mother's ringtone. Pulling it out of my pocket, I answered it.

"Mom, now is not a good time to—"

"Trevor! Your father... Something's happened to your father!"

My heart dropped. "What do you mean something's happened to Dad?"

"He called me from his cell. I couldn't understand him. I thought he said he couldn't breathe! I don't know where he is on the ranch. He took Wild Bill out for a ride after breakfast."

"I'm on my way. Call Steed, Mitchell, and Wade. Have them start looking."

"I already did. I saw you leaving earlier, so I knew you weren't on the ranch, but Steed's worried. He's going up in the plane to look from above."

My heart was racing. Scarlett stood by my side, her hand on my arm, worry in her eyes.

"Call me if anyone finds him. I'm leaving Lilly's now."

I hit End and looked at Scarlett. "I'm sorry, angel, I need to go. Something's happened to my dad."

She nodded. "Okay. Go! Please let me know if he's okay?"

Without even thinking, I leaned down and kissed her on the lips. "I will."

Running back to my truck, I pulled out my phone and called Cord.

"Cord!"

"I'm already on my way, just left my place."

"Fuck, what do you think happened?"

There was silence on the other end. "Cord!"

"I don't know, Trevor. Mitchell just called and said he was almost to the house. Just be careful driving and get there in one piece, all right?"

The phone went dead. Dropping my cell on the seat, I gripped the wheel and pushed down on the gas.

"Don't fucking do this to us, Dad. *Don't*."

CHAPTER 7

Trevor

By the time I got to the house, Steed had spotted Dad from the plane in the east pasture, leaning up against a tree. Wade and Mitchell had gotten to him within minutes after Steed called in the location. The ambulance was already at the house, and by the time I got out of my truck and over to it, they were getting Dad out of the Jeep.

"I broke something and got the wind and my pride knocked out of me. I'm fine. This isn't necessary," he said.

I let out the breath I hadn't realized I'd been holding.

"What happened?" my mother cried out, kissing my father on the lips and hugging him, making him moan.

"I fell off the horse. Damn thing reared up at a bob cat. I wasn't expecting it, and I hit the ground. When I called you…well, I still hadn't been able to catch my breath from the damn wind getting knocked out of me."

My mother sagged in relief and held her hand over her chest.

"John Parker, you gave me a fright! I thought you had a heart attack, you asshole!"

There was no way I could hold back the laugh, and neither could everyone else around us, including the two EMS folks who tried to assess Dad.

Steed jogged up, taking in the situation. "He's okay, sort of. He got thrown from Wild Bill and thinks he broke something. Said the wind was knocked out of him," Mitch said.

About that time, Waylynn and Jonathon came running over. Jonathon was holding Liberty.

"Daddy! Are you okay? We were heading to San Antonio and turned around when Momma called."

"I'm fine, Waylynn. Just need to nurse my pride and maybe a rib or two."

She let out a sigh of relief. "Someone call Amelia!"

"I did already, and Corina." Paxton stood close by with a very scared Chloe next to her, along with a sleeping Gage in her arms. I walked up and took Gage, while Steed picked up Chloe and told her Granddaddy was okay.

"I'll take Gage inside. Dad, you need me to go find Wild Bill?" I asked.

My father glanced to Wade, who shook his head, and said, "I'll get him. Don't worry."

"Mr. Parker, we need to get you into the ambulance and to the hospital," one of the EMS workers said.

"I'm not getting in no damn ambulance!" My father stated as Waylynn and Mom started helping my father toward the back of the ambulance.

"Yes, you are, John Parker," Mom said with a firm voice.

"Daddy, stop being a jackass," Waylynn added. "Jonathon, are you okay with Liberty? I'm going to ride with my mom in the ambulance."

"Yes, go! We're fine," Jonathon replied.

My father groaned. "For the love of Christ, women. I'm fine."

The door to the ambulance shut, and the EMS driver said, "This ought to be fun."

We all chuckled and watched as they drove down the driveway.

"Holy shit," Mitchell said next to me.

"Bad words, Uncle Mitchell," Chloe announced.

"Sorry, pumpkin. The situation called for it."

"Don't even!" Steed said to Chloe. She put her finger to her mouth as if saying she would remain silent. Then her face turned serious.

"Is Granddaddy going to be okay, Daddy?" Chloe asked, her big blue eyes looking up at Steed.

He kissed her cheek. "He's going to be sore, but okay."

Two hours later, we all sat in the living room of my folks' house, everyone minus mom and Waylynn. My father had made it clear no one else was to come to the hospital. He had two broken ribs, a bruised ego, and wasn't in the mood to deal with us. It had been hard not to go, but Mom made us all promise we'd listen to his wishes.

Pulling out my phone, I glanced down to re-read Scarlett's last text to me.

Scarlett: *I'm so glad your dad is okay. Give him my love and let me know if y'all need anything.*

I had replied with a simple, *okay*. But now, as I stared at it, I wanted to tell her I needed her. I needed to feel her in my arms, to see her smile up at me. To smell that vanilla scent that always seemed to be around her. I needed a fucking candle with that smell.

My hands shook as I typed a new reply.

Me: *I'm sorry about breakfast. I was pretty shaken up, but I'm glad it wasn't worse.*

Scarlett: *I'm glad too. Make it up to me tomorrow?*

Smiling, I replied.

Me: *Yes.*

"I'm starving!" Amelia stated as she stood. "Let's go to Lilly's for something to eat."

Chloe jumped while shouting. "Yes! All of us! A big family lunch!"

I reached down and picked up Gage who laughed and told me no tickles. I, of course, didn't listen.

Harley stood and pulled at Tripp to join her. "Lunch sounds amazing. This baby needs food!"

"Then it's settled. We're all going to Lilly's," Cord declared, Maebh tucked up against his side.

"I'll call ahead to give Lucy a heads up we need a table for thirteen adults and four kiddos!" Steed said as we all piled out of the house.

It felt good to be around my family. To see how happy they all were. I knew that was what I wanted, and I wanted it with Scarlett. When I parked, I texted Scarlett that the entire family was going to Lilly's for lunch and that if she wanted to join us I'd love to see her. She didn't live far from the town square, a couple of blocks. She could be there in less than five minutes.

As we got closer to Lilly's I saw her. I slowed my pace as I took in the sight before me.

Scarlett, in *our* booth...with Eric. He reached across the table and placed his hand over hers, causing her to smile warmly.

"What is that eejit doing?" Maebh muttered, looking at the same scene as me.

"Fuck," Cord mumbled when I pushed past everyone and walked into the café.

"Trevor! Trevor!" Maebh and Cord both called out. When Scarlett heard my name she looked up. Her hand instantly pulled from

Eric's and she smiled at me. It faded, however, when she saw how pissed off I was.

Slipping out of the booth, she stopped me before I got to Eric.

"Trevor, I just got your text."

I swallowed hard. "Is something going on between the two of you?"

Eric stood, and Scarlett cast him a warning look. What the fuck was that about?

"Trev, let's go sit down. Scarlett, you're more than welcome to join us if you want," Cord stated.

"Eric, I think you need to leave," Maebh warned. "*Now*."

He stood defiantly, his arms crossed over his chest. "I'll leave if Scarlett wants me to leave."

My eyes narrowed. "What in the hell does that mean?"

"Trevor, you need to calm down this instant." It was Amelia now, pulling my arm toward the table Lucy had set up for the family.

Eric decided to grow some balls. "It means, I've been here for Scarlett when she needed someone. You haven't."

"Eric! Enough!" Maebh said, stepping between us.

"No, Maebh. This asshole thinks he can come and go as he pleases in Scarlett's life, and he can't. I've already told her I'd take care of her and the…"

"Eric!" Scarlett shouted, causing him to look her way.

"*You'll* take care of her?" I asked with a laugh. "I'm the one who loves her."

Gasps could be heard across the whole damn restaurant. Maebh spun around and looked at me, her mouth gaping open. Then she smiled.

"You love her?" she whispered.

Glancing at a stunned Scarlett, I replied, "Yes. Very much."

"You love her? If you loved her you wouldn't treat her like a whore," Eric practically shouted.

Scarlett moved in front of Eric right as I went at him. I accidentally knocked into her, pushing her almost to the ground, but Cord caught her just in time. Wade was there, stopping me before I was able to get to Eric. Pulling me back by my arms, I fought to get out of Wade's hold.

Eric turned to Scarlett. "Are you okay, sweetheart?"

The endearment caused me to try to get after him again, making Eric face me. Tripp stood between us, his hand on Eric's chest, keeping him at bay. He now seemed like he wanted a piece of me as much as I wanted a piece of him.

"You stupid fool! You could have hurt the baby!" Eric shouted.

I stopped resisting Wade. Eric's words bounced around in my head for a few moments before they sank in. Then it hit me like a brick wall. Wade's hold on me loosened. He must have heard it as well.

Eric rushed to Scarlett when he saw me stop resisting.

"Are you okay?" he asked, holding her and giving her a once-over. She looked like she was in a state of shock as she stared at Eric.

"What...what did you say?" I asked, looking between Eric and Scarlett.

Scarlett's eyes pierced mine, and I'd never seen her look so sad in my entire life.

Eric took a step toward me. "She's pregnant, you arsehole, and you almost knocked her to the ground."

"Eric, *why*?" Maebh yelled, glaring at Eric. She turned to me sadly, and I knew that she knew. She *knew* Scarlett was pregnant.

The whole room started to feel like it was closing in on me, and I couldn't breathe. I swallowed hard, trying to figure out why my vision was getting blurry.

Maebh reached for my hands, attempting to steady my wobbly body. "Trevor, you need to sit down. Please. Wade, help him. He looks ill."

I stared at Scarlett. A single tear slipped from her eye and slowly made a trail down her cheek. That one tear felt like it had reached into my heart and ripped it out.

"You're...pregnant?" I asked, the words barely audible.

Eric wrapped his arm around Scarlett's shoulder, and it all made sense. The realization hit me like a MAC truck. Scarlett was pregnant with Eric's child. A sickness rolled over my entire body, almost making me bend over and throw up.

"H-how long have you been sleeping with him?"

Scarlett sucked in a breath, and Maebh looked over her shoulder. "Eric! Knock it the feck off. Cord, get him out of here. He's only making this worse!"

It was like a light went off in Scarlett's eyes, and she stepped out of Eric's hold. Her gaze pierced mine, a desperate pleading for me to understand, but I didn't understand. I couldn't understand. My mind went back to almost two months ago when we had been together. Was she pregnant then?

Oh. God. I need out of here.

She shook her head. "Trevor, it's not what you think. *Please.*"

I looked around the café. My entire family stood there, looks of horror, sadness, and disbelief on everyone's faces.

Turning, I made my way out of the café.

"Trevor! Wait!" Scarlett called out, only making me walk faster. I needed to leave.

"Trevor!"

I was about to get sick.

"Dude, wait!" Wade called out as he reached for my arm.

"Wade, I need to get out of here."

The second I burst through the doors of the café, I did the only thing I could think of doing.

Run.

I ran hard and fast. Not stopping until my lungs burned and my legs felt like jelly.

Leaning over, I placed my hands on my knees and dragged in one deep breath after another. When I glanced up, I saw I was at the local park and playground. My gaze instantly fell on a mom pushing her little girl on a swing.

"Jesus Christ, Trevor. Are you trying to give me a heart attack?" Wade panted as he caught up to me. "Do you know how hard it is to run that fast in cowboy boots?"

I stared at the woman and the little girl, and my chest burned with the strangest sensation.

Scarlett's pregnant.

The ground swayed, and I leaned back over.

"Trevor, let's sit down. I need to catch my breath and you look like you're about to pass out."

I followed Wade over to a group of benches. Four little kids ran by, playing what looked like tag. Their laughter carried through the air filling a space in my heart I didn't know needed filling. It reminded me of all of us kids playing on the ranch. How free life was then. No pressure, no confusion. Simpler, happy times. I longed for that again.

I wasn't sure how long we sat there in silence before Wade finally spoke.

"It's not his baby, Trevor. You know Scarlett better than that."

Jerking my head to the left, I stared at my best friend.

"What makes you come to that conclusion?"

"I see the way Scarlett looks at you. The way she can't seem to focus on anyone or anything when you're near her. The look in her eyes when she realized you thought the baby was his. You may not want to believe this, but she loves you."

Closing my eyes, I shook my head. "Yeah, well, I've seen the way she's been hanging all over this Eric asshole. The way he had his arm around her like he was claiming her."

Wade rubbed the back of his neck and went to say something, but stopped.

My eyes wandered back to the kids playing. A strange ache started to build in my chest that I'd never felt before, like I had not only lost Scarlett, but something else. It was the emptiness I felt the day she drove away from me at the café all those years ago, but ten times stronger.

"You ready to be a dad someday, Wade?" I asked.

He was watching the kids too, a smile on his face. "Yeah. Can't wait."

The corners of my mouth tugged slightly. He looked happy, and I wanted that. I hadn't realized before this moment how desperately I wanted it.

"Amelia's pregnant," Wade said.

"What?" This time a wide smile grew over my face. "Holy shit, Wade, that's awesome."

He looked at me, tears in his eyes. "I'm pretty happy about it. We haven't told anyone yet. She's not very far along, fourteen weeks."

I pulled my best friend into a hug, and I gave him a couple hard slaps on the back before I let go.

"Congratulations, man."

"Thanks, Trevor."

The moment of happiness quickly left. "Scarlett and Amelia will be pregnant at the same time."

His smile grew bigger. "Yeah. I guess they will be."

I sat back on the bench. "I really want to be alone, Wade."

"Trevor, I think you need to talk to Scarlett. Don't let that jerk make you second-guess her. It's not his baby."

Scrubbing my hands down my unshaven face, I sighed. "Not right now. I can't even think straight. I need some time to process this."

Wade placed his hand on my shoulder. "Call me if you need anything, okay? And do me a favor."

When I looked up, Wade was wearing a serious expression. "Don't go off and fuck someone thinking it will make you feel better."

I flinched. That's what I would have done months ago. Hell, it was what I did after that first time I was with Scarlett.

Breaking our stare, I nodded. "I won't."

"Good. I'll see ya around."

With a quick nod, I replied, "See ya."

Once I was left to myself, I watched the kids running and playing. The mom pushing her daughter in the swing as the dad took pictures on his phone. Another dad tossed a ball to his son, both of them laughing when he swung and missed, spinning damn near in a complete circle.

I felt like I was lost in a storm on the sea. Trying to keep from going under in the giant waves, as something dark was pulling me deeper down.

Every single memory of being together with Scarlett flooded my mind. From that first dance in middle school to the night we made love this past summer—and I panicked. It was the first time I realized how much I really loved her. How much I needed her. The way we felt together when we made love. I knew she felt it too, and it was so damn powerful it scared me senseless.

My stomach dropped at the next thought. We'd had sex with no protection that night. The baby had to be mine. Scarlett said nothing was happening between her and Eric, and I believed her. Why did he seem so hell bent on making me think it was his baby, though?

The vibration in my pocket made my thoughts halt. I pulled out my cell and saw her name.

Scarlett: *Please call me or come back. Please!*

Closing my eyes, I took in a deep breath and hit reply.

Me: *I need to know one thing. Is it his baby or mine?*

Scarlett: *Please don't make me tell you over a damn text, Trevor.*

Me: *I need to know, Scarlett.*

Scarlett: *Then you don't know me at all, Trevor Parker. The baby is yours. I'm ten weeks pregnant.*

Everything stopped. I no longer heard the kids playing in front of me or Mr. Henderson's lawn mower across the street. I heard nothing but the beat of my heart in my chest.

CHAPTER 8

Scarlett

I stood there, my body numb as I watched Trevor bolt down the street, Wade right on his heels.

"Scarlett, sweetheart, come sit down."

Paxton's voice was soft and gentle.

"I need to go after him!" I finally managed to say, pulling my phone out from my back pocket and hitting his number.

"Let Wade go. You need to sit down and get something to drink," Corina demanded.

I let them both usher me over to the large group of tables pushed together. I watched as Maebh laid into Eric outside the café. Her finger was jabbing into his chest while Cord was trying to pull her away. I tried calling Trevor a few more times, but each time it went to voicemail.

My eyes closed, and I tried to forget the look of pain on Trevor's face, but it only became clearer. My heart ached. I knew it must have hurt him to find out like that. It was not how I planned to tell him.

"Why did he do that?" I whispered.

"He was upset and in shock. He'll be back," Corina said, taking my hand in hers.

I shook my head. "No. Eric. *Why* would he tell Trevor I was pregnant?" They exchanged looks and Paxton turned to glare at Eric. The anger was clearly written all over her face.

"Paxton?" I asked, urging in my voice.

When she looked back at me, she took in a deep breath. "He did it on purpose, Scarlett. With the way he acted, putting his arm around you defensively, I'm sure it has people wondering who the father of your baby is. Including Trevor."

I gasped. "What? It's Trevor's baby! I'm only friends with Eric. That's it!"

Paxton quickly sat down, relief washing over her face. "I thought so, but Scarlett, I had to ask. Eric made it look like he was the father, I think that was part of the reason Trevor reacted the way he did."

Tears spilled down my cheeks. "I didn't want him to find out like that. I was going to tell him today. Then everything happened with John, and Trevor had to leave. I swear, I was going to tell him today."

"*Shhh*, it's okay," Corina said, pulling me against her side. The whole family was now seated around the table. Everyone but Trevor, Wade, Jonathon, Waylnn, and their parents. Maebh had come back in from bitching out Eric. I was hoping she'd left an impact.

My gaze swept over everyone. "This wasn't how I wanted you all to find out."

Maebh and Cord smiled gently.

Cord laughed. "I'm pretty sure Maebh just tore Eric a new asshole, if that makes any of this better."

I groaned as Maebh started talking in Irish.

"Ah, hell, you know she's pissed when she starts that." Tripp chuckled.

"Do you mind if I ask when you're due?" Corina asked.

I chewed on my lip. "Um, well, I wanted to tell Trevor first, but since everyone seems to know I'm pregnant anyway, why not? I'm due May 25."

Steed, Tripp, and Mitchell looked relieved. They hadn't heard my conversation with Paxton and Corina, so this was their confirmation that the child I was carrying was indeed Trevor's.

Harley squealed. "Scarlett, this is going to be so much fun, both of us being pregnant! John and Melanie are going to die!"

I snuck a peek at Amelia. Wade was still gone, probably with Trevor. We exchanged a secret smile.

"Well, now that the drama has settled, what can I get everyone to eat?" Lucy asked, trying to avoid looking at me. I'm sure she was wondering, just like Paxton had been, who the baby daddy was.

"I'm going to go ahead and go home," I stated.

Everyone's eyes snapped over to me.

"What? Why?" Paxton asked.

With a half shrug, I replied, "I'm not feeling very well, and to be honest, I need to be alone for a bit."

Steed stood. "Let me get you home, Scarlett."

Standing, I shook my head. "No thank you, Steed. It's a short walk and the air will do me and my stomach some good."

Everyone took turns giving me a hug goodbye and congratulating me on the baby. I tried to ignore the stares from other people in the café as I walked out. I was both physically and mentally exhausted.

As I set out for my house, I texted Trevor. I was desperate to speak to him. I couldn't have him thinking that Eric and I had slept together.

Scarlett: *Please call me or come back. Please!*

The dots started to bounce on the screen, and I held my breath.

Me: *I need to know one thing. Is it his baby or mine?*

Was he serious?

Scarlett: *Please don't make me tell you over a damn text, Trevor.*

Me: *I need to know, Scarlett.*

I stopped walking and stared at his text. He honestly thought there was a chance the baby wasn't his? Tears pricked at the back of my eyes as I typed my response.

Scarlett: *Then you don't know me at all, Trevor Parker. The baby is yours. I'm ten weeks pregnant.*

Pushing my phone into my pocket, I picked up the pace. My mind raced as I thought about how badly all of this had gone down. The plan had been to tell Trevor about the baby. Tell him I wasn't expecting anything from him, but that I wanted him to be a part of our baby's life. Now he was doubting if the baby was even his because of a stupid move Eric made.

I walked up my porch steps and stopped when I found him sitting on my porch swing. Anger swept over my entire body.

"You are the *last* person I want to see," I spat out.

"Scarlett, let me explain."

I held up my hand. "No, you don't get to explain how you just tore this from me, Eric. You stripped something away that was supposed to be a beautiful moment. This was *mine* to share, and you announced it to everyone."

He honestly looked sick to his stomach.

"I…I didn't mean to do it. It slipped from my mouth."

With a roll of my eyes, I shook my head. "Why did you make it seem like the baby was yours?"

He had the decency to look regretful. "I don't know. A part of me doesn't think Trevor deserves you or this baby."

"It's his baby, Eric!" I practically shouted.

"And *I've* been the one here for you. *I've* been the one to hold you in my arms when he hurts you. Which he will do over and over again, Scarlett. Do you think him finding out he's going to be a father means that he's going to suddenly change his ways? Tigers do not change their stripes, Scarlett, and you know that."

His words felt like a slap across my face.

"I don't know what is going to happen, but the fact remains that you took this away from me. You stripped me of being able to tell Trevor that he is going to be a father. The worst part is you announced it in front of…"

My voice trailed off, and I covered my mouth with my hand as the reality of what happened really hit me.

My parents. What if someone from the café tells my parents? What if people get on the prayer line and started to talk?

Eric rushed over to me, placing his hands on my arms.

"He can be in the child's life, but Scarlett, let me help you with this. I'm falling in love with you, and I want to help you raise this baby."

"Wh-what?" I pulled out of his hold.

"I'll marry you tomorrow. I don't care if we go to the courthouse, we can do it however you want."

What in the world was he talking about?

"Eric, we're friends. That's all. We've only known each other a few short weeks. You don't love me like that."

"I do. I'll marry you and spend the rest of my life making you happy, Scarlett. You have to trust me."

My fingers pinched the bridge of my nose as I exhaled. "Eric, wait. Just stop."

"I'll take care of both of you. I'll never make you cry like he does."

"Please, stop!" I said, louder this time.

He took a step closer, and I held up my hand. "I can't marry you!"

"Why not? Afraid you'll be happy with me?" he asked, a playful smirk on his face.

I frowned. "I can't marry you because I don't love you. I *love* Trevor."

Eric's smile faded. "You love a man who treats you like dirt?"

"You don't know anything about how he treats me." The memory of Trevor sitting on my bed last night, whispering he loved me, replayed in my mind. I'd seen the other side of Trevor that no one else ever sees. The person who took care of me when I was sick. The man who sat for hours next to my bed when I hardly had the energy to even move.

I saw the struggle in his eyes and heard his whispered words when he made love to me…about how he didn't deserve me. But I couldn't deny that Trevor had also hurt me on more than one occasion, regardless if he meant to or not.

"He fucks other women and comes to you when he can't find anyone better to be with."

Eric's words cut deeply. I slapped him across the face, instantly making my hand sting.

He didn't even move, only closed his eyes. "I'm sorry. I didn't mean that."

"Leave. I need you to go. *Right now*. Trevor is not the one hurting me. You are."

"Scarlett, I'm sorry. I get so angry when you let him get away with things."

"Right now, he is *not* the one who has me upset. Leave, Eric. Please."

His entire body sagged. Dropping his head, he slowly shook it. "I don't understand what you see in him, love."

Exhaustion was beginning to overtake my body.

"Please, will you just go? I want to be alone."

Eric headed down the stairs. I didn't even bother with a good-bye. I turned and unlocked my front door. The second I got in and shut it, I headed to the sofa. Sitting down, I immediately laid on my side, grabbed a blanket, shut off my mind, and drifted off to sleep.

CHAPTER 9

Trevor

The last twenty-four hours I'd gone through every emotion possible. Shock. Anger. Hurt. Frustration. Now the anger was back...but not at Scarlett. At myself.

I was a stupid idiot.

I didn't want to believe that Scarlett had been with Eric, but I hadn't given her much reason not to be with another man. I'd walked away from her that night we'd made love. Like a complete asshole. I'd thought it was better to leave than show her how freaked out I was. I was afraid she'd see how much I loved her. Know how much I wanted every night to be like that night.

Looking back on what happened over these last few hours, it had nothing to do with not wearing the condom. It had everything to do with how I'd fallen in love with her. Hell, I was pretty sure I fell in love with her when I kissed her our senior year of high school. No one woman ever made me feel the way I felt when I was with Scarlett...when I thought about her, made love to her, heard her laugh, saw her smile. Especially when I was the one who making her happy.

My chest did a weird flutter thing as I closed my eyes.

"You're such a fucking asshole," I spoke out loud.

"I can agree with that."

Opening my eyes, I found Aunt Vi sipping a cocktail while floating in my folks' pool. She'd been the only one to actually force me to talk to her yesterday when I got back to the ranch. I didn't want to go back to my place alone, so I sat with Aunt Vi and told her everything while we waited for my mother and Waylynn to bring my father back home.

"Thanks, Aunt Vi. I actually didn't mean to say that out loud."

She took another drink before saying, "Now that you've admitted it, what are you going to do to fix it?"

"I have no clue. As far as I know, Scarlett doesn't want anything to do with me."

Vi scoffed. "Please, the way that girl looks at you, she's madly in love. Anyone can see it. Well, anyone but you obviously. *Dick*."

That last word she attempted to mumble under her breath. At least, I thought she meant to mumble it. I would have been shocked, but we are talking about Aunt Vi here, after all.

Glancing to my right, I saw my cell phone sitting on the side table. I reached for it and pressed the button on the side, turning it on.

"It's about goddamn time. What is it with you Parker men? My God, does a damn lightning bolt need to come out of the sky and strike your penis for you to get your other head on straight?"

"I needed time to think," I said defensively.

"Hmm, your phone had to be off for you to think?"

"Yes."

"Sounds like you didn't think very much then, Trevor. *Dick*."

I rolled my eyes. "Okay, you do know that I can hear you calling me a dick."

"If the cowboy boot fits."

I sighed and said, "I don't think it is his baby, but I'm not sure if they haven't struck up something other than friendship. He's always with her and they looked...comfortable the few times I've seen them together."

"Maybe he's just being a friend to her. Sounds like she needed one."

Now it was my turn to let out a gruff laugh.

"May I give you some advice, Trevor?"

I faced my aunt again. "Yes."

"Go to her in person. Don't do this over the phone. The first thing you need to do is tell her you're sorry for being a..."

"Dick?"

She smiled. "You said it, not me."

With a nod, I returned her smile with one of my own. "Thanks, Aunt Vi."

I made my way back toward the house. I'd go see my father before heading back to my place.

"Trevor, before you go to her, change and shower, you stink."

"Don't you have a pool at your own house, Aunt Vi?"

She laughed. "What fun would that be?"

My hand rubbed the tension in the back of my neck. "If they don't already know, will you not say anything to my folks? I want to be the one to tell them."

"Well, if it makes you feel better, the Oak Springs prayer chain hasn't asked for God to strike you down dead yet, so...you've got that working for you."

I was positive my eyes were wide as saucers before I chuckled. "Right. See ya later, Aunt Vi."

"See ya!"

I found both of my folks crashed on the sofa, and I didn't want to wake them so I headed back to my place to shower before making my way into town. When I pulled up to Scarlett's house, I saw her BMW in the driveway. I pulled in a deep breath and got out of my truck. Glancing across the street, I couldn't help but notice Mrs. Johnson talking to Mrs. Croft. They both looked my way and waved, while giving me a smile that clearly said they already knew the news. If they knew the scuttlebutt, then who else also knew it?

"Fuck," I mumbled as I smiled and waved back.

Taking the porch steps two at a time, I rang Scarlett's doorbell and held my breath. If Eric was here I was going to rip him in two.

The door opened and my breath caught in my throat. Scarlett stood in front of me in a pair of worn-out jeans and my old T-shirt I had left over here. The best part of all was a paint smudge on the tip of her nose and one on her forehead.

Fucking hell, she looked gorgeous.

"Painting?" I asked with a smile. She didn't return the smile. She simply pushed the door open and walked into the living room.

That wasn't a good sign.

I followed her through the living room and then up the steps. My heart was pounding, not because I was secretly hoping she was taking me to her room and we were going to have the most amazing make-up sex, but because this woman was carrying my baby.

Our baby.

That did something to my heart, and I couldn't explain what. It was a good thing...but it was also a scary thing.

She walked past her bedroom and into the room down the hall. When I walked in, I looked around. She was painting it a light yellow. There were strips of painter's tape going across the room half-way down the wall and across to the floorboards.

"Scarlett, I can help you paint this room."

Spinning on her heels, she glared. I instinctively took a step back.

"This *room* is the nursery."

My stomach did that weird flutter thing, like it always did when Scarlett smiled at me, but this was better. If there could be such a thing.

"Oh," I whispered, not sure what else to say. Then I found my words.

"I'd love to help you with the nursery."

Her face softened, and she lifted her chin. "So you don't still think the baby is Eric's?"

I shook my head. "I'm sorry. I was confused and he made it seem like y'all were together. The whole thing completely caught me off guard and I wasn't thinking clearly."

Scarlett stared down at the floor. "We're only friends. Eric and me."

Her voice sounded off, as if she was telling me the truth but also holding back.

"You don't sound convinced of that."

Snapping her eyes back up to mine, she replied, "I only see him as a friend. He, on the other hand…well…he admitted to having feelings for me."

I swallowed hard. "Oh."

It was the only damn thing I could say.

We both stood there for a few moments, neither of us knowing what to say.

"When did you find out? About the baby?" I asked, clearing my throat. She looked panicked for a quick moment and looked away.

"Can I get all of this cleaned up before we talk?"

Moving farther into the room, I took the paint brush and roller. "I'll clean up. You might want to jump in the shower. You have paint on your face."

Reaching up with my hand, I tried to rub it off of her forehead. Scarlett drew in a breath and locked her brown eyes on mine.

For a moment, I thought she was going to lift up on her toes to kiss me, but she did the opposite. She stepped away from me, putting distance between us that I felt in my very soul. It nearly killed me.

"Thanks," she whispered before leaving the room.

I closed my eyes and cursed. Things were totally fucked up between us, and it was all my fault.

CHAPTER 10

Trevor

After I got the paint lid back on and cleaned the brushes and the roller, I made my way downstairs and into the kitchen. Scarlett always had lemonade. While everyone else loved sweet tea, she loved lemonade and I really loved her lemonade.

I looked everywhere in the refrigerator and couldn't find it.

"What are you looking for?" she asked, making me jump.

"Shit, you scared me. Um, the lemonade."

She slid onto a chair at the large kitchen island.

"I don't drink it anymore. All the sugar isn't good for me or the…baby."

I leaned against the counter. I had to admit I wasn't as freaked out about the baby as I had been twelve hours ago. I had been out by the pool rocking back and forth on the lounge chair while Steed and Aunt Vi looked on, concern on their faces. They'd been smart enough to leave me alone. The only time Aunt Vi approached was when I started chanting, *A baby. Holy shit. A baby.*

Moving around a bit on the stool, Scarlett placed her arms on the island and then seemed to think twice about keeping them there. She was nervous, and I was trying my best to act calm. I had no idea what was going to happen between us. The last thing I wanted was for her to see how fucking scared I was.

Scarlett handed me a piece of paper. "So, um, that's the baby's first picture. It was a sonogram they did when I found out I was pregnant. The baby is due on May 25."

My breath caught, a bit of panic raced through my veins, but I did my best to hide it. The picture looked like a little blob, but it was the most beautiful blob I'd ever seen.

"So, you're not that far along."

"No," she replied. "Like I said in the text I sent, I'm about ten weeks. I'm guessing it was that night we…when you…"

"When we made love with no condom?"

She nodded, her hands wringing together. "I'm not looking for anything from you, Trevor. I want you to be a part of this baby's life, but I'm not going to force you into anything."

A sharp pain hit me square in the chest, and for a moment it felt like I couldn't breathe.

"You honestly think I'd walk away from my own child?"

Her sad eyes lifted to meet mine. "You don't have a problem walking away from me."

A bout of nausea hit me. "I guess I deserved that."

Her brow lifted, something like resignation showing on her face.

"I need you to know something. I haven't been sleeping around."

She scoffed. "I've seen you flirting with women. That girl you walked out of Lilly's with. That was the day I found out I was pregnant. Do you know how it felt to see you flirting with her after I had just found out I was carrying your baby?"

"Nothing happened. I was being nice to my buddy's fiancé's maid of honor. That was all."

Scarlett looked away, wiping a tear as she shook her head.

"Maebh knows about the baby, doesn't she?" I asked.

When she didn't answer, I went on. "Does Cord know?"

Scarlett swallowed hard.

"Well, a few things make a bit more sense now. Like how Maebh wanted to rip my head off."

Glancing my way, she said, "I asked them not to say anything to you, so please don't be mad at them. I wanted to tell you myself. I was going to tell you yesterday morning before you had to leave. Then when you said you were going to Lilly's for lunch, I was going to see if we could take a walk, but Eric showed up, and well…we know how that all went."

My own fucking brother knew before me. My stomach rolled.

"When did Eric find out?"

Scarlett looked like she didn't want to answer. "The day I did. Maebh had gone into his office to call Cord because I had cried myself to sleep in hers and…"

I sucked in a breath. I fucking knew she had been upset when I saw her that day. I figured she thought I might be hooking up with someone. It was the whole reason I went over to Aisling to talk to her. That asshole lied to me when he said they weren't there.

Prick.

"He lied and said you weren't there. I knew you were upset, and I wanted to explain to you who that was, but he lied and said you weren't there."

Her eyes filled with regret.

"I'm…I'm sorry."

With a frustrated groan, I shook my head. "Why didn't you just fucking tell me?" Anger laced my words.

"I was going to but then I saw you making out with that stripper and Eric started telling me how you were never going to change, and I…I was confused, Trevor. You haven't exactly made this relationship…or whatever was between us, very easy."

"Was?" I asked, feeling my heart practically stop at that one word. Had she given up on me? On us?

Scarlett wrapped her arms around her body and stared at me. My eyes scanned her, and I caught sight of a spot of yellow paint still in her hair. Walking up to her, I picked up the piece and smiled.

"You have paint in your hair."

The way she looked up warmly gave me hope that maybe she hadn't given up on me, but she surprised the hell out of me with her next set of words.

Scarlett shook her head. "I can't do this with you anymore. One minute you're hot, the next you're cold. I have to think about my baby."

"Our baby," I corrected.

Her eyes closed, and she whispered, "Our baby." Opening them, her eyes filled were full of sadness. "Since that first moment you asked me to dance with you when we were just kids, I've had feelings for you. I thought maybe you did too."

"I did. I do," I quickly added.

"You don't know what you want, Trevor. I can't do this with you. I refuse to be the type of woman who sits at home and wonders how many women you're flirting with, or how many more are on your mind."

I took a step back. "I'd never cheat on you. I mean, we were together Scarlett, but I never said we were exclusive. Still, I haven't been with anyone else in months."

"Have you tried? To be with another woman?"

Guilt ripped at me, my silence her answer.

"Right now, I need to focus on me and the baby."

"Where does that leave us?" I asked.

With a half shrug, she replied, "Two people who are going to have a baby."

Closing my eyes, I balled my fists and counted to ten before I looked at her.

"That's it? What are we, Scarlett? Friends? Lovers? Two people trying to figure this out and start over?"

"You've hurt me more than once, Trevor. I know you didn't promise me anything, but I felt something between us and I let myself fall in…"

Her voice trailed off.

"You let yourself fall in what?"

Tears pooled in her eyes. "It doesn't matter."

"The hell it doesn't. I fucked up, I get that. I was confused. Hell, I'm still confused. You're the only woman in my life who has ever made me want more and that scares me, Scarlett. I left the bar the other night to find you, to tell you I'm sorry I messed things up with us. To beg you to give me one more chance. I was scared of my feelings, and I finally admitted it to myself. That night I realized how much I cared for you, I was scared."

"Why?" she asked, her voice almost a plea.

"Why what?"

"Why does that scare you?"

"I don't know! Because if I give you my heart and you leave me, I honestly don't think I'll be able to survive. It would destroy me, Scarlett."

She inhaled sharply and a tear fell, then another. My whole damn world felt like it was tipped over because I was upsetting her.

I pulled her into my arms and held her.

"Please don't cry, baby. I hate making you cry, and I do it all the damn time."

Her hands came up and she gripped onto my T-shirt as she buried her head into my chest.

"You have to know I've never done this before, Scarlett, and I don't know what I'm doing. I'm going to fuck up, but I swear to you I'll never hurt you again."

When she pulled back, she bit down on her lip before saying, "I wish I could I believe you. You have no idea how much I wish I could believe you, but I can't."

My legs about went out from under me.

"What?" I whispered, a feeling of dread settled into my chest.

"At least, not right now. There's so much going on, and I'm not sure if you're feeling this way because you feel obligated to the baby."

"Scarlett, I lov—"

Her hand covered my mouth. Shaking her head, she whispered, "Please don't say it. Not now. Not when we are in this weird, unknown place. The only time I ever want to hear you say that again is when you know one-hundred percent that the words you speak are from your heart."

I closed my eyes and shook my head. I knew I loved her. Hell, I fell for her that day outside of Lilly's when I kissed her.

"Please, Trevor."

I pulled her hand away from my mouth. "I'm not going to promise you that I won't tell you I love you, because I do love you."

Her eyes closed.

"Scarlett, look at me."

She swallowed hard, then opened her eyes.

"I love you, and I'm sorry I didn't say it sooner. I didn't have my shit figured out and it took a while for me to come around. I can't change any of that. I need you to know, though, I wanted to tell you this the other night before I found out about the baby. The night I saw you at Maebh's restaurant."

A tear slipped down her cheek. I gently wiped it away.

"Do you love me, Scarlett?"

Her head dropped, and I lifted her chin so that she was forced to look at me.

"Do you love me? Please just answer that one question."

Trembling, she whispered, "Yes, I love you."

I let out the breath I was holding. Then she stepped away from me.

"I don't know what's going to happen, but I can't play tug of war with you anymore, Trevor. I want you to be a part of the baby's life, but right now, I don't think you can be a part of mine."

"Scarlett, please."

My voice cracked as she shook her head.

Turning away, I closed my eyes and tried to take a few deep breaths. The back of my throat burned as I fought to keep my own tears at bay.

I wasn't sure how long we stood in her kitchen before Scarlett finally spoke.

"We need to tell our parents before they hear it from someone else."

With a nod, I turned and looked at her. She looked tired and worn out.

"Okay, let's do that together."

"My father is going to expect things, and I think we need to be prepared for him to be rather upset when he finds out we're not getting married."

I swallowed hard. The thought of marrying someone just a month ago would have made me break out in hives. Now everything was different.

"I'd marry you in a heartbeat if you'd have me."

Scarlett's eyes widened in surprise. Then she looked angry as hell.

"Let me get this straight, Trevor Parker. I can't get you to commit to just dating me, and then all of sudden you'd marry me?"

"You're having my baby, Scarlett."

She shook her head. "Is that the only reason you'd marry me, Trevor? Because you knocked me up, and it's the proper, southern thing to do?"

"What? No! I mean, if things were different, I'd, of course, want to date. Especially since I've never really dated anyone. I think things would move slower, but…I guess I messed that up."

Scarlett opened her mouth but snapped it shut quickly. After pacing for a few moments, she faced me.

"Should we tell your parents first or mine?"

"That was a change of subject."

Tilting her head, she glared at me.

"Mine?" I said, a hint of fear in my voice.

"I think we should do this today."

"Wait," I said, putting my hand up to my face and scrubbing over it. "Don't you think we need to figure some things out before we tell our parents? Do we move in together? Where will the baby live?"

"No. And here."

"Okay, well, don't you think I should have a nursery at my house too?"

She chewed on her lip.

"You are going to let me see my own child, right?"

Her mouth fell open, and she stared at me in shock. "Of course I am!"

"Okay, because I'm pretty sure the first thing my folks are going to ask is when we're getting married. We need to have something else to tell them. A plan of how we intend to share custody of the baby."

She instantly began chewing on her thumbnail. "Right. They'll ask questions."

"I think we should be honest with them."

Laughing, she faced me. "What? Tell them you're a dick and wouldn't commit to a relationship with me before I got knocked up? And what else should we tell them? We had unprotected sex and when you realized it, you ran out? Without so much as a '*thanks for the fuck*'?"

I flinched. "Don't do that. Don't make that night seem like it didn't mean something."

"Did it? Because all I do is give and all you do is take. I gave myself to you that night and you took me. Then you left."

"I...I got scared because of the intense feelings I was having for you, Scarlett. I know I shouldn't have left like that, but I didn't know what else to do. That night was the best night of my life, and we made a child that night. Please don't let my stupid mistake take away from that."

She stood there, something I didn't understand etched on her face. A part of me thought she might kiss me, the other part was ready for her to slap me.

Glancing down, she placed her hands on her stomach.

"I'm so angry at you, Trevor." When she looked again, her eyes were filled with tears. "And I don't know if I'll ever be able to forgive you for hurting me like you did."

My very soul was stunned by the reality of her words. I took a step closer, framed her face in my hands, and leaned down. Kissing her gently on the lips, I whispered, "I'll wait forever if I have to, Scarlett."

CHAPTER 11

Scarlett

We drove in silence. Trevor navigated his truck through the streets of Oak Springs out to the country roads. I loved being farther out of town. Not that being in town was bad; it wasn't. But something about the silence of the country soothed my soul.

Clearing my throat, I said, "I talked to Corina about working for her."

I could feel Trevor's gaze. "Did you lose your job?"

"No, but I got to thinking about when the baby is born. I don't want to put him or her into daycare. If I helped at the bed and breakfast, I could use the nursery that Mitchell had put in for Merit. Plus, her mother works there full time, so she could help me with the baby."

When I looked at him, he was staring straight ahead.

"Trevor? You know you're stopped at a stop sign, right?"

This time, he cleared his throat. "Yeah, sorry. I got to thinking. How would this work? Will we just share her?"

My stomach flipped when he said *her*. Did Trevor hope for a girl? Did he even realize he had said that?

"Yes, of course. I mean, if you feel like you want to do something legally, we can have Tripp write up a custody agreement."

His face went white as a ghost. "What? No, I don't think that's necessary, do you?"

I smiled. "I don't think so."

"Is your insurance good at work? What about after the baby is born?" He rubbed his neck, his habit for when he was thinking about something important or really stressed out.

"It's okay. It won't cover everything, but most of everything. Corina said she has a small insurance plan that her mother is on that I can be added to. It will be more expensive, but I think I can make it work by not having to pay daycare."

"Whatever it doesn't cover for the birth, let me know, and I'll take care of the rest. We can always add the baby onto my insurance."

My chest squeezed. "Are you sure?"

Trevor reached for my hand, but when I pulled it away, he stopped.

"Of course, I'm sure." The hurt in his voice wasn't hard to hear. I felt guilty, but Trevor had a way of sweeping me off of my feet. As much as I wanted him to hold my hand, we needed to go slow.

Closing my eyes, I let out a sigh before glancing out the window. I wasn't sure if I felt relieved at his calmness or scared at his one-eighty about this situation.

"Has it sunk in that you're going to be a father?" I blurted out, a little on the bitchy side.

Trevor chuckled. "Yes."

"You seem calm. Accepting this way better than I thought you would."

He full-on laughed this time. "Did you not see me run like a bat out of hell at Lilly's yesterday? Wade is still texting me about the blisters he got from running after me in his boots."

I tried not to smile, but I did.

"Of course, if you need confirmation of my freak out, just ask Steed and Aunt Vi. I'm pretty sure they took turns watching me last night by the pool."

"Why?" I asked.

"Might have been me sitting in the lounge chair rocking back and forth chanting something about a baby."

This time I did laugh. "You were not."

"I was. Tell me you didn't sit in a corner and rock a few times when you found out."

Our eyes met, both of us smiling. "I might have for about ten minutes...or an hour, possibly longer."

Trevor's laughter filled the truck and it made my entire body warm up. Especially deep down in my belly. Stupid betraying body.

"Are you scared?" he asked, his voice barely above a whisper.

"Yes."

He nodded. "Me too. I don't want to suck as a father."

This time, I reached for his hand and squeezed it. "You won't. You had an amazing example growing up."

His jaw twitched and this time, he withdrew his hand. But it was only to hit the button on the gate that led to the Parker family ranch. My heart was thumping.

"I hope the prayer chain hasn't gotten to them."

"Well, Aunt Vi said no one had sent out a request for lightning to strike me down, so that's a good sign that the prayer chain hadn't been activated yet."

I covered my mouth as I attempted not to laugh.

We both remained silent while Trevor drove down the long driveway and finally pulled up in front of the house.

"Is anyone else here?" I asked, my hands wringing in my lap.

"No, their cars would be parked out front. Only Dad and Mom pull around to the back."

I nodded.

Trevor got out of the truck and made his way to my side. He opened the door, and I reached out for his hand but froze.

"I can't do this. Your parents are going to hate me. Think I trapped you or want money or think I'm a whore or…"

Trevor lifted me out of his truck and gently put me on the ground, leaning as close to me as he could without pressing his body onto mine.

"Stop it. My mother adores you and wouldn't think any of those things and neither would my father. Scarlett, it takes two to make a baby, remember?"

"I know, it's just—"

His mouth covered mine, and he kissed me. Damn it. I wanted to push him away, but Trevor Parker was my weakness. One little kiss wouldn't hurt anything, as long as he didn't deepen it.

When he pulled away, not taking it further, I felt a sting of disappointment.

What in the heck is wrong with me?

You don't want him. You do want him. Hell, I'm probably more confused than Trevor.

"Ready?" he asked, his sweet southern voice pulling me from my thoughts. My hands ached to touch his strong, broad chest. To feel his muscles under my fingers.

Ugh. Scarlett, get it together.

"As I'll ever be."

John and Melanie Parker were sitting in the family room and I came to an abrupt halt when I saw my parents sitting across from them.

"Oh, shit. Joyce and Dalton are here. It's a two-for-one kind of day," Trevor whispered from behind me.

My parents stood and faced us. As I scanned their expressions, I knew they already knew. Where in the heck was their car when we pulled up?

"So this is how we find out you're having a baby? Through Oak Springs gossip?" my father stated, anger etched in each word.

"We were planning on telling you all today, that's why we're here." My voice sounded shaky, but when Trevor placed his hand on my lower back, I gained new strength.

John stood slowly, holding onto his side.

"So, it's true? You got Scarlett pregnant?" he asked, his eyes piercing Trevor's.

Trevor went to speak, but I responded first. "Excuse me, but with all due respect, Mr. Parker. It does take two to tango."

My father shook his head and turned from me. Tears pricked at the back of my eyes, but I refused to let them fall.

"The due date?" my mother asked in a harsh tone that made me flinch. Even Melanie looked surprised. She should know the type of woman my mother was. After all, she had been her best friend for years. Joyce Littlefield was all about impressions and what people thought of her and her family.

Trevor reached for my hand, and I let him take it this time. My entire body was shaking, even my voice, and I needed something to calm me. His touch worked.

"May 25," I managed to get out with a steady voice.

Melanie smiled sweetly at me.

With a sigh, my mother replied, "Well, looks like we're going to have to make plans here pretty quick."

"Plans for what, Mrs. Littlefield?" Trevor asked.

"The wedding, of course!" my mother scoffed.

"Wedding?"

That synchronized response came from me, Trevor, and Melanie. John stood silent, shooting a glare at Trevor that made my knees shake. My father stood next to John, giving Trevor the same look, just not nearly as bad as his own father's.

Melanie cleared her throat, moving to stand closer to my mother. "Joyce, I think we're jumping to conclusions here. Let's all sit down. Scarlett and Trevor can help me get some tea and scones I picked up earlier from the bakery."

Trevor squeezed my hand as Melanie headed our way.

"Kids, will you please help me?"

Trevor nearly pulled my arm out of its socket as we followed his mother through the house and into the kitchen.

Melanie spun and faced us the moment she stepped into the kitchen. "Trevor Parker, I'd like to put you over my knee and spank you!"

My mouth twitched with a smile, even though I knew it wasn't funny.

"Me? Why me?"

Jabbing her finger into his chest, she shot him a dirty look. "Wrap the stick! Didn't we always tell you to use protection?!"

Then she turned to me.

"Scarlett Littlefield, I'm so confused with how I should be feeling because I'm over-the-moon happy, but also sad. I feel like I pushed you two together, and I've heard rumors and…well…"

She turned before we could see the tears fall.

"Wh-what are your plans, so I can help diffuse this situation?" she whispered.

Trevor and I exchanged a look before I drew in a breath.

"We're not getting married. I think we both need time to let this all soak in, but for right now we plan on sharing custody. I'll have a nursery at my house, Trevor will have one at his house."

Melanie stared at us, her mouth open in shock. "You mean, you're not even moving in together? Are you at least still dating?"

I swallowed hard and looked away. The heaviness of Trevor's eyes left a feeling of emptiness in my chest. I couldn't even find the words to tell her the truth.

"Not right now we're not, Mom."

"Oh, Lord. Trevor get the tea out of the refrigerator. Scarlett, come help me put these on a plate."

The three of us worked in silence as Trevor got a tray and put the cups on it. Once Melanie had taken a few deep breaths, I figured we were heading back into the family room, but she walked to the window that looked out over their pool.

"Your fathers are going to both be disappointed. Scarlett, I'm not sure what your mother is going to say."

"Mom, we can't be forced into a marriage," Trevor said. "That wouldn't be right."

Melanie faced Trevor, her eyes narrowing. "Is this because you won't give up your style of living? Is that why Maebh was so angry at you that night? What have you done, Trevor?"

Trevor jerked back like his mother had slapped him.

"No, Melanie, this is about me. Trevor and I have been off and on and we were really never committed to each other. It's complicated right now. Trevor wants more. I'm the one who needs time."

Trevor stepped in front of me, his blue eyes looking down into me. The sadness on his face nearly made my knees buckle.

"My mom is right. I've hurt you in more ways than I could ever make up to you. And I'll tell my mother like I told you, Scarlett." He turned and faced his mother. "I'm not giving up on us."

"You only feel this way because of the baby, Trevor," I said, unable to stop myself.

His eyes closed, and he shook his head. "I told you I came looking for you the other night to tell you I wanted to be with you before I even knew about the baby. Why can't you believe that?"

Memories of looking out the window at Trevor standing there, staring at me like I had just ripped his heart out hit me. It was true, he had been begging me that day to talk to him. He said he needed to tell me something and I was positive he was going to tell me he loved me. Why was I so afraid to take the leap?

Pulling from him, I stared at his chest. "I need a little time."

"Then I'll give you time. I'll give you the rest of my life if I have to."

Melanie walked up to us and placed her hands on both of our arms.

"I think you need to word your plans differently when we walk back out there."

Looking at her, I asked, "What do you mean?"

"Your parents and John are going to expect Trevor to do the right thing and marry you. Now I think that's a bit old fashioned, but if you tell them you're not even dating, heads will spin. This is what you're going to do. Tell them that y'all are taking things one day at a time. You'll make all the major decisions when both of your heads are clear, and you're not making emotional, knee-jerk reactions."

Her brow lifted as she said that last part and I couldn't help but wonder if that was directed at me.

"Now, let's get back in there before they come searching for us."

Melanie took the tray of perfectly placed scones, directed me to get the pitcher of tea and Trevor to get the tray of glasses and plates.

I started to move toward the tea when Trevor stopped me. Lifting his hand, he brushed a piece of loose hair away from my cheek.

"I'm not going to say I'm sorry for this. When it hit me the other night that you were the woman I wanted to be with, this wasn't the way I wanted things to happen."

My heart dropped.

"But this is the plan that was made for us, and I'm not lying to you when I say I'm both scared shitless and excited as hell."

A small smile tugged at my mouth.

"You don't want me to say I love you because you don't think I mean it, but I love you, Scarlett. I have since the moment I first kissed you at eighteen. I just want to make sure you know that before we walk out there."

No words would form on my lips, so I gave him a soft smile. Trevor grabbed the tray and headed out of the kitchen, pausing to wait for me.

Closing my eyes, I focused on keeping the pitcher in my hands still, while I said a silent prayer that things wouldn't go the way I feared they were fixin' to.

CHAPTER 12

Scarlett

Melanie poured a glass of sweet tea for everyone as I brought the tray of scones around. This felt so gosh darn formal, and I hated it. Not what I pictured when I dreamed of telling my parents about a baby.

I sat down next to Trevor, all eyes on both of us. It was Trevor who spoke up first.

"Dad, Mr. and Mrs. Littlefield, I know you all think the right thing to do would be to get married right away. Scarlett and I need to take some time to let this process. I'm sure you know this wasn't a planned pregnancy. Nonetheless, this child is wanted by both of us, and he or she will be loved unconditionally regardless of what Scarlett and I decide to do. I hope that our excitement is something we share with y'all."

I instantly saw bodies relax.

"Of course, it is!" my mother exclaimed. "It was a shock, that's all."

"As it was to both of us," I added. "We understand the reckless way we behaved, and we take full responsibility. Trevor and I have decided that we're going to take this one day at a time. That goes with our relationship, as well. We're not rushing into something. We also are not moving in together as of right now. Trevor's going to help me with the baby's room at my house, and we'll also have one at his house."

My mother moved uneasily in her seat as she took a sip of tea.

John cleared his throat and looked at me and then Trevor. "My gut reaction is to tell you that you have a responsibility to marry Scarlett, but I agree with you both, and I'm glad to see that you're thinking with open minds and that you appear to be in this together."

Trevor took my hand. "We are. Very much so."

"I expect you're going to stop working at your brother's bar then?" my father asked. I could hear the dislike for Trevor in his voice.

"Yes, I actually made that decision before I found out about the baby."

Everyone nodded, clearly glad.

"The expense of the birth?" John asked.

"My insurance will cover a good portion of it and Trevor's already said he'll pay for what isn't covered."

John smiled for the first time. It hit me that since they had found out about the baby, not one of them had congratulated us. Feeling sick to my stomach, I pressed my lips together and quickly stood.

"If you'll excuse me."

Trevor was right behind me as I rushed out of the family room and down the hall. I wasn't even sure where I was going. When I got to the end of a hall, I stopped and wrapped my arms around myself, letting the tears I'd been holding back finally fall.

Warm arms engulfed me, holding me while I let it all out.

"*Shhh*, it's okay, baby."

Shaking my head, I turned to Trevor. "They didn't even congratulate us! This wasn't how I pictured this, Trevor. Not at all. I feel like I've been robbed of so much already. I didn't get to tell you the way I wanted to, our parents are mad at us for being reckless and irresponsible and although they are being cordial, they totally expect us to be married before next May. I just want to feel happy about this. I'm tired of crying! I'm tired of being sad. I want this baby, and I can't even feel happy about it."

Trevor pulled me to him, letting me bury my face in his chest.

"I swear I'll make it up to you, baby. I swear."

He couldn't make it up to me though. Those moments would never come back. The happy tears, the room filled with laughter and joy. I would never get them for this baby and that nearly shattered my already broken heart.

Trevor used his finger to lift my chin, so I was looking up at him.

"Let's me and you go out tonight and celebrate."

I smiled and wiped my tears away. "Really?"

The way he smiled back left me breathless. I knew this man cared deeply for me. I'd heard him whisper in the darkness that he loved me. Why couldn't I let my heart believe he'd be happy with me and our baby?

Why?

Trevor pulled out his phone and sent off a text message as I wiped my tears away.

"Yes, really. We're having a baby, and not only could I use a hard drink, I want to do this over again. Tonight you're going to tell me I'm going to be a father. This is our do-over."

I smiled, feeling a lightness in my body I hadn't felt in weeks. Trevor looked at his phone again when a message came through. Maybe he was already making plans for our dinner. I felt giddy for the first time in a long time.

After pushing his phone in his pocket, Trevor slipped his fingers between mine. I didn't have the strength to pull away, and I didn't want to. I needed him right now, and I was going to be selfish and take what I could.

"Thank you, Trevor."

He winked and tugged me gently.

"Let's go tell our folks we're leaving."

I let Trevor lead the way back to the family room. When we walked in, my mother and Melanie both stood up.

"Scarlett and I are leaving. Y'all may not want to celebrate this news, but we definitely do."

Melanie's hand covered her mouth and John did his best to stand. My father was standing in front of me before I even knew he had moved.

"Scarlett, you don't believe that we're happy?"

"You all certainly don't seem like it. This wasn't the reaction I'd hoped for when I told you about the baby."

"Darling, we were shocked. That's all," my mother said, pulling me to her and wrapping me in her arms.

I watched as Melanie hugged Trevor and John did the same. Trevor was careful not to hurt his dad with his broken ribs.

"Why don't we all go out and celebrate!" Melanie said. "John, are you feeling up to it?"

"Hell yes, I am. There's another grandbaby coming, so let the party begin!"

Trevor leaned down and kissed his mother's cheek. I couldn't hear him, but I saw him say thank you. Trevor must have sent *her* the message in the hallway. The way our parents did a one-eighty was nothing short of a miracle. I made a note to ask him what he had done to make this happen.

A small piece of my heart felt like it was mending.

"Let me take Scarlett home so she can change and then we'll meet...where?" Trevor asked.

"How about Lane's Grill? Waylynn knows the owner and said the food is amazing," Melanie said with excitement.

Trevor winked at her. "Make it happen."

After kissing and hugging everyone, Trevor and I made our way out of the house and back to his truck. We drove in silence most of the way back into town. I could tell Trevor was thinking, and I didn't want to interrupt whatever he was working through in his mind. When he finally spoke, I jumped.

"So, I've got an idea."

"Shit! You scared me," I said with a chuckle.

He smiled but didn't look my way. "Want to hear it?"

"Of course, I want to hear it."

"The nights that I normally worked at Cord's Place, I'll plan on coming over to your place." He turned to me and winked. "See what I did there?"

I giggled and nodded. "I did see that."

The fun side of Trevor. I loved this side of him and wondered how many women had actually gotten to see it. As much as I wanted to not remember the good times with Trevor, I couldn't forget them. It wasn't like he only showed up on my doorstep for sex. When I was sick he came over for almost a week straight and did nothing but watch reruns of *Friends* with me. The random days he would show up after I went for a run and sit on my porch and just talk to me. The canoe ride we took were he made friends with an old man who was trying to save a duck…which landed Trevor in the lake and he hadn't even cared. The way he pulled over once and asked if I wanted to swing on at a playground.

That was the Trevor I fell in love with. The man no one else ever saw. I even knew back then he was afraid of committing. He told me more than once, but I couldn't push him away. Trevor Parker made his way into my heart when I was only eighteen years old, and I knew he would forever be its keeper. He had still hurt me, though, and I was not going to make this easy for him. No matter how badly

I wanted him, I needed to know he was truly ready to commit to not only the baby, but to me as well before I let him back in a hundred percent.

I had been so lost in my thoughts, I hadn't heard a word Trevor said.

"What do you think?"

"Um, I was completely lost and may or may not have been listening."

Trevor laughed. "Is that the pregnancy brain I hear my sisters-in-law talk about?"

"Ha! Maybe, what did you say?"

"I was saying, how about if I come over here and get the nursery set up. That way you don't have to be inhaling any fumes or moving furniture or anything. You tell me what you want, and I'll do it."

Chewing on my lip, I tried to ignore the way he made my insides melt. I didn't want to seem too eager for his help, but I didn't want to deny it either. It was going to be important for us to spend time together.

"You don't mind?"

"No, not at all. Do you want to do the nursery at my house in the same theme?"

Good Lord, how does this man even know about nursery themes? Ugh. He's going to make this paying him back thing very hard to do.

"Um, I haven't really thought about a theme. I just liked the color yellow I saw in a magazine!"

Trevor lost it laughing. "Well, do you want a theme?"

Giddiness filled my entire body. *Are we really talking about nursery themes right now?*

"You don't think we're jinxing anything by planning the theme this early, do you?"

Trevor's smile vanished, and he rubbed the back of his neck. Clear sign I had just given him something to stress about.

"Shit, I didn't think about that. Maybe we should hold off?"

I shrugged. "Well, I did buy this little Winnie the Pooh stuffed animal the other day."

"Pooh Bear?"

Thud. Why did that sound so damn sexy and make me instantly ache between my legs?

"Yep!" I said, trying not to sound like two sweet, innocent words from him had instantly turned me on.

"Jesus, I used to love Winnie the Pooh. Ask my mother. I was obsessed with him for years."

I smiled warmly as he got lost in a childhood memory. "Do you want to do the nursery in that theme? I mean, when the time comes to do it."

Trevor was stopped at a stop light and turned to look at me. There was no doubt I saw something in his eyes. Was that…excitement?

"How about we do that theme at my house, and you pick out something you love for your house?" he said. Clearly, he was claiming Pooh Bear.

"Two themes! You're living on the edge, Trevor Parker."

He went to reach for my hand but stopped himself. A tinge of regret pulsed in my chest and I wanted to extend my hand to him, but I knew we needed to move slowly. I wanted to believe with all my heart that Trevor would change, but even I had my doubts that a leopard could change his spots that quickly.

Trevor pulled into my driveway, still laughing about living on the edge. His smile came to an abrupt halt. I turned to see what he was looking at and nearly gasped when I found Eric sitting on the bench on my front porch. When he looked up and saw me in Trevor's truck, he frowned.

"What in the fuck is he doing here?" Trevor demanded. "Did you know he was here?"

"No! Of course not." Turning to Trevor, I watched his jaw flex. I was so angry at Eric for just showing up and waiting for me like this. He and I needed to have a talk. I had no idea why he was acting this way. I never led him to believe I thought of him as anything more than a friend.

"Let me handle this, please."

"How can you not be pissed at him after what he did?"

I sighed heavily. "I am angry, Trevor, but Eric was there for me when I needed a friend, and I can't turn my back on him because you don't like him."

The grip Trevor had on the steering wheel tightened so much his knuckles turned white.

When he met my gaze, I gasped. His blue eyes looked grey and I could feel the anger in them. "I *would* have been here for you had you *told me* about the baby."

Placing my hand on his arm, I gave it a squeeze. "I thought we were starting over. Let's not do this, especially in front of Eric."

Trevor's body relaxed, and he shook his head, probably to clear his mind of the things he was plotting to do to Eric. "You're right, I'm sorry. It's just, seeing him makes me want to throat punch his ass every single time."

I chuckled. "Stop it. Are you going back to your place to change?"

Trevor looked at me like I was insane. "Hell no. I'll run over to Cord's and grab a shirt from him and shower and change at your place."

I raised an eyebrow.

"What?" he asked, giving me a fake, innocent smile.

"Behave, Trevor Parker, do you hear me? We're in this situation because I couldn't say no to you."

He winked, and I tried to ignore the butterflies in my stomach.

"Let me get the door for you."

There was no use in arguing, Trevor insisted on helping me out of the truck every single time. I watched as he walked around the front, ignoring Eric along the way.

A part of me was disappointed that Trevor didn't try to hold on-to my hand as we walked up the steps to my porch. I was positive he didn't want Eric to see if I pulled my hand away. I wouldn't have. I didn't need to give Eric any ideas that he might have a chance with me.

"Eric, what are you doing here?" I asked. Trevor stood next to me, his hands in his pockets. The way he was staring at Eric should have made him drop to the ground.

"I wanted to make sure you were okay."

"She's fine, so you can leave now," Trevor stated.

When I shot a warning look in his direction, Trevor sighed.

"Trevor, why don't you run over to Cord's? I need to talk to Er-ic."

He opened his mouth to protest but stopped when I pleaded with my eyes.

Trevor leaned down and kissed me on the forehead like it was second nature. He whispered, "I'll only be a minute."

I watched him head down the steps to his truck. It wasn't hard to notice that he paused before climbing in. I knew it had to be hard for him to leave me here with Eric.

Smiling, I watched him back out of the driveway and head to the square. I figured I had about fifteen minutes or less to get things settled with Eric.

"So, I see you've just let him back into your life. Where were you?"

For the first time since I'd been friends with Eric, I didn't want to see him. Let alone talk to him.

How dare he treat me this way?

With my keys in my hand, I faced my door and unlocked it. "Would you like something to drink? How long have you been sitting out here?"

Eric huffed and followed me in. "I'd love some water. I've been here about thirty minutes. I saw your car and figured you went for a walk."

Making my way into the kitchen, I pulled out two bottles of water and handed one to Eric.

He opened the water and nearly drank the whole bottle before sitting on a stool and waiting for me to talk.

"First of all, Trevor is always going to be in my life because we're having a child together. As far as where we were, it's honestly none of your business, but I'll tell you anyway. We told our parents about the baby."

His brows shot up. "Wow. How did that go?"

With a shrug, I replied, "It could have gone better. Our folks are going out to eat with us to celebrate, so I need to make this quick so I can get ready."

Eric's eyes looked sad.

Before I had a chance to speak, he started in.

"Scarlett, a man like that doesn't change his colors overnight."

"How do you know?"

He sighed. "My God, are you that desperate for him?"

I gave him a warning look.

"I'm sorry, but I find it hard to believe that you would just take him back."

"That's where you're wrong, Eric. I haven't let Trevor back in. We're not a couple, at least not right now."

His eyes flickered with something that looked like hope. "Oh? Why not?"

"I told Trevor I needed time to figure out how to forgive him. Make sure he wasn't doing all of this because of the baby. He said he wanted to be with me exclusively before he even found out about the baby."

With a rough laugh, Eric said, "And you believe him?"

Folding my arms across my chest, I nodded. "I do. I saw the look on his face that night when he saw me at Aisling and thought I was with you. He was devastated. He'd been trying to call me all that day, and I kept ignoring him. When I finally did answer, he told me he needed to talk to me. That's when we made plans to meet that next morning."

"How do you know he didn't already know about the baby?"

This time I was the one who scoffed. "I'm sorry, do you not remember when you dropped the baby bomb on him? His reaction alone says he didn't know."

Eric had the decency to look like he regretted his part in all of that.

"Fine, so let's say he had some sort of epiphany, do you think he is the type of man to stay faithful to you, love?"

I thought about his question for a few moments before answering.

"Deep down, my heart is answering yes. My head is still a bit confused."

"I'd listen to your head and not your heart."

"Eric, you'll never know how much I appreciate you being there for me, and I don't want to lose your friendship. I need you to understand something, though. I love Trevor and I may not be ready to fall into a relationship with him, but we owe it to each other to see where things go. We're having a baby together and I know that's not the only reason for us to be a couple, but I want to try. I can't explain it to you other than to say that I gave that man my heart a long time ago, and I don't think I'll ever be able to give it to someone else, at least not any time soon."

He shook his head. "How can you say that after everything he did?"

With a shrug, I spoke the truth. "Because you only saw the bad. He never promised me anything, and he was always up front from the first moment I went with him to his family's benefit dinner. He's always been honest about that."

"So you were okay hooking up with a guy who whores around?"

Flinching, I looked down at my hands and then back to Eric. "I can't help the way my heart feels, Eric."

Looking away, he stood. "You're being foolish and acting like a silly girl with a high school crush."

My body heated with anger. "Excuse me?"

"Foolish! You think he is going to change, and you are wrong. A man like him cannot stop being with countless women. He likes the chase and the adventure too much."

There was no sense in arguing with him. Even if I told him Trevor hadn't been with other women, he'd argue that Trevor was lying.

"If that's your opinion of me and of Trevor, there's nothing I can do or say to change your mind."

Eric sighed. "For Christ's sake, Scarlett. Can't you see I would always take care of you and love you?"

"Can't you see how unhappy you would be? Why would you want to be with a woman who loves another man?"

"You'll learn to love me."

"Please don't make me keep doing this, Eric. I don't want to hurt you."

Eric walked over to me and pulled me to him, crushing his lips to mine.

I knew he was hoping for a spark that might give him the slightest hint that there was something between us. I didn't kiss him back and just stood still in his embrace. The kiss was nothing like when I kissed Trevor. It lasted five seconds, at the most, before I pushed him away, and I wiped my mouth.

"You don't feel anything for me? Nothing when I kissed you?"

My heart ached to hurt him. Slowly shaking my head, I replied, "No, I'm sorry."

Swallowing hard, he started out of the kitchen.

"When he hurts you again, don't come to me for a shoulder to cry on."

"Eric, please don't leave like this. I'd like to be friends."

His hand was on the doorknob. "I don't want to be your friend, Scarlett. I wanted more than that."

"I'm sorry, but that's all I can give you."

With that, he walked out the door, softly closing it.

I stood in my living room, staring at the door. I was sad to lose a friend, but I needed him to know, once and for all, where I stood with my heart.

I slowly made my way up the stairs, then stripped out of my clothes the second I hit my bedroom. A hot shower was exactly what I needed.

CHAPTER 13

Trevor

By the time I got back to Scarlett's house, Eric was gone, and she was upstairs getting ready. As I made my way to the guest bedroom, I got the last reply from the group text I had sent out about dinner. I was bound and determined to make this day up to Scarlett and I needed my family to help me.

I headed to the bathroom off the spare room. The temptation to jump in and take a quick shower won over as I soaped up and rinsed off the day's grime.

Turning off the shower, I opened the curtain and glanced around for a towel.

Damn it. I should have looked before jumping in. The door to the bathroom opened, and Scarlett walked in. She screamed when she saw me and then stood perfectly still. Well, most of her stood still. Her eyes slowly roamed my wet, naked body, and I couldn't help smirking when I watched her lick her lips like she wanted a taste of what was before her.

"You wouldn't happen to have a towel, would you, darlin'?" I asked.

Scarlett's eyes lingered on my dick which was now growing hard from her gaze.

"Scarlett?"

Jerking her head up, she cleared her throat. "Um…what? Wait. Hold on! What are you doing in here and why are you naked…and wet?"

Fuck if I didn't want to ask her if she was wet. I knew she was. The way this woman was giving me fuck-me eyes was testing my goddamn willpower.

But Scarlett wanted things a certain way and I was going to respect that. I needed to earn back her trust and if that meant ignoring the way she kept licking her lips and glancing at my cock, then that's what I would do.

"You were upstairs when I got back, and the front door was open, so I came in. A shower was too tempting, but you don't have a towel down here."

Her eyes were now everywhere but on me.

"A towel?"

I laughed. "Just a reminder of what you said earlier. I'm standing here naked and wet."

Her eyes swung back, except this time she kept her gaze on mine.

"Towel. Um. I, ah, have one, I think…"

My eyes moved up to the towel on top of her head. "Can I use that one?"

Her hand moved up to the towel. "It's wet."

"I don't mind wet. I don't mind wet at all."

Did a moan just slip from those perfectly bee-stung lips of hers?

Like a robot, Scarlett lifted her hand, pulled the towel off and handed it to me. My cock jumped against my abs as I watched her dark hair fall around her shoulders.

Fucking hell. What I wouldn't do to run my fingers through that wet hair and pull her head back so I could kiss the living shit out of her.

Not today, Trevor. Not today.

With a smile, I wrapped the towel around my waist, took a step closer to her and kissed her on the forehead.

"Thanks, babe. I'm going to get dressed now."

When I walked around her, she mumbled something I didn't understand, but I chose to ignore it as I walked back into the guest bedroom.

I could feel Scarlett's eyes on me as I pulled the towel free, dried off quickly, then slipped my jeans on.

"Wait. You're not wearing underwear?"

Glancing over my shoulder, I lifted my brow. "If you get to stand there and watch me get dressed, do I get to watch you?"

Her cheeks turned red and she walked back into the bathroom and quickly came out with a hair dryer.

"Forgot this was down here. I'm sorry I walked in on you."

Scarlett rushed by me but not fast enough. I reached for her hand and pulled her to a stop. Drawing her close to me, she placed her hand on my chest and looked up at me with eyes that were silently begging me to kiss her. Her jaw, on the other hand, was firmly clamped shut.

I used my thumb to wipe away the white cream that was on her face.

"You had something on your face. Conditioner, maybe?"

Her entire body trembled as I held her. Her warmth disappeared when I stepped away. It took everything I had not to reach out and hold her steady when she wobbled a bit.

"Th-thanks. I'll, ah, go get dressed and dry my hair some."

I nodded, grabbing the shirt I borrowed from Cord. It was hard as hell to ignore the internal desire to beg her to kiss me. Beg her to let me feel her in my arms. Make love to her. But I had to. There was no way I was fucking this up.

"Sounds good. I'll wait in the living room for you."

Scarlett took a few steps back, her eyes still locked on my bare chest. The only thing that broke her gaze was me putting my shirt on. She spun around quickly and rushed out the door.

Once she was gone, I sat down on the edge of the bed and dropped my arms to my knees.

"Jesus, this is going to be hard," I whispered to myself.

After taking in a few deep breaths, I pulled out my phone and sent Corina a text.

Me: *You able to get something for dessert?*

She responded immediately.

Sis-in-law #1: *Of course, I did! Mrs. Johnson loves me and had something just for the occasion!*

Me: *Have I ever told you you're my favorite sister-in-law?*

Sis-in-law #1: *Nope, never.*

I took a screen shot of her name I had stored in my phone.

Me: *See? It even says you're #1*

Sis-in-law #1: *Could it just be that my name comes before Paxton's in the alphabet and that is how you put us in your phone?*

Me: *Minor detail....*

Sis-in-law #1: *See you soon, jerk!*

I walked around the living room. I'd been in this room so many times, but I never really paid attention to everything in it. The sofa I already knew was comfortable as shit. I'd fallen asleep on it during the few nights I stayed with Scarlett when she had the flu. I smiled when a memory hit me.

I'd fallen asleep after watching some documentary Scarlett was into. It didn't take much to wake me up when I realized my girl was crawling on top of me. Her warm body pushed down on the bulge in my jeans.

Slowly opening my eyes, I smiled when her chestnut brown eyes met my blue.

"What are you doing?" I asked, a smirk on my face.

"I think that medicine kicked in. I'm feeling better."

Dropping my hands to her hips, I lifted up into her. Scarlett dropped her head back and moaned.

"Trevor, please."

"Baby, you're sick."

She rotated her hips and dropped her gaze back to mine.

"Please. I want to feel you inside of me. I feel loads better, I swear."

I closed my eyes and prayed for the strength I needed to tell her no, but I couldn't. Scarlett was like a drug. And I needed a fucking fix.

She saw it in my eyes when I looked back at her. Lifting up, she worked quickly at getting my jeans undone. I lifted my hips and pulled them down, letting my hard cock spring out. Scarlett reached for my wallet on the side table and handed it to me. When I got the condom package out, I ripped it open with my teeth and slid the condom over my cock.

With a wide smile, she crawled back onto me and slowly guided my dick inside her warm pussy.

"Jesus," I hissed, my head falling back against the sofa. "Scarlett, you feel so good."

Leaning her forehead to mine, she smiled. "I'd kiss you, but I've got the flu."

"Fuck the flu," I grunted, wrapping my hand around her neck and capturing her lips with mine.

Scarlett moved up and down on my dick, slow at first and then faster.

Our kiss was heated and full of passion. I'd never come with someone on top of me like this. Never. Hearing the way Scarlett moaned, feeling her body tighten around mine, feeling this fucking connection that both thrilled and scared me to death, I let go when she started to come.

"Trevor," she gasped against my mouth as I pushed in deeper with my hands on her hips.

"Christ," I grunted and came so fucking hard I saw stars.

When our bodies finally came to a stop, our foreheads leaned against one another. My chest was rising and falling as much as Scarlett's.

"What are you doing to me, Scarlett?"

Pulling back, she stared into my eyes. The question was serious, my mind racing as I tried to figure out what was happening between us.

With a smile, she replied, "I believe I just fucked the flu right out of my system."

Laughing, I pulled the condom off, wrapped it in tissue and then dropped her onto the sofa. My body stayed barely off of hers while I kissed her until she was breathless. At that point I didn't give two fucks if I got the flu or not. I needed her mouth on mine.

There was no way I could ever get Scarlett out my system and it took everything I had in me not to admit it to her.

"You look lost in thought."

Scarlett's sweet voice pulled me from the memory as I stared at the sofa.

"Thinking about something."

She grinned. "Must have been something good. You have a huge smile on your face."

Rubbing the back of my neck, I nodded. "Yeah, it was. Really good."

Her gaze fell to the sofa and she smiled before looking at me. We had fucked and made love on that damn thing plenty of times.

"So, do you think we should head on out?" she finally asked.

My eyes roamed over her body. The simple black skirt fell past her knees, but had a split that would show off her legs when she walked. Simple, yet sexy as hell. The white top she had on mimicked the look of her skirt, simple and sexy, as it dropped down her shoulders and was held on by two thin straps. Scarlett knew how to dress. Even in a pair of jeans and a T-shirt she looked amazing. But knowing she was carrying my baby made her ten times sexier.

"You look…beautiful."

Dropping her gaze to assess her outfit, she said, "You've seen me in this before. I wear it to work sometimes."

"You wear *that* to work? Oh, fuck no. You're not allowed to wear that to work."

Pinching her eyebrows, she placed her hand on her hip and tilted her head. "Is that so? Who says?"

"Um, the man whose baby you're carrying. You look fucking hot in that outfit and the fact that you're carrying our child makes you look even hotter, so I'm going to need you to dress in sweats and T-shirts from now on. Y'all have a casual dress code at the courthouse, right?"

Her laugh filled the room and the tightening my chest didn't go unnoticed. I loved that I was making her laugh and not cry. I'd made her laugh plenty of other times, but for some reason, the times I made her cry stood out more. I needed to fix that.

When she stopped laughing, her teeth sank into that plump red lip of hers. "Did you really mean what you said?"

Keeping my eyes fixed on hers, I asked, "Which part? The sweats? Yes, I meant every word of that."

Her cheeks turned the most beautiful shade of pink as she chuckled. "No. The part about me looking hotter."

My pants felt like they'd grown about two sizes too small.

"Of course, I meant it. You look beautiful, Scarlett. I honestly can't wait to see our baby growing inside of you as you get bigger."

Her nose scrunched up. "*That* is a lie!"

I made my way over to her and placed my hand on her stomach, causing her to pull in a sharp breath. My own damn breathing picked up, but I tried like hell to act normal.

"I'm not ever going to lie to you, especially about our child. Seeing your stomach grow bigger means we're that much closer to meeting her."

Her eyes pooled with tears, and she quickly started blinking to keep them at bay. "Her?" she whispered.

I shrugged. "Or him. I don't care which. As long as they're healthy and have your eyes."

Scarlett looked away and cleared her throat. "We should probably get going."

I stepped away, and my heart felt like it was about to be ripped from my chest. I hated that she was keeping a wall between us. She didn't know it, but I was going to fight like hell to tear that thing down. Piece by damn piece if I had to.

"Did you want to follow me over there, so you'll have your car? Or I can bring you back home. Totally up to you."

Seemingly surprised by my offer of having her drive by herself, she paused for a moment and then shook her head.

"Would you mind if we drove over together? That way I don't have to drive back in the dark. The deer and all."

"I don't mind a single bit. Let's head on out."

The drive to Laney's Grill was quiet before I broke the silence. "Do you think I can go with you to your next doctor's appointment?"

I felt her eyes on me almost instantly.

"Of course, you can. I have one next week."

"Perfect. Should we meet there?"

Scarlett fiddled with her hands in her lap before answering me. "If that's what you want."

"It's up to you. I don't want to push you into something you aren't comfortable with or ready for."

I saw her pull in a deep breath. "It might be better if we meet, that way you don't have to bring me back to work and can head back to the ranch."

Disappointment hit me hard. "Okay."

The silence returned and when I couldn't take it any longer I turned the radio on, drowning out the overthinking in my damn head.

When we finally pulled up to the restaurant, I parked and shut the truck off. When I went to get out, Scarlett grabbed my arm.

"Wait."

Turning back to her, I gave her a smile. "Everything okay?"

"Yes. No. Trevor, I'm not trying to hurt you by keeping a little distance between us."

"I know that."

"Do you?" she asked, her brows pinched together.

"I do. I'm not going to lie and act like it doesn't hurt that you don't want to be near me, but I respect that."

She shook her head before returning her gaze back to me.

"It's not that. I want to be near you, but when I'm near you I want more. A lot more of you, and I can't do that right now. I need this to go slow, because God knows, Trevor, all you have to do is kiss me and I think we both know I'm yours."

Taking her hand in mine, I squeezed it. "That's why I've been stopping myself today. You have no idea how much I wanted to push you onto that bed today and make love to you. But I respect what you've asked from me. I'm not giving up on us, Scarlett, so don't take my behavior as giving up because I'd love nothing more than to do just the opposite of what I'm doing right now. But I'm giving you space."

She smiled.

"I'm going to fight for us. It might have taken me forever to figure out that what I had in front of me was what I needed, and I may have lost you, but I'm not giving up until you look me in the eyes and tell me you don't love me. I can't live without you, babe. I'm not sure if you'll ever be able to believe me, but I'm going to do my best to show you…and to show our baby."

"I want desperately to not feel scared and unsure about us. To stop wondering if you're in love with me…or simply in love with the feeling of us. My mind and my heart are all over the place," she said.

We sat for a few seconds just staring at each other before she cleared her throat. "We better get in there before our folks come looking for us."

With a nod, I climbed out of the truck. Every possible emotion felt like it was running through my body. I needed to get it under control in less than two seconds or Scarlett and our families would be able to see that her words had just rocked me to the core.

CHAPTER 14

Scarlett

Trevor's face wore an emotion I'd never seen on him before.

Fear.

"Damn it," I whispered as I watched him plaster on a fake smile as he opened the door. If I kept Trevor at a distance for too long, would he give up? I'd heard so much conviction in his voice that I knew that wouldn't happen. Then why was I so afraid to let him in?

Because if you give him your whole heart he'll have the power to hurt you again.

My head was spinning. Trevor had hurt me more times than I could count, but he had also never promised me anything before. I knew how much he cared about me from his whispered confessions, but he hadn't been ready for more. Was he truly ready now?

"Ready?"

The word made me stall for a quick moment. I smiled. "Ready."

"Let's go celebrate the fact that my super sperm got you pregnant on the first run!"

Laughing, I hit him in the stomach. "Super sperm? Okay, Clark Kent," I said as my cheeks heated.

"What? It's true. I've heard some people have to try for months or even years to get pregnant. We did it in one round and weren't even trying. I think that says something about my sperm and their super-potent abilities."

"We had sex at the right time of month is what that means."

Trevor took my hand, and I didn't pull it away. I needed to give him a little encouragement, and I liked the warmth of his body against mine in whatever small way I could get it right now. Trevor calmed me. And even though we had already told our parents, I was still feeling uneasy about this dinner. I couldn't help but wonder if my parents were putting on a happy face simply for the Parkers.

"Good evening. How are y'all doing?" the hostess asked as she smiled at me and then Trevor.

"We are doing great! Here to celebrate. You should have a reservation for Parker."

A bigger smile erupted on the young girl's face. "Oh! Yes, the rest of your party is here. Y'all are in the back room we reserve for private parties."

"Private parties?" I asked, looking up at Trevor.

He shrugged. "Mom must want to get drunk and loud."

I laughed. "I can't see that ever happening."

Trevor rolled his eyes, "Oh baby, you just wait. You're now stuck forever with this family and let me tell you, my momma can knock back the booze and let her hair down. You have met my sisters, right?"

The hostess chuckled. "If y'all will follow me, I'll show you to the room."

Trevor placed his hand on my lower back, making my lower stomach pull with more than desire. Lust. Want. Need. This man was driving me insane, and I wasn't sure if it was simply because we hadn't been around in each other in weeks or because he was purposely trying not to touch me. Either way, my libido was through the roof.

Trevor stopped us as we drew closer to the room. He leaned down and placed his mouth to my ear. A shiver ran down my spine when I felt the rush of warm air. I held my breath as I waited for him to speak.

"The only thing I ever want to do from this point on is make you happy."

I went to ask what he meant, but he guided us into the room. I was still looking up at him confused as I heard a chorus of people yell out.

"Congratulations!"

Jumping, my hand went to my mouth, and I let out a scream of surprise. I scanned the room and saw the entire Parker family, my folks, *and* my grandparents.

A huge, handmade sign in pink and blue hung behind them that read, "Congratulations, Trevor and Scarlett."

Pink, yellow, and blue balloons were everywhere. Before I had a chance to let it all process, a sea of Parkers rushed me. Each one hugged and kissed me on the cheek. I tried to hold my tears back, but finally gave up when little Chloe walked up and handed me a box.

"It's got a surprise in there for you, Ms. Scarlett!"

I bent down to get eye level with her while quickly wiping away the silly tears that had gotten loose. "I love surprises!"

Her face lit up and those Parker blue eyes beamed. "Me too! I think the baby will love the little goat toy I'm giving her! I bought it with my own money!"

Glancing at Trevor, I widened my eyes. I wasn't sure if Chloe realized she had given the surprise away or not, but I was over the moon. He winked.

Focusing on Chloe, I pulled her in for a hug. "I can't wait to see it! I'll open it before you leave."

She squeezed me, then pulled back. "Does this mean I get to call you Aunt Scarlett?"

My heart jumped to my throat. Before I had a chance to reply, Trevor intervened. "Yes, pumpkin. You can call her Aunt Scarlett."

"Yay!"

Chloe ran off across the large room declaring she had a new aunt and couldn't wait to tell the kids at school. Trevor watched her do a few jumps and twists, then said, "Well, that should get the rumor mill goin'."

I groaned.

"My phone should be blowing up any minute now from the prayer chain asking for folks to pray for your quickie marriage," Waylynn stated.

Spinning around, I stared at Waylynn. "What?"

She laughed. "Oh, man, this relationship is going to be so much fun to watch play out."

Waylynn pulled me in for a hug. "Don't wait too long to get back with him. I've got a bet going with Paxton, and I really, really need to win."

My shocked expression made Trevor frown, but Waylynn pushed me back at arm's length and gave me a knowing smile. "Just remember what we talked about at the pool party. Being big. You get my drift, girl."

My cheeks felt like they could heat up the entire room.

"I bet people will forget all about Old Lady Hopkins walking in on us having…S-E-X," Jonathon said as he cradled a sleeping Liberty.

"That spells sex!" Chloe called out from across the room. Jonathon closed his eyes and cursed under his breath as he and Waylynn moved to the table to sit down.

"Dude, they teach them to spell a lot younger these days, not like when we were in school," Trevor reminded him.

When my grandparents walked up to me, the tears almost started to flow. My grandmother hugged me so tenderly. This was what I had wanted when everyone found out. Happiness. Not shock, not expectations of what we were going to do. Just simple happiness.

"Some words of advice, sweetie. Suck on peppermints to help with the morning sickness."

"Thank you, Granny."

She smiled and added, "Be sure to drink lots of water. The baby needs it."

Granddad nodded and smiled at my grandmother. This January they were going to celebrate their fifty-fifth wedding anniversary, and I knew I wanted a love like theirs. That kind of love was very rare, a unique relationship of give and take, of love and loss. I looked around at the Parker family and knew that every couple in this room was cut from the same cloth as my grandparents. My eyes landed on Trevor and I silently hoped that he was also cut from that same cloth as his parents and siblings…someone who would fight for a love that endures every hardship. Only time would tell with me and Trevor, and we had the next seven months to figure it out.

"Lots of water and peppermint, Granny. Got it."

Granddad shook Trevor's hand. "You better take care of my granddaughter or I'll kick your ass from Texas all the way to Canada."

"Yes, sir. I promise to take care of both of them."

"That's what I want to hear," Granddad said, giving Trevor a firm slap on the back that caused Trevor to stumble a few steps.

Trevor cough-whispered, "Damn, the old man is strong. He nearly brought up a lung."

I covered my mouth to hide my giggle as my parents walked up to us.

It was as I expected it would be. Formal. As was everything with them. But I wouldn't let that diminish my happiness in this moment. I did get a hug from my mom, though, so there was that.

"Scarlett, darling, we're so happy. Not how we wanted this to happen per se, but we are happy nonetheless! I cannot wait to shop for baby clothes together." I could tell my mom was truly happy in her heart, but she had that worried edge to her words.

"Trevor, I expect you to do right by my daughter and grand-child," my father added.

With a nod and a firm handshake, Trevor replied, "I will indeed, sir. I promise you that."

When the last two people walked up to us, it finally hit me what had just happened. I got my celebration. Everyone was here to cele-brate our baby news, and it was all because of Trevor. He made this happen and he did it for me. My heart felt like it was about to burst. I was so excited and appreciative for everything that he had done. I was almost on the verge of being speechless knowing what he'd pulled off in such a short period of time.

Melanie took me in her arms and pressed her mouth to my ear. "Congratulations, sweetheart. We really are so happy for you both. I can't wait to be a grandmother again!"

"I can't...wait...either," I said between sobs. I hadn't even bro-ken down when my own mother hugged me, but there was some-thing in Melanie's voice. In her embrace. Something that told me everything was going to work out the way it should. That this wasn't a mistake, that it was God's plan, and everything would truly be okay with me and Trevor and our baby.

John waited patiently until I got the tears under control, then gave me a hug and also gave one to his son, hitting him on the back just as hard as granddad did. I had a feeling there was more to those slaps than I knew or could understand.

When we stood alone, I looked up at Trevor. He had a huge smile on his face as he scanned the room.

"Were you surprised?" he asked, looking down at me, the smile not faltering.

No words would form, and if they did, I knew I would start crying the moment I spoke. I nodded, covered my mouth and began to cry anyway.

Trevor wrapped his arms around me, allowing me to bury my face in his chest while I got my stupid pregnancy emotions under control. Inhaling his woodsy cologne, I closed my eyes and got lost in the feeling of being in his arms.

"I did it for you, Scarlett."

I replied in a muffled voice, "I know. Thank you. You'll never know how much this meant to me."

Trevor stared down at me. "All I want is for those to be happy tears. Are they?"

"Yes!" I said, wiping them from my cheek. "Thank goodness I wore waterproof mascara."

What Trevor did next made my heart stop. Hell, it made everything in the room stop. He leaned down and kissed my left cheek softly, then my right, and finished it with a kiss to my forehead. When he turned to walk over to everyone, I took hold of his arm and stopped him.

On tiptoe, I placed my hand on the side of his face, letting him know I wanted him to kiss me. He looked unsure at first, almost afraid. But he lowered his face and our lips met. It was soft and tender. Like the very first kiss this man ever gave me. The one that sealed my heart to him. When I opened my mouth to his, he groaned and just barely slipped his tongue into my mouth before he bit my lower lip and pulled his mouth away.

It hadn't been much, but it was what he needed, and I was more than happy to give it to him.

"Thank you," he whispered before guiding us both over to the large table that was set up in the room. Everyone was taking their seats and when Chloe called the seat next to me, I felt a warmth spread over me I'd never felt before.

Love.

A completely different type of love that was so foreign to me. And one I never wanted to let go.

"It's going to be fun being pregnant with you, Scarlett!" Harley said. She and Tripp were sitting directly across from us.

"I think so, too! We can see which one of us eats more pints of ice cream or who has the craziest cravings, right?" I couldn't contain the grin that spread from ear to ear when I looked at Harley.

I snuck a peek at Amelia, but she was lost in a conversation with Paxton. She looked beautiful. Her smile nearly lit up the room. When my gaze caught Wade's, he winked at me. He knew what I was thinking. I wished the whole table knew about Amelia's pregnancy, as well.

"I can't believe you're going to be a dad before me," I heard Cord saying to Trevor.

"I can't help it if my sperm are better than yours. That takes STAM-IN-A, Cord. I can give you some hints if you need any on how to improve the stamina, just say the word."

Cord smacked Trevor upside his head and everyone within earshot started laughing.

I stared at Trevor, my mouth gaping. "Really, Trevor? Right here you're going to bring that up?" I whispered as he laughed.

"Whatever, little brother. You believe what you want, Farmer Smurf."

Steed lost it laughing, as did Tripp.

"Farmer Smurf?" I asked, looking at all the guys who were now in hysterics. Well, all of them except for my father and John. John, however, did have a slight smile on his face.

"Hey, unlike the rest of you bastards, I'll take that title proudly, thank you."

They all stopped laughing and stared at Trevor like something monumental had just happened. Clearly, I didn't get it.

"Wow. I'm not sure what to say to that, Trev," Wade added, looking at his best friend with the same expression as his brothers.

"What's happening right now?" I asked, glancing around the table.

"Don't ask. It is some stupid thing they all have going on. There are some things better left unknown, Scarlett. Best you figure that out now," Harley said as Waylynn nodded in agreement.

"What's going on?" Mitchell asked, sitting back down at the table and placing Merit in her high chair.

"I think Trevor just accepted his Smurf name, proudly and without argument," Jonathon stated, surprise in his voice.

"Smurf name?" I asked, confused as all get out. I tried to heed Harley's advice, but the way the guys were acting made me curious.

"No shit!?" Mitchell said with laugh.

"Uncle Mitchell swore!" Chloe yelled as Paxton covered Chloe's mouth, clearly expecting something else to follow.

"Boys! How many times do I have to say no swearing! There are going to be more and more children at this table who can repeat that stuff!" Melanie exclaimed.

Suddenly, Gage busted out his rendition of Mitchell. "No...chit!"

Steed and Paxton both gasped, while hushed snickers erupted around the table.

"Oh! Gage, you said a bad word!" Chloe declared.

"Lord help me," Steed stated as he looked down at his son. "We do not say bad words, Gage."

The little boy stared up at his father, big blue eyes filled with happiness. A smile that would melt anyone's heart.

"Patches!" Gage shouted.

"That's just as much of a bad word," Waylynn said softly while taking a drink of wine.

The entire table erupted in laughter. Even I knew about Patches. Chloe, on the other hand, smiled proudly.

"I taught Gage that word!" she stated with pride.

The rest of dinner was filled with endless conversations happening all around the table. How Liberty and Merit slept through it all was beyond me. I guess they were used to loud crowds. With this family, I would think they would have to get used to it.

Trevor leaned down and bumped my shoulder.

"What are you thinking about?"

I decided to tell him the truth and not brush it off.

"How amazing your family is. They are loud, and crazy, and a million different conversations are happening all at once and half the kids are asleep through all of it. Chloe is adorable, Gage has stolen my heart, and oh my goodness. Liberty and Merit."

Looking Trevor in the eyes, I grinned. "I can't wait for this baby. I'm so happy, Trevor."

My breath stalled. Trevor was looking at me with an expression I'd never seen on his face before, or at least, had never noticed it.

"I am too, Scarlett. I can't wait to add to the crazy."

He kissed the back of my hand before turning to Jonathon who asked him something about a tractor that needed fixing. He didn't let go of my hand, placing them both on the table between us. I also didn't make an attempt to pull back. When I glanced around the table, I took everyone in.

Harley and Tripp. The ultimate second-chance love story. I didn't know the complete history, but I did know by looking at the two of them that they were meant to be together.

Moving my gaze to Jonathon and Waylynn, I couldn't help a smile as I watched Waylynn stare down at her sleeping daughter. Liberty was seven months old and a precious little thing.

Melanie and John were at the end of the table with my parents and grandparents. Chloe had been sitting next to me at first but moved next to her mother because Gage needed help and that was what big sisters were for—according to Chloe. My grandmother was currently sitting to my right. Past Trevor was Cord and Maebh. Maebh was talking to Paxton across the table while Gage sat in Paxton's lap. He was attempting to use the entire red crayon on the coloring sheet Paxton had placed in front of him. He was a little over a year and such a handsome little boy. He stole my heart the first time I ever met him.

Next to Paxton was Steed, looking at Paxton like she hung the moon. My stomach dropped at the sight. It was beautiful to watch a man look at the woman he loved like that.

Next to them, Wade and Amelia exchanged secret words. The smile on both of their faces almost screamed *We have exciting news too*. I couldn't wait until they shared it.

The last couple was Mitchell and Corina. Baby Merit had crashed in Mitchell's arms. She was only about four months old, and my goodness did she have the bluest of blue eyes. I wanted to walk over and ask Mitchell if I could hold her, but Daddy was not about to let his little one out of his arms. Corina caught me staring and smiled.

"Want to hold her?" she called out across the table. I jumped up, taking the invitation without hesitation.

"Do you mind, Mitchell?"

He laughed. "Not at all. She may be little, but she gets heavy after a while."

Mitchell stood and placed Merit in my arms. She didn't wake up. Corina and I walked off to the side as I stared down at the baby in my arms.

"Are you nervous?" she asked.

I nodded. "Yes. A bit scared, really. I mean, they're adorable when they're other people's!"

She chuckled.

"Thank you for letting me come work for you at the bed and breakfast after the baby is born. It's going to help out so much."

Her smile was genuine. "Of course! It will be fun having you there, plus it frees up more time for me. My mom helps a ton, but it will be nice for her to be able to take a day off, as well."

I rocked back and forth while staring at Merit. She was so precious. Everything about her was perfect.

Glancing up at Corina, I asked, "Do you know what the guys were talking about with the Smurf thing?"

She grinned. "Cord started it, I think, with Steed or Mitchell. I'm not sure. He said once the guys fell in love they walked around with this goofy, happy expression. Cord said they had been Smurfed."

"Why Smurfs?" I asked with a little giggle.

"Smurfs are happy little people. Cord's given each of them a name. So when he called Trevor Farmer Smurf and Trevor didn't argue with it, they were all surprised. He was basically saying he's happy and in love, according to the guys' secret language."

My eyes snapped over to Trevor. He was talking to Wade and Steed off to the side of the table. I watched him nod at something Wade was saying. He was so handsome he took my breath away. Lowering my gaze, I sighed internally at the way the man filled his jeans. It honestly made my mouth salivate knowing he didn't have anything on but the jeans. Moving my gaze up to his button-up shirt, I could see his muscles move underneath the fabric.

Damn. The man was hot as hell.

"He loves you, Scarlett. I know he hasn't always showed it, but we've all seen him struggle since last spring with his emotions about you."

The sting at the back of my eyes was becoming familiar, but I pushed it away.

Focusing on Corina, I smiled. "It's…complicated."

"Why?" she asked her voice so sincere. But it was a question I wasn't even sure I could honestly answer.

"I don't know. I mean, he pushed me away for so many months, yet at the same time I felt like he didn't want to push me away…if that makes sense."

She nodded. "It does."

"I see another side of Trevor coming out that he only ever shared with me. It's confusing because I try to think it's not about the baby, but I still do. That insecurity is slowly fading away. I just need time."

Corina tilted her head, a slight smirk on her face.

"I have never doubted that Trevor was in love with you, Scarlett. I think we all saw, everyone but Trevor. He was scared, but the thought of you being with Eric was the punch in the stomach he needed to see the light. I don't doubt for one second that Trevor wouldn't be there for you and the baby. He's a Parker, and his parents expect him to take care of their women and always be there for them. But this!"

She motioned to the room.

"This he did because he wanted you to be happy. He told his family you were robbed of celebrating this miracle and asked if we could be here tonight."

I swallowed hard, my eyes drifting back to Trevor. He was laughing at something Wade was saying.

Her hand landed on my shoulder and she gave it a squeeze. "I'm not telling you to rush into his arms. I'm sure he did things that hurt you. I'm just saying, no man would do all of this for a woman he didn't love with all his heart, and I'm pretty sure he'd only do it for the one he hoped he'd get to spend the rest of his life with. Don't let it make your guard go up because you feel like he changed overnight. Love does some pretty crazy things to people, especially when they think they've let it slip through their fingers."

Turning to her, I nodded. "I know you're right. Thank you, Corina."

"Go slow, get to know each other better. You're both about to have your world turned upside down, but in the most amazing way."

Chewing on my lip, I let her words settle in.

"Mind if I hold my beautiful niece?" Trevor asked, causing my stomach to twist in knots. Did this man have any idea how he made me feel?

"Of course, you can!" I said, smiling as I carefully handed over Merit. Trevor, on the other hand, handled her like a pro. He took her from me, spun her to the other side of his arms and started walking off with her. My mouth dropped open.

"He just handled her like he does that every day!"

Corina laughed. "Trevor is an amazing uncle. Just ask Chloe. Did you know once a week he has a standing tea party with her?"

My jaw was on the floor. "What? You have got to be kidding. That man, at a tea party?" I couldn't help the chuckle.

Corina nodded. "Paxton told me. Trevor makes time every Thursday afternoon when Chloe gets home from school. I'd love to see it! Can you see tattooed muscle-man Trevor sitting at a tiny table sipping tea from plastic cups surrounded by stuffed animals and baby goats?"

We both chuckled before I glanced over to Trevor and watched him rock his niece slightly back and forth. He was talking to Mitchell, and he looked like this was something he did every single day. Second nature.

A warm feeling filled my chest as I stared at Trevor, and I whispered, "I actually *can* see it."

CHAPTER 15

Trevor

I walked Scarlett to her door and stopped as she fumbled with the key. Once she had it unlocked, she stepped into her house.

"I'm going to head on home," I said, watching her expression fall just the slightest.

"You are?"

With a half shrug, I replied, "You've had a busy day. I figured you were tired."

Scarlett chewed on her lip. "Thank you for tonight. It meant a lot to me that you did all of that."

"Well, our baby deserves to be celebrated, right?"

"Yes!" she replied with a soft laugh.

"If you need anything, call me?"

"I will. I promise."

Stepping into the doorway, I kissed her on the forehead. "Good-night, Scarlett."

"'Night, Trevor."

Walking away from her was the hardest fucking thing I ever had to do. I wanted to pull her into my arms and hold her. Tell her how much I loved her and that I wanted this more than she'd ever realize.

My hand was on the truck door when Scarlett called out my name.

"Trevor?"

I glanced back at her. "Yeah?"

"*Um*, thank you again."

I gave her a wave and climbed up into the truck. Scarlett stood at the doorway until I pulled out of her driveway. My heart was pounding in my chest the entire drive back to the ranch. Instead of driving to my house, I headed to my folks' place, hoping my father would still be up.

When I saw the lights on in the house, I parked out front and made my way to the family room. My mother was curled on the sofa, book in hand.

"Trevor, is everything okay?"

I stepped into the room and gave her a warm smile. "Yeah. Thank you for helping me today with the dinner, Mom."

Her book went to her lap as she focused on me. "Of course. I knew the moment I got that text from you that we needed to turn things around. I don't want Scarlett feeling like this baby is a mistake."

With a nod, I blew out a breath.

"I know you're scared, Trevor, but I also know you love that girl. Do you know why I initially pushed the two of you together?"

With a scoff, I answered, "Because you're nosy and like to butt into your kids' lives?"

"Yes, well, but no, that wasn't the reason. Eight years ago, I watched my youngest son kiss a girl. A beautiful young woman whom I had grown to know very well. The way he looked at her, watched as she drove away, stood there like his entire world had just shifted, made me smile."

"You saw me kiss Scarlett?"

"I did," she replied. "I also remember when the two of you were about eight years old, and you made a pledge to Scarlett. You probably don't remember, because after that, you started saying you were too old to play with a girl."

Sitting on the sofa, I laughed. "I don't remember a pledge. I hardly remember even playing with Scarlett."

My mother's face was soft and beautiful. I could see where Amelia and Waylynn got their stunning looks from. Her brown hair was pulled up into a ponytail and those grey eyes were focused completely on me.

"You had both been in the backyard here and Scarlett had fallen, cut her knee up pretty good. I was watching her for Joyce that afternoon. When I walked out with a Band-Aid you were holding Scarlett's hand. At eight, I could not believe the way you were looking at her. It actually made me stop and watch the two of you together."

"I was a charmer even back then, huh?"

She rolled her eyes. "Very much so. You kissed her forehead and told her not to cry, that you couldn't stand to see her cry because it made your stomach feel really bad."

I laughed. "It still does."

Her brows rose. "I'm sure it does."

"What did I promise her?"

Setting her book to the side, my mother stared into my eyes and said, "I'll never forget it."

My heart was pounding, the memory coming straight back. All these years, all the times I'd been with Scarlett, and I hadn't remembered. Until now.

"You kissed her forehead and then said…"

With a whispered voice, I said, "I'll love you forever."

She nodded. "I knew you were only eight, but the way you said those words to her, Trevor… It was as if you meant it from the bottom of your soul. When I saw you kiss her outside of Lilly's Café, I knew you still meant it. I'm sorry if I pushed you two together but it seems that Fate intervened a long time ago and I was just helping out."

My breath caught, and I leaned back into the sofa. When I was finally able to speak, I stood up, walked over to her and kissed her on the cheek.

"I'm not, Mom. I'm glad you're a busybody."

She hit me in the stomach and laughed.

"Your father is in his office. I'm sure that's who you were hoping to find."

"I'm glad I found you first. I love you, Mom."

"I love you too, darling. Now let me get back to my book. It's getting to a steamy part!"

I grunted. "Gross, Mom. Gross."

Quickly escaping before she told me what she was reading, I made my way to my father's office. I tapped lightly on the door, and he looked up from his reading.

"I figured you'd be making your way to me either tonight or tomorrow." He leaned back, made his fingers into a steeple under his chin and said, "Come on in."

"Do you just keep getting wiser the older you get?" I asked, making my way to the large, leather chair opposite his desk.

"I think so. It's a power I don't take lightly, but it is fun. Especially when I get to use it against my children."

I dropped into the seat and let out a breath.

"Thank you for not getting angry with me."

"Angry over a child? Never. Am I upset how it all went down? Yes. I'm not here to judge you, though, son. That's not my job. My job is to make sure you do what is right for both Scarlett and your baby."

"Dalton pulled me to the side tonight and demanded to know when I planned on marrying Scarlett."

My father rolled his eyes. "I never did like that asshole."

"What?" I said, my brows lifted. "Mom and Joyce are best friends."

"That doesn't mean I have to like the guy. Let me ask you something, Trevor, why do you think a man insists that his only child be sent off to a boarding school in Boston?"

I shrugged. "I don't know, a better education?"

"You don't think there are good boarding schools in Texas? Closer to home?"

My brows pulled in tight. "What are you saying, Dad?"

He lifted his eyes past me, to the door, then focused back on me.

"What I'm about to tell you stays between us, do you understand me? You don't even tell Scarlett. Understood?"

I swallowed hard. "Yes, sir."

Standing, my father walked to his office bar and poured us each a whiskey.

"Dalton Littlefield is not Scarlett's father."

It felt as if the entire room emptied of air.

"What?"

He handed me the drink and sat in the chair next to me.

"Dalton and Joyce dated off and on through high school. Things broke off in college, but when she came back, they struck up a friendship. Dalton asked her out, and Joyce told him she was three months pregnant. It was the reason she came back to town. The guy she was dating didn't want the baby and told her to never contact him again. He signed away all rights as a parent. Dalton told her at the time he didn't care and that he would marry her. They had a quickie marriage, but after Scarlett was born, Dalton changed. He started to resent the fact that Scarlett wasn't his. When he and Joyce tried for a baby of their own, it never happened."

"Can he not have kids?" I asked.

"Don't know. He would never find out even though Joyce begged him to. Dalton never treated Scarlett badly. He just couldn't accept that she wasn't his. The older she got, the more she began to look like her birth father. Dalton demanded that Joyce send Scarlett off. She held off as long as she could, until high school."

"Why didn't she just tell the fucker no?"

My father looked at his drink and then back to me. "He told her he was going to tell Scarlett the truth, and Joyce didn't want to break her daughter's heart."

I lifted my glass and nearly drank the entire thing.

"So he wanted her gone because she was a reminder of *what* exactly?"

"I'm not sure. Some men aren't...well, let's just say I don't care for him and never have. Your mother and I have both told Joyce that he has cheated on her, and she refuses to listen. I think in some weird way, she feels like she owes him something. Her life and Scarlett's has been a good one, and it might not have been if Dalton hadn't married her. I'm sure Joyce would have struggled. Her folks didn't have much, and she worked for Dalton's parents. I think she felt she owed them to stay with their son."

"That's messed up."

"I think Dalton tries, and I have no doubt that he loves Scarlett. Not like how your mother and I love you kids, which is a shame."

Rubbing my hand over the tight muscles in my neck, I asked, "Why did you tell me all of this, Dad?"

"I wanted you to understand why Scarlett's parents reacted the way they did earlier today. Why they seemed so...disappointed. I knew Scarlett was upset, and I have to tell you, I'm proud as hell of how you took things into your own hands tonight."

"You don't think this pregnancy was a mistake, do you?"

He shook his head and flashed me a bright smile. "This was not a mistake. I've heard rumors around town about your rather loose lifestyle when it comes to women."

My cheeks heated. "Since Scarlett and I have been together I haven't been with anyone but one other woman and that was a mistake."

He shrugged. "The past is in the past, Trevor. The only thing you need to focus on now is what's in front of you. Now, how are things with you and Scarlett?"

I finished my drink and set it on a coaster. "That's why I'm here. I needed to talk to you. I need your advice, Dad."

"I'm listening."

I slowly pushed out a deep breath. "Scarlett has put a wall between us, and for good reason. I never promised her a relationship, but I know I gave her mixed signals. I wanted to be with her but didn't want to commit."

His brow lifted.

"I know. Believe me I've already gotten lectured by all of your other sons and daughters on more than one occasion."

"Good. Now keep going."

"When I finally came to my senses about Scarlett, it was before I found out about the baby. I thought she was with another guy, and I realized that I couldn't live without her in my life. The only problem is, she thinks I've changed my tune *because* of the baby."

"Did you explain to her that wasn't the case?"

"I have, but I understand why she has her guard up. I hurt her, Dad. Not on purpose, only because I was a complete asshat."

"Let me ask you something, Trevor. Where do you see yourself in five years?"

Leaning back in the chair, I smiled. "That's easy. Running the ranch with Scarlett by my side, maybe another baby by then. I don't know what Scarlett wants in the way of kids, but I know watching my other siblings that it would be pretty cool to have at least two."

A smile grew over my father's face. "Do you realize what you just said, son? The ranch has always been in your blood, always something you knew you were going to do, but almost all of that had to do with Scarlett and kids."

Pinching my brows, I looked down in thought. "Who am I and what happened to fun, carefree Trevor?"

His head dropped back as a burst of laughter came out. When he finally stopped, he looked at me.

"Out of all my sons, you remind me the most of myself, Trevor."

Warmth filled my chest.

"That's a compliment, Dad."

"Thank you, son. But seriously. I had the same ideas about life when I was younger, but when I met your mother I fell hard on my ass and life did a one-eighty. Everything that once revolved around me, went right to her. Still does."

"You and Mom have a beautiful love story, Dad."

He winked. "We do, but so do the rest of your siblings. What have I always told you kids about life?"

"That we all live on borrowed time and to make the most of every moment."

He pointed to me. "Exactly. Take each day as it comes. If Scarlett needs slow, give her slow, but let her know how you feel every single day. Be honest with her. If you're scared, nervous, unsure of something, tell her. The key is being open. Why do you think your mother and I have been so happy all these years? I'm not afraid to tell her the truth. When I found out she was pregnant with twins, I nearly ran for my life."

My eyes widened in shock.

"I wouldn't have, but for one brief moment, I panicked. How in the hell would I be able to run this ranch, help her with Waylynn, Tripp, and twins? I gave myself ten minutes and a few shots of Jack Daniel's and I made my way to her and told her I was scared to death."

"What did she do?"

"She laughed and started to cry and admitted she was scared, too. I'm sure Scarlett is scared, just like I know you are. A relationship is a lot to take in, and then throw a baby into the picture. The only thing you can do is let her know you're here for her...for as long as she needs you to be."

I nodded.

"Do you know what I'm most scared of?"

He shook his head. "What?"

"Not being a good dad like you and not being able to make Scarlett happy like you make Mom."

My father's gaze stayed locked on me for the longest time before he shook his head, looked down at his drink then finished it off. Setting the glass onto the desk, he leaned forward, his elbows resting on his legs.

"I'm going to let you in on a little secret, Trevor. Listen to me closely, do you hear me?"

"Yes, sir."

"I've made plenty of mistakes as a husband and a father. Lots of them. Especially in the beginning. Do you want to know what I did when I found out you got your first tattoo?"

Smiling, I answered, "You probably shit your pants."

He chuckled. "Something like that. I flew off the handle and told your mother I was going to make you go into the military because you needed to have some discipline."

My eyes widened in shock. "Dad, I was eighteen."

"I know. But do you know who stopped me from acting like a complete idiot and kept me from storming into your room and ripping you a new one?"

"Mom?"

He smiled, and it lit up the room. "I'm the father I am today because you have a mother who is amazing. Who loved me beyond everything. Even with my mistakes, my short temper, my over-controlling ways. Your mother and I are a team. Sometimes she's the coach and sometimes I am, but no one is perfect and you're going to make mistakes. It's okay to make them, son. That's how we learn. The most important thing you can do as a father, and a husband, is to make sure your children and the woman you love know that they are number one in your life. Everything else is below them."

He leaned forward and pressed his hand on my chest. "What do you feel in here when you think about Scarlett?"

Closing my eyes, I pictured Scarlett. I opened my eyes and looked directly at my father.

"A fire. A blazing fire."

He nodded. "*Yes*. Don't be afraid of it. Step off into the deep end, I promise, the water won't put it out."

The slight knock at the door caused my father to pull his hand back. With a wink, he said, "Come on in."

"Boys, it's getting late, I'm going to bed."

I stood along with my father and shook his hand.

"I'm leaving, Mom. Thanks for letting me borrow him."

My mother wrapped her arm around my father.

"Always happy to share him."

I watched my father gaze down at my mother with so much love on his face. For a moment, I think they forgot I was even there.

Finally clearing my throat, I said, "'Night y'all."

"'Night, sweetheart."

"Trevor, are we on for south pasture this week?"

Laughing, I nodded. "Yeah, Dad. I've got it all under control."

He gave me a thumbs up. "That's my boy."

Walking out of my parents' house I knew exactly what I had to do to prove to Scarlett I was in this come hell or high water.

She was the love of my life, and I was never letting her go.

CHAPTER 16

Scarlett

"Ms. Littlefield?"

Trevor nearly jumped out of his seat when the nurse called my name. I stood and walked toward her, smiling. She looked past me to Trevor. I expected her to smile at him, like most women, but her gaze fell back to me and she smiled. She mouthed, *wow,* and we both let out a small chuckle.

"How have you been feeling?" the nurse asked while motioning us into a room.

"Pretty good. Morning sickness is pretty intense, but other than that I feel good."

She motioned for me to sit down. After taking my blood pressure, she made a few notes in my chart.

"Are you the father?"

"Yes, Trevor Parker."

She wrote Trevor's name in the chart then asked for the best phone number to contact him.

Standing, she turned back to us. "Looks like you'll be getting a sonogram today. Go ahead and take your pants and panties off and cover up with this blanket. Dr. Buten will be doing a sonogram today as well as a nuchal translucency test if you want one."

"What's that test for?" Trevor asked. When I looked at him I could see both excitement and a bit of fear.

"It tests for Down syndrome, certain heart defects, as well as other chromosomal abnormalities. It's a two-part test that consists of a blood test and the sonogram."

"Okay," I said softly.

"Dr. Buten will be right in."

"Thank you so much," Trevor and I said at once.

The second the door shut, Trevor started pacing while I got situated.

"Why are you pacing?"

"I'm not pacing."

I followed him with my eyes. "Trevor, you are pacing. Are you nervous?"

"Yes. What if something is wrong with the baby?"

Reaching out, I took hold of his arm and pulled him to a stop. "Why would you think something would be wrong?"

My breath stalled in my chest when I saw tears in his eyes.

"I was such a prick. I don't want karma to come back on me."

Closing my eyes, I took in a deep breath. I could hear the fear in his voice. Grabbing Trevor's hands, I held onto them.

"God doesn't work that way, Trevor. You're making me nervous, so for me, will you please sit down?"

His eyes widened. "Shit, I didn't mean to make you worry. I'm sorry, baby."

Kissing my forehead, he sat in the chair while I leaned back on the table.

His endearment went straight to my chest, and then down to my belly where it flipped a few times. I knew I wasn't far enough along to feel the baby. I was simply feeling butterflies from this man.

"Scarlett, do you remember when we were about eight and you fell and scraped your knee at my house?"

Frowning, I shook my head. "No. Why?"

"Mom told me a story, and I hadn't remembered it until she brought it up."

"What was the story?"

Trevor grinned while looking down at the floor. "Mom said you had fallen and she was coming out to check on you. She said she saw me holding your hand and then I kissed you on the forehead and told you I'd love you forever."

The blood rushed through my veins until I felt dizzy. Trevor was always kissing me on the forehead. The very first time I remembered him doing it was at the benefit dinner when he excused himself to get us drinks, like it was second nature for him.

Warmth settled in my chest, and before I could say anything, a knock on the door had us both sitting up.

Dr. Buten walked in and smiled. I could feel Trevor tense up.

"You're the doctor?" he asked, looking at me and then back to the young doctor.

"I am." He leaned his hand out and introduced himself. "Dr. John Buten."

Trevor stood. "Trevor Parker."

The doctor's grin grew into a full-on smile. "Parker, you say? Related to Cord, Tripp, Mitchell, and Steed. Correct?"

"Yes, sir. All older brothers."

He nodded. "Well, this should be interesting. You Parker men know how to keep me on my toes."

I tried not to chuckle as Trevor looked at me with a confused expression.

"I think Maebh nearly kicked Cord out at her yearly appointment," I said.

Dr. Buten laughed, then sat down and started going through my chart.

"Okay, so, we need to complete another sonogram. Let's see, the last time you were here we came up with the due date of May 25. That would put conception end of August beginning of September. Are we sure on that time frame?"

"Yes. I can pretty much give you the exact date," I said. To the doctor's credit, he didn't let my statement faze him.

Pulling a machine closer to the table, he said, "Well, I'll take some measurements today. We took a few on your last sonogram, but let's see how baby is growing so that we can confirm that due date one more time."

Glancing up at Trevor, he said, "You're more than welcome to film this with your phone if you want. I'll give y'all a few pictures, but you might want the heartbeat recorded."

"Heartbeat?" I said at the same time as Trevor.

Dr. Buten grinned. "We will be able to hear the heartbeat. We can sometimes hear it earlier but since you only had a vaginal ultrasound on your first appointment, this time the heartbeat is much clearer."

I breathed in deeply and tried to relax. Dr. Buten turned the monitor so that both Trevor and I could see it. I peeked at Trevor. He had his phone out and ready to go.

"The black area is your uterus and the amniotic fluid. You look right about where you said, eleven or twelve weeks."

I blinked rapidly, trying to keep the tears at bay as I looked at the baby pop up on the monitor. She was so much bigger than the last time.

"That is your baby. There is the head, the body and right here and here...those are the arms, and down here, looks like we have two little leg buds. Looks like we have an active little one. The baby is moving all over the place."

I laughed and so did Trevor.

"And see that right there, that is your baby's heart beating."

"Holy. Shit."

Dr. Buten chuckled and looked at Trevor. "Yeah, it's something else, isn't it? Let me take a few measurements."

I stared at the screen while he clicked around. The baby kept moving and making Dr. Buten start over again.

"Yep, Scarlett, you're right. You're eleven weeks, five days. Now let's take a look around. Oh! Look at this baby moving! Y'all are getting a treat. Okay, let's listen to the heartbeat if we can get him or her to slow down a bit. Did you see that? Your baby just waved to you."

"I can't even believe this. I never dreamed we'd see her so clearly, or that she'd be moving like this," Trevor said in amazement.

I fought to keep my tears back.

"So precious," I whispered.

Dr. Buten clicked on the little beating heart. "Finally, let's see if we can get it."

The beat that filled the room was the most beautiful sound I'd ever heard.

"Let me measure the heart rate."

More clicks and Dr. Buten said, "A hundred-and-seventy-six beats per minute. That's perfect."

He looked up at Trevor. "Did you get that recorded? Some dads get stunned by the sound and they forget to hit record."

Trevor nodded. "I wouldn't mind hearing it again, though."

Dr. Buten grinned. The sound filled the air again, and I watched as tears built in Trevor's eyes. He closed them and seemed to get lost in our child's beating heart. When Dr. Buten stopped it, I pulled in a shaking breath as I looked back to Trevor. He was staring at me, smiling. He surprised me by leaning down and kissing me gently on the lips.

More tears slipped from my eyes as I quickly wiped them away.

"I'm so sorry."

"Don't be. This is a happy time and that sound should bring tears to your eyes. That's your baby." Dr. Buten said.

Trevor sat down next to me, grabbed my hand and laughed. "She looks like a gummy bear."

Dr. Buten chuckled. "Yep, sure does. The baby isn't much bigger than a gummy bear either!"

"Oh my goodness," I whispered, squeezing Trevor's hand.

Dr. Buten finished the exam and I sat up. We went over what I could be expecting in the way of weight gain, and the nausea hopefully easing up, as well as what would be happening with the baby over the next month and when I should be back.

"I think we're for sure safe to keep May 25 as your due date. I'll see you back in four weeks. In the meantime, any questions from either of you?"

The door opened and the nurse walked back in. She reached down and tore off the pictures of our baby and handed them to Trevor.

I gave a polite smile. "No questions from me. Trevor?"

Trevor stared at the photos, a new smile on his face that made me fall in love with him even more. To see him already so in love with our child did something to me. Broke down another layer of that wall I had erected.

"Trevor? Any questions?" Dr. Buten asked.

He looked up. "When will we be able to find out the sex of the baby?"

"Between sixteen and twenty weeks."

Trevor looked at me. When he winked, I felt that familiar pull in my lower stomach. It was happening more and more. When I saw

Trevor, when I thought about Trevor, when I closed my eyes and dreamt about Trevor…

"I'm not sure I want to find out the sex."

Trevor looked at me, his mouth open. "What?"

I grinned. "I wanted to be surprised."

When he gave me that sexy as hell grin, I nearly melted. Then he spoke the words I wanted to hear, and I was a puddle on the floor. "If you want to be surprised, then we'll be surprised."

Dr. Buten also seemed pleased with Trevor's response. "Any other questions?" Dr. Buten asked.

I shook my head and Trevor did as well.

"Okay, then, I'll let you get dressed and we'll see you in four weeks."

"Thank you, Dr. Buten."

Trevor reached his hand out and also thanked him.

"That's what I'm here for you. The nurse will take some blood-work from you and let you know when the test results come back."

"Thank you, Dr. Buten."

Once the door shut, and we were alone, Trevor cleared his throat and wiped at a few tears.

"You ready to head home?" Trevor asked.

"Would you mind if we stopped at Joe's Bar-B-Que? I'm dying for a brisket sandwich."

Trevor flashed a brilliant smile. "Of course, that sounds good. Gotta keep this baby growing and the momma happy, after all."

We made our way to the front desk where I made another appointment. Trevor and I put it in our phones and headed to his truck.

After stopping at the food truck in the parking lot of Hank's Hardware, Trevor and I headed back to my house.

"You mind if I eat mine at your place before I head on back to the ranch?"

My heartbeat picked up and my hands started to sweat. Never mind the fact that my head was slightly spinning at the idea of Trevor coming inside and eating with me.

"I don't mind at all."

The last week and a half had been busy for both of us, and this was the first real time alone we'd spent together. Trevor called me at least once a day, and offered to stop by, but I knew things were busy on the ranch and I had been working overtime at the courthouse, not getting home until almost nine at night.

"How's the baby's room plan coming along?" Trevor asked while he took the food out of the bags and spread it out on the kitchen island.

"Good. I was wanting to change out the light, but I think I'll wait a bit."

"Let me know when you want it changed, and I'll do it. I don't want you on a ladder doing that kind of stuff."

I laughed. "Trevor, I wouldn't have the faintest idea how to change a light fixture, so that job is one-hundred-percent all yours."

He winked. "Well, I didn't want to make the assumption like I didn't think you could. Just let me know, okay?"

"I'll let you know. Hey, can you forward that video you took today of the baby?"

He grinned. "The Gummy Bear?"

I groaned. "Oh no, you're going to call her that from now on, aren't you?"

"Hell yes. That's what she looked like," he said with a chuckle while pulling up the video on his phone.

"Want to watch it again?" he asked, setting it down so we could both keep eating and see it. When we got to the heartbeat, Trevor turned the sound up and I started crying again. This time, though, Trevor pulled me into his arms. I had a sneaky feeling it was because he was crying as well and didn't want me to see.

Being in his arms, with my emotions all over the place, I did something stupid. I grabbed onto his shirt and held him tighter. The feel of his body against mine was driving me insane. I wanted him, but my stupid head was telling me I couldn't have him. Not yet.

"Tell me what you want from me, Scarlett. I'll do anything."

I pulled in a deep breath. How could I keep denying what I wanted?

"Just hold me for a bit, will you?"

"There's nothing more I'd rather be doing, darlin'."

Trevor gave me exactly what I wanted. He held onto me like he was afraid to let me go—and a very large part of me never wanted him to let go.

CHAPTER 17

Trevor

"Uncle Trevor!"

Glancing up from my desk, I smiled as Chloe burst through my office door.

"Chloe Parker, how many times have I told you not to just run into Trevor's office?"

With a quick glance at her mother, Chloe yelled out, "Sorry!"

"Hey, Pumpkin!" I said right as she launched into my arms. It was a damn good thing I pushed away from my desk in time, otherwise she would've landed right on top of my desk.

"Are you ready for our tea party? Mommy said it's such a beautiful November day and we should have it out by the pool."

I looked at Paxton who wore a smile that said she was up to something.

"I think outside sounds wonderful. Let's go!"

Chloe grabbed onto my hand and dragged me out of the office and through the entire house. Paxton was next to me, clearly with something on her mind.

"So, want to tell me what your brain is thinking so loudly, Paxton?"

"What? I have no idea what you're talking about."

I flashed her a look that said I didn't believe a damn word she was saying.

When Chloe finally got us out by the pool, I looked at the table all set up.

"Okay, we just need to wait for our other guest," Chloe said, sitting down and neatly setting her napkin on her lap.

I groaned and faced Paxton. "Please tell me Patches isn't coming. You know what happened the last time he came to a tea party. Do I have to remind you about mom's broken crystal vase?"

Covering her mouth, Paxton attempted to hide her laugh.

"It's not Patches, Uncle Trevor!"

"Then who is it, princess?" I asked, ruffling Chloe's hair, only to have her push my hand away.

"Am I late?"

I smiled when I saw her. "Scarlett?"

She made her way toward us, dressed in a beautiful, long, pink skirt with a white flowing top.

"Scarlett, you look beautiful!" Paxton said, giving her a quick hug.

"Hey," I said, kissing her on the forehead. "What in the world are you doing here?"

Scarlett smiled at Chloe. "Well, I got a call today at work asking if I was able to join a certain young lady for a tea party and there was no way I could turn that esteemed invitation down."

Chloe smiled. "I called her, Uncle Trevor. I heard you telling granddaddy how much you missed her and that you hadn't been able to leave the ranch to see her. So I asked Mommy if we could invite her today. I didn't think you would mind since you love her and all."

Scarlett's face turned red.

"Chloe, honey," Paxton started to say something, but Chloe wasn't having it. She had already ratted me out about missing Scarlett…my niece was on a roll. I swear to God, it has to be something in the blood with these Parker women.

"It's okay, Mommy! Uncle Trevor told Granddaddy he loved Scarlett more than the air he breathes, which is funny cause he needs air to breathe. You know that…right, Aunt Scarlett? Do you love Uncle Trevor that much, too?"

Scarlett's stunned gaze went from Chloe to me. We stared at each other for a few moments before Scarlett finally spoke.

"I do know that, Chloe. And yes, I love your Uncle Trevor that much, too. Thank you for sharing your special time with him at your tea party."

My heart slammed against my chest as I stared at Scarlett. Wishing like hell we were alone.

Paxton seemed pleased and quickly dismissed herself so that we could get on with the tea party.

I watched as Chloe and Scarlett instantly hit it off. Chloe poured us all a glass of iced tea in our fancy glass tea cups.

"Wow, you busted out the fancy tea set for Scarlett, huh?" I asked while holding up the miniature tea cup and saucer. "I guess I know where I rank, huh, kiddo? I only get the plastic."

"Mommy said this was a special tea party and that our plastic set wouldn't do."

Scarlett tried to hide her smile but failed.

"Yup, bottom of the pecking order," I mumbled while taking a sip.

"Thank you so much, Chloe. I appreciate it, and might I say, this is a beautiful tea set."

"Santa brought it for me last year! This year I'm hoping he brings me a boyfriend. Rip, if possible. If not a boyfriend, then another goat will do."

I choked on my tea. Scarlett had to reach over and hit me a few times on the back.

"You okay?" she asked.

"No, I'm not okay." Pointing to my niece, I said, "Chloe, if you ever want to leave the house again, do not put that on your list to Santa."

Chloe tilted her head and stared at me. "But why?"

"Who is Rip, Chloe?" Scarlett asked, taking a sip of tea and winking at me over the small cup.

I had to grab onto the table because it felt like the entire world had shaken from that one, sexy-as-fuck wink.

"Well, I have two Rips in my life, Aunt Scarlett. My horse I got from Santa, and Rip, my future husband. He's Wade's younger brother. He's in my class and I love him. He doesn't really know it, though."

"Oh. I see." Scarlett peeked at me, and I nodded.

"Yeah, exactly."

Scarlett focused back on Chloe. "Do your mommy and daddy know about Rip…the future husband?"

"Yep! Daddy told me I'm not allowed to look at Rip or talk to him, but I know he was just kidding."

"That's what you think," I whispered.

Chloe laughed cutely. If only she knew the plans her father was making to threaten the poor boy when he was old enough to know what his penis was for.

"Well, you have plenty of time for boyfriends," Scarlett said. "I think you and Rip should be friends first."

"Are you and Uncle Tripp getting married now that you're gonna have a baby?"

Scarlett and I froze.

"Well, your uncle and I are, *um*, we're…" Scarlett looked at me for help, but I leaned back in the chair and smiled, not offering one bit. After what she'd just said to Chloe about loving me, I wanted to see how she got out of this without stumbling.

"You're what?" Chloe asked, almost with a bat of her eyes. "Boyfriend and girlfriend? I would think so if y'all love each other. Are you going to live here on the ranch when the baby is born?" Chloe jumped out of her seat. "I hope you do! Patches would love another friend to chase around."

She placed her hand on her hip, tilted her head, and looked up in thought.

"Let's see, what was the other question I was supposed to ask?"

Scarlett's mouth fell open as I let out a laugh.

"What do you mean, 'the other question you were *supposed* to ask'?" I pulled Chloe over to me.

Chloe giggled and covered her mouth. "Aunt Waylynn and I practiced the questions before y'all got here, but I think I forgot a few. Momma's gonna be upset with me because those were the important ones, too."

When Scarlett's head whipped around and looked at me with a *what the hell* look, I shrugged. "Welcome to the family."

"Son-of-a-bitch!" I yelled out, throwing the wrench onto the ground and scrubbing my hands over my face.

"Trevor, why don't we just call Hank's friend who works on tractors and we can get this thing fixed."

"Because I need it fixed now, Wade. Not in a week. Right the fuck now."

He held up his hands and took a few steps back.

"Okay, I surrender. But while you're throwing a hissy fit, you want to tell me the real reason you're in a piss mood today? Hell, you've been in one for the last week."

Walking away from the tractor, I took in a few deep breaths and tried to cool off. I was pissed and it had nothing to do with the damn tractor.

"I haven't seen Scarlett in a week. I stopped by her house last night without calling, and she was sitting on her porch talking to that fucker."

Wade folded his arms over his chest.

"That's the code word for Eric, right?"

"Yes, there are many code words for Eric. Fucker, douchebag, dickhead, bastard. I could keep going."

"So, did you stop?"

"I pulled into her driveway and stopped the truck. Scarlett came up and said she and Eric were catching up. Turns out he's stopped by her house a few times, but she didn't tell me."

"Was she supposed to tell you?"

I rubbed the back of my neck. "No, I guess not."

"You know there is nothing going on there, right?"

Blowing out a frustrated breath, I nodded. "I know, Wade. It doesn't erase the fact that I'm no closer with Scarlett now than I was a month ago. She's still keeping me at arm's length and when I go for long stretches like this, it just…"

"It just what?"

"I don't know what it does, dude. I'm trying to give her space and time, but I don't want her to think I don't care, so I call each day and the last two days I've gotten her voicemail. She texts back, but it feels distant. Then seeing her with him… I guess I'm jealous she has time to sit on the front porch and drink tea with him, but she can't take a call from me. Christ, I sound like a pussy."

Wade slapped me on the back. "You've been working way too much."

"There's a lot to do. I mean, we've got to get this place ready for winter, we've got the new project Mitchell is working on with the breeding, and hell, whatever else we got going on."

"Didn't you say one of your friends from high school was having a party this afternoon? Maybe that's what you need, a day at the river just hanging out with some friends."

"Yeah, maybe. You want to come?"

He laughed. "Are you kidding me? I've got to meet with Steed to go over the books from last quarter. I've got some marketing ideas for the breeding program and I wanted to see what he thought about it. Hopefully it will fit into the budget for next spring."

"Do y'all need me there?"

"No, Trevor, take a damn Friday off. You finally quit working at Cord's Place and all you've done is work your ass even harder on the ranch, if that's at all possible."

"Busy is good for our business. You know that."

He slapped the side of my arm. "Why don't you call Scarlett? See if she wants to go and just relax. Have some fun. Lord knows once the baby comes y'all won't have the opportunity to be going to river parties."

I smiled. "Hey, speaking of baby, how is Amelia? Y'all didn't come to the family dinner last weekend."

"She's doing great. She had a draft of her book she wanted to finish. The plan is for her to try and get a few books ahead, so when the baby comes she can just concentrate on being a mommy."

"That's awesome. She feeling okay?"

Wade laughed. "Oh yeah, she's feeling more than okay. Is Scarlett feeling a little more...frisky? When they say pregnant women get more...you know...they aren't lying."

I frowned. "What?"

He shrugged, trying to blow off what he had just brought up. "Nothing. I shouldn't have said anything."

"Wait, are you trying to say your wife is horny because she's pregnant? First off, gross that's my sister, and second, is that really something that happens?"

"From what I've read. Haven't you been reading any books?"

I rolled my eyes. "I'm not the one married to a writer, dude."

"For your information, asshole, I picked them up on my own. I wanted to know what all was happening with Amelia and the baby. It's pretty interesting. Anyway, in one of the books they said a woman is more…you know…horny when they're pregnant."

"Well, since Scarlett is keeping me at a distance, I wouldn't know."

Wade frowned.

My phone rang and I pulled it out of my back pocket in a hurry, only to see that it was James Larson, my old buddy from high school.

"Hey, James, what's up?"

"Dude! You coming to the party? It's going to be a blast from the past. A few of the guys have come into town."

"I'm not sure if I can make it."

"Trev, come on. I'm getting married in two months and this is the last party I'm throwing. Just come and have some fun. Some of these girls from high school are still looking pretty hot."

"Yeah, I'm not interested in that, James."

A roar of laughter came through the phone. "That's right! Rumor has it you're settled down. I have to admit, I was sort of stunned that you stopped working at your brother's bar, I thought you loved it there. What a place to blow off steam."

"My priorities changed."

Wade smiled and shook his head.

"Well, what the fuck ever. Just come for a little bit."

"Fine, I'll come, but I'm not staying long."

"That's what I wanted to hear. Feel free to bring anyone. I'll see ya soon."

The phone went dead, and I pulled up Scarlett's number. Walking away from Wade, I hit dial. I sighed when I got her voicemail.

"Hey, Scarlett, it's me. Listen, I'm taking the rest of the day off and heading to James Larson's river party down at his place. I was just wondering if you wanted to go with me? I know you said you had today off from all the over time you had been working. I'll be leaving here in a bit so if you want to go, just give me a holler and I'll pick you up."

I hit End and pushed my phone into my back pocket. I glanced out over the vast Texas hill country. For as far as the eye could see, it was our ranch. I loved this place, but something felt missing. Something was off, and I couldn't shake the uneasy feeling brewing deep in my soul.

CHAPTER 18

Scarlett

"Come on, Scarlett! You never do anything fun anymore."

I sat on my living room sofa, my feet tucked under my body, a pint of ice cream in my hand. My hormones had been off the chart the last few weeks and my emotions even worse. I'd been putting off seeing Trevor because I wasn't sure if I would break down and cry...or what I would do.

"Lynn, I'm pregnant. Going to a river party when it's hot as hell out is not my idea of fun."

"Okay, so I'll admit the eighty-eight degrees in November thing sort of sucks, but you have to come. This will be your last fun time out before you get a giant basketball in your belly and you start to waddle like a duck."

I shot her a dirty look.

"I talked to James just a little bit ago. He said Trevor was coming so I figured that meant you were, as well. I mean, are you not pregnant with his baby?"

That got my attention. "Trevor's going?"

Her smile faded. "Are y'all not together? I mean, you're not dating? Because Trevor has made it very clear to everyone he is off the market. When Margret and Darcy saw Trevor at the feed store, Darcy said Trevor didn't flirt with them once! He said hello when they said hi and he kept right on going. Sort of pissed Darcy off, but Margret told her about you and the baby."

"Wait, Darcy was trying to put the moves on Trevor? When?"

"The day before yesterday, I think it was."

I snarled. "That bitch! She works in Dr. Buten's office! She knows I'm pregnant with Trevor's baby."

Lynn half-shrugged. "Well, you didn't go to high school here, girl. Darcy was the poster girl for class slut. She didn't care if a guy had a girlfriend or not. She's been trying for years to hook up with Trevor Parker and hasn't been able to."

I lifted a brow. "Really?"

With a nod, she replied, "Yep. Now go change and let's go."

Sighing, I threw the blanket off and headed to my room, finishing off the chocolate ice cream as I climbed the steps.

Once I got to my room, I found my phone on the nightstand. I'd forgotten I left it there to charge. Picking it up, I saw a new voicemail from Trevor.

Hitting speaker, I listened to it while I changed into a pair of shorts and a light blue sweater tank top. Once I heard that Trevor had invited me to the party, a new feeling swept over me. I was actually excited to go. I was bummed I'd missed his call and would have much rather gone with him, but I knew I would be seeing him there. After the whole thing with Eric being at my house and Trevor showing up, I had been wanting to talk to him. I'd seen it on his face and heard it in his voice. He was worried I was growing more distant. I hadn't meant to be pushing Trevor back; it was just hard to maintain control when he was around. Plus, I had been working a lot of overtime to save money so I could pay bills when I went on maternity leave. Grabbing a sweater, I made my way down the steps.

"Trevor called and said he was going to the party."

Lynn pinched her brows together. "Hello, I already told you that."

I grabbed my keys and some cash. "You telling me and Trevor inviting me are two totally different things."

She rolled her eyes. "I don't understand your relationship with him. I truly don't."

"Can I just drive over with you? I'm sure I can get Trevor to give me a ride back."

"Sure! You ready?"

"Yep. Let's go have one more fling before we all have to grow up."

Lynn laughed as I locked my door and followed her to her Honda Accord.

"Amen to that!"

Thirty minutes later we were driving down the gravel road that led to the river. I had texted Trevor, but he hadn't returned my text. The closer we got the river, the more nervous I got. What if I showed up and Trevor was talking to someone? Or worse yet, flirting with them?

"Maybe I shouldn't have come. I'm starting to feel a bit sick."

Lynn huffed. "It's probably the pint of ice cream you sucked down and that Snickers bar you made me stop and get. Jesus, where are you putting all this food, girl?"

"I don't normally eat like that, but I was craving the Snickers, and the ice cream was just…well, it was good and I wanted it."

"You're not actually eating for two, you know. You don't need to double up what you're eating."

"Yes, doctor."

Lynn hit me on the leg. "I'm just saying, eat healthy."

"I do. But every now and then I deserve a damn Snickers!"

She laughed. "You do. I can't even imagine being pregnant. Ugh."

Before I had a chance to ask why she felt like that, I saw all the cars and trucks. Trevor's was hard to miss; it was the last one in the row and Lynn pulled up and parked next to it.

"Okay, let's go have some fun. I'll drink whatever beers you can't."

Getting out of the car, I pointed to her. "Hey, isn't that the same as the eating double thing?"

"Nope. That rule does not apply to beer. When your friend is pregnant, you're allowed to drink her allotted quantity of beers." Lynn grabbed our bags out of her trunk.

"That's not true."

Hooking her arm with mine, we made our way down the path. I could hear shouting and music the closer we got. My heart started pounding and I stopped.

Lynn turned to face and me, and her smile vanished.

"What? What's wrong, Scarlett?"

I shook my head and took a few steps back. "I can't. What if he's...what if I see him with someone?"

"Trevor? Scarlett, are you out of your damn mind? Listen, I get that he acted like a complete dick after y'all hooked up, but I'm pretty damn sure he is not here sucking face with some girl when you are carrying his baby."

My hand came up to my mouth as a wave of nausea hit me. "I'm going to be sick."

I rushed over to the bushes and threw up. It didn't take long for everything I had consumed to come rushing back.

"Christ, Scarlett! You're making yourself sick thinking about this."

Standing up, I placed my hand over my forehead. "I feel dizzy."

"Let's get you some water and get you to a chair or something."

Fear gripped me as Lynn took my arm and led me closer to the party.

Why couldn't I just trust Trevor? Why did I let these stupid doubts creep into my brain and wedge themselves in?

When we came around a bend, I got a clear shot of the whole party. I quickly started to scan the crowd. It didn't take long to spot him.

"I told you! You had nothing to worry about."

A rush of air came out—I hadn't even realized I had been holding my breath. Trevor was standing off to the side talking to about four or five guys. Girls were everywhere, walking around in swimsuits and shorts that left little to the imagination.

Trevor was focused only on the guys he was talking to. His back was toward the river. He held a beer in his hand, and when I looked him over, I started to laugh.

"What in the hell is he wearing?" I asked.

"Christ, looks like he just walked out of Mrs. Johnson's calculus class!"

We both started to laugh, and it was like he knew I was there. His head turned and our eyes locked. He smiled, and then his smile faded when he saw Lynn with her arm around me. Trevor rushed over.

"What's wrong?" he asked, placing both hands on my arms and giving me a once-over.

"She threw up as we were walking down here," Lynn said, giving me a wink.

"You threw up?"

His hand went to my forehead, followed by his cheek.

"It's just something I ate, I think."

"A king-size Snickers bar on top of a pint of chocolate ice cream."

"Lynn!" I cried out, giving her a dirty look.

"Trevor, she might need to lay low today. She said she was dizzy."

My mouth dropped open as I stared at the woman who used to be my one and only best friend during high school and college. I was going to give Chloe Parker that new title.

"Come on, let's get you some water. There are some hammocks around the trees, away from everyone. We can go rest there."

"Trevor, I don't need to rest."

He led us over to a row of coolers. He opened the first one and reached in, grabbing two bottles of water. Then he started walking off, away from the party.

When we rounded the corner, I saw about four hammocks spread out in the trees.

"How did you know these were here?" I asked as we made our way to the one farthest away.

"James had a lot of parties in high school. I would come back here and lay in these when I wanted to get away, which was often."

"Really? I sort of pictured you as a party guy."

Trevor laughed. "Don't get me wrong, I liked to party, but sometimes I wasn't in the mood."

"Speaking of high school, what in the world are you wearing?"

Trevor stopped walking and looked down.

"What? This was my party outfit in high school. Black T-shirt and ripped jeans."

I let my eyes roam over his perfect body. "Trevor, it looks like you have patches on your jeans. And not just plain patches, striped ones. And you're in sneakers. I don't think I've ever seen you in sneakers."

He laughed. "I was in the mood for a change. Plus, that asshole James said to dress like high school. Dick."

"I'd say."

As we started walking, I felt that familiar feeling in my mouth. The one where saliva builds right before you get sick.

"Um, Trevor? I think I may throw up again."

Before Trevor could react, I turned and threw up. I was surprised I still had anything left in my stomach and the force with which I threw up scared me.

Trevor held my hair back and rubbed my back while I leaned over. It instantly made the nausea ease up.

"Oh God, can you come do that every morning cause you're making it go away."

"I'd be more than happy to."

After a few minutes, it passed, and I stood up.

"Shit, you got it all over…hold on."

Trevor pulled off his T-shirt and opened the bottle of water, pouring some of it onto the shirt. He then wiped around my mouth and chin.

I closed my eyes and groaned. "Did I have throw up on my face?"

"Yep!" he said with a slight chuckle.

"How embarrassing," I stated, taking a drink of water and rinsing out my mouth.

"Nonsense. The woman carrying my baby couldn't possibly do anything that would embarrass her. Come on, babe, let's lie down."

I wasn't going to argue. For one, I still sort of felt like crap. I was suddenly hit with a heavy feeling of tiredness, and Trevor was shirtless and wanting me to lie next to him in a hammock. Not to mention he had just called me babe. I loved when he called me baby or babe.

Loved. It.

Trevor laid down on the hammock then pulled me onto it. I kicked off my flip flops and snuggled up against him.

"Wow, this hammock is big," I said, throwing my leg over his and letting him pull me up against him. His arm was wrapped around me in such a protective way. His other hand held onto my arm, almost as if he was afraid I'd get up and leave. I breathed in his scent.

"You smell so good."

His unshaven face scraped against mine, relaxing me even more.

The feel of his bare skin on mine was amazing. This whole thing felt amazing.

It felt right.

I could feel myself slowly drifting off.

I decided to start pulling the wall down.

"Trevor?" I whispered.

"Yes?"

"I haven't been purposely avoiding you. Well, maybe I have because my emotions have been all over the place."

He held me tighter and whispered, "It's okay, baby."

My heartbeat picked up a bit more. Here we go, time to knock the wall down.

"I want more."

His body flexed under me.

"More?"

Nodding, I said, "*Mmm-hmm*. I need you in my life, and I need you to be more than the baby's father."

He kissed my forehead. "Nothing would make me happier. I love you, Scarlett."

With a smile, I replied, "I love you, too."

"New beginnings, right?" he spoke against my lips.

"Yes, new beginnings. Will you promise me something, though?"

"Anything."

"Don't wear those jeans ever again, okay?"

My body shook as he laughed. Kissing me once more, he answered. "It's a deal."

CHAPTER 19

Trevor

Scarlett fell asleep lying next to me in the hammock. I didn't make a sound, but inside I was doing a fucking Irish Jig. She had no clue how happy she had just made me. When she finally started to stir, I woke her all the way up.

"Hey, you feel better?"

Those beautiful eyes locked on mine. "I do, but I know something that will make me feel even better?"

I raised a brow. "Another Snickers?"

She laughed, but then started to run her fingers over my bare chest. My entire body felt like it was on fire from her touch.

Her smile faded to a sexier-than-hell smirk. "I was thinking more along the lines of you and me back at my house."

My heart dropped to the bottom of my stomach.

"Are you sure?"

Closing her eyes, she took in a deep breath then blew it out just as slow. Her warm breath on my bare skin nearly had me taking her right there.

"I'm so very sure, Trevor. I want you, desperately, and I'm tired of denying myself."

That was all I needed to hear. I got up and quickly walked around the hammock. Grabbing her flip flops, I picked her up in my arms, causing her to let out a small yelp.

"Trevor! What are you doing! I can walk."

"I can walk to my truck faster."

Her arms wrapped tighter around my neck.

"Scarlett, are you sure about this? I don't want to rush you."

She gave me the sweetest grin. "Trevor, I love you and you've been so patient. I know I've been acting stupid and…"

"No, you haven't."

With a nod, she replied, "I have. The last few weeks you have been amazing and so patient, but I can't take it any longer. I need you inside of me, and I really, really need to come. This pregnancy is making me want it all the time. Between that and the morning sickness, it's been torture."

"Jesus Christ," I mumbled, nearly tripping and dropping her.

By the time we got back to my truck, my cock was hard and begging for me to let him out of these fucking jeans.

"My place is closer," I said, starting my truck.

She gave me a shy smile and nodded.

It took everything I had to drive the speed limit. We hadn't even told anyone we were leaving, but we'd been away from the party in that hammock for about an hour while Scarlett napped, so I doubted anyone would have even have missed us.

Pulling into the driveway, I pushed the button for the automatic gate. Scarlett's knee bounced up and down while we watched the gate slowly swing open. Once it was open, I floored it and took off down the driveway. I headed down the gravel road that went around the main house. I lived in the foreman's house, but I had since claimed it as mine and had started to remodel it slowly.

When I finally got to the turn that led to my place, I hit the gas a little more. The road was fairly flat, so I knew it wouldn't be too rough for Scarlett.

"Trevor," she whispered when she saw the house.

"I know, baby. I feel the same way."

Throwing my truck into park, I ripped the keys out. Scarlett wasn't about to wait for me, she jumped out of the truck and raced up the steps. The door to my place wasn't locked, and we burst through it. I kicked it shut with my foot, my mouth on hers. The kiss was hot and passionate. This wasn't the time for sweet and romantic, even though I had envisioned something like that for our first time back together.

Scarlett's hands were frantically trying to undo my jeans as I kicked off my sneakers.

"I'm so horny. God, I've been so horny," she whispered against my lips.

I growled into her mouth. "From now on, when you want to come it's only me who makes you come. It doesn't matter the time or day, you tell me."

She nodded as she dropped to her knees, pulling my jeans with her. When my cock sprang free, she looked up at me and grinned.

"I really like it when you don't wear underwear."

"I'll remember that."

Her hand wrapped around my cock, and I knew she was about to put it into her mouth. I couldn't let her do that.

"No. If you put me in your mouth I'm going to come faster than you can even get me down your throat. Plus, this isn't about me, baby. It's about you."

She sucked in a breath as I pulled her up and quickly got her undressed. Soon she was standing before me naked.

"Sit down on the table, Scarlett."

"The table?"

"Yes."

"But I'm not wearing any clothes."

I pointed to the table. "Sit. Now."

She quickly did what I said. Dropping to the floor, I pulled her legs up and over my shoulders.

"Jesus, Trevor." Her cheeks were a beautiful pink. Her chest rose quickly with anticipation.

"Fucking hell. I can smell how turned on you are, baby."

Her hands went to my hair and she tugged. Her silent way of begging me to fuck her pussy with my mouth.

I slowly licked through her soft folds, groaning while I did it.

Scarlett moaned and pulled me closer to her.

"Please. Oh, Trevor."

My girl wasn't going to have to beg me. I buried my face into her and licked and sucked until she started screaming my name.

"Yes! Trevor! Trevor! Oh God, I'm coming."

When her body finally settled, I kissed her stomach then slowly made my way to her mouth. She didn't stop me when I went to kiss her. She wrapped her arms around me and moaned when she tasted herself on my tongue.

"I need to be inside of you, baby. Now."

She nodded. I pulled her up from the table and picked her up into my arms. My house was a one-story, with my bedroom to the right of the living room.

Gently lying her on the bed, I pulled open the side table and grabbed a condom. Scarlett sat up and reached for my arm. When I looked at her, she was smiling.

"Trevor, that horse has already left the barn. I'm pregnant already, I think you can save the condom."

Glancing at the square package in my hand, I laughed and threw it back into the drawer. Crawling onto the bed, I settled my body over Scarlett's, careful not to put too much weight on her.

"Fuck. I'm apologizing to you right now, before we even get started, because I'm going to come embarrassingly fast."

Her index finger traced along my jaw line.

"I'm sorry for making you wait so long."

I rubbed my nose against hers then kissed her forehead and replied, "I'd wait forever for you."

A tear slipped from her eye and trailed down her cheek. Leaning in, I kissed it.

"Happy?"

Closing her eyes, she nodded. "So very happy."

When I pushed slowly into her, we both moaned.

"Damn it, Scarlett. You feel like heaven."

Her arms and legs wrapped around my body as I kissed her softly. Our tongues intertwined in a dance while I moved slowly in and out of her body.

I'd never felt anything so good in my life. I could tell she had another orgasm building, and I knew the moment she came around my bare cock, I would come too.

Breaking our kiss, I looked into her eyes and slowed to a stop. I was buried deep inside of her, our breaths coming fast and hard, even though I was making love to her as slowly as I could.

"You're mine and I'm yours. Do you understand that?"

"Yes," she whispered.

"I mean it, Scarlett. There is no other woman I want, but you. I love you and someday I'm going to marry you when you're ready to have me as your husband."

Sobs slipped from her mouth as she covered it with one hand, keeping her other hand wrapped around my neck.

"I. Love. You," I said as I pulled out and slowly pushed back in.

"You're mine, Trevor…and I need you to move faster because I'm almost there."

My pace picked up, and Scarlett matched me move for move.

"Yes, Trevor, God, yes."

Her feet hooked around my ass, pulling me in deeper as she cried out my name. Leaning my forehead to hers, I felt my own orgasm hit me. It was like nothing I'd ever felt before in my life.

"Scarlett, I'm coming."

She grabbed my face, pulling my lips to hers. I kissed her as I came inside of her, feeling her body shake right along with mine.

When I stopped moving, Scarlett dropped her legs from around me. Slipping off to the side of her, I laid on my back, breathing in much-needed air because I'd almost blacked out from the force of my orgasm.

I'd never in my life, not even the night we made love and I forgot the condom, felt anything like that.

Reaching for her hand, I laced our fingers together.

"That was…I don't even have words to describe how that was."

Squeezing my hand, Scarlett rolled to her side and rested her head on my chest.

"I'm starving now."

"You're hungry? I'm absolutely exhausted."

"I'm that, too. And I'm also feeling so…blissfully amazing. I don't want to move."

Wrapping my arm around her, I pulled her closer to me. "Then we won't move, baby. We can lie here the rest of the day and night if you want."

"*Mmm*, sounds like heaven. But I'm going to need food."

"That's my pregnant princess talking. I wonder if Lilly's will deliver way out here?"

CHAPTER 20

Scarlett

When my eyes opened, I felt the delicious ache between my legs.

Trevor.

Peeking up, I stared at the man who had taken me to heaven with some mind-blowing orgasms not too long ago. He slept so peacefully.

Lifting my head, I rested my chin on the back of my hand. A dull pulse started between my legs. I wanted more. I *needed* more of him. Hell, we had lost time to make up for, and I wasn't about to let it slip by. I had a naked Trevor, and I was going to take full advantage of that.

Carefully moving the sheet off of us, I crawled on top of him. When I rubbed myself over his cock, I smiled at his hardness.

His hands went to my hips, and he let out a low growl before he whispered my name.

"Scarlett."

A wider smile broke out over my face when he opened his beautiful blue eyes and looked at me.

Slowly lifting, I used my hand to guide him inside of me. Working him in, I dropped my head back and moaned. Once I had myself fully seated, I rocked back and forth. His body rubbing against my clit was heaven.

"Fuck, yes," Trevor hissed, making me look down at him.

"Baby," he grunted as he lifted his hips. "You horny?"

I nodded. "I told you…it seems to happen a lot now because of the pregnancy."

He winked. "I know exactly how to take care of that then."

Lifting up before I pushed back down, I made both of us moan.

"So do I," I purred as I dropped my hands to his chest and started to ride him. It didn't take long for me to come. Trevor carefully moved me and got on top where he made love to me again, kissing me softly on my mouth, chin, neck, and down my chest. When he moved his lips back up to my ear and whispered that he loved me, I came. I knew he was coming right along with me when his breath turned quick and hard.

Trevor stayed inside of me long after he'd finished. Both of us staring into each other's eyes. We didn't need to say anything, I saw it all in his eyes and he in mine.

"Move in with me, Scarlett."

My eyes widened in shock. "What?"

"I can't stand being away from you. I want to wake up with you in my arms each morning and I want to fall asleep with you in my arms after I make love to you."

Swallowing hard, I searched for my voice.

"Trevor, I don't know. I have to get up early to be at the courthouse and…"

"Quit."

With my hands on his chest, I pushed him back so I could get a better look at him.

Letting out a gruff laugh, I said, "Trevor, I need my insurance! I need a job."

"Work here, for me on the ranch. I can cover the cost of the baby."

I rolled my eyes. "Okay, yeah, you can cover the cost of the baby's birth? Trevor it will be thousands of dollars. Why do you think I've been working so much overtime?"

He smiled. No, actually, he *smirked*.

"I love how completely innocent you are, Scarlett. It's one of the things I love about you."

Frowning, I pushed him harder, making him finally pull out of me. I scooted off the bed and grabbed the blanket to cover up.

"Innocent? I beg your pardon, but I have the estimate of how much this baby is going to cost, and it's not going to be cheap. Trevor, I need my insurance. I need a job to pay for things like diapers and formula. I'm not going to be dependent on you for those things."

Trevor climbed out of bed, not even caring that he was still completely naked. He walked to my side and took my hand. My eyes roamed his perfectly toned body. The way his muscles moved felt like a sin. God, he was sexy.

Trevor reached for the blanket and pulled it off of me.

"Let's take a shower."

"That's not going to wash away this conversation."

"Nope, it's not, but it will feel good to shower. Let me wash your body while I explain that money is not a problem."

"Oh, really?"

He laughed again. "Nope."

"You're not the least bit worried about the cost?" I asked as Trevor reached into his large, walk-in shower and turned it on. Water rained down from the faucets on the ceiling. I was in love with his shower and honestly wouldn't mind using it every day. Or soaking in the giant soaker tub next to it.

"I'm always worried about the cost of things. I don't throw my money away, and that's why I'm worth a few million."

He pulled me into the shower, and I stood there, staring at him as the water fell onto me.

"What did you just say?"

He leaned closer, placing his lips on my neck and gently sucking while his hands grabbed my ass. I dropped my head back when he pulled my body against his. He was hard again. My goodness, this man's stamina was going to keep me fit during this pregnancy.

"Damn, you feel so good," he whispered against my skin, causing my body to erupt in goosebumps. My mind went fuzzy, and for some reason I didn't care what we had just been talking about. Not when Trevor lifted my leg and slowly pushed back inside of me, deliciously slow.

"God, help me, I'm not going to be able to walk for a week," I panted as he moved in and out of me, this time at a faster pace.

"That's the plan baby. That's the plan."

I smiled when I opened my eyes and saw I was in Trevor's living room. An amazing smell was coming from the kitchen. I headed that way.

Trevor was talking to someone on the phone in a hushed voice.

"So, you'll do it for me? I owe you one, buddy."

A slight chuckle came from Trevor before he started talking again.

"I need to feed my girl first and probably take her back to her place to change, but we'll meet y'all there around nine?"

Clearing my throat, I walked into the kitchen.

"Speaking of, she just woke up. Okay, tell Amelia I love her, and hey, congrats again, dude."

Trevor hit End on his phone and flashed me a panty-melting smile.

"How did you sleep, baby?"

"Wonderful. I don't think I've slept that good in a long time and I wasn't even asleep that long."

He laughed. "I'm making us tacos. Does that sound okay?"

My stomach decided now was the perfect time to growl. I giggled and said, "That sounds amazing."

"Your stomach feeling okay?"

Nodding, I sat on the stool at the counter and watched Trevor move around the kitchen. "Do you need any help?"

"Nope, I've got it all. Just waiting for the taco shells to heat up."

With a contented sigh, I placed my chin on my palm and watched him. He was shirtless and only wearing a pair of shorts. Letting my gaze move lower, I couldn't help but smile at him in his bare feet. Something about Trevor made me want to demand that he kiss me, then make love to me again.

"Amelia and Wade told my folks about their pregnancy."

I gasped. "They did! What did your folks say?"

"Wade said they were over the moon and kept talking about how they were going to have four new grandchildren to spoil!"

"Four?" I asked, taking a drink of the water Trevor placed in front of me.

"Yeah, Tripp and Harley are having twins."

"Oh my gosh, I completely forgot that Harley said she was having twins! How exciting."

Trevor stopped and faced me. "Don't say that. It runs in the family. I'm okay with one baby but throw in two and I don't know what I'll do!"

I chuckled. "Deal, I won't even say the word, but I'm right there with you."

He winked, and my stomach dipped.

"I'm glad we're on the same page with that."

The buzzer for the tacos went off and Trevor took them out of the oven. I decided to make a taco salad while he practically inhaled four tacos.

"Where do you put all the food you eat, Trevor?"

He shrugged. "I work hard on the ranch, plus work out. I burn it off pretty easy."

I wiped the corners of my mouth with my napkin and set it on my now empty plate. I crunched up three taco shells and piled on the taco fixings and nearly ate it the whole thing in five bites. In my defense, I was starving.

"Earlier, when you were talking about me not working, or coming to work for you…"

My voice trailed off.

"Yeah, what about it?" Trevor asked, standing and taking both of our plates.

"You said you had a few million. What did you mean by that?"

Trevor rinsed off the plates, then put them in the dishwasher before he turned and leaned against the counter. He folded his arms over his massive chest. I wanted to lick my lips, but somehow managed to stay in control. Hard as it was.

"You already know my parents are pretty wealthy."

I nodded.

"Well, my father has taught me how to invest my money. Plus, I pretty much run the ranch now that my father has stepped down even more. I get the most in the profit sharing, plus I have a few things on the side. Cord paid me while I worked at the bar and all of that money I used to invest in shit."

"Invest in shit?" I said with a chuckle.

"Yep. I've always been good with money, Scarlett. I've got a pretty good nest egg saved up."

I chewed on my lip. "I understand that, but I won't be living off of you."

"You wouldn't be. Work for me. Lord knows I could use an assistant with all of the office-type shit. I hate doing that. Steed takes care of the books and Paxton works part-time here too. Wade and Mitchell could also use some help, I'm sure. You'd sort of be like the administrative assistant to all of us. Mom used to help a lot, but since Dad has pulled back, so has she."

"You're being serious?"

Trevor walked up to me and took my hand in his. I slipped off the stool and stood in front of him.

"I'm being dead serious. I want you near me. Especially with you being pregnant, I'd feel better."

My mouth opened and closed a few times before I found my voice. "Trevor, this is all happening so fast. I mean, we just got back together, and you want me to move in with you and work for you. Are you even sure you're ready for this step?"

He pushed a stray piece of hair that had fallen out of my ponytail behind my ear.

"If I didn't want this, I wouldn't have asked you. And don't worry about the money to pay for the baby. If you come work for us full-time, you'll have insurance."

Closing my eyes, I tried to let all of this sink in.

"Think about it, okay?"

I opened my eyes and found him staring deeply into my soul.

"I'll think about it, but I want you to think about it as well. I don't want this to be a knee-jerk thing because we shared an amazing moment together. Remember what your mom said."

He leaned down and kissed my forehead, and it made my heart skip. "I don't need to think about it, but I will if it makes you feel better."

"It would."

"Okay, so now that we got that out of the way, everyone is headed to Cord's Place tonight to celebrate Amelia and Wade's news. You feel like going out? Maybe doing a bit of dancing with me?"

Smiling, I placed my hand on the side of his face. "I can't think of any other place I'd rather be. I need to go home and change, though."

With a wicked smile, Trevor said, "See? Another reason you need to move in with me. Your clothes would already be here!"

CHAPTER 21

Scarlett

It was hard not to notice the people staring at Trevor and me. Let me correct that, *the women* glaring at me.

"Is it just me, or is every woman in this bar staring?" I called up to Trevor. He glanced around and then looked down at me.

"It's just you, babe."

Turning to Corina, I asked her the same question. If anyone was going to shoot me straight, it would be her or Maebh. Hell, any of the Parker women would shoot me straight.

"Am I being paranoid or are women staring at me?"

Corina laughed and yelled over the music.

"Nope, they're staring. Mostly at the way Trevor has a death grip on you!"

Maebh stopped in front of us, pulling me in for a hug. "You look beautiful! Did Trevor fall over when he saw you in this dress?"

Glancing down, I smiled. If I was still able to dress sexy, I was going to. I had on a light blue cocktail dress that hugged me in all the right places. It also showed off my little baby bump. My black stiletto heels made my short legs look like they went on forever. Being five-foot-three inches, I always felt a tad bit on the short side. And standing next to Trevor without heels, I felt even shorter. Tonight, when I walked down the steps from my bedroom, Trevor nearly dropped to the floor when he saw me. His first reaction was to tell me to go back up the steps and change. But once I told him why I wanted to dress a bit on the sexy side, he understood. Then he proceeded to tell me that he was not letting me out of his sight, and if one man touched me he would kill them.

"He told me to change!"

Maebh laughed as she looked at Trevor who was talking to Cord. Three large tables had been reserved for all of us. It was starting to be a rare occasion to have everyone together.

"Come on, let's sit down!" Maebh said, gently pulling me to the middle table. Harley and Tripp were already sitting and completely lost in one another. I got tears in my eyes when I saw Tripp's hand on her stomach while he talked to her.

"Can you not keep your hands to yourself, Tripp? We're in public!" Trevor called out, slapping his brother on the back and leaning down to kiss Harley on the cheek.

Tripp shook Trevor's hand, then leaned over and gave me a hug and kiss on the cheek.

"You look beautiful, Scarlett," he said with a sweet grin. Harley stood and wrapped me in her arms. I couldn't believe how much bigger she had gotten in the last few weeks.

"I agree, you look stunning, sweetie!"

"You look beautiful, Harley!" I said, placing my hand on her swollen belly. "How are you feeling?"

She laughed. "Tired! I can't believe how tired I am. I think I'm going to have to bring in another vet earlier than I thought to help me out."

"If you need any help, I'd love to help out! Once upon a time I wanted to be a vet."

She wore a surprised expression. "Seriously? Why didn't you?"

I waved it off. "Long story, but I'd love to come volunteer to help out in any way I can."

"I'll take you up on that, but you'll be paid."

Narrowing my eyes, I shouted, "We'll talk about it later!"

She pointed to me. "Deal!"

Trevor pulled my seat out and I sat down. Glancing around the table, I smiled. The entire Parker clan was now here. Paxton and Steed were at the table next to us. They looked happy to be out on a date night. The way Steed leaned in and whispered every so often in Paxton's ear was adorable. Especially when she would blush at something he said. Then you had Mitchell and Corina. His arm was around her chair and the way he kept twisting a piece of her hair in his fingers showed how much he wanted to touch her in any way he could. I sighed and kept my gaze moving.

Cord and Maebh. New love in full blossom. Cord looked at his fiancée like she hung the moon and she did the same. It was a beautiful thing to watch, the two of them. Their hands were locked together on the table as they spoke to one another and then drifted off to other conversations.

Then there was Wade and Amelia. My goodness, she was glowing and looked positively radiant. Her hands were going every which way as she talked about telling John and Melanie that they were expecting. I laughed at how animated she was. No wonder she was an author; she was an amazing storyteller.

Jonathon and Waylynn sat as close to each other as possible. They laughed with Amelia, and every now and then, Jonathon would lean over and say something in Waylynn's ear. The two of them looked like the perfect couple. The happiness that radiated off of them was hard to miss. It was almost as if they had their own little secret that kept them connected.

"Taking it all in, baby?"

Trevor's deep voice pulled my attention away from his sister and brother-in-law and back to him. His cornflower blue eyes stared deeply into my own.

"You have an amazing family, do you know that?"

He quickly scanned everyone. "I do know that. They're your family now, too, babe."

I sank my teeth into my lip only to have Trevor reach up and touch my mouth.

"Stop doing that or I'm going to take you to my brother's office and fuck you."

Gasping, my mouth dropped open. "Trevor!"

He winked, "What? I can't help it if you turn me on, Scarlett. Every little damn thing you do makes me want to sink my…"

Reaching my hand around his neck, I pulled his mouth to mine and kissed him before saying against his lips, "Stop talking like that in public before I take you up on that offer!"

He laughed and twirled one of the curls framing my face. I swore his eyes looked like they were twinkling.

He leaned his forehead against mine and said, "I love you, baby." Then he placed his hand on my stomach. "I love both of you."

I was lost to this man. Everything seemed to drift away, and it felt like it was only the two of us.

The band stopped playing and I heard Cord talking. Drawing back, I turned to face the stage that was set up toward the back of the bar.

"It's been awhile since we had this guy on stage, but he's been asked to sing a special song tonight. I'll let him jump on up here and tell y'all about it."

The crowd started to clap as Wade jumped up on the stage. I peeked over at Amelia. She was clapping like crazy and screaming out her husband's name.

"Hey, y'all. So, Cord's right, I haven't been up here to sing in a while. I've had a lot going on in my world. I got married to the most beautiful woman in Oak Springs, Mrs. Amelia Adams."

The crowd went wild as Amelia screamed out, "I love you, Wade!"

I couldn't help but laugh, along with the rest of the Parker clan. Trevor placed his arm around my shoulders, pulling me closer to his side.

"Hold on, I've got even better news. We're expecting out first baby this April!"

More cheers erupted as Amelia blushed then blew a kiss to Wade.

"You're probably thinking I'm up here to sing a song to my beautiful wife, but someone else very close to me asked me if I would sing a certain song for him and dedicate it to the woman he loved."

I glanced around the bar and then around the table, wondering who had asked Wade to get up and sing.

"There isn't anything I wouldn't do for this guy. He's my best friend and has been by my side through thick and thin, so when he called me today and asked if I could sing this song with the band to-night, I didn't hesitate to say yes."

Swallowing hard, I looked at Trevor. He was staring straight ahead at Wade, a wide grin on his face. His thumb moved softly across the exposed skin on my shoulder, causing my entire body to shiver.

"I called Mike, the lead singer, asked him if he thought we could pull this song off and his response was, 'Hell yes.' So after a few hours of being up here practicing, we're going to attempt to cover this one."

The crowd cheered again, clapping and letting out whistles and hollers.

"Trevor?" I asked, squeezing his hand that was holding mine.

He faced me and winked. Standing, he pulled me up.

"Dance with me, Scarlett?"

I was suddenly hit with déjà vu. A feeling from so many years ago came rushing back all over again. It was the first time Trevor Parker had kissed me and stolen my heart. The moment I fell in love with him, and I felt like I was hitting the lottery and getting to experience it for the first time all over again.

"Trevor," I whispered, my chin trembling and my throat burning as I attempted to hold back my tears.

He led me through the crowd to the dance floor which had opened up, leaving a space for the two of us. I didn't even care that all eyes were on us.

Wade strummed his guitar and said, "This song is dedicated to Scarlett from Trevor."

Trevor gently took me in his arms and held my body against his. Pressing his mouth to my ear, he said, "I couldn't even begin to say how I feel about you better than the words of this song."

When the music started, I lost my battle. Tears instantly steamed down my face the moment I recognized the song.

Trevor pulled me against him as we danced. Wade and the band were doing a cover of Daughtry's "Deep End." I listened to every single word while the man I loved held me close to his body.

Trevor's hand came up and cupped my neck, causing me to look up at him. When he sang the chorus with Wade, my body shook with sobs. He used his thumbs to wipe away my tears, kissed me on the forehead, and took me back into his arms. It felt like we were the only two people in the room, in the entire world. My gaze locked with his while we moved to the song.

This man didn't even have to say a word because I saw everything in his beautiful blue eyes. And I knew that whatever our future held, as long as Trevor was next to me, I could do anything.

Lost in the words and music, I held onto Trevor like my life depended on it. Hearing him sing the words along with Wade made my chest tighten in the most amazing way. This love was a powerful, amazing, once-in-a-lifetime thing.

When I glanced back up at him, I knew I wanted everything with this man. That meant giving him one hundred percent of myself.

When the song was coming to an end, Trevor stopped swaying, cupped my face in his hands and smiled at me with the most stunning smile I'd ever seen on his handsome face.

"I love you, Scarlett Littlefield. Will you please do me the honor of moving in with me? Let me take care of you and the baby?"

A sob-laugh came out as I answered him. "Yes, yes I'll move in with you, Trevor."

He pressed his mouth to mine. My arms wrapped around his neck and all I heard were people cheering. I didn't even care that the entire bar was watching us. As far as I was concerned it was only the two of us.

Breaking our connection, Trevor gave me a wink before saying, "We're leaving now."

Not one to argue, I let him lead me off the dance floor, to the table to grab my purse, and out the door. I barely had time to say goodnight to everyone and we didn't even get to hear Wade sing any more songs.

"What is the rush, Trevor Parker?" I asked with a giggle.

"I'm taking you home, and we're making love all night."

"What if I told you my body is exhausted."

He stopped walking, concerned on his face. Even in the dark of night, I saw the fear in his eyes.

"Are you okay? Did I hurt you?"

"What? No, not at all. I'm just tired, that's all."

"Then we're going home to sleep. I don't care what we do, as long as you're in my arms."

I couldn't hide the smile on my face if I'd tried. Glancing over my shoulder, I caught a glimpse of someone coming out of Cord's Place. It didn't take me long to realize it was Eric.

I turned back to Trevor. This was the man I loved and wanted to spend the rest of my life with. I could only hope that Eric had seen that tonight and finally realized I was happy. My phone buzzed in my purse and I knew it was him. Not wanting to ruin this amazing night, I decided to ignore it. I'd talk to Trevor about Eric tomorrow.

Tonight I simply wanted to be lost in his arms.

CHAPTER 22

Trevor

My mother stood in front of the Christmas tree in the family room, a box in her arms. It was December 9. The annual Parker family decorating day.

"Okay, everyone knows what to do. Harley, sweetheart, you're on popcorn string duty."

"Hey, that's not fair! She gets to sit down the whole time!" Tripp argued.

Giving my brother a stern look, our mother cleared her throat. "Well, the minute we find out you're six months pregnant with twins, then you can sit and string popcorn, Tripp."

"Noted." Kissing Harley on the cheek, Tripp grabbed the box and sat on the floor with a very curious Gage.

Scarlett peeked around the corner and smiled when she saw me. "Trevor? How long do the cookies stay in the oven?"

"Ten to twelve minutes," I replied, heading in her direction. Scarlett was sixteen weeks pregnant and had the cutest baby bump. I loved running my hand over it when we were in bed. I couldn't wait to feel the baby move for the first time. Her morning sickness was tapering off, but Amelia's had kicked up. I smiled when I saw my sister in the kitchen. Amelia was closer to reaching the twenty-week mark and you could for sure see her baby bump.

"Mom said she wanted tacos, so tacos it is," Waylynn said with a roll of her eyes. "Amelia, do you want to shred the cheese?"

My baby sister slipped off the stool, grabbed the block of cheese and got to work on shredding it.

"These look perfect!" Scarlett stated, pulling my butter pecan cookies from the oven.

"When can I eat one?" Waylynn asked, staring down at the pan of cookies, a hungry gleam in her eyes.

I rolled my eyes and pushed her out of the way. "Don't you have a child and husband to take care of?"

The doorbell rang, and Waylynn jumped.

"That's Liberty!"

Scarlett looked confused for a moment before it dawned on her. Liberty was the birth mother to Waylynn and Jonathon's adopted baby girl who shared the same name as her birth mom.

Amelia gasped and then cried out, "Oh. My. God. Holy. Shit."

Everyone looked at Chloe who held up her hands. "I wasn't going to say anything!" Chloe declared.

"What's wrong?" Scarlett asked Amelia, taking the cheese and grater out of her hands and guiding her to the table. Tears were forming in my sister's eyes, and I started to have a semi-freak-out moment.

"Amelia, are you okay?" I asked, dropping down to eye level with her.

She nodded. "Can you please go get Wade?"

"I will!" Scarlett said, rushing out of the kitchen. Less than a minute later, she was back with Wade. He dropped down next to me, so I stood and backed away.

"Baby, what's wrong?" He looked down at her hands on her stomach, nothing but fear in his eyes.

"I felt the baby."

Scarlett let out a breath of air at the same time I did.

"What?" Wade asked, a huge smile covering his face.

"The baby, I felt her...or him. I kept feeling something all morning and when I felt it again, I knew it was the baby. It felt like gas sort of, but different."

I glanced over to Scarlett, and we smiled at each other.

"What's going on? Is everything okay?" Mom asked, walking into the kitchen and looking at all of us.

"Aunt Meli felt her baby!" Chloe announced.

"What!? Oh my goodness, Amelia!"

Our mother rushed over to Amelia, nearly knocking Wade out of the way to pull her up into a hug.

I reached for Scarlett's hand and kissed the back of it. When I stepped closer, I placed my mouth at her ear. "You're next."

Her hand went to her stomach. She nodded then whispered, "I can't wait."

Harley walked into the kitchen and declared, "Well, I already ran out of popcorn. I keep eating it." She looked around and then stopped moving.

"Here! Here! Put your hand here!" she yelled out, pointing to her belly.

The sight before me was like nothing I'd seen before. Parker women came from everywhere, each pushing and shoving to place their hand on Harley's stomach to feel one of the twins kicking.

Chloe won. Her little hand was on Harley's stomach and she let out a squeal when she felt one of the babies kick.

"Get out of the way, kid. It's my turn!" Amelia said, pushing our niece out of the way. Then it was Corina, who had appeared out of thin air. Waylynn was next, along with Paxton.

"Where did you all come from?" I asked, glancing around the kitchen. My mother was laughing while putting hamburger meat into a large frying pan.

"Darn it. The baby isn't moving anymore," Waylynn said with a pout.

Liberty laughed, then made her way over to my mother where she took over cooking the hamburger meat.

"Thank you, Liberty, sweetheart," my mother said, giving her a kiss on the cheek and making her way back out of the kitchen. I loved that Waylynn and Jonathon had made Liberty such a huge presence in their life. I thought it was pretty cool that they had planned on letting little Liberty know who her birth mother was once she was old enough to understand, if that was what Liberty wanted.

Scarlett made her way over to Liberty and reached her hand out. "Hey, I don't think we've ever met before. I'm Scarlett Littlefield, Trevor's girlfriend."

Damn, I liked the sound of that. I wanted it to be fiancée, but we were still doing that damn slow thing.

"It's a pleasure to meet you, Scarlett. I hear you're pregnant, too!"

Scarlett laughed. "Yes! Something must be in the Oak Springs water."

"Must be!" Liberty agreed. She glanced over my way and gave me a polite smile. I knew she was still trying to feel at ease with all of us, a pretty daunting task with this rowdy bunch.

Waylynn walked over to Liberty. "Liberty, you don't have to cook. Why don't you go see baby Liberty? She's with Jonathon, I think, in the formal living room working on that tree."

Her brows pulled in some. "Is there more than one tree?"

Scarlett and I looked at each other before I turned my attention to Liberty. "Don't ask, just go with it. You may want to avoid my mother, though. Whatever room she is in, stay out of it."

She gave me a puzzled look. "Why?"

Corina peeked her head into the kitchen. "Scarlett, Mom told me to tell you that you must have left your reindeer ears in the other room. Here they are!"

With a pout, Scarlett took the strap-on ears from Corina, who was wearing a Santa hat that kept singing "*Jingle Bells*".

Corina squeezed the tip of Scarlett's antlers, causing everyone to jump to the sound of "*Santa Claus is Coming to Town.*"

"I think I see why," Liberty whispered as she took the spatula out of my hand and went back to cooking the hamburger meat.

"Smart girl. I like you already," Scarlett said with a smile.

"Come on, we need help with the Disney tree," Corina said, wrapping her arm up with Scarlett's.

"Have fun! I'll stay here and keep making cookies!" I called out.

Glancing over her shoulder, Scarlett shot me the evil eye.

I laughed, then started to take the cookies off the cookie sheet to put more dough on.

"I love your family," Liberty stated.

"Yeah, they're a good bunch. Have you spoken to your folks at all?"

Her smile faded as she shook her head. "Mike and Wanda feel more like my folks these days. They're amazing and have helped me so much. I don't know what I would have done without them."

"Yeah, they're good people. They were there for Wade when he lost his family."

Liberty nodded, then smiled. It was clear she was fixin' to change the subject.

"So, let's see. Harley is pregnant with twins and due in March?"

"Yep."

"Amelia is due in April and Scarlett is due when?"

I grinned. "May 25."

"You must be excited."

"Very."

She turned to face me with a serious look. When she glanced over my shoulder, I couldn't help but wonder what was on her mind.

"May I ask you something, Trevor?"

"Of course."

She swallowed hard and glanced at the floor before catching my gaze with hers. "How is Waylynn handling the pregnancies?"

My chest constricted. I was a fucking shit brother for not even thinking about that. I hadn't once thought about how Waylynn might be handling all of this.

"I, *um*, I'm not sure. Christ, I hadn't even thought of it." My hand ran over my head and I cursed under my breath again.

"Don't beat yourself up about it. She is such a strong woman, and I know she doesn't show her emotions all the time. I was just wondering if you had an idea of how she was dealing with it all."

"I don't. I'm sorry. If I get a chance to talk to Jonathon today I will."

She nodded. "Me too. Wanda was asking, as well."

I slipped the cookies into the oven, then shut it and leaned against the island.

"Liberty, I wanted to tell you that I think you're very brave."

She stopped what she was doing and faced me with a confused expression.

"Why?"

I shrugged. "I can't imagine giving up a baby, but I know why you did it, and I think that was a very brave thing to do."

"Thank you, Trevor. It was hard, but I knew it was the right decision and I think baby Liberty is going to have the best life possible."

"Waylynn and Jonathon love her."

She grinned. "I know they do."

"What about you? How are you doing?"

Her grin grew to a wide, full-blown smile. "I'm doing great. I've sort of met someone. I haven't told anyone yet. I was going to tell Waylynn and Jonathon soon. It's been crazy."

My brow lifted. "Crazy good?"

The way Liberty's face lit up, I already knew the answer.

"So crazy good. He's such a nice guy, I was honestly beginning to wonder if there were any left. He knows about baby Liberty and he didn't judge me at all. That was important to me. He supports my dreams and encourages me all the time."

"Sound like a good guy."

"Who's a good guy?" Waylynn asked. The giant Christmas tree hat on her head was blinking its lights off and on. Liberty busted out laughing the moment she saw it.

Waylynn rolled her eyes. "Laugh all you want but wait until my mother gets to you. Now, who are we talking about and why are you standing in the kitchen gossiping with my baby brother?"

I pushed off the counter and kissed Waylynn on the forehead. "Can we talk out back for a second? Just the two of us?"

She looked confused. "Okay."

I motioned for her to lead the way and followed. We walked over to the rocking chairs and each took a seat.

"Is everything okay, Trevor?" she asked, her voice void of its normal humor and feistiness.

I reached for her hand. "Waylynn, are you doing okay with all of this?"

She snarled. "Do any of us do okay with mom's crazy behavior at Christmas time?"

Chuckling, I shook my head. "No. Harley, Amelia, and Scarlett...all being pregnant."

Her eyes softened, and she squeezed my hand. "I love you for being concerned, Trevor. It was hard at first when I found out about Harley and Scarlett, but I quickly got over it every time I looked at Liberty. I will admit I felt a bit of jealousy when I found out that

Amelia was pregnant. I think her being our sister made it all hit home a bit more. I've been talking to a counselor and that's helped. I think I've come to terms with it, but there will always be a piece of me that feels empty."

"I'm sorry, Waylynn."

"Please don't be, Trevor. I really am happy, and I believe there is a reason for everything. Jonathon and I are talking about maybe adopting another baby."

I smiled. "You are? That's amazing, Waylynn."

She nodded her head. "Just talking right now. We'll see. I love you for caring."

The heat on my cheeks had to have been obvious to her. "Honestly, it was Liberty who asked. She wanted to make sure you were okay, and I felt like a complete asshole because I hadn't even thought of asking you myself."

Waylynn laughed. "God, I love that girl. That was sweet of her to be concerned."

"She loves you too, Waylynn."

"I know she does. Now come on. Let's get back in there. You probably have to save Scarlett from Mom."

Groaning, I opened the back door for my sister. When Liberty caught my eye, I nodded. She looked relieved.

Clearing my throat, I said, "So, Liberty met someone. Now get to girl talking. I'm going to find Scarlett and save her."

Waylynn gasped, then turned to Liberty. "Oh my God! Tell me everything!"

With that, I made my way out of the kitchen and through the house. Each room had some sort of action going on. My father was at the bar in the family room pouring himself a shot. I couldn't help but laugh. He acted like he hated this day, but we all knew he loved it. There wasn't anything he wouldn't for my mother.

Walking up to Corina, I tapped her on the shoulder. "Hey, do you know where Scarlett is?"

"She's one of the lucky ones. She snuck out before your mom started the craft area. I believe she is hiding out on the swing on the front porch."

I frowned. "Craft area?"

With a low groan, Corina held up a hand-decorated ornament. "Chloe's idea a few weeks back. Melanie jumped all over it, and there is now a designated area in the dining room for everyone to make an ornament."

My mother walked into the room, and I ducked behind Corina. "I need a distraction, Corina, or she'll suck me in!"

Corina pointed a finger. "You owe me, Trevor Parker. You owe me big."

As she walked away, I dove behind the sofa out of sight from my mother.

"Melanie, can you show me how you made that angel?"

I could hear my mother squeal in delight. "Yes! Oh, I could kiss Chloe for coming up with this idea!"

They walked out of the room and I jumped up, only to find Chloe standing in front of me.

Letting out what my brothers would call "a girly scream," I placed my hand over my chest. "Chloe! Jesus, you scared me. What are you, a ninja? You're everywhere."

"You need to come make an ornament, Uncle Trevor."

Panic hit me. The last thing I wanted to do was craft. I needed to think of something and fast. Chloe was staring at me like she was about to call out for my mother any moment.

"I will, pumpkin, as soon as I find Scarlett. She'll want to make one for the baby."

Chloe smiled big, and I felt a little guilty. Just a little.

Reaching for my hand, Chloe tried to pull me into the dragon's lair, but I stood firm.

"I need to find Scarlett, so she knows the plan."

Chloe narrowed her eyes like she knew I was lying. The moment her hand went to her hip, I was screwed. What was it about these Parker women? They were bred to sniff out a lie.

"Um, well, I better go find Scarlett."

"Want me to come?"

"No! I mean, no, pumpkin, you go and have fun. It won't take me long to find her at all. She'll be excited. She loves to craft and shi...um...stuff."

That seemed to be what she wanted to hear.

"Okay!" Spinning on the heels of her bright pink cowboy boots, Chloe called out, "Grammy, Uncle Trevor and Aunt Scarlett are gonna make the baby an ornament."

That was my one and only chance to escape. And escape I did.

CHAPTER 23

Scarlett

I sat on the porch swing with my eyes closed, taking in the sounds of nature. It was so quiet and relaxing...unlike the crazy that was unfolding inside the Parker house. From behind, a noise made me turn around. Trevor came around the corner of the house as fast as he could.

"Trevor? What are you doing?"

"I had to sneak out while Corina distracted my mother. I almost got pulled into the dining room to make a handmade craft by Mom and then Chloe. I narrowly escaped Chloe. We need to leave. Now."

My hand went to my mouth as I attempted to hide a laugh and failed.

"You laugh now, but Chloe already told my mother we want to make an ornament for the baby."

Dropping my hand to my stomach, I smiled. "That might be fun."

Trevor sat down next to me on the swing, draped his arm around my shoulders and groaned. "Yep, right along with getting a tooth pulled."

I hit him lightly on the stomach before dropping my head onto his shoulder.

"You okay?" he asked, kissing the top of my head.

"Yeah, I'm just tired. I feel like I need to nap."

"You want to go home?"

The temptation to say yes was strong, but I shook my head.

"I need a few minutes of calm, then I can go back in."

"My family is a lot to take in, especially for someone who grew up as an only child."

A giggle slipped from my lips. "They *are* a lot to take in. How do you keep up with all of them? I mean, there are so many, and the family is growing by leaps and bounds. I think I need a chart, and I grew up knowing your family."

Trevor laughed. "Well, it's all the babies that keep getting thrown into the mix. I'm honestly waiting for Cord and Maebh to say they've got a bun in the oven or Mitchell and Corina to announce they're pregnant again."

"What about Paxton and Steed? Are they going to have anymore?"

"I think they want one more."

We sat for a few moments in silence before I spoke.

"I'm scared I'm not going to be a good mother. I look at your mom, Waylynn, Paxton, and Corina and they all seem to be so good at it."

Trevor pulled me close. Six months ago, if someone had told me I'd be having this conversation with Trevor I'd have told them they were insane.

"Trust me, they mess up all the time. We're going too also, but I think we learn by making mistakes."

My hand rested on my stomach. "I want to feel the baby so badly."

"Soon, baby."

Chewing on my lip, I pulled back to look at Trevor. "I keep having this nightmare that something happens to me. Like I'm stuck in water and I can't get out. I'm not pregnant in the dream, and I just keep screaming for someone to help me. I'm surprised I haven't woken you up when I have it. I sit up sweating and can hardly breathe."

Trevor frowned, then got in front of me and dropped to his knees. He took both of my hands and gently kissed each one.

"You're going to be an amazing mother, and I'm going to be a great dad and we're totally going to screw things up. As long as we don't drop the baby, forget to feed 'em, or leave the house without them, I think we're going to be fine."

I chuckled. "Now you have me worried I'll drop them."

He shook his head and leaned up, his hand moving behind my neck.

"Listen to me, Scarlett, you're going to be the best mother ever."

"I know. I'm scared, that's all."

"So am I, baby. Fucking terrified. All we need is you, me, and our little Gummy Bear. That's all we'll ever need."

Tears pricked at the back of my eyes, but I laughed at Trevor's nickname for the baby.

"Sometimes I feel like this is a dream and I'll wake up and none of it will be real."

Trevor pulled me close, our lips touched, and we were soon lost in a kiss.

A throat cleared from behind Trevor, causing us to break the connection. I missed his touch as soon as he fell back on his heels. He gave me a sexy wink and stood.

Steed was standing on the front porch, a smile on his face.

"Hate to interrupt, but Chloe sent me looking for the two of you."

Trevor groaned. "No! Tell her you can't find us."

"I'm not lying to my daughter, dickhead."

"Dude! She wants me to *craft*! Me!"

Steed walked up to Trevor. "Do you know what I had to do the other day?"

"Kiss Patches?" Trevor replied.

"Ha. And for the record, I've had to do that. No, what I had to do was sit in my dining room, while Chloe laid out every single piece of make-up Paxton owned. It was make Daddy look like a princess day. By the time my daughter was finished, I looked like a drag queen down on her luck. Here. I even have the picture to prove it."

Steed pulled out his phone while I made my way over to them. When he turned it around, Trevor and I both lost it laughing. Steed had on a wig that looked like it came from the movie *Frozen*. He had pigtails, bright pink lipstick, purple and pink eyeshadow, ruby red cheeks, and fake, plastic diamond earrings that dangled from his ears. To top it all off, he had on a tiara.

"What in the fuck?" Trevor asked, bending over to laugh. "Please send me that picture. God, I'll give you five hundred dollars to send me that picture."

"Screw you, Trevor. The point I'm trying to make is, once you become a dad, you're going to be doing shit like this."

Glancing up, Trevor whispered, "Please let me have a boy."

I punched him on the arm.

"Just come in, make an ornament and then Mom and Chloe will be off your back."

"Scarlett's tired."

I pointed to him. "Oh no, you are not putting this on me, Trevor Parker. I think it will be fun to make the baby an ornament."

Steed motioned to me. "See, your girlfriend wants to make one for your baby, so let's go."

He headed into the house and I followed. Trevor reached for my hand, pulling me to a stop.

"Steed, we'll be right there. I want to ask Scarlett something first."

With a nod, he headed into the house, leaving me and Trevor alone on the front porch.

"You know I love you, right?" he asked, his face serious.

"I know."

"You know I'm not leaving you or the baby. I'm in this with you forever and always."

Smiling, I placed my hand on the side of his cheek. His unshaven face felt good against my hand. I wanted to feel it between my legs as I called out his name. Over and over.

"I know."

"Then marry me, Scarlett."

My heart dropped to my stomach. Everything felt a little off, like the entire world had tilted a bit.

"What?" I softly asked.

"I don't want people to call you my girlfriend. I want them to know you're mine. And I'm yours."

"Trevor, I think…I mean…this is all so sudden. You're moving fast and I'm not sure if you're doing it all for the right reasons."

"Right reasons? Because loving you and wanting to make you mine isn't the right reason?"

I shook my head. "No, because your brother just called me your girlfriend, and you think we need to be something more. That this, what we have, needs a permanent title. We don't have to be married to be parents to our baby. Things are different now and when we get married it's going to be because we love each other, not because I'm pregnant."

"That's not why…"

Placing my fingers to his mouth, I closed my eyes and shook my head. I wanted more than anything to tell him I'd marry him. I wanted to scream out *yes*! But I knew in my heart we needed to wait.

I opened my eyes and smiled. "I want nothing more than to be your wife."

His eyes lit up and a huge smile moved across his face.

"But now isn't the time to ask me."

"When is, Scarlett? I almost lost you once, and I refuse to risk losing you again."

Leaning up, I kissed him gently on the lips. "You're never going to lose me, Trevor Parker."

He wrapped his arms around me, pulling me flush against his body.

"Promise me that, Scarlett."

"I promise I'll never leave you."

He kissed the tip of my nose. "And I promise I'll never leave you. I love you."

"I love you too."

The screen door flew up and little feet came running out.

"Uncle Trevor! Come on! I've got the glue gun ready to go!" Chloe declared.

With a groan only loud enough for me to hear, Trevor forced a smile and wrapped his arm around my waist.

Trevor plastered on a smile "We're coming and *so* ready to do this!"

Chloe jumped while clapping. "Yay! Let's go! Wait till you see the crown I made you, Uncle Trevor!"

Trevor tried to turn around, but I pushed him into the house.

"Come on. This is good Dad practice!" I said, trying my best to hide my laugh.

"I'm sure going to miss you, Scarlett!"

With a grin, I kissed the cheek of my co-worker and friend, Mia. We worked together at the courthouse and I had to admit, a part of me was sad I was leaving. Only a small part.

Once Harley found out I was quitting my job and going to work for Trevor, she begged me to come in and work two afternoons a week at the vet clinic. I was over the moon when she asked. Trevor thought it was a great idea, too. I was a little giddy at the idea that I would be working at a vet clinic, especially since my dream had been to go to vet school.

Of course, my parents thought it was a bad idea and that I was being reckless with the pregnancy. They reasoned that a dog could bite me, or I could get sick. When that didn't work, they tried rabies, and when that didn't work, my father simply told me I was stubborn like my mother. He never once compared me to him. Everything had always been "like my mother." Like he had no bad qualities or quirks, only the females. It had bothered me when I was little, but it didn't bother me anymore.

"I'll miss you too, Mia."

"Promise you'll still come in and have lunch with us? And make sure you invite us to the baby shower!"

I nodded and smiled. "I promise I'll do both."

Mia leaned against my desk. "I wish a tall, dark and handsome man would sweep me off my feet. Although, I could do without the knocking me up thing. I don't want kids."

Frowning, I placed the last personal item from my desk into the box.

"You don't want kids?"

"Nope. No, thanks. I think they're gross. I mean, I like them for all of about an hour. Then I'm ready for them to be seen and not heard."

"That's terrible, Mia!" I said, shaking my head and letting out a chuckle.

"It's true."

"Don't ever go over to the Parker house for family night, then."

She grinned and gave me a thumbs up. "Noted."

"Scarlett?"

Turning, I found Eric, hands tucked inside his pockets and a shy smile on his face.

"Okay, who is *this* hottie?" Mia whispered in my ear.

"A friend," I responded.

"Single?" Mia asked.

I nodded. "Yep! Eric, what are you doing here?"

He glanced down at my desk and then back at me. "I had to come and see if it was true. The bastard is really making you leave your job and your home?"

Mia took a few steps back. "*Um*, I think I'm going to go grab a coffee."

I glared at Eric. Lately, he'd had a habit of doing things to embarrass me in public, especially saying things about Trevor that I didn't appreciate.

"Thanks, Mia," I said, squeezing her hand to let her know I was okay.

Once she was around the corner, I faced Eric.

"You need to stop doing this."

"Doing what? Speaking the truth, love? I heard Maebh telling Cord you were renting your house out. What in the hell are you doing? I thought you were going to live there, and Trevor was going to have a room at his house for the baby? What are you doing, Scarlett? Why are you setting yourself up for heartache?"

Rolling my eyes, I threw my purse into the box and picked it up.

"Wait! Let me walk you to your car," Eric nearly shouted as he took the box from my arms.

"Fine, but after this, you will stop with this nonsense."

Eric followed behind me as I made my way through the courthouse. When we got to my car, I popped open the trunk.

After placing the box inside, Eric shut the trunk and faced me. "Tell me why you're leaving your job. Why you're giving up your house."

"I'm not giving up my house, and I moved in with Trevor last month. He offered me a job at the ranch, working as his assistant. I'm also going to be working with Harley a few days a week at the vet clinic."

Eric scoffed. "His *assistant*? Really? He's that insecure that he has to have you under his thumb by moving you in and making you leave your job?"

"No, dickhead," said a voice from behind me. "I love her so much that I want to be near her as often as I can. We got a problem here, Eric?"

As I spun around, my heart felt like it stopped mid-beat. Trevor stood before us, arms folded over his massive chest, a look of pure hatred plastered on his face and pointed directly at Eric.

Shit. This was not going to end well.

CHAPTER 24

Trevor

Scarlett seemed surprised to see me, but Eric almost seemed gleeful.

What in the fuck was this guy doing here?

"Trevor, what are you doing here?" Scarlett asked.

I let my body relax some and smiled at her.

"I wanted to make sure you didn't need any help."

The way she returned my smile made my knees weaken.

"How nice, the hero rushing in. Tell me, Trevor, what did you do to force Scarlett to give everything up and fall at your feet?"

"Eric!" Scarlett gasped. "What in the world has gotten into you? You promised me you were going to stop this the last time we talked."

It felt like someone had punched me in the gut. Scarlett had been talking to Eric since I found them sitting on her porch months ago, and she hadn't told me? It wasn't like I didn't trust her, but I didn't trust this asshole standing in front of me. He was obsessed with Scarlett, and she couldn't see it. Even Cord said Maebh was beginning to be concerned with his behavior when it came to Scarlett.

"Talked? When did y'all talk?"

Eric looked pleased with himself as he waited for Scarlett to answer.

"Eric stopped by here a few times to see how I was doing. I've assured him I'm perfectly fine and that he needs to stop acting like this. I'm happy, we're happy, and his butting in is not doing any good."

I smirked as I looked back at Eric. Did he really think I was going to be pissed at Scarlett because he was essentially stalking her?

Fucker.

"I care about Scarlett, that's all."

"And I don't?"

With a smug look, Eric shrugged. "I don't know. Does a leopard really change its spots or is this all just a show because you thought Scarlett might be falling for me?"

"Wait, what? Eric, what in the world are you talking about?" Scarlett asked.

I'd had enough of this prick. It was time to set him straight.

I got in his face.

"You need to stay the fuck away from her. She's off limits, understand?"

"You going to put a collar and leash on her, as well?"

"Eric!" Scarlett shouted.

Grabbing him by the shirt, I pulled my fist back only to stop when Scarlett pushed us apart.

"Stop this! Eric, I've told you before, and I'll tell you once more, I'm in love with Trevor. I'm having his baby. After I move the last of my things out of my house I'll officially be moved in with him. I'm working for Frio River Ranch, not just Trevor, and I'm excited about it. I don't care if you agree with that or not."

Eric rolled his eyes and shook his head in disbelief. I knew how hard it was for him to believe I could have changed. Hell, even I couldn't believe it until the moment I realized that I could lose Scarlett, that she was the only woman I'd ever loved and would ever love. I didn't expect this jackass to understand that. He had Superman syndrome. He saw a woman in destress and felt like he had to fly in and save her.

"Scarlett, I care about you," he said. "I've seen you hurt, and I just want to make sure you're okay."

"I don't need this stress from you, Eric. What I need is for you to accept that I'm happy. *Very* happy. Won't you just be happy for me and move on? I think this friendship is over, Eric. I really need you to leave and let me live my life with the man I love."

Eric pulled in a deep breath. When he looked back at Scarlett, he didn't say a word. He simply turned and walked away.

Scarlett sighed and faced me. Before she could say anything, I cupped her face in my hands and kissed her.

When she wrapped her arms around my neck, the kiss deepened, but we both had the good sense to stop since we were standing outside the courthouse.

Drawing back, I grinned. "I honestly would have thought it would be some crazy girl from my past causing us heartache, not this Eric guy."

"Ugh, don't even say that, Trevor Parker. Come on, let's head to my place so I can pack up the last few things to bring to your house."

Before she had a chance to walk away from me, I took her hand in mine.

"Thank you for doing this. I know you didn't have to move in with me or give up your job."

Her smile practically melted my heart. Scarlett Littlefield had a way of making it seem like it was only the two of us no matter where we were. I knew what she was giving up, and I also knew she didn't do it because I'd forced her into it. We loved each other and if Eric couldn't see that, then that was his problem.

"I didn't give up my job, Trevor. I'm doing this for us."

Kissing her forehead, I smacked her on the butt.

"Meet ya at your place."

She giggled and got into her car. I watched as she buckled up and pulled out of the parking lot. Jogging over to my truck, I heard my name.

"Trevor! Trevor Parker!"

Stopping, I turned to see Kenzie Lewis, one of the reporters for the *Oak Springs Gazette*.

"Hey, Kenzie, what's going on?"

She smiled as she headed my way. "Rumor has it you're off the market."

With a frown, I looked directly into her eyes. "I didn't think you ran the gossip column, Kenz."

She laughed. "I don't. This is off the record. I'm curious, that's all. Is it true? Are you and Scarlett settling down together?"

"What is happening with me and Scarlett is no one's business. Period."

"Seems like there are a lot of broken hearts in town. Especially with you quitting over at Cord's Place. It appears all the Parker men are off the market now."

I forced a smile and opened my truck door. "It appears so."

"Tell me, Trevor, are you the type of guy who can actually settle down with one woman?"

Staring at her, I laughed. "Let me guess, Kenzie. You've been talking to Eric."

She smirked. "As a matter of fact, I have been. He thinks there may be a story in there somewhere."

With a smirk, I took a step closer to her. "I'm disappointed in you."

Her face went pale. "Excuse me?"

"A piece of advice for you, Kenzie. Let the town gossip mill stay with the prayer chain. This bullshit you're trying to pull, it doesn't become you."

Lifting her chin, Kenzie forced a smile. "Well, if things don't work out between y'all—"

I shot her a look that instantly had her shutting her mouth.

"Oh, it's going to work out. See ya' around, Kenzie."

With a lift of her hand and a fake ass smile, she waved. "See ya' around, Trevor."

I started my truck and pulled out of the lot. Anger quickly had my body heating up. That fucking Eric. What in the hell was that guy's deal? Shaking off all thoughts of that dickhead, I focused on Scarlett and getting the last of her things out of the house. Christmas was in a couple of days and the sooner she was with me, the better I'd feel.

CHAPTER 25

Scarlett

The smell of bacon had me opening my eyes and letting out a soft moan.

"Oh God, bacon."

Throwing the blanket and sheet off of me, I slipped my robe on and headed to the bathroom before making my way to the kitchen. Trevor knew I had been craving bacon and had been making it every single morning since I officially moved in a few days earlier. Before that, I'd pretty much been staying at his house every night and slowly moving my things in over the last month.

The moment I stepped into the kitchen, Trevor turned to face me. It was like he'd sensed I was there.

"Good morning, baby."

I walked over to him and planted a kiss on his lips. "Good morning. You know, you're going to spoil me with this bacon every morning."

He grinned and every nerve ending tingled. We had come such a long way in a short amount of time. I still felt like I needed to pinch myself to believe this was all happening.

"I would have brought it up to you, but the smell must have woken you up."

"Actually, it was your child pushing on my bladder that woke me up."

Trevor beamed and placed his hand on my stomach. The look of pure happiness in his eyes was hard to miss.

"Gummy Bear causing trouble already, huh?"

"Yes! Apple doesn't fall far."

With a quick bend down, Trevor kissed me. It was soft and sweet, but still sent a zap of desire to my lower belly.

"I know what I want for Christmas," I whispered against his lips.

"What's that, baby?"

Placing my hands on his bare chest, I looked up into those beautiful blue eyes.

"You."

The once-soft blue instantly turned darker, and before I knew it, Trevor was turning off the oven and I was in his arms. He headed back to our bedroom where he gave me the best Christmas gift a girl could want: three orgasms coupled with slow passionate love making.

Nothing would ever top this first Christmas together.

Presents laid in neat piles across the large family room. I watched as Mitchell attempted to get Merit to crawl toward him. Liberty was now crawling. I couldn't help but laugh every time I watched her take off and Jonathon and Waylynn had to go after her.

Maebh and Cord were glued to each other like two peas in a pod. It was the cutest thing to watch them together. Maebh's father Aedin was in town and completely lost in a conversation with Aunt Vi. There was something going on between the two of them, and I made a mental note to ask Trevor about it.

My eyes roamed the room and found Corina talking with her mom, Lori, and Melanie. Lori was now running the bed and breakfast for Corina and when I had decided to go work for Frio River Ranch, Lori hired a part-time girl to help out. She ended up being fantastic with the guests and the perfect fit. She freed up time for Lori to be with Corina and Merit. It was obvious how much Corina loved having her mother here.

Moving my attention around the room, I found Steed playing hide and seek with Gage, while Amelia, Wade, and Paxton played a board game with Chloe.

"Taking it all in?" Trevor whispered as he came up behind me.

Laughing, I nodded. "Everyone is scattered. It's hard to keep up with all the bodies."

Trevor pointed over to Maebh and Cord. "Except for those two love birds."

"They're probably talking wedding plans. It's romantic that they're getting married in Ireland."

Sitting next to me, Trevor took my hand in his. "Do you think we'll be able to go? With the baby being so young and all?"

I shrugged. "I guess we can talk to the pediatrician about it, but I don't see why we wouldn't be able to. Maebh tried to push it out knowing when I was due. Amelia and Wade are planning on going with their little one who is due three weeks before us."

Trevor laced his fingers with mine. "Then I say we plan on going as well. We can do business-class on the flight over, so it will be more comfortable for the baby and us."

Turning to face him, I smiled. "Who are you and what did you do with Trevor?"

Trevor laughed. "Well, the old Trevor realized what a stupid idiot he was after months of fighting the truth. He wised up and went after the woman he loved. Then when he found out said woman was carrying his baby, something else was set off inside of him."

I raised a brow. "And what exactly was that?"

Placing his finger on my chin, he brushed his lips against mine and whispered, "A love so powerful it knocked me on my ass. A love so strong it woke me up and showed me what I truly longed for."

Tears pricked at the back of my eyes. "Trevor Parker, you are truly the most romantic man in this room."

A crooked smile formed on his beautiful face. "Don't tell my brothers that. They'll try to show me up."

"We can't have that," I softly replied.

"No. We can't."

His lips pressed to mine, and I had to remind myself we were in a room full of his family.

"Gross! Uncle Trevor put his tongue in Aunt Scarlett's mouth!"

We both laughed as we broke the kiss and sat back.

Trevor pulled Chloe to him and started covering her in kisses. She screamed in delight and laughed as Trevor tickled her. I couldn't help being overwhelmed by emotions. Pushing it all down before I got too worked up, I smiled as I watched the man I loved more than anything playing with his niece. I pictured him playing with our little one and loved how that made my entire body warm.

"It's time to open presents!" Melanie called out as cheers erupted in the room.

"I hate to break up the beauty of all of this," Aunt Vi said as she walked into the room.

Everyone turned to her, the cheers dying out.

"Patches is currently in the kitchen. Eating *all* the food."

I'd never seen so many people move so fast in my life. The only people who didn't jump up and run were me, Harley, and Amelia. The three of us looked at each other and laughed.

"Ah, the joys of being pregnant," Harley stated as she waddled out of the family room.

Amelia hooked her arm with mine as we walked calmly toward the chaos.

"Welcome to the Parker family, Scarlett," she said with a smile.

CHAPTER 26

Trevor

I knew the moment she walked into the barn. It wasn't because I smelled that sweet vanilla of her body lotion; it was the way my heart jumped a little in my chest. My body just knew when she was around.

Glancing over my shoulder, I tossed the hay bale up to Mitchell.

"Hey there, beautiful."

Scarlett stood before me, her face lit up like she'd just walked into something amazing.

"I felt the baby move."

I stopped and stood, staring at her.

"Are you serious?" Mitchell said as he jumped down from the loft where we had been stacking the hay. "Feel like a little flutter?"

Scarlett nodded. "I've been feeling something, I just wasn't sure if it was the baby or not."

I felt myself smile, but I couldn't move. She had felt the baby move. Mitchell slapped me on the back and laughed.

"Dude, snap out of it. You should be able to feel Gummy Bear move soon. It didn't take very long before I could feel Merit moving around. Best damn thing ever."

I rushed over to Scarlett, pulling off my work gloves as I moved.

"You felt the baby?" I asked, grinning like a fool.

"Yep! I know now what it feels like, so next time I'll be ready. I don't think you can feel it yet, but like Mitchell said, we're getting close!"

I pulled her into my arms and hugged her before framing her face with my hands and kissing her.

"Hey, why don't y'all saddle up a few horses and enjoy the afternoon," Mitchell said. "I can get Wade to help me with the rest of this, Trevor."

Turning to my brother, I asked, "You sure? I don't want to leave you high and dry."

"I'm sure. Wade won't mind."

"I heard my name."

Wade walked into the barn, already wearing his work gloves. He must have been coming down to help out.

"You already finish up that project you were working on?" I asked, giving him an arched brow.

He grinned.

"I've got what I need from the land survey samples. Comparing the numbers, I have a better idea of the density of the livestock grazing in the southwest pasture. I think we can increase the number slightly and still not have to worry about a shortage of grazing area."

"What does that even mean?" Scarlett asked with a giggle.

Tossing my gloves onto a bench, I replied, "It means Wade likes playing with grass and dirt and seeing how many cows can graze in a pasture based on what is grown there."

I swore Wade stuck his chest out. I was ready for him to beat on it and declare himself master of all things dirt and shit.

Scarlett smiled at Wade. "Oh, sounds…interesting."

"It is," Wade stated at the same time Mitchell and I said, "It isn't."

Scarlett laughed.

"Come on, let's get some horses ready to ride. You feeling okay today?"

"I am. It's the first day in a while I haven't had a back ache, or an upset stomach, or felt like I had to pee every five minutes."

Wade groaned. "Enjoy it. It won't last. Amelia started sleeping in the guest room because she's afraid she's going to wake me up with how much she gets up and uses the restroom."

It was Scarlett's turn to groan. Laughing, I took her hand in mine and led her down the barn.

"You want to ride Candy Cane today?"

I watched her face light up as she ran her hand down the side of the horse's neck.

"Can we still ride her with her being pregnant and all?"

"Yep, once she gets to about three months before foaling, we won't ride her. Harley said she is about six months pregnant. This will probably be her last ride, to be honest. I don't want to risk anything with her."

I ran my hands over the horse, causing her to toss her head up a bit, telling me she wanted some scratching.

"What is it with you and females, Trevor Parker? Even the girl animals love you."

Laughing, I tugged Scarlett over. "The only female I care about is you."

She smiled, and my knees felt weak. Damn, this woman had no idea the control she had over me.

"You're sure the straps won't hurt her, right?"

With a wink, I replied, "I promise you. If I thought it was unsafe for her or the foal, I'd let you know. Just keep your legs light, not because I think you'll hurt her, I just don't want her trotting with you on her."

She grinned. "I'm pretty sure the four of us would be okay."

I stopped moving and looked at her. "The four of y'all?"

"Me, Gummy Bear, Candy, and her foal."

Walking over to her, I leaned down and kissed her. "Oh, that's right. I love you, Scarlett."

She grinned. "Wow, well, I love you too. What was that for?"

Shrugging, I replied, "I just wanted to tell you that."

"Y'all going to stand there in Candy's stall and stare at each other or actually go riding?" Mitchell called out.

A blush hit Scarlett's cheeks, and she looked down at my bare chest.

"You are going to put your shirt on, right?"

Lifting a brow, I asked, "Why? Is this distracting?"

She nodded. "Yes. Very."

"Then I'm keeping it off."

After I got both horses ready to go, I helped Scarlett onto Candy Cane and jumped onto Rex. He was one of my favorite horses, and he loved to be ridden any chance he could.

"Ready?" I asked.

"Yep."

We started off at a slow pace. There was no way I was going to risk anything with Scarlett up on that horse. I didn't care that she was an experienced rider, or that Candy was a calm horse. That was my girl and baby on that giant, gentle beast.

Walking along the trail in silence, I closed my eyes and let the peaceful sounds of nature relax me. Rex instantly knew when I was relaxed because he slowed the pace down.

"Trevor? Is it okay if we stop for a bit?"

I brought Rex to a stop and jumped off. Draping the reins over his back, I let him walk around and graze while I helped Scarlett off her horse.

"You okay?"

She nodded. "Just wanted to take a little walk off of the horses, if that's okay."

"Of course, it is. Let me get the reins up on her so she can graze with Rex."

Candy instantly made her way over to Rex. They rubbed their heads and softly spoke to one another.

"Did Candy mate with Rex?" Scarlett asked, watching the two horses interact.

"I'm not sure. She was out in the pasture with Rex and two other studs."

Scarlett smiled and looked up at me. "Oh, yeah, those two are momma and daddy. Look at how he keeps nudging her and how close he is to her. Trevor! That's so sweet!"

I shrugged. "Or he just knows she's pregnant, and he thinks she's horny and he wants a piece."

Her hand punched my stomach, causing me to let out a sharp breath.

Laughing, I grabbed Scarlett's hand, and we slowly walked in the open field.

"What's on your mind, baby?"

She sighed. "Everything."

"Want to talk about it?"

Her gaze dropped to the ground as we walked, and it took her a few moments before she finally looked up.

"I'm scared. I have this feeling and I can't shake it. It's like I'm waiting for the floor to fall out from under me. This all feels too…perfect."

I frowned. "What feels too perfect?"

"This!" she said, stretching out her arms. Then pointing to me, she added. "You. For years I used to dream about that kiss, Trevor. The way you made me feel. When you asked me to the benefit dinner and we slept together, I was even more in love with you. Then all the crap we went through and…well…all of that."

My chest ached knowing I had hurt her so many times.

"Scarlett, I'm not going to pretend I wasn't a dick, because I was. I wasn't sure how to handle the way I felt about you. It scared me. Sometimes it still does, but there is one thing I know for sure. I love you. I've loved you from the first moment I kissed you. You don't think I'm terrified that I'm going to fuck this up and hurt you? Every damn day I wake up I worry I'm going to mess up somehow or someone is going to see you on the street and tell you how she hooked up with me and how I'll never change. That all scares the piss out of me."

I took her hands and smiled. "When it hit me that I might be losing you, I decided then and there that that wasn't going to be an option."

She nodded. "I know, and I feel stupid for being insecure. I don't know if it's just my hormones or what."

"I'm not with you because of the baby. I'm with you because you are the love of my life. Our baby is just a bonus. You are the very reason I take each breath. I know I pushed you to move in with me and work here on the ranch. Call me greedy. I want you with me every single day. I have time to make up for and I don't wanna waste another day."

Tears filled her eyes, causing her to blink rapidly in an attempt to keep them back.

"I used to have this crazy idea that I didn't want to be with one woman. At least, not anytime soon. But when the right one came along—you—it scared the fuck out of me. I tried to stay away so that I didn't hurt you and all I ended up doing was hurting you."

"I should have told you about the baby right away."

"None of that matters. What matters is this very moment. You and me. The baby. I'd give my last breath for the two of you, don't ever forget that."

A tear escaped her eye as she whispered my name. "Trevor."

She took in a deep breath before focusing back on me when she spoke.

"God answered my prayers when he made this baby. I'll never regret that night. I'll never regret anything that brought the two of us together, no matter how winding the road was. We both ended up at the same stop exactly when we needed to be there."

Brushing a stray piece of hair away from her face, I kissed her. Slow at first. Whispering against her lips how much I loved her.

"I love you with every beat of my heart. You're my everything, Scarlett Littlefield."

Her arms wrapped around my neck, and in a breathy voice, she replied, "I want to be Scarlett Parker."

Heat surged through my body as I drew back and gazed into her gorgeous, chestnut brown eyes. The flutter in my chest quickened as I asked, "What did you say?"

"I want to marry you, Trevor."

I was positive my smile couldn't possibly grow any bigger. "You're serious? You'll marry me?"

Nodding, she giggled in delight. "Yes! I want to be your wife when our baby is born. I don't want to wait another second."

"Oh baby, you just made me the happiest man on Earth. I need to let you know…you're gonna have to wait a few seconds, though."

Her brows pulled in some as she stared up at me. "Why?"

"Because I'm about to make love to you."

"Here? Out in the field?"

"Yep, the first tree I get you to, I'm burying myself inside of you."

Scarlett's eyes turned dark with desire. Picking her up, I walked over to a tree, gently setting her down, and made good on my promise.

CHAPTER 27

Trevor

My father and mother sat on the sofa opposite me, staring like I'd just told them I had found the cure to cancer. I got it…at first. They were shocked. Scarlett and I had told them we were taking our time, not rushing into things. From the outside looking in, it probably looked the opposite. She'd moved in with me. Started working for me. And now we were talking marriage.

"Let me understand this, because a few months back, marriage wasn't on the table," Dad reminded us.

"It's always been on the table for me, Dad. I wasn't pushing Scarlett, that's all. I wanted her to be ready, and she's ready. She wants to be married with the Parker name when the baby is born."

My mother smiled as she took my father's hand.

"Are we talking a big wedding?"

"No, small. We'd like to get married here on the ranch. I need to still ask her Daddy for his permission."

"Well, considering you knocked up his daughter…"

My mother hit my father in the stomach, causing him to bend over and let out a breath.

"Damn, woman, I was only being honest. My ribs still hurt from my fall, by the way."

Rolling her eyes, Mom focused back on me. "Trevor, I think it's wonderful you want to get married. I just worry you're doing it for the wrong reason."

I frowned. "The wrong reason?"

"The baby?" she prompted. "I know you love Scarlett, but a year ago, had you been sitting across from us and told us you were getting married, I'd be looking for the cameras and…"

Turning to my father, she asked, "What's that young boy's name who pranks people?"

He glanced up and thought about it. "What is his name? Alan? No, wait…Axel?"

"Axel?" I asked in a stunned voice.

"No, that's not it. It starts with an A, and he's handsome."

"I know!" my father declared, "Justin Timberlake."

"That's not an A, John. That's a J. He was in that show about the three little men or something."

"Alan!"

My mother snapped her fingers. "That's it! No, wait."

"Ashton Kutcher, y'all. His name is *Ashton* Kutcher!"

They both pointed to me. "That's him!"

Jesus, this was more painful than I'd anticipated.

"This isn't a game, and I know before Scarlett I was…different."

Mom raised her brow, smirking. "Different?"

With a chuckle, my father added, "If my memory serves me, the prayer chain called it something else, son."

I groaned and dropped back in my chair. "Why can't y'all be happy for us? Can't you see how much I love her and want to be with her? Having her here on the ranch has made me the happiest I've ever been."

"Sweetheart, I do see it. Honestly, I do. I know you fell in love with Scarlett before you found out about the baby, but don't deny that you were confused. Your brothers told us you pushed her away for the longest time."

I made a mental note to get back at each of my brothers for talking to my parents about Scarlett and me.

"I'm not denying any of that. I was messed up, but when it hit me, it hit me hard. I won't lose her. I'll fight with everything I have for her whether we're married or not, and no one is going to stop me from loving her."

My father walked over to me. I stood and waited for what he was about to say. I was stunned when he pulled me to him and hugged me. After a hard slap on the back, he said, "That's the man I raised. That's the man you've always been and, the one I always will be proud of. You know your mother and I support y'all in whatever you decide to do."

"Of course, we will, Trevor. If it's a marriage you want, by golly, we'll give y'all a wedding you'll never forget."

Dad laughed as he added, "And we'll even throw in Patches for free entertainment."

"Yeah, no," I said, taking a step back. "No Patches. No goats… period."

"Were you not there when Steed got married? Or Mitchell?" Mom asked.

With a scoff, I replied, "Yes, Mama, I was there. I was there when that damn goat crashed Waylynn's welcome home party, Christmas, countless dinners, not to mention the number of times I've walked into my office and he's on my desk eating papers."

Covering her mouth, my mother tried not to laugh, but failed.

"He'd make a lovely attendant in the wedding, Trev," Dad said, slapping me on the side of the arm and heading out of the family room.

"Wh-what?!" I shrieked like a damn teenage girl. "Mom! Mom, no. No Patches."

My mother placed her hand on the side of my face and winked. "Baby boy, the only way that goat isn't going to be a part of this wedding is if you go off to another state. Heck, maybe even another country, like your brother Cord is doing."

Scarlett walked into the family room, a smile on her face. "What's John laughing so hard about?"

That was when Mom lost it laughing.

With a chuckle, Scarlett looked from Mom to me and then back to Mom. "What's so funny, Melanie?"

She laughed even harder while holding her side and heading out of the room.

Holy shit. When had my parents turned so evil? So...cruel?

Scarlett giggled before turning to me. "What's so funny?"

"Listen, baby, how serious are you about getting married here on the ranch?"

"Serious. I thought we agreed on the ranch. Have you talked to my daddy yet? Is he pushing for somewhere else?"

I shook my head. "No, I'm afraid we've got a bigger issue than your father."

Her brows pulled in tight. "Who?"

"More like what."

"Okay, what?"

"One word. *Patches*."

Scarlett had been living on the ranch long enough to know about Patches' reputation for being a troublemaker. And he was Chloe's best friend.

Covering her mouth, she gasped. "Oh no!"

"Oh. Yes."

I knocked on Steed's office door and smiled when he looked up.

"Hey, what's going on?"

With a half-hearted shrug, I walked into his office. "Not much. What are you doing?"

"Going over the next quarter's budget. Fun times. What's wrong? You look like you have something on your mind."

Taking a seat in the chair, I decided to cut to the chase.

"Scarlett and I are getting married."

A wide smile spread over his face as he stood and made his way around his desk for a quick hug.

"That's amazing, dude. Congratulations. Can't say I'm not surprised, but I'm glad y'all are going for it. Before the baby is due?"

I nodded as I sat back down, and he returned to his desk.

"Yeah, we're thinking Valentine's Day. We'd like to do it before Harley has the twins."

"Valentine's Day? That's right around the corner. Y'all sure you have time to plan a wedding that quick? That won't be too stressful for Scarlett?"

"Scarlett and I want a simple wedding. Family and close friends only, so it won't be hard to plan. Mom, Waylynn, and Joyce have all agreed to help Scarlett with the planning. Plus, we're having it here on the ranch so that makes it simple."

Steed's smile dropped, and he leaned forward. Worry etched across his face instantly. "Um, here? On the ranch?"

"Yeah, that's why I was stopping in to talk to you."

Leaning back in his chair, Steed let out a breath. "Patches."

"You hit the nail on the head, dude. Listen, I love Chloe with all my heart, and the whole Patches thing is funny...most of the time. Dude, Mom said the damn goat was going to be *in* the wedding."

He rubbed along his jaw, like he was trying to figure out how to break the bad news to me. "Mom has pretty much accepted the fact that the damn goat is a member of the family."

"Isn't he?"

"Okay, so you're here to talk about how we can keep Patches out of the wedding?"

I nodded. "Yes."

"Well, we could keep the wedding a secret from Chloe. Spring it on her last minute, throw her off-guard so she doesn't have time to make any plans."

The tension in my shoulders lifted. This was a halfway decent plan. "That might work. Keep the youngest Parker woman out of the loop. I like this."

"But Waylynn is still somewhat bitter about all the occasions Patches has crashed the party. She may spill the beans to Chloe just to get back at you."

"For what?" I exclaimed. "I haven't done anything to her."

Steed lifted a brow. "It's Waylynn. She doesn't need a reason."

I nodded. "That's true."

"For all we know, she's already planning the outfit Patches will wear to the wedding."

We both shuddered. "God, I hope not."

"Maybe I have Mom and Joyce give Waylynn the wrong day for the wedding."

"That might work," Steed agreed.

A throat cleared behind us and I turned to see Paxton standing in the doorway, her arms crossed over her chest.

"Hey, baby! What brings you here? Where's Gage?"

"With your mom. What in the world are the two of you doing?"

Steed made his way to his wife and kissed her on the lips. "Trevor and Scarlett are getting married here at the ranch on Valentine's Day."

Paxton smiled and hugged me. "Trevor! This is so amazing! I'm so happy for y'all!"

"Thanks, Paxton. I know it's fast, but Scarlett wants to get married, and we figured Valentine's Day would be nice. We thought about March, but with Harley due, we wanted her to be able to be there."

"Harley was put on bedrest today. Tripp said she hasn't stopped bitching in Spanish since they left the doctor's office."

"What?" I said at the same time as Steed.

"I mean, she might be able to come to the wedding if she asked the doctor. They just don't want her going into labor too soon."

"Are the babies okay?"

"Yep! They're doing great, but Harley's little body is taking a beating with those two. It's just a precautionary thing."

I sighed. "Damn. Then maybe we should move it to March?"

"Why don't you talk to Tripp and Harley? It might be sort of nice to do it during the spring fling, when y'all first officially dated. Then you can dance with her as your wife."

I smiled. "You're saying get married right before the spring fling?"

Steed clapped his hands together. "Or what about during it? Y'all could get married right at the beginning of the benefit dinner. You know Mom will have Patches locked away for that. There is no chance of Chloe sweet talking her out of it."

A rush of renewed energy ripped through my body, and I grabbed my brother. "You're a fucking genius! Not only will Mom love this idea, but it will take care of Patches without having to hurt Chloe's feelings. This is brilliant!"

"You are both terrible. Poor Patches. He only wants to be a part of the family."

"He can be. He just can't be a part of my wedding."

Paxton grinned. "Oh, have you not met Patches? Where there is a will, there is a way."

"Not on my wedding day."

"Hey! We're all making rhymes, how divine!"

Paxton faced Steed. "I didn't rhyme, babe."

He frowned and thought about it for a moment before whispering, "Damn."

Shaking my head, I focused back on Paxton. "Mom will not allow that goat to ruin her one and only time of year where she gets to pull out all the bells and whistles. Patches isn't going to be an issue. Now, I'm going to head off and talk to Scarlett about pushing the wedding to March!"

As I walked out of Steed's office, I heard Paxton say, "How foolish he is to believe that our little Chloe won't succeed."

Waving, I called out, "Good one, Paxton."

CHAPTER 28

Scarlett

Hands wrapped around my body and landed on my swollen belly. I instantly warmed everywhere, especially between my legs.

Hot breath hit below my ear. "Happy Valentine's Day, baby."

Dropping my head against Trevor's chest, I smiled and replied, "Happy Valentine's Day."

"I have something for you," he whispered, rubbing his hands over my stomach.

"Oh, yeah? What is it?"

"You'll have to…"

The baby kicked, and I smiled. Trevor stopped talking the moment Gummy Bear kicked.

I lifted my head and glanced back at him.

"Did you feel the baby move?" I asked, turning to face him. Trevor hadn't felt the baby move yet, and it was killing him—especially with me being twenty-six weeks. He kept telling me that in all the books, they say he should have felt the baby by now. He placed his hands back on my stomach and stared at it. My heart raced when I saw the tears forming in his eyes.

Another kick, this one harder. I knew for sure he felt that one.

"I felt it," he softly said. Reaching up, I gently brushed away the tear rolling down his face. "Holy shit. I felt Gummy Bear. I've never felt anything so beautiful in my life."

Now it was my turn for tears to fall.

"Make Gummy Bear do it again!" Trevor demanded, a smile on his face as he looked into my eyes.

"I wish I could, but this baby is a Parker and stubborn as hell. He won't perform on demand."

Trevor laughed and dropped down to his knees. "Hey there, baby. We still don't know if you're a boy or a girl, and Mommy wants to be surprised, but Daddy wants to know. If you're a boy, kick twice. A girl, kick once."

Laughing, I shook my head as I stared down at him. "It doesn't work that way, Trevor."

"Why not? You're twenty-six weeks and Dr. Buten said the baby responds to voices now."

A very strong kick happened right were Trevor's hand was. His mouth dropped open, and he fell back onto his ass.

"That was a coincidence!" I stated, my heart beating a bit faster.

Trevor pointed to my stomach. "Holy fuck, our kid is a genius!" He dropped his head into his hands and groaned. "And a girl. Oh my God, I'm having a girl. This is God's way of getting me back."

I stared down at him.

"We don't know what we're having and as much as I would love to believe the baby understood you, I don't think that's the case, Trevor. Now get up and get ready for our date!"

He sat there, his arms draped over his knees. "Think about it. All of my brothers so far had girls first. Steed had Chloe. Mitchell had Merit. Tripp is having...well...we don't know what they're having, but I bet it's both girls."

"Amelia's having a boy," I stated.

Trevor looked up at me. "Don't you see? That's Wade's sperm. He isn't a Parker! My parents had a girl first. That's it, Scarlett. We're having a girl."

Excitement bubbled up inside of me, but I pushed it away. I would be happy with a boy or a girl. As long as they were healthy and happy. That was all I cared about.

"We don't know that."

"She kicked my hand! She. Kicked. My. Hand. Only a woman could put me in my damn place. I'll be having tea parties all the damn time now."

With a roll of my eyes, I headed to our bedroom. "I'm going to get dressed, Mr. Parker. If you still intend on taking me out, I suggest you do the same."

As I walked into the bedroom, I pulled my shirt over my head and folded it neatly. I removed my pants next. The white pair with royal blue flowers was my favorite. The matching royal blue shirt was the other half of my favorite outfit. I wore it all the time and Paxton had even asked me if I had bought more than one pair. I'd laughed like she was insane. I would never admit I had four pair of the same pants and shirts hanging in my closet. I couldn't help it! The outfit was comfy.

Warm hands landed on my hips, causing me to jump. Trevor's lips on my neck instantly made my panties damp.

"Do we have time?" he asked while placing light kisses over my neck.

"Yes," I breathed out, even though we would run the risk of being late for our reservations. There was a new Italian restaurant in town that I had been wanting to eat at. I was craving lasagna so bad.

The moment Trevor's hard cock touched me, I forgot about food. I forgot about everything but his hands on my body.

"I want you from behind, is that okay?" he asked softly in my ear.

"I don't care how you take me. I just need to come."

He chuckled as he slid my panties off and motioned for me to get on the bed.

Crawling onto it, I lifted my ass and waited for him to fill me. It seemed like I was horny all the time. Maybe I just couldn't get enough of Trevor. His touch. His warmth filling me completely. Making me whole. Sex with Trevor Parker was never dull. The scruff of his always present five-o'clock shadow was a turn on by itself. Everything about my future husband made me horny.

Trevor's hands roamed over my ass, then around to my stomach where he rubbed gently while placing kisses on my back.

"I fucking love seeing you naked. You've never looked as beautiful as you do with our baby growing inside of you."

Moaning at his words and needing him to touch me, I pushed back against him. He let out a chuckle.

"Horny?"

"Yes! Trevor, please, I'm so ready for you."

He didn't make me wait long before he slid inside, inch by delicious inch. It felt like heaven every time he entered me.

"Yes," I gasped when he filled me completely.

"Jesus, baby. You feel so good."

Reaching his hand around, Trevor played with my clit while moving in and out at a slow pace. I knew it wasn't going to take long. I could feel the build-up starting in my toes.

"Trevor!" I cried out, needing him to give me more. "Please!"

"You're so beautiful like this Scarlett, God, it turns me on so fucking much."

He pressed on my clit harder while picking up the speed. It wasn't going to be long now. Any second and I was going to come.

"Yes! Yes! I'm so close!"

Trevor rubbed my stomach. Then he went completely still.

"What…what happened? I was about to come! Why did you stop?" I panted out.

"She moved. I felt her move. Oh my God, I'm having sex and my daughter just moved. Our daughter knows we are having sex right now. Maybe she felt my cock! Oh fuck!"

Trevor pulled out and backed away, staring down at me in horror.

"What are you talking about? She didn't feel you! Now get back inside of me and finish what you started, damn it!"

Looking like he had just seen a ghost, Trevor shook his head. "I can't. I was fucking you and our baby moved. This is exactly what I NEVER want our daughter to do...what kind of a role model am I being to her?"

"So what, Trevor? The baby is happy because Mommy is happy. Now finish making Mommy happy!"

Trevor quickly walked out of the bedroom, his hands running frantically through his hair.

"Where are you going?" I called out.

"I have to make an emergency phone call!"

"To who!" I asked, dropping my body onto the bed in frustration.

Trevor walked back into the bedroom with his phone in his hand.

"Emergency meeting. Now. I'm getting everyone else on the phone."

I lifted my head and stared at him. "Who...are you...talking to?"

"Steed."

My eyes widened.

"And Mitchell. Emergency meeting. I need to get Tripp on."

"Oh my God! What?" I cried out, sitting up in bed. "You're calling your brothers now?"

"Yes, that was Scarlett," he said into the phone. "She's a bit upset with me. I stopped sex right before she came."

Horror washed over my face as I laid down and groaned into a pillow. There was no way I was going out to dinner now. No way. I had never been so embarrassed in my entire life.

"Okay, everyone is on. Yes, Steed, I know she's going to be pissed, she already is. Here is the problem. We were having sex, and I felt the baby move when I placed my hand on her stomach."

I cried out, "Why, God? Why!"

"Yes. It was really cool finally feeling her, I'll have to tell y'all all about how smart she is. But the thing is, I was having sex and she kicked and I have to know, can she feel me?"

Tossing the pillow at Trevor, I sat up. "Hang up that phone right now!" I yelled.

"No, Tripp. She's just a little hangry."

My mouth dropped open. "Hangry? I'm hangry? No! I'm horny!"

Trevor covered the phone. "Scarlett! I'm talking to my brothers, they don't need to hear you talk like that!"

I was pretty sure the look on my face was pure dumbfoundedness.

Is that even a word? It is now.

"Are you sure, Steed? Tripp, your take on this? You're sure? Mitchell? Okay, so it's all safe? The baby can't feel me jabbing her head or anything?"

"Okay, that's it," I said as I climbed off the bed and headed into the bathroom. By the time I'd peed and pulled on a T-shirt that was on Trevor's sink, the mood was completely gone.

When I stepped into the bedroom, Trevor was lying on the bed, a sexy smile on his handsome face. It took everything I had to walk past him.

"The baby can't feel me. Mitchell said Merit moved all the time during sex. We're good to go."

I lifted a brow. "Good to go?"

He nodded. "Yep. You want on top so you can come faster?"

Placing my hands on my hips, I glared at him. "I don't want your penis anywhere near me. Not against me, not in me, not within five feet of me."

Trevor sat up. "Why? What did I do?"

"What did you do? *What* did you *do*?"

Throwing my hands in the air, I screamed in frustration and stormed out of the bedroom and directly to the kitchen. I needed ice cream, maybe another Snickers bar.

"Scarlett! Wait!"

Trevor was behind me in an instant, bringing me to a stop right before I reached the kitchen. That was twice this evening he'd blocked me from something I really needed and wanted.

"Okay, so maybe I shouldn't have called my brothers, but that freaked me out."

I closed my eyes and slowly shook my head. "You should have talked to me, Trevor. I've read every pregnancy book I could get my hands on. I've read about sex during pregnancy. We can have sex, and it's not going to hurt the baby. She may move around and that's okay. I get it that you had a moment of panic, but your first reaction was to call all your brothers at once? That was a bit extreme, don't you think?"

He nodded. "It was, but this is new territory for me. I'm sorry."

My shoulders sagged, and I leaned into him.

With a sigh, I said, "I'm embarrassed, Trevor. I don't even want to go out to eat anymore."

"What? No! Let me make it up to you. Come on, let me give you what you want."

It was hard to resist this man. It always had been, and I knew it always would be. Between the blue eyes and that body of his, I was screwed.

"Fine, but I want two orgasms!"

He laughed and picked me up. Carrying me back to our bedroom, he made sweet love to me and not only gave me two orgasms but added in a bonus round. By the time we left for dinner, very late, I was in an orgasmic-induced bliss. I quickly forgot all about Trevor's freak-out.

CHAPTER 29

Scarlett

Trevor and I walked up to the entrance of La Madia. My stomach growled, and the baby gave a good little kick. Gummy Bear was getting stronger every day and that was evident in the frequency and strength of the kicks.

"You hungry, Scarlett?" Trevor asked, his hand on my lower back, leading me through the door to the hostess.

"I'm starving."

"Is that you or the baby's stomach?"

"Gummy Bear really wants some lasagna."

Trevor chuckled, and the hostess smiled as she glanced between the two of us.

"Welcome to La Madia! The newest restaurant here in our little growing town of Oak Springs!"

Wow, this girl puts the P in peppy.

"Hi there!" I said, in an equally excited voice.

"Reservations, I hope? It's a busy day today."

Trevor replied, "Parker for two."

"Okay, um, I have a few reservations for Parker for two." She blushed.

"Trevor, and do me a favor, put us the farthest away from the other Parkers."

She frowned. "Bad blood?"

I attempted to hide my laugh.

"Well, since Cord got out of jail, he hasn't been the same. A little moody, if you know what I mean."

My eyes widened just like the hostesses.

"Then you've got Mitchell, he's the one you have to look out for. He was a cop. He says he quit, but we think he's now doing undercover Secret Service, involved in the types of things that no one wants to talk about."

"I know him! He used to come talk to our high school!"

Trevor shrugged. "Don't let the charm fool you."

She grabbed two menus while motioning for us to follow her. When she turned her back, I hit Trevor in the stomach.

"What are you doing?" I whispered.

"Having fun. It's what we do."

Sighing, I shook my head. "I'll never understand this family."

We were tucked back into a corner that was pretty much secluded from the rest of the restaurant.

"Here is the table you requested, Mr. Parker."

I rolled my eyes. This girl had actually listened to his plea to be far away from everyone.

"Thank you, and one last thing, if Steed Parker shows up, I'll give you a hundred bucks to tell him and his wife that the special for tonight is goat."

"Goat?" the girl asked.

"Yep. A hundred bucks."

She grinned. "I'll do it!"

Sitting, I whispered, "Good Lord."

Trevor laughed and leaned down to kiss me on the cheek before taking his seat. As soon as we were seated, our waitress took our order and left us with two glasses of ice water and fresh bread with dipping sauce.

"Bread!" I gasped, taking a piece and nearly pushing the whole thing into my mouth.

Trevor snarled. "Jesus, you really were hangry."

"I really was. Plus, you worked up even more of my appetite."

He grinned and gave me a sexy wink that made my insides tremble.

Trevor ended up getting the lasagna along with me. The waitress brought back our side salads and asked Trevor if he would like any wine.

"No, thanks. Not drinking tonight."

She smiled. It was almost like something passed between the two of them, something I wasn't privy to, and I couldn't help but wonder if Trevor knew this girl.

"Do you know her?" I asked, deciding to just ask instead of driving myself mad wondering.

"Nope. Never seen her before in my life. She does, however, resemble a guy I went to high school with. Could be his little sister."

I nodded and glanced over my shoulder but didn't see her.

Oh, for the love of all things good, Scarlett. Stop this insecurity. Where in the world is it coming from?

I ate my side salad in record time, feeling a bit guilty that I was practically inhaling my food.

The main course came out, and Trevor and I were lost in conversation together. We talked about the ranch, the baby's room that Trevor was currently painting, the crib that Jonathon was making as a wedding gift, and the wedding itself.

"Everything seems to be pretty much taken care of. Do you need help with anything?"

Shaking my head, I replied, "What I haven't taken care of already, Mom, Melanie, or Waylynn have on their list. It sort of makes it easy having the wedding right before the dinner. Everything will look beautiful just from that. The lights and all the flowers your mom is bringing in."

"Yeah, she always makes it look beautiful. You're sure you don't mind sharing all of this with the dinner?"

"Not at all. I'm glad we're doing the actual wedding ceremony in the pasture, though, just you and me. I mean, I guess we're really having two weddings, but the first one feels so intimate, like it's just for the three of us."

Trevor reached for my left hand and brought it to his lips.

"Speaking of the wedding ceremony. I think it's about time I put a ring on that finger, don't you?"

My heart felt like it dropped right out of my chest. The sounds of the restaurant vanished and the only thing I could hear was my heartbeat, racing like a hummingbird.

"What?" I managed to get out. Trevor and I had talked about rings, but we had yet to go and pick any out, not because we weren't ready; we just hadn't made our way into San Antonio yet to look.

Reaching into his jacket pocket, Trevor pulled out a small box.

My eyes landed on it, and I couldn't help but notice how old it looked.

"This ring belonged to Aunt Vi. It was my grandmother's ring and when I found out you were pregnant, Aunt Vi was one of the first people to be there for me. She showed me the ring and said it was mine if I wanted it. A few months back I asked her if I could give it to you."

Trevor opened the box, and I inhaled a sharp breath at the sight before me. A beautiful princess cut diamond encased with smaller diamonds sat on the most exquisite band I'd ever seen. The band almost looked like a feather with the intricate details on it. It wasn't a normal, smooth band, it had so much character.

"This is Aunt Vi's?" I asked, staring at it.

"This is yours, Scarlett."

He reached for my hand and slipped the ring on. It was a perfect fit and I didn't even bother holding back my tears.

"Scarlett Littlefield, will you do me the honor of becoming my wife?"

Covering my mouth with my right hand, I nodded. "Yes! Nothing would make me happier!"

Tears streamed from my eyes and I silently thanked the hostess for sitting us in this corner.

Wiping my tears, I let out a laugh. "Good thing we're in a corner!"

"I came in the other day and looked around the restaurant. I asked for them to seat us here."

My mouth dropped open. "I thought she did that because you said to seat us away from everyone."

Trevor laughed. "No, I did it to divert you, but I'm glad you didn't catch on."

Opening my mouth, I was interrupted by a voice. A female voice.

"Trevor Parker. I see the rumors are true."

I watched as Trevor's stunning blue eyes turned cold. Glancing up, he shot the woman a dirty look.

"I guess you don't respect folks' privacy?"

A part of me didn't want to look to see who was standing there. I was positive I knew her. Even though I didn't go to school here in Oak Springs, I grew up with most of the people who were still living in town.

"Can't an old *friend* stop over to congratulate you both?"

A sickness rolled through my stomach.

Lacy Miller. The homecoming queen, the prom queen, the captain of the cheerleading team, and the girl I'd overheard more than once when I was home, bragging about sleeping with Trevor.

My eyes lifted. She wasn't looking at me. She was smiling at Trevor. The look on her face clearly said she wanted him.

Somehow, I dug deep inside and pushed all the doubts and insecurities to the side and found strength. Honestly, my strength was sitting across from me, and he was still holding the hand he had just put an engagement ring on.

Trevor loved me. He'd only ever loved me and he had proved it time and time again. I could freak out, withdraw into myself and pout, but what good would it do? I was the woman this man loved and wanted to spend the rest of his life with. I was the woman carrying his baby.

Not Lacy Miller.

She could smile and bat her eyes at him all she wanted. I saw the way he looked at her. It was nothing like how he had been looking at me moments ago.

Clearing my throat, I said, "Lacy Miller, right? It was sure nice of you to come over and interrupt our Valentine's dinner to give us both your well wishes."

Lacy let her smile drop for a quick moment before plastering a fake one on. "I'm sorry. I don't remember you. Did you go to school here in Oak Springs?"

I laughed. "Well, I guess it's not unusual to forget your best friend from fifth grade, is it? Scarlett Littlefield. I went to a private high school in Boston."

She narrowed her eyes at me. "That's right. You're the one who set the trash can on fire outside the courthouse."

I pointed to her. "That's me! You probably didn't recognize me when you came in to file for a divorce from your husband, Drake. I was the one who filed the paperwork for you."

Her face turned white, then went red.

"I didn't realize that was you."

"Lacy, is there something you needed, other than to congratulate us?" Trevor asked, clearly frustrated.

She fiddled with a strand of hair as she focused on Trevor. Then she laughed. "I never pictured you as the settling down type of guy. You were always the settle-between-their-legs sort of fellow."

My eyes widened in shock.

"I was waiting on the one woman who made me want to settle down. Whores are a dime a dozen, but a woman who captures your heart? Once in a lifetime."

Lacy's expression turned cold as stone. Then a sweet-as-pie smile moved across her face and she turned to face me directly.

"If you want to know the type of man you're marrying and having a baby with, ask him about the time he fucked me and my best friend Kim. At the same time."

An audible gasp slipped from between my lips as I watched Lacy spin around on her expensive high heels and saunter off. I could barely hear Trevor cursing; I was too focused on the woman. Knowing Trevor had been with her. Obviously more than once. And a threesome? Oh my God. That was more information than I needed. Or wanted. My stomach rolled and the lasagna I just ate was threatening to come back up.

"Scarlett. Scarlett!"

Trevor's voice snapped me out of my daze, drawing my gaze back to him.

"Let's go."

I nodded as numbness washed across my body. As much as I was trying to ignore the woman's hateful words, they kept replaying in my mind. Jealousy ran rampant throughout my body and there was nothing I could do to stop it, no matter how hard I tried.

Trevor tossed a few hundred dollar bills onto the table, took my hand and led me out of the restaurant. I forced myself to smile as I looked straight ahead, in case Lacy was watching us leave. I remained focused on the door that led me to fresh air. It was getting harder to breathe and it felt like someone was sitting on my chest.

"What's happening to me?" I whispered, as Trevor glanced back and gave me a concerned look. Stopping, he cupped my face in his hands.

"What's wrong?" he asked, worry etched in his beautiful blue eyes.

"Need fresh air. Now."

It was all I could get out, and I felt bad because I saw not only worry in his eyes, but fear, too.

The moment the fresh air hit my face, I took a deep breath. Trevor walked us over to a bench, where I sat and closed my eyes. I focused solely on breathing, tuning everything else out except for my breath, heartbeat, and the feel of our baby moving inside of me.

"Scarlett? You're scaring me."

Trevor's voice pulled me out of the quiet moment. Opening my eyes, I faced him with a forced smile.

"I'm okay. I think I was having an anxiety attack. At least, that's what I always pictured an anxiety attack would be like."

"Look at me," he demanded.

"I am looking at you."

He took my hands and squeezed them. "I want you to look at me, not through me. Look at me."

Our eyes met. A calm sensation drifted over me like a cooling mist during a hot summer day. Other people walked by us. They stared like they were dying to know what in the world was going on.

"It's okay, Trevor. I'm okay, I promise you. I just wasn't ready for a crazy ex of yours to cause a scene in a restaurant."

"She was not an ex. I've never dated anyone, Scarlett. Only you. She was a mistake, like all the others, but I can't change my past. I'm sorry I couldn't protect you from her."

I lifted my hand and placed it on the side of his cheek. "So much has happened to us this last year."

He scoffed. "That's the truth."

"I'm not going to lie and say I can bury that jealous side of me that hates knowing you were with other women. No woman would ever be able to do that. It's human nature. I can promise you, though, that nothing will ever change my love for you. Nothing."

Closing his eyes, Trevor pressed his mouth in a tight line.

"We just got engaged. The last thing I want to talk about is what just happened in there with that vile woman."

Sitting up, I placed his hand on the side of my stomach. The baby was going crazy, and I was sure Trevor would feel at least one kick, maybe two.

His brows lifted, then he smiled. "What is she doing?"

"Gummy Bear is pissed we walked out before dessert."

This time Trevor tossed his head back and let out a hearty laugh. One that rumbled right through my body and straight to that lower part of my anatomy that ached for him.

When he stopped laughing, he stood and took my hand. "Come on. let's get my girls some dessert."

"You're hell bent that this baby is a girl, aren't you?"

"Yep. And I've accepted the fact that I'll have to be on my toes twenty-four-seven around you two."

With a shake of my head, I let Trevor lead us to the truck. With my silly moment of jealousy past, I let myself relax into the knowledge that life had never been so beautiful. The small little kick to the left of my stomach told me the baby agreed.

CHAPTER 30

Trevor

Lifting my cowboy hat off my head, I wiped at the sweat. It was the hottest day on record for March and the damn month had just begun.

Mitchell let out a groan and leaned against the truck. "Shit, I don't remember it ever being this hot in March. Mother Nature is being a bitch."

I chuckled. "Yeah, she is. At least a small front is moving through next week for the spring fling. It won't be so terrible."

"How is Harley liking the vet who came in to work while she's out?" Wade asked Tripp, who was currently throwing bales of hay into the back of the ranch truck.

He stopped, took off his hat, and poured his bottle of water over his head. Standing back up, he answered Wade.

"She likes her. Plus, with Scarlett helping out, things have been running pretty smooth. Of course, Harley doesn't want to hear that. She broke down crying yesterday and said she was sick of being at home and felt like a beached whale. I feel really bad for her."

"I'm honestly surprised she's made it this close to her due date!" Mitchell said.

"Yeah, so are we. Dr. Buten is saying we need to induce, and Harley is perfectly fine with that. With her due date in less than three weeks, she is more than ready to get those babies out."

We all laughed.

I took a drink of water and looked at Tripp. "What do you think you're having?"

He shrugged. "I don't care, as long as they are both healthy, I'm good with anything."

"Girls. I bet you're having girls," I declared.

A look of terror washed over his face. Steed slapped him on the back. "Girls wouldn't be so bad."

"One, maybe, but two?" Tripp said, a shake in his usually calm voice.

Cord rode up on Bullet and jumped off the damn horse before it even came to a stop.

"It's about time you showed up to do some work, asshole!" Mitchell called out.

Cord headed straight to Tripp.

"You need to get home. Harley's been trying to call you, and your phone is going straight to voicemail."

Tripp pulled out his phone and cussed. "Fuck, it's dead."

He looked at Cord, fear etched all over his face. Mitchell and I pushed off from the truck and headed over to Cord.

"What's going on? Is Harley okay?" Tripp asked.

Cord smiled. "Dude, her water broke, and her folks are taking her to the hospital."

We stood there stunned. Not one of us saying anything.

"I called Mom and Dad back up at the house. They're making all the calls to family, but you need to get your ass going!"

Tripp smiled and then he started jumping like a five-year-old. I'd never seen my brother act that way before. He leaned over, his hands on his knees, taking one deep breath after another.

Steed walked up to him. "Tripp? You okay?"

He shook his head. "Holy shit. Oh my God. I'm about to be a father. To twins." Glancing up at all of us, he shouted. "Twins! What the fuck am I supposed to do with that?"

Wade leaned over and whispered, "Talk about a delayed reaction!"

I chuckled.

Steed's face stayed neutral, and I had to hand it to him because I was fighting to hold back a laugh and to crack a joke, and I knew everyone else was as well. "You're going to get into the truck and let us take you to the hospital. This shit can wait."

Jonathon pulled up in his truck and honked the horn. Waylynn rolled the window down and yelled out. "Woohoo! The babies are on their way! Come on, Tripp!"

Steed helped Tripp to Jonathon's truck. Waylynn jumped out, a look of concern on her face.

"What's wrong, Tripp?" she asked, motioning for him to get into the front seat. I glanced back and saw Liberty in her car seat. A wide smile formed on her face, and she waved at me. I opened the back door and leaned in.

"Hey there, beautiful. You have a kiss for Uncle Trevor?"

She giggled and puckered her lips. I gave her a quick kiss while Steed and Waylynn got Tripp into the front seat. Jonathon shot me a questioning look and I laughed. "I think it all just became real to him."

"*Ahh*, I see!" Jonathon said, grinning. "Poor bastard."

"I can hear you, assholes!" Tripp said.

"Tripp Parker, do not swear! Liberty is in the truck!" Waylynn stated with a slap to Tripp's head. Liberty giggled along with me and Jonathon.

"Bye, sweet girl," I said, giving my niece a peck on the cheek and moving so Waylynn could get in.

"Y'all be careful driving," Steed said as he shut the front door and I shut the back.

"We'll be right behind y'all," Mitchell called out from behind.

I watched as Tripp dropped his head back against the seat while Jonathon drove off.

"Poor bastard. He's in for a ride," Steed said with an evil laugh.

Blowing out a breath, I turned to the rest of the gang. "Let's finish this up quickly and then head on back up to the house."

Wade, Mitchell, and Steed looked at me like I was insane.

"You want us to finish this while our brother heads to the hospital to have babies?" Mitchell asked.

I shrugged. "What? It will take us ten minutes tops and it's done."

Bobby McDaniel pulled up in one of the ranch trucks and jumped out, making his way toward us.

"Let the FNG do it," Wade said.

Bobby was a seventeen-year-old who had just started working for us on weekends.

"He can't load all this hay by himself," I said.

With a quick look around, Bobby's brows pinched together. "What does FNG stand for?"

Wade chuckled and hit Bobby on the back. "Fucking New Guy, now come on and help us so we can get this finished."

The way Bobby stood straighter and smiled made me chuckle. He seemed to like his new title.

Mitchell and Steed mumbled under their breath, but I ignored them. It would take us less than ten minutes to finish loading up this hay and then it would be done.

When the last hay bale was tossed onto the trailer, Steed wiped his forehead.

"There, finished. Now let's head back to the house. I want to pick up Paxton before heading to the hospital."

Mitchell walked past Steed, sniffed him and said, "Dude, take a shower. You fucking stink."

Pushing Mitchell, Steed replied, "So do you, asshole."

Mitchell pushed Steed again, and it quickly became a brawling match with the two of them rolling around on the ground.

Wade shook his head and walked around them while Cord and I broke up the fight.

As Wade walked past, he said, "I'll never understand this family. Ever."

Six hours later, the entire Parker family was sitting in the waiting room of the hospital. Scarlett had her head on my arm, sleeping peacefully. Paxton, Cord, Maebh, and Waylynn had gathered up the kids and taken them outside to the courtyard to play for a bit.

My eyes wandered over to Amelia. She sat with her hands resting on her belly as she stared at me.

"Why are you staring at me, Amelia?"

She smiled. "You look happy."

I gave her a grin. "So do you."

"I am! But I really wish y'all would just find out what you're having. It's killing me not to know!"

With a roll of my eyes, I glanced down to the beautiful woman next to me. Her brown hair was pulled up into a ponytail. Her cheeks were a beautiful pink, but not from make-up, it was just her natural glow. She'd always had it, but ever since she'd gotten pregnant, it seemed brighter. I couldn't resist the urge to kiss her, so I did. I placed a soft kiss on her forehead and looked back at Amelia.

"She won't budge. Says she wants to be surprised."

Amelia let out a huff. "Just like Harley."

Mom stood and stretched. "Leave the poor girl alone. If she wants to be surprised, let her be."

Turning her attention to Amelia and Wade, my mother tilted her head and asked, "Have y'all picked out a name?"

I watched as Amelia turned to Wade. The way he smiled at my sister warmed my heart. You could see the love between them as clear as day.

Not taking her eyes off Wade, Amelia replied, "We thought John Michael. John for daddy, and Michael for Wade's daddy."

An ache filled my chest as I watched my best friend fight to hold back his emotions. I hated that his entire family was gone. Taken in a car accident because some asshole kid was texting and driving. I knew his two little sisters, Grace and Anna, would have loved Amelia. And his parents would have fallen in love with her the moment they met her.

My mother covered her mouth to hold back her own emotions as my father walked toward Amelia and Wade. They both stood, and my father pulled Amelia into his arms, then Wade.

"I'd be honored to share your daddy's name."

I looked away, the raw emotion causing an ache in the back of my throat as I fought to keep it together. Scarlett sat up, yawned, and saw the display in front of her.

"What's going on?"

Attempting to speak, my voice cracked. Clearing it, I answered her. "Amelia just told my folks they're naming the baby after dad and Wade's dad. John Michael."

Scarlett pulled in a soft breath. She turned to me. "How sweet is that! Oh my, that makes me want to cry."

I nodded.

We watched the scene play out as everyone settled back in their seats. When I looked at Scarlett, she was chewing on her lip, lost in thought.

"What are you thinking about, baby?"

Her eyes were focused on Amelia and Corina. They were both talking about some knitting class that Corina wanted all the girls to take.

"Our baby. I think we should find out the sex."

I nearly jumped out of my seat I was so happy. "Yes! I have been waiting for you to say that!"

"Did I hear you want to find out the sex of the baby?" my mother asked, a hopeful look in her eyes.

Scarlett nodded. "I think so!"

"Finally!" Amelia exclaimed, rushing over. She pulled Scarlett out of the chair and dragged her over to where she and Corina had been talking. I glanced over to Wade and we both smiled.

A weird feeling came over me. Happiness was spilling from everywhere. Now I knew how Scarlett had felt when she said she was waiting for the floor to drop out from underneath her.

I closed my eyes and said a quick prayer that everything was okay with Harley and the twins.

A voice cleared, drawing all of our attention to Dr. Buten and Tripp. They both wore wide smiles, which instantly put my fears at bay.

Dr. Buten spoke first. Gus and Maddie, Harley's parents, and Mom and Dad, all stood the moment they saw Tripp. The four of them looked nervous as they waited to hear how Harley and the babies were.

"Harley and both babies are doing amazing. Harley did a great job delivering them both naturally. Dr. Buten had to help turn one of them around, but it all worked out amazing! They were about three minutes apart."

Turning to Tripp, Dr. Buten motioned for him speak. I watched as tears rolled down my older brother's face and I couldn't help but feel a frog in my throat as I tried to keep my own emotions back.

Everyone stood. Scarlett was back at my side, her hand curled in mine as we waited.

"I'm happy to say that Rose Adelita Parker was born at 7:01 and Maximiliano Tripp Parker was born at 7:04. A girl *and* boy. I couldn't have asked for anything better."

The entire waiting room erupted in cheers. Scarlett looked up at me and I raised a brow. "I told you. Girl first. It's that Parker sperm."

She laughed and reached up on her toes to give me a kiss before making her way to Tripp.

I hadn't noticed the rest of the gang come back with the kids, but Chloe was letting Tripp know that Rose could have all of her clothes after Liberty and Merit wore them.

Tripp bent down and hugged her. "Thank you, Chloe. I know Rose will love anything she gets from her cousins."

"Oh, dear," my mother said with a slight chuckle. "Six grand-babies down, two more to go!"

My father wrapped my mother up in his arms and kissed her. I could see the happiness practically dripping off of the two of them.

"Can you imagine what Christmas is going to be like in the next few years?" Steed said with a laugh.

I couldn't help but catch the way Mitchell looked at Corina. I'd seen that look before. Plenty of times. When he caught me looking at them, I gave him a questioning stare. He gave me a quick wink, then a nod, and reached for Tripp's hand to shake it.

"Holy shit," I whispered.

"What?" Scarlett asked. Leaning down, I placed my mouth to her ear. "Corina's pregnant."

Scarlett gasped.

"Don't say anything. I totally just guessed it and Mitchell confirmed."

Glancing between me and Mitchell, she gave an incredulous look.

"How did you guess it and he confirmed it when y'all are standing ten feet apart and haven't even spoken?"

With a wink, I replied, "Baby, the Parker men have more than one talent."

She rolled her eyes and made her way to Chloe where she quickly got pulled into a conversation about how Chloe was going to bring Patches up to date as soon as she got back to the ranch.

"I'm going to head back in with Harley," Tripp said. "If y'all will give us just a bit more time with the babies, then we can start letting folks in to visit."

"The grandparents are first," Gus called out.

My father pointed to Gus. "Yes, what he said."

CHAPTER 31

Scarlett

Patches.

Holding up my bouquet, I stared at the half-eaten flowers and wanted to cry.

"It's okay. We can fix this," Waylynn said. "Look, here comes Maebh now."

The moment I saw Maebh I relaxed. We had become close since last fall, and by now she felt more like a sister to me than anything. The fact that she pushed her own wedding out a few weeks into July so that Trevor, me, and the baby could be there, meant the world to me.

"Look! See, it's even more beautiful than the other one. That arse of a goat couldn't pull one over on us today!" Maebh declared as she held the flower up in victory.

When she set the bouquet down, she glanced out the window. I followed her gaze. Trevor, Cord, and Wade were all chasing Patches in the yard. He had already tried to get into the backyard and Melanie had nearly had a fit.

Maebh laughed. "Look at those eejits. All they have to do is give the beast food."

Waylynn let out a sigh. "I'm going to need to get...what's the word for drunk again, Maebh?"

"Langered."

"I'm going to need to do that after this week. Between the spring fling yesterday, the wedding today, and the dinner tonight, I'm knackered."

"Very well done!" Maebh exclaimed as Waylynn smiled.

With a giggle, I went to stand and stopped. A strange feeling I'd never felt before rolled over my stomach. A contraction, maybe? Harley and Amelia had told me about the Braxton Hicks contractions. I hadn't had any yet, so maybe that was what it had been.

"Are you well, Scarlett?" Maebh asked.

Nodding, I smiled. "I think I might have had a Braxton Hicks contraction."

"Well, take it easy and sit down. You don't need to head over to the pasture for another thirty minutes."

The sound of Trevor yelling outside made me look again. Chewing on my lip, I watched as Wade did an impressive dive and grabbed Patches.

"They got him!" I said. Relief sweeping over me. The last thing I wanted was for that goat to cause more problems. I knew Chloe loved him, and her feelings had been hurt when Trevor and I had said Patches couldn't be a part of the wedding because it was set up too close to the dinner. She understood, but it killed me to see the disappointment on her face.

"Do you know how many diaper bags I went through because of that damn goat? I swear, if Chloe didn't love it so much I'd..."

"Don't say it!" Paxton said, walking into the room with a bottle of water. She handed it to me and placed her hands on my stomach.

"Thirty weeks and some change. Oh my gosh. You're getting closer!"

"I know! I've been having the strangest dreams."

Paxton nodded. "I did too, probably around the same time as you. Heartburn was a bitch for me."

"I don't have that, but I know Amelia has been cutting back on certain foods because of heartburn."

Corina pinned a loose curl back as she spoke. "Well, at least you aren't swelling. I was so swollen from thirty weeks on."

My eyes met hers, and she smiled. Mitchell and Corina hadn't told anyone, but it was obvious she was pregnant. I didn't want to push her, since she might be very early on. Melanie and John were going to be over the moon.

Corina took my hand in hers and squeezed it. "Hey, are you okay?"

Digging my teeth into my bottom lip, I nodded.

"I think I'm nervous. Excited. I don't know. I feel a bit...off."

"Off?" Maeabh asked as she held my veil over my head. She looked in the mirror as she settled it down on my hair.

"Yeah, I can't explain it. I think it's just nerves."

Paxton took a seat on the bed, looking at me in the mirror.

"I think that's normal. I mean, just dealing with the weird emotions of being pregnant, and then having a wedding on top of it. It's got to be a strange mix of emotions."

My eyes caught Waylynn's, and although she wore a smile, I saw the sadness in her eyes. It must be hard for her to hear all this talk about pregnancy. I didn't want to complain because I knew she'd trade places with me any day for the chance to carry a child.

I felt another jolt in my stomach and tensed.

"Braxton Hicks?" Paxton asked.

Shrugging, I replied, "I guess. I haven't felt these pains before."

"Is your stomach getting hard and tight?"

"Yes, and a weird pain. I'm sure it's nothing. Just too much excitement the past week."

Maebh leaned over and rested her chin on my shoulder as she gazed at me in the mirror.

"You look so beautiful. Trevor is going to pass out when he sees you," she said.

Our eyes locked. "Are you excited about your wedding with Cord?"

Her face lit up. "Yes! It can't get here fast enough."

Waylynn walked over to the window. "Four more months, and we'll all be in Ireland for the wedding. Crazy to think how far we've all come in just a few years."

Turning, she leaned against the windowsill and smiled.

"Maebh, it's going to be crazy at your wedding. You know this, right? Four babies! All of them under four months."

Amelia burst into the room, completely out of breath.

"Waylynn Parker! How could you not tell us! *How*?"

A wide smile grew across Waylynn's beautiful face. "Tell you what?"

"Jonathon just told Wade, who called and told me!"

Paxton looked between Waylynn and Amelia. "What are y'all talking about?"

Amelia laughed as she placed her hands on her stomach. The poor thing had practically grown overnight. She only had six weeks left until she had her son. She looked like she was ready to pop now.

"Are you going to tell them, or am I?" Amelia asked, brow arched.

Pushing off the windowsill, Waylynn waved her hand in the air. "Fine, I'll tell them. Jonathon and I will become parents for the second time this summer. August to be exact."

Gasps could be heard across the room.

"Oh my God!" Paxton screamed out.

"What! What?" Corina said, jumping around like mad.

Maebh joined Corina jumping around before she rushed over to Waylynn.

"You're adopting again?"

Waylynn wiped her tears away and nodded. "Yes. It was a pretty stressful process this time, but we've known for a few weeks. The birth mother picked us out of about four couples. He's due August 3."

I made my way to Waylynn, joining the other girls to congratulate her.

"I'm so happy for you Waylynn! I don't know how you were able to keep that a secret!" I said, giving her a hug.

She laughed. "Mom and Dad knew. We had to tell someone or I felt like I was going to burst! I can't wait to meet her."

"Do y'all have a name picked out?" Amelia asked.

"We have a couple, but I think once we see her, we'll know."

"Is it the same arrangement you have with Liberty?" Maebh asked.

Waylynn shook her head and looked sad for a brief moment. "No. The mother, I guess, hooked up with her best friend in a drunken night of passion. They're both lawyers, well on their way to becoming partners in their own firms. She's planning on taking a leave of absence when she starts to show. They both agreed that neither one of them were ready to be parents and decided on adoption. They interviewed four couples, and they both liked Jonathon and me. I think it was because of Liberty, to be honest with you. The mother said she felt a connection with me."

The knock on the door had all of us jumping.

"Jesus, that scared the shit out of me!" Waylynn said, discreetly wiping away a tear.

"Ladies, it's time!" my mother said, popping her head into the room. "Scarlett, your daddy is wanting to see you."

I thought the nervous energy I had been feeling would come back, but when I saw my father and the smile on his face, I felt peace instead.

"Daddy," I whispered as he walked into the room and the last person stepped out.

He made his way over to me and wiped at a tear that had escaped from his eye. "You look beautiful."

"Thank you," I replied as he kissed me on the cheek. He was tense and acted as if he had something he wanted to say to me.

"My little girl is getting married."

I smiled. "I'm sorry I'm doing it backwards."

He frowned. "Don't you dare apologize. Everything happens for a reason. I spoke with Trevor earlier. The boy is over the moon. I have to admit, I had my doubts in the beginning and thought you were moving too fast, but he's proven me wrong."

He closed his eyes and shook his head while letting out a soft chuckle. Focusing back on me, he went on.

"Any fool can see how much that man loves you. The way he looks at you is proof enough. I'm happy if you're happy."

Blinking rapidly to keep from crying, I pressed my lips together before getting myself in check.

"I'm so happy, Daddy. I've never been this happy before in my life."

He chuckled. "You're fixin' to prove yourself wrong when you say I do. And then in about nine or ten weeks, you'll prove yourself wrong again when you hold your child in your arms."

"Dalton Littlefield, you better not be making her cry! Her makeup!"

Glancing over my father's shoulder, I smiled at my mother. A look passed between the two of them. When my father looked back at me, I could see it in his eyes. He was keeping something from me.

"Dalton, please." My mother implored. With a nod of his head, the look vanished and was replaced by pure happiness.

"After the wedding, Scarlett, I'd love to have lunch together. Just the two of us."

I smiled, an uneasy feeling settling in my chest. "Okay. I'd love that."

When my gaze caught my mother's, she smiled. "It's time, sweetheart."

"Oh, gosh," I replied, pulling in a long deep breath and shaking off the last minute of weirdness. "I'm ready. Daddy, you ready?"

He paused and looked back at my mother. She seemed to give him a look. Turning back to me, he smiled. "I'm ready, baby girl."

As we walked through the Parker house, I couldn't contain my excitement. My nerves had been replaced by a bubbling of happiness deep in my chest. I couldn't wait to see Trevor. Couldn't wait to become Mrs. Trevor Parker. Couldn't wait to finally be his completely.

The drive to the pasture felt like it took forever. When we pulled up, Daddy jumped out of the truck and around to help me down. The event planner Melanie had hired for the benefit dinner was also helping with the wedding. It was perfect since we were combining the dinner with our reception. We ended up only having family and our closest of friends at the wedding ceremony. It was small and intimate, exactly how I wanted it. Of course, it also reduced the risk of some crazy woman running into the ceremony and crying out, "I object!", which really would have sucked.

The wedding party was also small. Since Trevor didn't want to have to pick one of his brothers and hurt the other's feelings, he ended up asking Wade to be his best man. It made sense in the end. They were best friends, after all. I had asked Maebh to be my maid of honor. She cried and started talking in Irish the afternoon I asked her over for coffee and donuts.

"Ready?" Daddy asked, extending his arm to mine.

The violinist we'd hired began playing the music and Daddy and I stepped out from around a giant oak tree. Trevor's back was facing me, but then he turned and our eyes met. He smiled the most breathtaking smile I'd ever seen. My chin trembled as I took him in. He was dressed in Wrangler jeans, a white button-down shirt and a pink tie. I chuckled when I saw the tie. We were going for an ultra-sound this week, and I couldn't wait to find out the sex of the baby. Trevor was still insisting it was a girl. I thought it was a boy, but it was only a matter of time before we knew.

When I finished checking out my future husband's amazing body, my gaze pierced his and we couldn't take our eyes off one another. His eyes were like an ocean that always knew how to draw me into their waves and not let go. I was captivated.

Daddy brought us to a stop, and I didn't even hear the preacher speaking. I was focused on Trevor, who was smiling at me like he hadn't seen me in years. I could practically feel the love pouring from every inch of his body.

My father lifted my veil and stepped to the side, allowing Trevor to stand in front of me.

He swallowed hard and bit down on his lip before speaking. "You look absolutely beautiful. I've never seen such a sight."

Smiling, I turned to the preacher. Then it happened. A sharp pain hit me so hard, I actually felt like I was going to drop to my knees. It started in my back and radiated around to my stomach.

"Oh, God," I gasped, grabbing Trevor.

"Scarlett?" both the preacher and Trevor said at once.

Then I felt it.

Something wet was running down my leg. Panic instantly set in. *No. No. No! I'm only thirty weeks. I still have ten weeks to go!*

"Scarlett, baby, I need you to tell me what's wrong," Trevor begged.

Looking into his eyes, I started to cry.

Trevor looked like someone had hit him, and the pain on his face nearly knocked me over.

"Scarlett, what is wrong?" he asked again before glancing around. "Someone help me! What's wrong with her?"

This time, I found my voice long enough to answer.

"I think my water broke."

CHAPTER 32

Trevor

Everything was a blur. I didn't remember how we got to the hospital. I didn't remember who drove. How we got to this floor or when they took Scarlett away and told me I had to leave the room.

Everything was a blur.

"Trevor, darling, why don't you drink some coffee."

My mother's voice penetrated the fog and caused me to glance her way.

"This is my fault."

Her mouth dropped open.

"What?"

Shaking my head in disbelief, I looked down to the floor. "This is my fault. This is my payback for the way I treated her."

Sitting next to me, my mother placed the coffees on the table next to the chair and reached for my hands.

"Look at me right this moment, Trevor Parker."

Forcing myself to do as she said, our eyes met.

"This is not your fault. This is no one's fault. You heard the doctor. Scarlett was in perfect health. The baby was fine; nothing was wrong. She went into labor early, that's it. God doesn't play games like that and you know it."

I shook my head. "If everything was okay, why did her water break and why is my wife being cut open and having our baby taken out? The baby isn't ready to come, Mom. Not yet. It's too soon."

Joyce sat on the other side of me, holding my other hand.

"Trevor, the survival rate of infants at thirty weeks is very good, especially if the baby is born healthy. They know what they're doing. The baby is going to be okay."

Tears streamed from my eyes as my head dropped. "Why did this happen? Why Scarlett? Why? If we lose this baby…it will kill her. It will kill me!"

My mother wrapped her arms around me, and I dropped my head to her chest and cried. I didn't give two shits who saw me, or who heard me. It felt like someone had ripped a hole in my chest and was attempting to tear my heart out piece by piece.

"Joyce, will you find John, please?"

"Yes, of course."

Rocking me gently, Mom whispered that everything was going to be okay. I wanted to believe her. I wanted to have faith, but it felt like my faith was slowly starting to slip away.

"John, take him to the chapel. Please."

My father reached down and pulled me up. "Come on, son. We're going to the chapel. Tripp, help me."

Tripp stood on the other side of me as the three of us headed to the hospital chapel. Was it a sign that it was on the same floor?

The moment the doors pushed open and I saw the giant cross, I dropped to my knees. Burying my face in my hands, I cried out with everything I had in me. I needed God to hear my pleas. I needed him to listen to me.

"God, don't do this to me! Don't you take them away from me. I'll do anything. I swear to you, I'll do anything. You can take me, but please don't take our child from Scarlett... P-please. I b-beg of you. God, *please* don't do this!" I cried out as I buried my face in my hands while sobs rocked my entire body.

Tripp was on the floor next to me. His arm wrapped around me, his voice shaking as he tried to tell me to stand up. I couldn't move. I didn't want to move. The only place I wanted to be was with Scarlett.

"I need to get to her. I need to be with her. She needs me!" I shouted, jumping up and trying to push past Tripp and my father to get out of the doors of the chapel.

"Stop, Trevor!" my father shouted.

Tripp grabbed my arms and pulled me onto the pew.

"Trevor, I know you're scared. We're all scared. But you rushing out there and trying to find Scarlett is not going to help anyone."

Looking up, I could barely see him. My vision was blurry.

"Tripp."

It was all I could manage to get out.

He looked down at me, his face softened, and he closed his eyes. "I can't imagine how you feel, Trevor."

He sat down next to me and stared straight ahead at the altar, just like I was doing.

"I know Scarlett and I know she is going to fight with everything she has, and I know Dr. Buten is not going to let anything happen to your baby. He won't."

I wiped my tears away and nodded. Dad sat behind us and placed his hand on my shoulder. The warmth from his love filled my body and eased my fears slightly, but not much.

"I'm scared," I whispered.

"I know you are, son. I know you are."

I closed my eyes and prayed to God. I tried to make deals with Him at first. Then I went to pleading. Then I simply went to reciting prayers I remembered from Bible school.

The doors to the chapel opened and the three of us spun around. Dr. Buten was standing there. He didn't wear a smile like he had when Tripp's kids were born. No, he wore a grim expression and his eyes looked tired.

I stood, wringing my hands. I swallowed hard and watched as he walked closer to us. My father placed his hand on my shoulder while Tripp placed his hand on the other shoulder.

My entire body trembled, and I wanted to run. In that moment, I wanted to turn and run away. I wasn't sure I was strong enough to hear what was about to come from this man's mouth.

"Scarlett is doing good. She's sleeping from the surgery. We had to sedate her. She was pretty upset, and it was making her blood pressure spike."

I felt sick to my stomach; I should have been with her.

"She should be up and walking later this evening, and I'd like for you to be in the room when she wakes up, Trevor. She's going to ask you a lot of questions."

Dread washed over me. He was about to tell me we lost our child.

"The baby?" My father asked when I attempted to open my mouth, and nothing came out.

"The baby is doing…okay. She's in an incubator and we're helping her breathe. She weighs three pounds, four ounces. She's fourteen-and-a-half-inches long."

My heart started pounding in my chest.

Scarlett and the baby were okay.

Closing my eyes, I shook my head to gather my thoughts.

"The baby is okay?" I asked in barely-there voice.

Dr. Buten smiled. "She is, but she has a long road ahead of her, Trevor. She's going to need help breathing for a bit, help eating until she can learn to suck, and we have to keep a close eye on her. Her body temperature and oxygen are key right now. I don't want you to be shocked when you see her. She's hooked up to a lot of things that are monitoring her.

Your pediatrician is with the neonatologist right now. Both of them will go over her treatment plan with you and Scarlett, but I believe she's going to be fine. What we need you and Scarlett to do is start bonding with her as soon as possible. That means skin-to-skin contact with both of you. Since the baby got taken right away from Scarlett, she didn't have that connection. Some parents may feel a bit distant from their baby because they didn't get the chance to experience her coming out and immediately holding her."

"I don't care about that. When can I see her? Hold her?"

He smiled. "Let's get you to Scarlett, then the nurses will take you to the baby. We didn't know the name, so right now she's called baby girl Parker."

It was then that it hit me that he'd told me the weight and length and said that it was a girl. "Wait. It's a girl? We had a girl?"

Dr. Buten laughed, knowing the history behind me telling Scarlett I knew we were having a girl.

"Looks like you were right, Trevor. She's a pretty special little girl."

My father pulled me into a hug and slapped my back. "They're okay, son. They're both going to be okay."

The moment he let me go, Tripp pulled me in.

"Trevor," Dr. Buten said, his voice turning serious. "I need you to understand that the baby is still in the NICU. She is strong, and I expect a favorable prognosis, but nothing is a guarantee. The next few days will be touchy, but I think she'll be okay. I just want you to understand that sometimes things…happen when we're dealing with preemies."

I nodded. "I understand. Do we know why Scarlett went into labor so early?"

Dr. Buten shook his head. "About twenty-five percent of women who go into preterm delivery have no known reason for it. Scarlett was fine medically, and the baby was too. I wish I had a better answer for you, Trevor."

Taking in a deep breath, I tried to wrap my head around everything.

"You ready to go see Scarlett?" Dr. Buten asked.

"I'm more than ready," I answered.

"Good. Let's get you to Scarlett's room before she wakes up."

Her eyes slowly opened, and she smiled when she saw me. Then her smile faded. Fear quickly etched on her face.

"The baby is okay," I quickly said.

Her hand reached down to her stomach.

"They had to take her, but she's in the NICU and in an incubator."

Scarlett's hand came up to her mouth, tears pooling in her eyes. Standing, I leaned over and kissed her lips.

"Scarlett, listen to me. She's okay. She's going to be okay. Please don't worry. I need you to stay calm, okay?"

A sob slipped from her lips. "She? We had a girl?"

With a wide grin, I nodded. "Told you it was a girl."

Her cries quickly turned to laughter, then she stopped. Pain crept into her eyes and she closed them.

"Ouch. I'm so sore."

Leaning over, I hit the nurse's call button. "Let me have the nurse come in, maybe they can give you medicine. They had to do an emergency C-section to get the baby out. The baby was in distress, and Dr. Buten felt the best thing to do was deliver her now."

"Oh my God. Trevor, she's only thirty-weeks old!"

"I know, but she's doing good. They have her in the incubator to regulate her temperature. She also has oxygen and a feeding tube."

Scarlett closed her eyes again, and I watched as a tear managed to slip through, drawing a path down her soft cheek. Reaching over, I wiped it away.

"Have you seen her yet?" she asked, still squeezing her eyes shut.

"No. I wanted to be with you when you woke up, so I could let you know what happened."

Her eyes flew open. "Trevor, you need to get to her. Touch her, talk to her. Let her know we're here. Please. Please go to her."

The monitor that measured Scarlett's heartrate was climbing. The door to her room opened and the nurse quickly walked in.

"Hey there, let's take a few deep, calming breaths, Mom. We need you to stay calm, okay?"

Scarlett nodded. "I'm so sorry. My…baby…" Sobs hit her again and I could tell they were both emotional and physical. She had to be in pain.

"It's okay, Ms. Littlefield. Once I get your pain under control, we'll get you into a wheelchair and bring you to see her. But not for a few hours, okay? You just had major surgery, so we need to take it easy."

With a nod, Scarlett took in a few deep breaths.

"Now, I'm going to give you something for the pain."

Turning to me, Scarlett forced a smile. "Trevor, will you please go see our baby?"

I glanced up at the nurse. She nodded. "I'll show you to the NICU as soon as we get Ms. Littlefield settled."

Scarlett and I exchanged a small smile. We never did manage to get married but that didn't matter. To me she was already mine, to hell about a piece of paper.

"We need to pick out a name for her," I whispered as I kissed the back of her hand gently, careful not to touch her IV.

"Well, we had it narrowed down to two."

The nurse grinned as she pushed the syringe into the IV port.

"What were the two names?" the nurse asked.

"Paisley or Aurora," I replied.

"Both are beautiful. I think you should see her first, then decide."

I shook my head. "No, I want Scarlett to decide."

With a soft smile, Scarlett said, "Take a video of her and we'll decide together."

The nurse smiled. "That is a perfect idea. Scarlett, that medicine is going to make you sleepy, and the more you sleep the better, okay?"

Scarlett nodded and closed her eyes. Before I knew it, she was back asleep.

Swallowing hard, I kissed her forehead. "I'm going to go see our baby girl."

Her eyes barely opened, and she mumbled, "Tell her Mommy loves her."

I fought to hold back my tears. This wasn't fair. I didn't want to see our baby without Scarlett.

"Will do."

Stepping back, I studied her. She looked peaceful and no longer in pain as she drifted off to sleep.

"Resting is the best thing for her, Mr. Parker. Let's go see your baby."

When we stepped out of the room and into the hall, I stopped walking abruptly. The nurse turned and faced me. Tilting her head in question, she studied me.

"I can't do it. I can't see the baby without her. It's not right."

"Mr. Parker, what you're feeling is natural, but I heard your wife pleading for you to go to the baby and I agree with her. The faster you connect with her, the better it will be for you and for the baby."

My hand rubbed the back of my neck. "She wasn't planned, and the first time I found out about her...wasn't exactly good. I just don't want the first time I meet my daughter to be...without Scarlett. We seem to keep doing everything backwards."

When my voice cracked, the nurse took a step closer and reached for my hand.

"I know what you're going through. The whole reason I became a nurse was because I went into labor at thirty-two weeks. I couldn't see my baby for five days, I developed an infection. My husband was scared to death to see that tiny little thing. He was afraid she would bond with him and not me. It was the hardest thing I ever went through, and I know it was for him too. Each time he came into my room, I saw the guilt on his face, but I promise you, I wanted him with our baby more than I wanted him with me. Scarlett feels the same way. Her mothering instincts have already kicked in, sweetie. I promise you, later this evening we'll get her up and take her to the baby."

I nodded and took in a few deep breaths. "Okay. Okay, I'm okay now."

She chuckled. "You don't sound like it, but I'll take your word for it. Let's go meet your daughter."

CHAPTER 33

Trevor

I felt numb washing up before heading into the NICU. The moment I walked in, I froze. The first thing I saw were incubators. About ten of them. Next to each one was a rocking chair. Nurses were tending to some of the incubators, while two nurses were sitting in the rocking chairs holding the tiniest of babies. My heart nearly dropped when the nurse pointed to the incubator with the pink blanket draped over it.

"Baby girl Parker is waiting to meet you, Dad."

Pulling in a deep breath, another nurse walked up to us.

"Kacy, this is Trevor Parker."

A wide smile moved across her face. "Baby girl Parker's daddy. She is the sweetest little thing."

I forced a smile and tried to get my heartbeat under control. My hands were shaking so bad, I had to ball them into fists.

"I'm going to leave you with Kacy, Mr. Parker."

Turning to the nurse, I reached out my hand. "Thank you so much."

One quick glance at her nametag and I added, "Emma. Thank you for taking care of Scarlett and me…and our baby girl."

"Of course. I'm on shift until eleven, and if I don't see you before I leave, I'm sure I'll see you tomorrow evening."

I nodded and turned back to Kacy.

"Mr. Parker."

"Trevor, please call me Trevor."

She nodded. "Okay, Trevor. I need to let you know that your daughter is hooked up to a lot of wires and machines. It's going to be shocking. She's very little and fragile, but not so fragile you won't be able to hold her."

"Today?"

"Maybe. She'll be on a schedule. Every three to four hours one of us will wake her, take her vitals and when the time comes, start to practice with her on taking a bottle. During these schedules, Mom and Dad are encouraged to be here. We like to do something called Kangaroo Care. This is where there is skin-to-skin contact with Mom or Dad. It helps with growth and bonding."

"Okay," I replied, as I glanced around the room. I felt so far out of my element and tried like hell not to cry. In the corner, a mom sat in a rocker, holding her tiny infant to her chest. Tears pricked harder at the back of my eyes.

"Are you ready to meet your daughter?" Kacy asked, pulling my gaze away from the mom.

My entire body trembled, and I had no fucking idea why I was so damn scared. I wanted Scarlett here. I needed Scarlett here. It wasn't fair I was getting to see the baby first without her.

"Trevor?" Kacy asked, squeezing gently on my arm. My eyes met hers.

"I wish Scarlett was here."

A soft smile moved over her face. "I know you do. I also know she would be here if she could. The first few days you might struggle bonding with the baby, or your wife might, but it's these first few days that are of the utmost importance."

"We're not married. We, um, we were at our wedding ceremony when Scarlett's water broke."

"I'm so sorry," Kacy said and I could hear the sincerity in her voice. "Scarlett might have a harder time bonding since she is not seeing the baby for a few hours after birth. I need you to know that we're here not only for the baby, but for you and Scarlett, as well. Any questions you might have or anything you might need, just ask."

"Thank you, Kacy."

She nodded and motioned for me to follow her.

"Now, you washed up good before you came in. You can reach into the incubator and touch the baby. I encourage it. Talk to her. Let her know you're here."

When we walked up, she lifted the blanket and I nearly dropped to my knees. My stomach lurched as I stared down at my precious daughter, wires and tubes coming out in every direction.

"Oh my God," I whispered as a sob slipped from my mouth. Pulling in a deep breath, I got my emotions quickly under control.

"Let me explain what we have going on here, okay?"

All I could do was nod.

"This is the ventilator, and we're hoping your growing preemie won't be on it long. She'll move to a CPAP when we remove this. This is the PICC line. She doesn't have the sucking motion down just yet, but once she does, we'll feed her with a bottle and this will be removed. We need to make sure her gut is ready before we start introducing Scarlett's milk. Right now she is getting something called Totally Parental Nutrition, or TPN. The nutrition bypasses the digestive system and goes right into her bloodstream. Just like it did when she was in the womb."

I nodded, trying to get the bile down in my throat.

She started pointing to different things and telling me what they were. My head was spinning. "This is her temperature monitor. This is her ECG and blood pressure monitor."

Gummy Bear was attached to so many things. "What is that?" I asked, pointing to the tubes that were wrapped around each tiny foot.

"The oxygen saturation monitor and one of the IV pumps. This is her umbilical artery catheter."

"Kacy, how in the world will we be able to hold her with all of this attached to her?"

She gave me a warm grin. "Trust me, you'll be able to hold her. Would you like to introduce yourself now? I'm sure she's ready to hear your voice, this time up close and personal."

Taking in a deep breath, I slipped my hands into the incubator and picked up my daughter's tiny hand, laying it in mine. It was so tiny, yet I could feel her strength.

"Hey there, Gummy Bear. It's Daddy. You decided to surprise me and Mommy by coming to meet us early."

When her little hand squeezed my pinky finger, I leaned my head on the incubator and cried. I wasn't sure how to deal with a situation that was totally out of my control. Kacy put her arm around me to let me know she was there.

"I read a quote once about preemies. It's always stuck in my mind. It said, *'Having a premature baby is like getting one of God's little miracles in the midst of their creation'*. I always loved that."

Through blurry, tear-soaked eyes, I stared at my daughter. Tubes and wires were everywhere in her incubator, but there she was, holding onto my finger. Telling me she wasn't going to give up. She was going to be strong.

"I'll never...I'll never leave you ever, princess. Never. Mommy and Daddy are going to be here for you always. I love you so much."

Clearing her voice, Kacy dropped her arm from me. "I'm going to let Daddy and daughter bond for a bit."

I blocked out everything around me and focused on the little miracle. A small pink hat was on her head and I knew immediately what I had to do when I left the NICU. For now, though, I was going to be right here with my daughter, letting her know we were with her and that her mommy was going to be there soon.

"Mommy will be here later. I think we'll get your schedule so they can time it. Maybe Mommy will be able to hold you because she's waited an awfully long time to hold you and see your beautiful face. Can you wait just a bit longer for her, princess? She wants to be here so badly."

Her little fingers gently squeezed my finger, and I fought to hold back the breakdown that was knocking at the door of my heart all over again.

Looking up, I took in the NICU. How long would we have to keep our daughter here? A month? Two? What would life be like once we did get her home? Could she travel with us to Ireland to the wedding? Would she need special medical care? I felt like I was caught between the bookends of this part of my life. I sort of knew where things were going, but I really had no fucking clue.

This wasn't supposed to be how things happened. Scarlett was going to carry the baby full term. She would be born and placed in Scarlett's arms right away. We were supposed to whisk her home, and everyone would go crazy over her.

My eyes landed back on my little Gummy Bear. She yawned and everything in that moment made complete sense.

I didn't know why things worked out like they had, but I did know with all of my heart that everything was going to be okay. I needed to be strong for my two girls. I'd give myself one moment to lose my shit when I left here, and the moment I walked into Scarlett's room, I was there for her one-hundred-and-ten percent.

A small shake of my shoulder had me opening my eyes. I had fallen asleep with my head on the baby's incubator. My hand still in the incubator with my daughter's fingers still wrapped around my pinky.

"You looked pretty peaceful sleeping and I hated waking you, but I figured you might want to get back to Mom."

I dragged my free hand down my face. "Yes. I'm sorry about that."

Kacy grinned. "Don't apologize. We're going to be waking baby Parker up in about an hour. If Mom is feeling up to it, she might want to hold her then."

Gently letting go of my daughter's hand, I stood. "Yes! She'll want to. Let me head back to her room."

With a slight chuckle, Kacy nodded. "Then I'll see you soon."

By the time I made it back to Scarlett's room, the nurse had already helped her out of bed, to the bathroom, and she was sitting her in the wheelchair.

"Shit, I'm sorry, baby. I wanted to be back here when you got out of bed."

Lifting her chestnut eyes to me, Scarlett tried her best to smile through the pain. Once she was seated, I could see her body relax.

"I had her stand up as straight as she could. It's best to stretch the incision while she is still somewhat numb."

Snarling, I replied, "Ouch."

Scarlett shook her head and added, "Numb, my ass."

Then she let out a breath and focused on me. "Did you take a picture of her?"

My eyes darted to the nurse and then back to Scarlett.

"Yes. Baby, I need you to be prepared when you see her. She's hooked up to a lot of things."

Scarlett nodded. "I asked for my phone and started to research some on premature babies once I woke up."

"Okay, good."

My stomach dropped a bit. Looking at pictures of other people's babies was one thing, seeing your own was going to be different. After I left the NICU I headed into the men's restroom and sat in a stall for a few minutes and cried my fucking eyes out all over again. It felt good to get it all out, and I knew at some point, Scarlett was going to need to do the same thing. For now, the only thing I could do was be by her side.

"May I see the pictures?" Scarlett asked.

I hesitated, not sure what to do. I pulled my phone out of my back pocket and walked over to her. I pulled up the one and only picture I'd taken of our baby. Handing my phone to Scarlett, I held my breath. She had asked for a video, but I couldn't do it. I'd barely been able to take the picture.

She sucked in a sharp breath and then stared at the photo. Tears formed in those beautiful eyes of hers. She handed me back the phone and wiped her cheeks.

"I need to see her, Trevor. Now."

"Okay, let's go see her."

CHAPTER 34

Scarlett

No matter how many pictures I Googled, or how many things I read, nothing could have prepared me for walking into the NICU.

I tried my best to keep my emotions in check as Trevor wheeled us to the incubator that had a pink and white blanket draped over one half of it.

The name "Baby Girl Parker" was at the end and that broke my heart in a million pieces. Our daughter was hours old and didn't have a name yet. Hadn't felt her mother's warm breath on her skin or heard my voice. Fear crept in.

What if she doesn't know who I am? What if she won't bond with me?

Trevor bent down in front of me, placing his hand on the side of my face. "Hey, don't get in your head. I did the same thing when I first walked in here. She's going to know it's you. You have been her home for thirty weeks, she's felt your love and heard your heartbeat since the moment she was a tiny gummy bear. I promise you, darlin', she will know her momma."

I nodded as he reached up and brushed a tear off my cheek with his thumb.

"Will you help me stand?" I asked.

"Of course, baby."

Trevor and the nurse both helped me up. My eyes were closed as I dealt with the pain, but the moment I opened them and saw my daughter, I felt nothing but love. Everything else vanished and the only thing I felt was pure and utter love, and I wanted nothing more than to protect our child.

"Ms. Littlefield, my name is Kacy. I'm the NICU nurse who's been taking care of your daughter."

Smiling, I extended my hand. "It's a pleasure meeting you. Please call me Scarlett."

"Like I told, Trevor, we're not only here for your baby, but for y'all as well. If you have any questions or concerns, please don't hesitate to ask me or any of the nurses on shift."

I managed to whisper, "Okay."

"Want to meet your daughter?" she asked, a smile on her face.

A part of me wanted to turn and run. I wasn't sure why I was suddenly scared to death.

Then I felt Trevor's arm around my waist and all the fear vanished. I knew with him by my side I could get through anything.

As I walked up to the incubator, I saw all the wires and tubes first. A sob slipped from my lips and Trevor held me closer.

"She's as beautiful as her mommy."

I looked at Trevor. He winked and leaned down to kiss me on the lips.

"It's all going to be okay, baby. I promise. Come on, she's been waiting for you and even though she may not physically be a part of you any longer, that connection will never be broken. She needs you now, needs to hear your voice and lie up against your heartbeat."

Turning back, I took another step closer. Tears instantly filled my eyes. Her little chest was moving up and down and she had tubes and wires coming out from all over her.

I felt weak, but Trevor held me up, a gentle touch around my waist. Kacy was at my other side.

"She's the best baby in here. Doesn't give me any trouble at all!"

Laughing, I replied, "She must take after me then."

Trevor chuckled. "Um, excuse me, I'm not the one who set the trash can on fire next to the courthouse."

"Well, I see getting to know you two is going to be fun," Kacy said.

My eyes scanned my baby's entire body as I took her in. Kacy proceeded to tell me about everything that was hooked up to the baby.

"Dr. Jackson, the neonatologist, will be by here shortly. I'm sure you'll have questions for her, please don't hesitate to ask them."

"How long do you think she'll need the breathing tube?" I asked.

"I'm not sure. The doctor will take a good look at her, listen to her lungs again and she'll make the decision when she feels like baby Parker will be able to at least move to a nose prong. We need to watch for apnea. Hopefully that won't be a problem."

"The feeding tube is just until she learns to suck?" I asked.

"Yes. Each time we take her out, she'll be worked with on different things. Sucking is one of those. The occupational therapists will be working with her as well on those types of things. We'll slowly introduce her to your milk, so that her digestive system gets used to it. I've already explained to Trevor what we are giving her, I'm more than happy to explain it to you as well."

"No, that's okay. I read up on it. TPN right?"

Kacy smiled. "You are absolutely right."

I was scared to ask the next question. "When can I hold her?"

"How about right now?"

Tears filled my eyes again, but this time I kept them back.

"Yes!"

"Trevor, why don't you help Mom into the rocking chair while I get baby Parker ready."

It felt like it took me forever to get into the chair, but when I finally did, I looked up to see Kacy holding the tiniest baby I'd ever seen in my life.

"Let's pull that gown open so that she can be up against your chest without any barriers, Mom."

The moment the baby was placed in my arms, I felt the most powerful surge of love. I feared it wasn't going to happen, but I felt the love flowing instantly between us.

Tears of happiness streamed down my face as I stared at her.

"Hey, beautiful girl. Sorry it took me so long to get here. You sort of took us by surprise."

Trevor was right next to me, taking a video on his phone. "Everyone is dying to see..."

He paused and looked into my eyes.

"What's her name, Scarlett? Do you know?"

I nodded. "Do you?"

He nodded and said, "Let's say it on three."

I grinned.

"What if we each say a different name?" I asked.

Trevor glanced at Kacy. "Then Kacy gets to pick."

Her smile faded. "What? No way."

"On three?" I asked, gazing back down at the baby.

Trevor cleared his throat and quietly counted. "One. Two. Three."

"Aurora."

We had both said the same name. Trevor looked relieved, and I felt like I was going to burst with happiness. I was still scared. For a million different reasons. Our daughter was in the NICU, she couldn't breathe on her own, and the future wasn't really known. But in that moment, with our daughter named, with the possibility of a beautiful future, I was happy. Happier than I'd ever been in my entire life.

Walking slowly into the NICU, I focused on Aurora's incubator and tried to tune all the other activity out. The first two days of her life I'd suffered from anxiety and broken down more than what I thought was normal. Trevor never left my side.

Cord and Maebh had come to see me and brought us clothes and essentials. They were the second group of people to see Aurora. Trevor's parents were the first grandparents to see her. Mine had been too worried they would make the baby sick and refused.

I was being discharged from the hospital and Trevor had rented a condo only a block away. He said there was no way we were going to be more than five minutes from Aurora.

I smiled when I got to the incubator. She wasn't in it. Instead, she was sleeping peacefully against her daddy's bare chest. She looked so incredibly small against Trevor's giant body. His large muscles nearly swallowed her whole. When he took his shirt off he got stares, not only from some of the nurses...I caught a mom peeking over once or twice.

Trevor and Aurora were both sleeping, and I couldn't help but stare at the two people I loved more than anything in this world. In the last two days Aurora had come a long way. She was now on a nasal cannula, and Dr. Jackson felt like she would be breathing without it any day. The PICC line was delivering her nutrients and medicine, if needed. The plan was for me to keep pumping breast milk for when Aurora was ready to receive it. Dr. Jackson said he hoped to be able to deliver that through a nasogastric tube soon.

"Scarlett, I have to be honest with you," Kacy, my favorite nurse who took care of Aurora, whispered. "That is a pretty darn sexy sight right there."

Laughing softly, I nodded. "It is. How long has he been holding her?"

"Not very long. He helped change her diaper and was asking about a bath for her. I wanted to wait until our next scheduled time frame to do the bath so you could be here. It always amazes me when most dads dive right in with the care of their little ones."

I faced her. "Most dads? Not all dads?"

She frowned. "Unfortunately, no. Even some moms are hesitant but that is very rare. Some of the fathers are in denial and won't even come and see the baby. Others, well, they come in to hold the baby during a lunch break and leave. I'd have to say a majority, though, are in tune with their kids and will do anything to help with their care."

"Wow, I mean, when I leave here, I get such an overwhelming sense of grief. The guilt of not being here if she needs me is a struggle and I'm hoping it will get better as the days go on. I trust y'all with her, please don't get me wrong. I just hate leaving her."

She placed her hand on my arm. "Trust me, I understand and you're not the only parent to feel that way. Here, I have something to give you. We were out of the caterpillar, and it's my favorite one to give to new preemies. Be right back."

Trevor opened his eyes. He smiled when he saw me.

"Hey, how are you feeling?"

"Good, I walked over here and, it felt good to move around."

His eyes roamed my body with lust. I glanced down at what I was wearing. Yoga pants and an oversized T-shirt that said Frio River Ranch.

"You look beautiful," he whispered.

I tilted my head and gave him a scowl.

"Don't look at me like that. You do, Scarlett."

"I haven't had a decent shower or washed my hair in days, and I don't have a stitch of make-up on. Plus, I look like a homeless person with leaky boobs."

Trevor kissed Aurora's head. "Like I said, you look beautiful. Doesn't she, princess? Mommy always looks beautiful, even dressed like a homeless person and especially with her leaky boobs."

Tingles swept across my body and I had the urge to walk over and kiss him. So I did. Then I kissed our daughter.

"Hello, sweet Aurora Belle. How is my baby girl this evening?"

Aurora moved, and I knew it was because she heard me. My heart melted at the sight, and it also broke in two. It killed me to see our daughter like this, but there were other babies in here in far worse condition, so I counted my blessings that our daughter was improving each day. I knew things could change, so I wasn't going to be picky with her progress.

"Mom won't stop calling me. She wants more pictures."

I giggled. "Who wouldn't want to see pictures of this beautiful little girl? My folks left before I came down. I signed all the discharge papers, so Daddy is bringing our stuff to the condo."

"Damn. I'm sorry I wasn't there, Scarlett."

"No, I'd rather you were here. Like I said, my folks were there, and they'll be at the house to help with things the first few days."

Trevor nodded, but I still saw the guilt in his eyes.

"Oh, good. You're up, Dad."

Slowly standing up from my bent-over position, I watched as Kacy held out a silver bracelet to me.

"What's this?" I asked as I took it from her. It looked like one of those bracelets you use for Pandora charms.

"This is called NICU Journey Beads. A NICU nurse came up with this as a way to celebrate milestones in the NICU. You start with the caterpillar bead and when you leave you'll get the butterfly bead. I also want to give you this one, the giraffe. It's the keeping baby warm in the incubator bead. Then we have this one!"

She threaded another bead onto the silver bracelet. "This is the Kangaroo for, of course, the importance of skin to skin. And this one is for you, Dad! The first diaper change. For each milestone Aurora has, we'll add another bead. She'll get to wear it as a necklace when she leaves the NICU for home."

My heart was overjoyed as I looked at the four beads on the bracelet. "We're at four already!" I softly said with excitement. One of the rules in the NICU was that loud noises were a no-no. Everything was kept at a controlled level because most of the little ones were still developing their hearing.

"Do we get one for a bath?" Trevor asked, a huge smile on his face.

I giggled. Who would have thought we would be so excited over beads? But each of these beads represented something monumental in our minds.

"You bet you do. She is scheduled for her first bath during the next scheduled round."

"I can't wait to help with the bath," I said with a grin

"Sorry, Dad, it's time for Aurora to head back to bed," Kacy said, taking Aurora from Trevor and placing her back in her incubator with practiced ease. Trevor yawned and ran his hands over his face.

"Why don't you head to the condo and get some sleep. I'll stay here."

"Scarlett, you had major surgery. You can't be hanging out in here. You need to rest."

"I'm fine. I don't want to leave her."

Kacy was busy writing something in Aurora's chart, not paying attention to us bickering. I'm sure it wasn't the first time, and it most assuredly wouldn't be the last that she'd hear parents having this same argument.

"Why don't you both head over and take a good nap. Her next scheduled time is in four hours. Go rest, you need to take care of yourselves. Let us do what we do best here, and that's take care of Aurora."

She reached for the beaded bracelet and tied it onto the incubator. "When Aurora leaves the NICU she's going to have a beautiful necklace to wear at home."

I pushed my arms through the incubator's opening and stroked Aurora gently.

"Mommy and Daddy will be back, princess. I promise. Sleep good for Kacy and the other nurses. I love you."

Trevor did the same thing. I could see the anguish on his face as we walked away.

When we got outside to Trevor's truck, I broke down.

Trevor quickly had me in his arms, holding me gently.

"We should have her with us, Trevor! We should be pulling out of here with our baby in the car seat and heading back to Oak Springs. Not to a rented condo in San Antonio *without* our baby!"

He stroked my head softly. "*Shhh*, I know. I know. But this is the card we were dealt, and we're going to make the best of it. That means going to the condo, resting, eating a good dinner, and then heading back in time to help with Aurora."

My face was buried in his chest. I wanted to rip off his shirt and touch him where Aurora had been sleeping against him. Anything to feel closer to her. Instead, I stepped back, wiped my tears away and nodded.

"Right. I'm sorry. It just hit me that we were leaving, and she wasn't coming with us."

Trevor nodded. "Don't be sorry. It hit me yesterday when I left to sign the paperwork for the condo. We're going to get through this, Scarlett. You, me, and our little fighter in there, because trust me when I say, our daughter is a true fighter."

The corners of my mouth rose slightly. "That's because she's a Parker."

"Hell yes, she is," Trevor replied, then kissed me gently on the lips.

After helping me into the truck, Trevor asked if I needed to stop and get any medicine.

"Nope, my folks picked up the prescriptions the doctor wrote. I'm going to start taking Motrin for the pain just in case they tell me they're ready for the breast milk."

"I hate that you have to pump and we are throwing it out."

"I know. We can't donate it, though, because of the pain meds."

"Still sucks, though."

We were at our condo four minutes later. Thank goodness it was on the first floor. I could walk upstairs, but the less I had to move, the better.

"Shower?" Trevor asked, wiggling his eyebrows.

"My parents are here, Trevor."

"No, they're not. I texted and said we were coming home and your mom said they ran to Oak Springs and would be back in a couple of hours. She wanted to get some indoor grill."

I groaned. "Oh Lord. The George Foreman grill?"

Trevor shrugged. "Maybe. I don't remember. All I know is, I've got a few hours alone with you, and I want you to sleep for most of it. So come on. Let me take you to the shower and clean you."

Letting him guide me through the condo, I glanced around as we walked through the rooms. It was beautiful and had to be costing Trevor a small fortune.

The moment we walked into the master bathroom, I gasped. It was like a spa. Trevor carefully pulled my shirt over my head. He reached behind me and unclasped my bra. I let it fall from my arms to the floor.

He dropped down and looked at the incision on my stomach. He frowned.

"It's a beautiful battle wound. It's okay, Trevor, I promise."

When his beautiful blue eyes looked up at me, I noticed how tired he looked. He'd been rotating between staying with me and being with Aurora. I would go down to the NICU as often as I could, but my nurses were keeping me on my own damn schedule.

"I'm sorry this happened," he said. "I'm so sorry."

Cupping his beautiful face within in my hands, I pierced his eyes with mine.

"You don't have anything to be sorry for."

He closed his eyes and dropped his head to the floor.

"Trevor, look at me."

When he lifted his head, I caught a breath. Tears rolled down his face, dampening his cheeks.

"This was not your fault. This was not my fault. This wasn't Aurora's fault. This is something that happened. Look at all those other families in the NICU. It happened to them, too. We're not alone in this, and we need to remember that. Aurora is a fighter; you even said so yourself. We're all going to be okay. All of us. What we need to focus on is that she's with us, and we didn't lose her and we're not going to lose her."

Trevor stood, pushed his hands through my hair, and pulled me to him gently. When his lips pressed against mine, I nearly melted into him.

The kiss was slow yet filled with passion. I wanted him, but I knew we still had six weeks to go before we were cleared for sex. Even though I wanted him, the thought of actually moving my body like that made me feel ill.

Trevor broke the kiss and leaned his forehead to mine.

"Come on, let's get you in the shower and to bed."

CHAPTER 35

Trevor

Aurora was five weeks old and we had gotten a plethora of beads. One for her bath. One for the first feeding. That had been stressful, especially when she was trying to learn to suck, swallow and breathe all at the same time. Aurora for sure earned that little pig bead.

We got one for her first clothes. It was a pink outfit with matching hat and socks. Her shirt said, "Parker Princess" and the hat had her name on it. I had asked Paxton to get it made the day Aurora was born. Scarlett and I couldn't believe how fast she grew out of it. That was another thing she got beads for. Weight gain.

Today she was getting a bead for a preemie open crib. Scarlett had been waiting for this bead—as had I. Actually, the bead I most wanted to get was the butterfly. It meant our princess was coming home with us, where she belonged.

"Good afternoon, Mr. Parker," Marge, who worked in the hospital cafeteria said. She wore a huge smile every single time I saw her.

"Is it afternoon, Marge? Feels like evening already."

She chuckled. "Long day?"

I yawned and replied with a sleepy, "Sure has been."

"How much longer will your little girl have to stay here?" she asked as she rang up two coffees.

"Hopefully not too much longer. She's breathing on her own now and has been for a few days. We just need her body temperature to stay where it's supposed to, and they said we'd start talking about bringing her home."

She gave me a warm smile. "Well, you are a good father. Your wife is a good mother, too."

I returned the smile with one of my own. I'd stopped correcting people about Scarlett and I not being married.

Lifting the coffees, I replied, "Thank you, Marge. Thanks for the coffee, too!"

"Any time, sweetie! Any time!"

With a long sigh, I leaned against the elevator wall as it brought me up to the fifth floor to the NICU. When the elevators opened, I saw Scarlett sitting in one of the chairs in the waiting room. Making my way to her, I sat down and handed her a coffee.

"Here ya go. One black coffee, minus the shot of whiskey you asked for. I figured the nurses might frown upon us getting drunk."

She laughed, but it was barely audible.

"What's wrong?" I asked, taking her hand in mine.

"I'm tired, Trevor. I want to go home. I want to take our baby home. I'm sick of sleeping in a stranger's bed when we do get a few quick hours of rest. I don't want to ask to hold her, goddamn it. I want to be able to hold her whenever the hell I want. I'm tired of people asking me why my last name is not Parker. I'm sick of seeing other parents cry. I can't keep tuning it all out. I want our family to all be able to hold Aurora and not stop to get badges and scrub in before seeing her. I want to have more than two people see her at once. I want this to all stop! All of it!"

A woman who was sitting in the waiting room looked over at us when Scarlett raised her voice.

"Baby, why don't you head on back to the condo and…"

"No! Stop telling me to leave. You leave. Why don't you just leave. Because none of this seems to be bothering you, Trevor. You just smile and keep going. I can't do it anymore. I can't!"

I leaned close, but she pushed me away. Balling my fists, I tried to keep my temper in line. I knew Scarlett was tired and stressed, and she was certainly due for a breakdown, but I was feeling the same exact way she was. I just took it out on the punching bag in the workout room of the complex each time I went back to the condo.

Before I said something I would regret, I walked toward the NICU.

I hadn't made it to the door when my phone rang. Pulling it out of my pocket, I saw my father's name.

"Hey, what's going on? Everything okay at the ranch?"

"Everything is fine. How is Aurora?"

"Precious as ever. It's Scarlett I'm worried about. She just lashed out at me, and I have no fucking clue why. I mean, I *know* why, but I don't know why. Christ, I'm not making any sense."

"I'm sorry, son. I know it's hard on both of you."

"It's okay, what's up?"

"Listen, I have double news for you."

"Okay, tell me it's good news because I sure could use some."

"It is. First one, Cord and Maebh eloped and got hitched in Ireland on their own."

"What?"

He laughed. "Yep. It killed Maebh that y'all weren't going to be able to make it to the wedding, so they decided to go over, get married, then have another wedding ceremony here for family."

Raking my fingers through my hair, I said, "Wow. I can't believe they would do that. Are they sure? I mean, Maebh has been talking about this wedding for months."

"And she's getting married over there. Vi went with them."

That made me laugh. "Oh, holy hell. Aunt Vi's got a thing for Maebh's dad."

My father chuckled. "Ready for the best news, though?"

"Hit me."

"Amelia went into labor last night."

"No shit!" I said, excitement washing over me for my baby sister.

"Has she delivered yet?"

"We're at the hospital now waiting to hear."

"Damn, Dad, that's amazing news. Is everything okay? No complications?"

"Dr. Buten said she was measuring about a week-and-a-half farther along than they first calculated, so she's really only a little over a week early."

Relief hit me. "That's great. Tell Wade and Amelia we wish we were there to welcome John Michael into the world."

"I will, son. I'm sorry no one called you earlier. I wasn't sure if y'all stayed at the hospital late last night or not. I didn't want to call too early."

I rubbed the tightness out of my neck and turned to head back to the hallway chair but found Scarlett standing there.

"Nah, Dad. No worries at all. You can call me anytime. Give Amelia my love."

"I will, son. Do the same for Scarlett and kiss Aurora Belle for me."

"Will do. Bye."

Hitting End, I looked at Scarlett. She looked white as a ghost.

"What's wrong?" I asked her.

"Amelia had the baby?"

I looked down at my phone and then back to her. "No, not yet. She went into labor late last night, I guess. Dad said everything is going good."

She gave a curt nod.

"Why don't you go be with her."

As she walked by, I reached for her arm. "Why are you pushing me away, Scarlett? What did I do?"

Her chin trembled, and she looked away from me. "You didn't do anything, Trevor."

"Then can you explain why you are acting like you can't stand the thought of being near me? I don't want to be anywhere but here with you and Aurora."

Jerking her head up, she looked stunned. Like she couldn't believe what I had just said.

"What?"

"Well, hell, I don't know. You keep telling me to leave. Seems to me you don't want me around."

Her mouth opened then quickly shut before she pulled her arm from my grip and headed toward the NICU. With a frustrated sigh, I followed her. The rest of the day was spent with Scarlett acting like I wasn't there. I was pretty sure even the nurses noticed. One of the moms even told me to not let it bother me, that it was normal. How in the fuck was that normal?

I wanted to call my dad, but by the time I left the hospital, without Scarlett, I was too exhausted to even talk. Wade had called me earlier this afternoon to tell me Amelia had delivered an eight-pound-one-ounce, healthy baby boy. I was so happy for them, but Scarlett seemed to shut into herself even more when I told her.

Taking a shower, I grabbed a blanket from the hall closet and my pillow and headed to the sofa. I had no idea if Scarlett was coming home tonight but the last place I wanted to be was alone in bed. A feeling of absolute dread moved over me as I tried to understand why the woman I loved, the mother of my child, was pulling away from me.

When I could no longer keep my eyes open, I fell asleep.

The next morning, I woke up before the sun. Grabbing a pair of shorts and a T-shirt from the dryer, I headed out for a run. I never did hear Scarlett come home from the hospital, so I was sure she was still there. She hadn't texted either.

After running for two miles, I stopped and sat down on a bench. I pulled my phone out and checked it. Nothing from Scarlett.

A woman with a large black dog came walking up. She sat down on the bench and took a long drink of water.

"Seems like something heavy is on your mind," she stated.

Turning to look at her, I forced a smile. "Nah."

With a lift of her brow, she gave me a look that said I was full of shit.

"Want to talk about it?"

I laughed. "To a stranger? No, but thank you."

"Sometimes talking to a stranger helps to put things into perspective."

I rolled my neck. "Okay, well my fiancée won't talk to me and is pushing me away like I did something wrong."

"Did you?"

"No. We have a five-week-old daughter in the NICU, and yesterday she decided she didn't want me around. I have no damn clue why."

Frowning, I faced the woman. "And I'm so sorry. I just unloaded all of that on you."

She laughed. "I asked you to. Plus, I have that kind of personality. I can read people as well. That's how I knew you were dealing with something."

"What are you? A mind reader?"

"Close. A psychiatrist."

This time it was my turn to laugh.

"So, did I hear you right, you have an infant in NICU? Five weeks, you say?"

I nodded. "Yes, she's doing great. She's even drinking from a bottle and trying to nurse. We had a small setback when she lost a couple of ounces, but she's gained it back."

"Son, I'm going to go out on a limb here, and I could be totally off, but this is my advice to you. When you see her today, talk to her, because I promise you she's scared to get *close* to you again."

Scoffing, I looked at the woman. "We've been close for the last five weeks. I don't think we've spent more than a few hours away from each other or from Aurora."

Her face lit up, and she smiled. "Your daughter's name is Aurora?"

"Yes, ma'am."

"Well, I'll be."

Looking up toward the sky that was slowly turning brighter, she laughed, then focused back on me.

"Son, that's not the kind of close I mean. What did the doctor say? Six weeks, no sex? You're coming up on that. She's scared. Maybe she's worried about her body or the way she looks. Maybe she's worried about being intimate with you like that because she's thinking she needs to focus on being a mother, or maybe she's just plain scared she'll get pregnant again. Having a preemie will do that to a woman."

My mouth hung open as I stared at this woman. Her damn dog was sitting there staring at me. Almost like he was trying to read my mind, too.

"Wait. You just met me, I told you very little about us, and that's what you came up with?"

The woman stood and shrugged. Then she gave me a wink. "It was just a thought. Unsolicited advice. Have a nice day."

She started to walk off, her dog trotting next to her. I went to start running again, away from the woman and her dog when she called out.

"By the way, my name is Aurora! Aurora Jean Bell! Good talking to you, son."

I stood there frozen in place. There was no fucking way that was the woman's name. Spinning around, I ran back to the condo. When I opened the door, I nearly dropped to the floor at the sight in front of me. Scarlett was sitting on the sofa, a blanket wrapped around her shoulders and her head dropped low.

When she looked up, she burst into tears, rushed over to me, and threw herself against me.

"Baby, what's wrong?"

Burying her face in my chest, she cried harder. I kicked the door shut with my foot, picked her up, and carried her to the sofa.

"Scarlett, what's wrong? Is everything okay with Aurora?"

She nodded. "Yes, she's fine. I'm sorry, I didn't mean to scare you about her. She's fine."

Framing her face with my hands, I wiped her cheeks with my thumbs. "Then why are you crying?"

"I…came home and you were gone. I thought you had l-left me."

My eyes widened in shock. "I would never leave you. Why in the world would you think that?"

Burying her face in her hands, she cried some more. "Because…I told you to leave. I treated you horribly yesterday and when I found out about Amelia's baby, this weird jealousy thing came over me. I got angry, and in my mind, I was blaming you. But it was just a way to keep you at bay because I was scared. I didn't mean to hurt you. When I came home, and you were gone…and you hadn't slept in our bed last night, I…"

She wiped her nose with the back of her hand. "I nearly lost it. I was so scared and the thought of driving you away about destroyed me."

"Hey, look at me," I gently demanded.

Scarlett lifted her swollen eyes and looked right at me.

"Do you remember what I told you all those months ago? I'm not going anywhere. I swear to you. Now, do you want to tell me what's going on? What was the matter yesterday?"

Scarlett chewed on her lip. "Dr. Buten's office called for my six-week check-up reminder."

I waited for her to keep going. "Okay. And?"

She gave me a look that said I should know what was wrong.

"Scarlett, baby, you're going to have to give me more information than that. Why did that get you upset?"

The words from the lady on the bench came rushing back. No freaking way was she right...

"Scarlett, are you afraid to be with me again? Sexually?"

Her eyes answered before she looked down at her hands. They were wringing together like mad.

"Why?"

She shrugged. "I figured you had a countdown on your phone and when I realized it yesterday, that next week we'd get the all clear, I freaked out. I'm afraid, Trevor. A part of me doesn't want any more kids. I overheard a mom talking the other day and she said her second child, she had six weeks early. Then this baby who was in NICU. She had him four weeks early! I can't do this again. I don't think I can do this again."

I grabbed her hands and brought them to my lips. "Stop. Take a deep breath, and just relax, will you?"

She did as I said. Closing her eyes, she took in a deep breath and slowly let it out.

"First, I've been a bit too busy to worry about the six-week countdown. Even though I'm ready to be back inside of you, and I was kind of hoping you felt that way too, I'd totally understand if that was the furthest thing from your mind, babe."

"I do! I look at you sometimes and I get so turned on. Especially seeing you with Aurora. You don't know how many times I wanted to jump your bones the last few weeks."

Laughing, I shook my head. "Okay, well, I've wanted to jump your bones, too."

Scarlett smiled for the first time since I walked through the door.

"Second, Scarlett, you're on the pill, and I can use a condom if you're worried about another baby. I think what we need to do is talk to Dr. Buten next week and ask him about the risks of another premature labor, if and when we get pregnant again."

Scarlett chewed on her lip, then dropped her gaze to my lips. I knew that look in her eyes.

"I'm sorry I acted like that. I think my emotions are all over the place, but that doesn't make what I did to you yesterday right."

"It's okay, baby. Let me jump in the shower and then we'll head over to the hospital."

She reached for my hand. Kissing the back of it, she whispered, "I love you so much."

"I love you more."

Quickly heading to the shower, I stripped out of my running clothes and stepped into the hot water. I knew it the moment she was there. The air charged with electricity, like it always did when she walked into a room.

Glancing over my shoulder, I smiled when I saw her step into the shower, naked.

"It hasn't been six weeks, baby."

"It's close enough."

Her arms wrapped around my neck, and I gently lifted her up. Wrapping her legs around me, she started to grind against my cock.

"Scarlett, I don't have a condom."

"No condom. I'm on the pill."

Our lips pressed together in a fierce kiss that was passionate, yet gentle.

"I don't want to hurt you," I whispered against her lips.

Drawing her head back, the corner of her mouth rose in a sexy smirk. "Then go slow."

I gently pushed my cock into her warm, wet pussy. We both moaned as I buried myself slowly inside of her, and then I just stood there, feeling her warmth all around me.

"Trevor. Oh God, I've missed you."

My lips peppered kisses along her neck as I slowly moved in and out of her, making sure I didn't hurt her. Scarlett had started going to a mommy yoga class at the hospital with a few other of the NICU moms and had recovered beautifully from her C-section. I still didn't want her to hurt herself, so I took it slow, even though I wanted to pull out and pound back into her, she felt so damn good.

"Trevor, please, go faster," Scarlett begged.

"Bedroom," I panted, turning off the water and walking us both soaking wet into our room. I gently placed Scarlett on the bed and made love to her. Reaching down, I pressed my thumb on her clit and watched as she fell apart around my cock.

It didn't take me long to tumble over the edge with her.

"Scarlett, I'm coming," I cried out as she squeezed my dick again. Pulling out every single drop of cum. This time her back arched off the bed as she cried out along with me. I loved how sensitive her body was to my touch. I'd never get tired of it.

When I was finally done coming, I rolled off of her and laid next to her, both of us trying to catch our breath.

Scarlett rolled over and ran her finger along my chest.

"That was amazing. I love you."

Turning my head to look at her, I raised a brow. "Want to do it again?"

Her eyes widened in shock before they traveled down my chest, to my stomach and finally to my semi-hard dick.

"As much as I would love a second round, we need to get to the hospital."

She crawled over me, placing her warm pussy right on my cock.

"But, I will take a rain check."

Laughing, I sat up and wrapped my arms around her.

"I'm going to hold you to that. And I'm also going to hold you to your promise to marry me."

Sadness filled her eyes. "I desperately want to marry you, Trevor. I hope you know that."

"I do. And I feel the same."

"Once we get Aurora home, let's try again. Something simple, family only."

"Deal. Come on, let's go see our daughter. She's probably wondering where we are."

CHAPTER 36

Scarlett

Kacy had come in early just so she could be the nurse on duty when we took Aurora home.

"And here is your going home bead. The butterfly."

A small tear slipped from my eye before I brushed it away. We had a bracelet full of milestones, each one holding a special memory for us that we would someday share with Aurora.

"Let's put it on her and take a picture!" Melanie said.

Two weeks ago, the same morning Trevor and I made love for the first time since Aurora was born, we got to the hospital and was told by Dr. Jackson that Aurora would be allowed to go home at seven weeks if she had reached her goal weight. She reached it a week early, but the plan was still to release her at seven weeks. I was bringing my daughter home, three weeks before my actual due date. It was surreal and exciting at the same time. A bit of fear was also mixed in.

"What if…"

Kacy held up her hand. "You've got this, Scarlett. You know this baby better than any of us do. You know her triggers, what to do to make her happy and believe me when I say that once you get her home you're going to be stunned by how much she thrives. You've got this."

I nodded. "I know. It's still scary to know Trevor and I will be the only two people taking care of her after she's had twenty-four-seven care by the most amazing nurses on the planet!"

Pulling me in for a hug, Kacy whispered, "You have a special little girl. Don't worry, you'll do great."

When we stepped back from one another, we both smiled.

"Thank you for everything you did for her."

It looked like Kacy was getting teary eyed. "Are you kidding? She was my favorite! Plus, I sort of liked watching her dad take off his shirt when he held her."

Laughing, I gave her a little push. One more hug and we were putting Aurora in her car seat. She was so little, it damn near swallowed her up.

I climbed into the back seat and waved goodbye as Trevor drove off, my mother in the front seat filming the whole thing.

Mom wiped a tear from her eye and said, "I can't believe the day has finally come. Aurora Belle Parker is finally heading home."

"Everything is ready with her room, right?" I asked. Again.

"Yes. For the sixth time. Melanie said Maebh did the final walk-through and everything is ready to go. Stop worrying. The bassinet has been placed in the master bedroom and Wade stocked up on preemie diapers when he went to the store for John Jr. Waylynn, Paxton, and Corina did a little shopping therapy for clothes since you hadn't had the baby shower yet. Aurora is all set."

My heart felt overfilled with gratitude and love for my future sisters-in-law. "That was so sweet of them. I wish we could have been at the family dinner when Corina and Mitchell announced she was pregnant."

"Oh, from what Melanie told me, she and John were ecstatic, and Corina's mother cried tears of joy."

My mother's voice trailed off, and I knew she was thinking about when Trevor and I first told our parents about Aurora.

Glancing into the rearview mirror, Trevor gave me a knowing smile. I reached up and squeezed my mother's shoulder. "Thank you, Mom, for being with us today. It meant a lot to me to have you here when we brought Aurora home. It's sort of scary knowing we're on our own now."

"Of course, sweetheart. I know Melanie wanted to be here as well. Heck, everyone wanted to be here. The one thing I know for sure, you will not be alone. Everyone is dying to see the princess who made such a grand appearance."

"Except Aunt Vi," Trevor said with a laugh. "Aunt Vi seems to have lost her passport in Ireland and is not in any hurry to find it. What a coincidence, right?"

I giggled and glanced at Aurora. She was sleeping like a perfect little angel. I swore she hardly ever cried unless she was hungry. For someone who demanded our attention from day one, she really was the best baby. Every nurse who worked with her said she was such a good baby.

Leaning my head back, I drifted off to sleep and didn't wake until I felt Trevor's arms around me, lifting me out of his truck.

"Baby, we're home," he whispered before placing a kiss on my cheek.

"*Mmm*...take me up to bed."

"I would, but your mom is currently standing in front of me holding Aurora."

Snapping my eyes open, I pursed my lips. "I didn't mean that! I meant for a nap!"

He laughed and set me down. Before I had a chance to walk away, he pulled me back to him. His hand softly cupped the side of my face.

"You know how much I love you, right?"

A warmth spread through my chest and settled in my belly. "Yes. You know how much I love you too, right?"

Trevor nodded. "I only want to make you and Aurora happy."

Lifting up on my tippy toes, I kissed him gently on the lips. "You make me the happiest woman on Earth. I love you."

"Love you, too."

When I turned back to my mother, she handed me Aurora in her tiny little carrier. All five pounds and eight ounces of her.

Trevor opened the door of the house and walked in. As much as I would have loved to have everyone here greeting us, Trevor and I asked that they let us settle in and wait a week before we had visitors. I was glad everyone had been so understanding.

It still was a bit sad to come home and have no one there to greet us, though.

Trevor and I walked into Aurora's room and I smiled. It was decorated in a Winnie the Pooh theme. Everything was ready, and I felt the tears building and an ache prick at the back of my throat.

"Her bassinet is in your room. Why don't you both take a nap?" my mother said.

Nodding, I walked to our room. I was scared to death to take Aurora out of her car seat and place her in the bassinet. With shaking hands, I did.

The moment I stepped back, I covered my mouth then looked at Trevor with a panicked look.

"What if…"

Placing his finger on my lips, he shook his head. "She's going to be fine. We're going to be fine. I promise you."

Chewing on my lip, I nodded.

"Come on, lay down and rest okay? I'll come in and check on both of you every few minutes."

"Promise?" I asked, my voice full of fear and anxiety I didn't want but couldn't shake.

"I promise."

After a week passed, Aurora was finally ready to have her first visitor.

Trevor walked toward the back of the house and looked out the window. He'd been doing it all morning.

"Don't you want breakfast, Trevor? At least something before my folks get here?"

"Yep, in a second. I want to head out back."

"Out back?" I asked, glancing over to him.

The doorbell rang, and Trevor quickly turned and answered it. Lori, Corina's mom walked in.

"Lori?" I asked, surprise laced in my voice.

"Oh my goodness, let me see the princess!" she stated as she walked over to me.

"What are you doing here?" I asked as she gave me a hug and peered down at Aurora.

"Trevor said you guys might need some help watching Aurora, so I'm here to help."

Peeking back at Trevor, I gave him an incredulous look. "We didn't talk about needing help with the baby just yet."

"No, we didn't. And we only need Lori's help for a little bit. Aurora isn't due for a feeding for another few hours. Let's get her in her bassinet and let me take you outside for some fresh air."

Trevor was terrible at secrets. I could tell by the smile on his face, he was up to something.

He lifted a brow at me as he walked back toward us. He picked up Aurora and headed to the master bedroom. Lori followed.

"Lori, what's going on?"

"Beats me."

"Liar. You're just as bad at this as he is."

I started for the back door, and she stopped me.

"Scarlett, let's get Aurora settled. You get changed and come out back. Please don't ask him any questions. He did this for you and wants to surprise you."

Biting my lip, I nodded. "Okay."

With quick steps, I headed to the bedroom. Trevor was gently placing the baby in the bassinet and swaddling her. She loved the way Trevor swaddled her so snug. He put her little heartbeat bear in with her and turned it on low. It was the sound of a human heartbeat. Aurora loved it and slept so well with it.

"I'll sit right here next to her while y'all go outside," Lori said, seeing my fear about leaving the baby.

"You won't leave her side?" I asked, biting on my thumbnail.

"Nope. I'm right here, and you're only going to be out back."

Trevor pulled my hand from my mouth, then held up a white sundress for me. "Do me a favor. Change into this, will you?"

"A sundress?"

"Please?"

I remembered Lori's words. A tingling feeling rushed across my body. What did the man have planned? Maybe a romantic breakfast out back? That would be so nice. A little bit of normalcy after the maelstrom we'd just endured.

"Of course I will. Give me a few minutes to freshen up?"

He nodded, then leaned down and kissed my forehead.

After giving Aurora one more once-over, I rushed into the bathroom and changed into the dress. There was a note on the counter with my name on it. Picking it up, I opened it and read the notecard.

Wear these. Please.

My eyes moved to the counter to see a pair of diamond earrings. Smiling, I picked them up and put them on. He was for sure planning a romantic breakfast. I wonder why he didn't pick dinner? Maybe the heat? It had been unusually hot for this time of year. The mornings were still cool and beautiful. I loved this man with all my heart, and I loved that he thought of something so sweet for us to share. This first week of being at home with Aurora had been stressful. But as we fell into a routine, my anxiety about her being okay slowly eased and everything felt like it was settling into place.

There was a pair of white Jimmy Choo pumps on the floor. With a giggle, I slipped them on. They fit me perfectly. When did he have time to do this? He must have had Waylynn pick all of this out.

I pulled up my hair in a loose bun and put on a small amount of mascara and some light-colored lipstick. Enough to make my lips look a little pink.

Another peek at Aurora and another confirmation from Lori that she wasn't going to leave her side, I headed out into the living room. Waylynn, Paxton, Amelia, Harley, Maebh, and Corina were all in the living room standing there with smiles.

"We washed our hands and none of us are sick!" Paxton whispered in excitement.

A lump formed in the back of my throat at the sight of them. It was so good to see everyone. My eyes landed on Corina. I made my way over to her.

"Congratulations, I heard."

"Thank you! I'm due September 7!"

"How exciting! What does Merit think about it?"

"She thinks she will be getting a new baby doll to play with."

I laughed, hugging her again. When Amelia stood in front of me, I hugged her tightly. "Where is John Jr?"

"He's with Wade."

"I can't wait to meet him."

"I can't wait for all the babies to have a play date! We're so lucky to have four of them all around the same age!" Harley said, giving me a quick hug and kiss.

Glancing over her, I shook my head. "You don't even look like you had twins two months ago!"

She laughed. "It's called five AM runs and taking care of twins!"

This time, the whole room laughed quietly.

Maebh walked up to me, the last one of the six girls to come congratulate me.

"Maebh," I whispered. "You didn't have to change your wedding."

"I did, and it actually turned out to be more perfect than I'd ever dreamed. The ceremony in Ireland was beautiful. Perfect. Cord and I knew we didn't need everyone there. We only needed each other. Of course, Aunt Vi and me Da, too."

I grinned, pulling her to me for a hug. "Thank you for always being there for me. I love you."

She held me tight and whispered, "I love you, too." Pushing me back to arm's length, she smiled. "Now are you ready?"

"For?"

"Let's head to the kitchen," Maebh stated.

Narrowing my eyes, I looked at each of them, noticing they were all dressed in similar sundresses, each in a soft pastel color.

Then it hit me.

"Oh. My. God."

Maebh squeezed my hand. "Hurry, the man has been waiting for almost two months to do this."

Both hands covered my mouth as I tried to keep calm and remember to breathe.

"Is this for real?" I asked, trying not to get any more emotional.

Waylynn walked up to me, gave me a once-over, and replied, "White dress. White Jimmy Choo heels, and diamond earrings that were our grandmother's. We'll let you decide on that one."

With a wink, she spun on her heels and followed the rest of the girls out of the living room and to the kitchen.

I glanced over at the large mirror that hung on the wall and looked at myself.

"Am I about to get married?"

"Scarlett, come on," Amelia pleaded.

With a deep breath in, I answered myself.

"Only one way to find out."

CHAPTER 37

Trevor

After Scarlett headed into the bathroom, I made my way to the guest bathroom, quickly changed, and headed outside. My heart nearly exploded at the sight in front of me.

When I'd told my parents I wanted to marry Scarlett right after we brought Aurora home, my mother went into immediate action, along with the rest of the girls.

I stood in my backyard and took in the sight. White lights were hung in the trees, lanterns were sprinkled all around. A beautiful arch was at the end of a small makeshift aisle, and it was covered in white roses. It was a miracle that Scarlett hadn't heard everyone back here last night and this morning. Of course, I'd done a good job of distracting her last night...

My four brothers and Wade stood there with smiles on all of their faces. Wade was holding his son, John Jr, who was only a few weeks old. I quickly made my way down to him.

"So, is this my new nephew?" I asked, peeking down to the sleeping baby boy in my best friend's arms.

"This is him. John Jr, meet your Uncle Trevor."

The baby didn't budge, except to suck on his pacifier a few times. Other than that, he was sound asleep in his father's arms.

"Damn, he's cute as a button."

"Uncle Twevor!"

Turning, I threw out my arms in time to catch Gage.

"Hey there, little buddy."

"Come pway whiff me, pwease!"

My heart melted. "I'm sorry, little buddy. I can't play right now, but I promise here in a bit, we'll play, okay?"

He stuck out his lip and pouted big time.

"This is what happens when the favorite uncle is away for too long," Steed said, laughing as he took his son from my arms. "Uncle Trevor has to do something really important and then I bet he'll play with you."

A smile reappeared on Gage's face.

"Where's Chloe?" I asked, looking around for my niece.

"Well, she is currently putting flowers on Patches."

Now it was my turn to pout. "Shit. There's no chance we can talk her out of it?"

Steed shook his head. "Paxton and I tried every trick in the book. Sorry, dude, the goat's in your wedding."

"Can't break tradition," Mitchell said with a chuckle.

I shot him a dirty look. "I hope you have twins."

His face went white. "Dude, that's not funny. At all."

Jonathon walked up holding Liberty, who was fussing to get down and walk on her own. She was over one now and all over the place.

"We are finally here. This is what happens when Mom leaves Daddy in charge of getting ready," Jonathon said, reaching his hand out to shake. "I'm glad y'all are finally back home."

"Me too. So, we never got to talk about the adoption," I said, reaching over and scooping Liberty from his arms. The moment I had her, she settled and started to rub her hands on my cheeks. She liked the slight stubble I always kept on my face.

"Unwell Twewor." She gave me a slobbery kiss, which I gladly accepted.

"Hey there, sweet little Liberty. I missed you. You have a new baby cousin, Aurora."

Liberty's eyes widened.

"Dude, Sleeping Beauty. She thinks that's who you're talking about."

I laughed and kissed her on the cheek.

"Anyway, back to the adoption," I said.

"August 3 is the big day. It's a couple in their late twenties. Both are lawyers, good friends who happened to get drunk and got a little carried away. She's taking a leave of absence once she starts showing, and she's actually coming to stay here in the main guest house until she has the baby. It was all in the agreement with the adoption. We're pretty excited. Found out she's having a boy, so that will make one of each."

"We're going to be overrun with females soon," my father said from behind me.

"Gandpa!" Liberty screamed out, pushing off of me to get to my father.

He took her and spun her around, making her laugh.

"Glad to see I'm still her favorite."

"Dad, you're all the kids' favorite," I replied.

He beamed. "You are all going to make me go broke if you keep popping out these kids. Your mother spoils each of them and y'all don't say a damn thing."

"Damn!" Liberty repeated as we all stilled.

"Waylynn is going to freak!" Jonathon said, quickly looking around for my oldest sister. "Where is she? Y'all are my witness, it was your dad who taught her that. Not me!"

Cord shook his head at his best friend. "Dude, what happened to you? You are the definition of pussy-whipped."

Jonathon went to say something to Cord, when Maebh called, "Cord! I need you to help me with something!"

I watched as Cord looked at me, smiled and said, "Welcome home!"

"Thanks, and congratulations on the wedding."

He grinned from ear to ear. "Thanks!"

"Cord?" Maebh called again, making my brother run off to see what his wife needed.

Jonathon scoffed and mumbled, "And he says *I'm* pussy-whipped."

My mother stood at the end of the aisle where Preacher Scott was standing. "Everyone! Come on and get in your seats! It's time! It's time!"

Maebh walked up to me, her eyes filled with tears.

"She was totally taken by surprise. Well done."

I kissed my sister-in-law on the cheek. "Thank you for helping Mom do this, and congratulations on the wedding. Y'all didn't have to do that."

"I know, but it all actually turned out brilliant. Now come on, your future bride is waiting, and you have a baby who is on a schedule."

Following Maebh down the aisle, I made my way to the end and shook Preacher Scott's hand.

"Let's try this once more, shall we?" he said with a smile and a wink.

This time, I stood up there alone. Everyone else was sitting in chairs that were covered in soft pink. It was the same color Scarlett had picked out for the original wedding. The lights from the trees gave off the perfect amount of light as the sun rose higher in the sky behind us.

The same violinist from our first wedding was here, too. I wasn't sure what my mother had to do to get her to come back to Oak Springs from Dallas, but I was glad she managed it.

The music started, and Scarlett made her way down the aisle. She was a vision in white. She hardly had any make-up on and was in a simple white sundress with the diamond earrings that had belonged to my grandmother.

Her eyes were focused on mine, until Chloe stepped in front of her with a completely tricked out Patches. The damn goat was covered in flowers. Scarlett's eyes nearly popped out of her head as chuckles came from nearly everyone.

"Patches?" Scarlett gasped, quickly looking at me.

"Doesn't he look beautiful, Aunt Scarlett?" Chloe asked, totally channeling that inner Parker woman guilt she already had down.

Scarlett's shocked gaze went from Chloe to me. I shrugged and started laughing. Soon Scarlett was laughing.

"Chloe, he looks amazing," Scarlett replied.

Chloe prompted Patches to start down the aisle, and I swore that damn goat looked like he was smiling. At one point, he seemed to stop and pose for the photographer. Scarlett followed Chloe and Patches, and I couldn't help but notice she kept a good amount of distance between her and the goat.

I didn't want to think about the last time she'd walked down the aisle toward me. Or the six weeks we'd spent away from the ranch, not once leaving our rented condo. I didn't know what I would have done if it hadn't been for our families. It was either my folks or Scarlett's who would came and stay with us, or it was one of my brothers or sisters bringing up more clothes, and food and essentials needed at the condo.

Most days and nights we were at the hospital, but every single time we went to the condo, fresh food or premade meals were waiting. Clean clothes to replace the ones we stripped off on our way to take a ten-minute shower. These people were a silent force behind the scenes, helping us more than they would ever know. I knew it was hard for them to take turns getting to see Aurora, and it was even harder for them to leave us behind when they returned to their normal lives, but I also knew they and everyone in Oak Springs were praying for our little girl.

Scarlett stopped in front of me and blew out a breath. "They say three times is a charm."

I laughed. "Well, let's not find out, this is only our second attempt. By the way, you take my breath away you're so beautiful."

Her eyes moved over my face before they landed on my lips and she bit down into hers. "And you are as handsome as ever."

"I have a bit of Liberty slobber on my cheek in case you were wondering."

Scarlett giggled. Pastor Scott cleared his throat and she turned to face him.

As Pastor Scott talked, I couldn't help but notice Patches moving closer and closer to Scarlett.

Leaning over, I whispered, "He's eyeing your bouquet."

Scarlett frowned and glanced between me and Pastor Scott, which made him pause.

"Not you, Pastor. The goat."

"The goat?"

I nodded.

"Shall I go on?" he asked, peeking over to Patches who was now playing innocent. I leaned back and looked at him.

"I'm watching you!" I whispered. Patches replied with a loud scream.

Scarlett started to laugh until Pastor Scott shot her a firm look.

"As I was saying…"

Then it happened.

The goat went for Scarlett's bouquet.

He snatched it from her hand so fast that Scarlett didn't seem to know it was gone for a few seconds.

Patches took off running down the aisle. I watched as Steed dove for him—thankfully he had handed Gage to Paxton. Then Mitchell went after the goat. Then Wade, who had given Amelia the baby. Patches had maneuvers a pro football player would die for.

Chloe sighed and shook her head, calmly walking toward her crazy goat.

"Here we go again. I told him to behave."

Scarlett and I busted out laughing.

"What is happening?!" Pastor Scott cried out.

"Patches is what is happening! Steed Parker, you better get that bouquet or I'm going to put that damn goat down myself!" Waylynn cried out, joining in on the chase.

Gage called out, "Wun Patches! Wun!"

The goat stopped and looked straight down the aisle.

"Oh. No," Scarlett and I said at the same time.

"Run! Save yourselves, he's coming for the roses!" I yelled out.

And, boy howdy, did Patches make the best effort he could to get those roses on the trellis behind the pastor. But he came to a halt. Turned, eyed the diaper bag sitting next to Harley and quickly grabbed it and took off running.

Now Tripp was on the chase.

Turning back to Pastor Scott, I grinned. "You should just keep going, maybe cut the things that aren't important."

He nodded. "Right. Let's do this again."

As the pastor quickly had us say our vows and exchange rings, he told me to kiss the bride. Before I did, Scarlett grinned. "Told you three times was a charm."

"Yes, you did, Mrs. Parker."

Scarlett

Seven months later—Christmas Day

Nine kids.

That was how many were lined up on the floor in front of the Christmas tree. Aurora was nine months old and sitting in-between Chloe and Merit. The three of them were thick as thieves. Next to Merit were Rose, Max, Gage, John, and baby Hudson, Waylynn and Jonathon's little boy who was born in early August. Next to Hudson was the youngest Parker baby, Shep. Mitchell and Corina delivered a healthy baby boy on September 12. Shep may have come into this world a little late, but he made up for it by being what everyone in the family declared the perfect baby. I didn't think I had heard him cry yet.

Melanie and John were both lying on the floor, attempting to get the perfect picture of their grandchildren.

"Mom, you'd better hurry. Look at all those hungry eyes scanning the presents."

"Oh, hush. Look at all my little angels. They're all so perfect!"

"Mom, you need to hurry. Someone pooped," Waylynn said, waving her hand in front of her face.

"Oh God, I smell it, too!" Mitchell said, making a gagging sound.

John chuckled and picked up Shep out of his carrier. "Glad you smelled it because it's your son."

Mitchell took Shep and kissed him on the cheek as he grabbed the diaper bag.

"That's my boy, stinking up the whole family room on Christmas morning. Just like your Uncle Cord."

Cord cried out and threw a pillow at Mitchell. "It was one time, Mitchell! One time! And I was sick!"

"Watch the baby, Cord Parker!" Melanie stated, pointing her finger at Cord.

I snuggled into Trevor's side, taking everything in. We'd spent our Christmas together earlier this morning with Aurora sleeping next to us. My favorite moment was when Trevor opened the picture frame that held a collage of photos of him and Aurora in the NICU. One of his hand and her clutching his finger. One of her sleeping on his chest. One of Trevor smiling as he put her first outfit on. And the last was Trevor putting her into her car seat, her NICU Journey beads sitting around her little neck. When he finally stopped staring at the picture, he looked at me and gave me the most beautiful smile I'd ever seen. I didn't want the moment to end. Now I wasn't wanting this moment to end.

Chloe was holding Aurora on her lap, explaining the process of how to open a present. Aurora glanced between Chloe and the plethora of presents under the tree and all the blinking lights, her eyes wide with excitement.

"Scarlett, I wish your folks were here to enjoy this first Christmas with us," Melanie said as she took Hudson out of his carrier and brought him to Waylynn. "Here, sweetheart, we don't want him getting trampled when the all-clear is given."

Waylynn beamed as she took her four-month-old son. Jonathon leaned over and gave the baby kisses all over his face, making him laugh.

With a soft sigh, I gave Melanie a half-smile. I'd finally cornered my father and asked him if he and mom were getting a divorce. Something had been strained between the two of them. When he confessed to not being my birth father, I thought it was odd I wasn't upset, or at least surprised. Instead, so many things made sense to me in that moment. "Yeah, I wish they were here too, but they've been wanting to go on a cruise for a while now."

Melanie gave me a sympathetic grin. My parents were not as close to Aurora as Melanie and John. In part, it was because Trevor and I lived on the ranch, and his folks saw her so much more. They'd helped so much after we brought Aurora home and bonded with her faster than anyone besides me and Trevor. Maebh had also bonded with Aurora almost from the day we brought her home. She and Cord were actually talking about buying land down from the ranch and building a house. I was secretly hoping they would and had let it slip to Melanie, who made sure to bring it up at least once an hour while in Cord and Maebh's presence.

"I'm going to grab Aurora," Trevor said, standing and walking to our daughter. When she saw her daddy, she lit up like she was a Christmas tree, too. She loved him and had that cowboy wrapped around her little finger. Her favorite thing to do was ride up on Daddy's horse each night. At first, it scared me, but I knew Trevor would never let anything happen to our little angel.

Chloe groaned in protest when Trevor took Aurora.

"She's still too little for the free for all, Chloe."

With a pout, Chloe nodded. "Grammy? Will you be Santa for the babies?"

"Of course, I will!"

Harley had grabbed Rose and Tripp had Max. Corina had already snagged baby Shep from Mitchell and was sitting next to

Mitchell on the love seat, rocking him while he continued to sleep through the craziness.

"Merit, do you need help, sweetheart?" Mitchell asked.

"No, Daddy! I'm a big gwurl!"

Mitchell smiled and replied, "Yes, you are, princess."

"Now listen up, little ones. No pushing, no shoving, and we take our time. What's the number-one rule, Chloe?"

"No Patches in the house on Christmas morning."

Everyone laughed.

"Yes, but what's the other rule?"

Chloe looked up. "No kissing Rip anymore on the playground."

"What!" Steed said, jumping up, only to have Paxton pull him back down.

"I was going to talk to you about that," Paxton said, chewing on her lip.

Steed stared at his wife. "When?"

Paxton shrugged. "When I absolutely had to."

I covered my mouth to keep from laughing too loudly.

Melanie did the same, then cleared her throat. "Chloe, what are the rules for opening a present?"

"Oh! After each present, you thank the person who gave it to you. Even Santa."

Pointing to her granddaughter, Melanie chuckled. "That was the rule I was looking for."

John walked up to Chloe and kissed her on the forehead. "I also second that other rule about Rip, by the way."

Chloe giggled, and Trevor moaned next to me.

"What's wrong?" I asked.

"That's going to be our daughter in a few years."

I chuckled. "I don't think we have to worry about boys for a good while."

"Max! You cannot pull the tree down, buddy!" Tripp said, jumping up and grabbing his son.

Rose laughed and clapped, almost as if she was cheering her brother on.

"I have a feeling those two are going to give you some stories," I said to Harley.

She let out an exasperated sigh. "You're telling me. I swear they sit up at night in their cribs and come up with things. Under one or not, these two are planners. It's like their brains are connected, I swear."

"Y'all thinking about more?" Trevor asked as Aurora snuggled into her daddy's chest and started closing her eyes. She wasn't the only one who felt safe in her daddy's arms.

Tripp scoffed. "More? God, no. No more."

I lifted a brow and looked at Harley.

"I'm with my husband. No more. These two are plenty. What about y'all?"

Trevor reached for my hand and squeezed it. My fears after we had Aurora had been strong, but as the months went on I got over them. Trevor and I had talked about another baby. In the end, we both decided for right now, we were happy with just the three of us. We would for sure try for another one, just maybe in another year.

"I think we want one more. Maybe in about a year or so."

"Smart!" Harley, Waylynn, and Corina said all at once.

Glancing over to Maebh, I smiled when I saw her against Cord, sound asleep. It was only eleven in the morning, but she was passed out.

"Maebh feeling okay, Cord?" I asked.

His face turned bright red, and he couldn't look me in the eyes. When he finally managed to look my way, I gasped, making everyone else turn and look at me.

"Oh. My. Goodness," I whispered.

"What's wrong?" Amelia asked, walking into the room with John sitting on her hip.

Cord pushed at Maebh, making her suddenly wake up.

"What! What's wrong! Did me da call?"

"No, but I think our little secret is fixin' to come out," Cord said as he pointed at me.

"What secret?" Amelia asked, sitting on the floor next to Wade.

"Are we ready to open gifts?" Melanie called out, and half of the kids yelled out yes.

I stared at Maebh, who looked at Cord, then me, then back to Cord. "You eejit! You told her I was pregnant?"

Melanie spun on her heels and yelled. "Wait! No opening of presents!"

Chloe groaned.

Cord closed his eyes and shook his head. "I didn't tell anyone anything."

Melanie walked over to Cord and Maebh, dropped onto the sofa next to them and stared at Maebh.

"Mom, what are you doing? That's creepy," Cord stated.

Maebh's eyes filled with tears, and she gave Melanie a smile that told the whole room that she and Cord were expecting.

Mitchell jumped up. "Holy shit! You're gonna be a Papa Smurf!"

Everyone in the room looked at Chloe and shouted, "No, Chloe!"

She held up her hands and said, "I wasn't going to say hell, shit, or fuck!"

Steed groaned while Paxton reprimanded Chloe.

"Chloe Parker!"

Covering her mouth, Chloe giggled. "Sorry!"

The attention returned to Maebh and Cord.

"So, are you going to be a Papa Smurf?" Trevor asked.

Looking at each other with so much love you could feel it pouring off of them, Cord and Maebh smiled for the longest time before Cord looked at the rest of the family.

"Maebh and I are going to have a baby in about seven months."

Cheers erupted around the room, making Aurora jump from her peaceful nap and causing Shep to cry for what I swore was the first time ever.

"Oh, come here, little man," Mitchell said as Merit ran over to her baby brother to make sure everything was okay.

While everyone was waiting to congratulate Cord and Maebh, the twins got busy with their previous plan for the Christmas tree.

"Um, Uncle Tripp, Aunt Harley?" Chloe said, loud enough to get everyone's attention. "Max and Rose are fixin' to pull the tree down."

The only thing I saw after that was Max's smile when the tree started to topple, and Tripp dove to stop it.

Smiling, I took it all in. Another beautiful, crazy, amazing day in the Parker family.

THE END

A Note from Kelly

Before I give y'all the epilogue and we close the book on this amazing Parker family I have grown to love so much, I want to tell you about something that touched my heart deeply as I wrote this book.

The NICU Journey Beads program is a real program that was brought to life by an amazing woman. Her name is Jodi Dolezel, a NICU nurse, who said she came up with the idea of the beads as a way to help the parents of preemies celebrate the progress of their babies in the NICU. She also saw it as a way to bring the nurses and parents a bit closer.

I was lucky enough to speak with her on the phone and I have to say she is someone I highly admire. As are all of the nurses and doctors who work in NICUs across the world. I'll be the first to say this wasn't an easy subject to research. I sat at my desk many times and cried as I tried to read through blurry tears. Then I stumbled upon a video of the Today Show that talked about the NICU Journey Bead program. I immediately emailed Jodi and asked her if I could include this in my book, and she said yes! What a better way to bring light to a beautiful thing.

If you would like to know more about the NICU Journey Bead program, or if you would like to donate to help families of these precious babies get their beads, please visit the links below.

Peek A Boo ICU website –
http://www.peekabooicu.com

NICU Journey Beads Program –
https://peekabooicu.org/content/7-nicu-journey-bead-program

(continued on next page)

Peek A Book ICU Facebook Page –
https://www.facebook.com/peekabooicuRN

To donate to the NICU Journey Beads Program –
https://www.youcaring.com/nicu-families-652202

Aunt Vi

John & Melanie Parker

Wingtipper & Toronthop   Steed & Paxton   Cord & Maeph   Amelia & Wade

Tripp & Harley   Mitchell & Carissa   Trevor & Scarlett

Liberty   Hudson

Chloe   Gage

Rose   Max

Meri   Shep

Kaityn

John Jr.

Aurora

Chloe

18 years old

My parents and Gage were the first to pull me in for a family hug. I'd done it.

Graduated with high honors from Oak Springs High School.

Oak Springs hadn't changed much since I moved here as a young girl with my father. It was still a small town, maybe a bit bigger than it used to be, but everyone still knew everyone. The only real difference was that they had built another building for the high school, and it was now completely separated from the elementary and middle school. A change most loved, but the older folks hated. It meant growth. I loved it, though. There was nothing like growing up in a small town.

The thought of going off to Texas A&M for college was daunting. I was excited, but everything was changing. For the good, of course, but it still meant I was leaving my family…and Rip.

My eyes caught a glimpse of him over my mother's shoulder. Rip Myers. My best friend and secret crush since kindergarten. He waved to me while my parents crushed the breath out of my body.

"Y'all, I can't breathe!" I gasped. Gage was the first to let go. My little brother wasn't really so little. Although he was six years younger than me, he was tall and beginning to fill out with muscles. Not only from his love of football, but from working on the ranch.

"I'm next!" Gage announced, doing a fist pump.

"And Merit and Liberty! But not for a few more years little brother," I added.

With an eye roll, Gage sighed then gave me a wink. "Minor details."

I glanced around. "Where is everyone?"

It was unlike the Parker clan not to be out in full force. I certainly heard everyone when my name was being called to walk across the stage. I was pretty sure my Uncle Cord and Uncle Trevor had been trying to see who could yell the loudest.

With a smile that said he was proud as all get out, my father replied, "They all headed back to the ranch. Granddaddy has the pit going and wanted to make sure everything was good with it. Your Grammy wanted to make sure everything was ready for the party."

The party of the century my Grammy called it. The first Parker grandchild to graduate high school and go off to college. I swear she'd been planning this for two years.

"Speaking of the party, we should head on back to the ranch," my mother said, giving me a kiss on the cheek. "You didn't drive. Do you want us to wait for you?"

Swinging my gaze back to Rip, I nodded. "Let me talk to Rip really quick… I'll meet y'all back at the ranch?"

My father turned to Rip. He smiled and asked, "Is Rip coming to the party?"

I shrugged. "Not sure. I'll ask."

"Don't be long, Chloe!" My mother called out as I made my way over to Rip and his family. Aunt Waylynn was standing in the crowd along with Uncle Jonathon, Rip's older brother. Liberty caught sight of me before Rip did and made a beeline right to me. She slammed her body into mine as we both laughed.

"You're free! I'm so jealous!" she quietly said.

Laughing, I stepped back from her. "Only a few more years, Liberty."

"Ugh, it can't come soon enough. The thought of being here without you makes me physically ill."

"You have Merit, Rose, Aurora, and Katlyn! What are you talking about?"

"I know, but you're the one who sneaks out with me to go swimming in the river."

"Please, Katlyn sneaks out all the time to the barn to ride that horse of hers. She'd be totally game to meet you for a night swim."

We giggled. "If Uncle Cord and Aunt Maebh find out about her nightly rides, she is in so much trouble."

Hudson walked up to me and engulfed me in a hug. "Congrats, cousin! How's it feel to be officially free of Oak Springs?"

I shrugged. "It doesn't feel as great as y'all think it will. Enjoy this time and enjoy high school. It goes by quick."

Hudson smiled. "We're going to miss you, but you'll be back for breaks and during the summer."

"Yes, of course I'll be back. I'm only a few hours away."

Dread moved over me. I hated the idea of leaving my family. Of leaving Rip. I focused back on him and saw him smile as my aunt and uncle made their way over to me. Aunt Waylynn hugged me.

"Chloe, I just can't believe it. It feels like it was just yesterday you were sneaking dogs home and trying to take over Aunt Harley's vet practice."

I laughed. "I think Rose is the one Aunt Harley needs to worry about. That girl is hell bent on becoming a vet and taking the fast track."

Aunt Waylynn rolled her eyes. "Sounds like a Parker woman. Listen, we need to get back to the ranch, or your grandmother will have a fit. Chloe, don't fiddle around too long."

"I won't. Mom and dad are waiting for me."

"I'll give her ride," Rip said, walking up and kissing me on the cheek.

My insides warmed like they always did when my best friend stood next to me. "You're coming over now?" I asked, glancing past him to his family.

"Yeah, we're not having a graduation party until Evie can get back to town. Probably next week. Your granddaddy invited us all over."

I smiled. Evie was Rip's oldest sister. She was married and living in Austin.

"Awesome! Let me text my mom and let her know I'm riding home with you."

After sending my mother a quick text, I said goodbye to my cousins and followed Rip through the small crowd that was still gathered outside of the high school.

Our ride back to the ranch was filled with talk, a lot of laughter, and a few promises that we would text or call each other every day. When we made it to Frio River Ranch, I smiled.

Home.

This place would always be home. I already knew the moment I graduated college I'd be making my way back to Oak Springs. Rip said the same thing. He was planning on working with Jonathon at his construction company, but as an engineer. He hoped to help him design the buildings for some of the bigger projects Uncle Jonathon did in Austin and San Antonio.

Rip pulled up and parked behind the plethora of trucks and cars.

"My gosh, did they invite all of Oak Springs to this party?" I asked while pushing open the truck door and sliding out. Rip was right there, waiting to help me out of the truck. That was one thing about living in a small Texas town, southern boys still had manners. Well, most of them did anyway.

As we climbed the steps to the ranch house, I turned to Rip. The excitement of today rushed back to me in one quick moment.

"We did it! Can you believe we did it?"

He laughed. "Nope. Feels like it took forever to get to this moment."

We faced each other. Our eyes met, and for once I wanted to tell him how I felt. Rip had made it clear early on that he only felt friendship between us. He never made any attempt to take our friendship beyond that, so neither did I.

I let out a quick breath and said, "Let's go party the Parker way!"

"Hell yeah, the only way to party!"

We made our way through the house and to the backyard. Tents were set up, much like how Grammy does it for spring fling dinner she throws each year.

My eyes scanned the crowd. My granddaddy was dancing with Grammy, and I felt my heart beat faster in my chest. I'd never seen two people so in love. Well, I had, but they were like the monarchy of the Parker family and the example of what true love really was and should be.

Then I saw my parents, looking directly into one another's eyes as they danced. So completely in love. It gave me hope that someday I'd find a love like theirs.

"Looks like they started without ya!" Rip chuckled.

"Yeah, looks like it."

Rip and I stood there and watched the scene play out. Each of my aunts and uncles were soon in each other's arms, cutting up the dance floor like it was nothing. They were all such amazing examples of what love was, following in the same footsteps as my grandparents—well, at least in their own way. They'd been there for each other through all of the good and the bad. I was blessed to have been raised in such an amazing family.

Rip pointed off to the left and I gasped at what I saw. "Oh my gosh! Aunt Vi is here with Uncle Aedin!"

"Wow, they came back from Ireland just for your graduation!" Rip said, making his way toward the crowd. He loved talking to Aedin. Rip's dream was to go to Ireland and learn everything he could about Aedin's business of making whiskey. Once Aunt Vi and Uncle Aedin married, they spent most of their time in Ireland. It was a treat for us all when they came to visit. Of course, poor Uncle Cord still had a heck of a time understanding his father-in-law and I'm sure that would never change.

I stood back and took everyone in.

My family was big, loud, and crazy at times, but I loved each and every one of them. I was going to miss them all.

As I went to step off the back porch to join the party, I saw a flash to my left. Turning, I stopped and stared at the disaster heading straight toward the tents.

"Oh, no," I whispered. "Patches!"

Patches, the goat I'd gotten from my granddaddy when we first moved to Oak Springs, was running at full speed. And behind him were three of his kids. All ready to crash the party.

"Daddy!" I yelled out and pointed. "He got out!"

Those were the magical words that everyone knew. Three simple words that spoke volumes. Everyone started for the food table. Even though Patches was up there in age, he was still a goat on a mission.

I covered my mouth with my hands and started to laugh as my childhood best friend and favorite goat in the entire world jumped onto the food table, the other three goats following their lead.

Gage and Merit both started yelling out, "Run, Patches! Run!" They had always been Patches' cheerleading team when he got into trouble.

After getting his fair share of food, Patches spotted his arch nemesis, Aunt Waylynn, and took off back toward the barn, his three kids following after him. Aunt Waylynn was hot on their heels.

"Patches! I swear to God, I'm going to kill you this time! I mean it!" Aunt Waylynn screamed out.

Rip walked up to me, laughing while tears streamed down his face as he draped his arm over my shoulders.

"Damn, Chloe. No one can throw a party like your family!"

Smiling, I agreed. "If that isn't the truth."

Rip wiped at his tears. "Wonder what party he'll crash next?"

I shrugged as I looked up at him with so much unspoken emotion in my eyes. "I can't wait to find out."

THANK YOU

Thank you to Kristin, Tanya, and Laura for being the first eyes on this manuscript!

Thank you to Kayla Miller for answering my questions about twin pregnancy.

Thank you to Julie for the amazing formatting…as usual!

Thank you to my editors, Elaine York, Cori McCarthy, and Amy Rose Capetta. Y'all are the best!

A HUGE thank you to all the readers who have invested their time in the Parker Family! It was such a fun series to write and I fell so in love with this family. I hope you all know how much I appreciate each and every one of y'all!

Thank you to Darrin and Lauren for sharing me with the Parkers! I love you both to the moon and back!

The playlist for *Reckless Love* can be found on my website – https://www.kellyelliottauthor.com/playlists.

From bestselling author Kelly Elliott comes the first book in a brand new series, the Austin Singles.

What happens when you're forced to seduce the one person you vowed never to love? You get screwed . . . in more than one way.

I walked out of Tucker Middleton's bedroom seven years ago, leaving him hurt and angry. Now I need his help; the only way I can get it is to make him think I want him back.

The only problem is we have silently vowed to hate one another for the rest of our lives. In order to get Tucker to help me – I have to seduce him.

Easy, right?

Charleston Monroe is playing me for a fool.

If she believes for one second I'm going to let her walk into my life to help her save the very job that ripped her away from me, she's got another thing coming.

She thinks she can seduce me, and I let her believe she can. After all, I'm getting what I've always wanted.

Her.